The Quiet Flame

Beloved, do not avenge yourselves, but rather give place to wrath; for it is written, "Vengeance is Mine, I will repay, " says the Lord.
Romans 12:19 (NKJV)

And this is eternal life, that they may know You, the only true God, and Jesus Christ whom You have sent
John 17:3 (NKJV)

Chapter 1

Nassau, New Providence, 1696

"Oooh" Gabrielle squealed, then quickly bit her lip and ran her hand over her rounded belly. 'Twas the hardest kick yet. There, something brushed across her palm. A foot? A hand? She wanted to smile at the life growing within her.

But all she could do was cry.

"What ye squawkin' 'bout, wench?" Lazy-eyed Smity leaned his shoulder against the iron bars of the cell across from hers and leered in her direction. "Yer brat givin' ye a what's what already?"

"Leave her be, ye bloated crank," Durwin said from the cell beside Smity's, eliciting further shouts and curses from other prisoners Gabrielle fortunately couldn't see and way-too-often wished she couldn't hear.

The small prison where she had been tossed nigh three months past consisted of a single filth-begrimed walkway, lined on both sides by cells too small for even a dog, let alone a human.

She offered Durwin a smile, and he nodded in return. The crusty old pirate had been kind to her since he arrived last month, though she could not fathom why. Perhaps he'd been taught to be a gentleman when he was younger, to treat a lady with respect.

Not that she was a lady. Not anymore.

Smity huffed and spat on the floor outside Durwin's cell. "She's nothin' but a pirate's whore, ye salty clod. An' I'll speak t' 'er any ways I want."

And there it was. *A pirate's whore.* Her new title.

From Lady Gabrielle Charlisse Hyde, daughter of Edmund Merrick Hyde, Earl of Clarendon, to naught but a strumpet. She lowered her chin. Hadn't her father always said her rash emotions would be her ruin?

The babe kicked again, and Gabrielle lowered to sit on the hay-stuffed mattress, ignoring the ache in her back and swelling in her ankles.

Smity snorted. "Ye'd be dead, wench, if it weren't fer that babe. But soon enough, soon enough."

His right eye floated off to the right, as it so often did, but his left one speared her with hatred. Why he detested her, she couldn't say, save perhaps some woman had broken his heart—if he'd ever had one. Or perhaps all pirates were simply evil.

"And you shall hang beside me, you insolent fool," she retorted.

Smity frowned.

Durwin chuckled.

But what did it matter? Smity was right, of course. She would have already met that unpleasant ending if they'd not discovered she was with child. Quite a surprise to her as well. Hence, she'd earned a four-month reprieve, if one could call her torturous existence in this prison a reprieve. In truth, death sounded a far better fate than another day in this place.

Tears burned behind her eyes. Yet with practiced control, she forced them back. She'd hated the child at first, hated the way his life had started. But over the months, as her belly swelled and she felt him move, she'd grown to love him…or her. But, no, 'twas a boy. Had to be.

She drew in a breath of air and instantly regretted it. She would never grow accustomed to the stench of this place, all putrid mold, decay, and death. A fly buzzed around her head, landed on her arm, but before she could swat it, it sped toward her uneaten dinner. If one could call the foul pile of regurgitated gruel dinner. She'd tried to eat as much as she could…for the babe's sake, but when her stomach threatened to eject what little she'd consumed, she pushed it away.

The sun withdrew its last golden rays from the slit-like window high above Gabrielle, pulling a cloak of gray over her cell. She rubbed her arms against a chill that had naught to do with the weather. She hated the nights worst of all. 'Twas when the shadows emerged from the stone walls like specters from graves, taunting her, reminding her of her foolishness, her naivety, her disobedience to God and her parents. 'Twas also at night that the prisoners grew more restless, more vocal in their agonizing screams, their obscene shouts, as if they, too, were haunted by demons from their past. And some, perhaps by demons of their future…a future hemmed in by a strangling noose and the jeers of an unfeeling crowd.

Terror spiraled through her, and she rubbed her neck. She had purposely avoided thinking about the horrors of being hanged. Her thoughts…and her heart…had been on her babe. Tears seared her eyes and, pressing a hand on her back, she struggled to rise and face the back wall, not wanting Smity to use her pain for entertainment.

Hanging her head, she ran both hands over her belly, allowing her tears to slide down her cheeks and spill onto her swollen womb. What would happen to her child? Who would care for him? Or would he be tossed in a run-down orphanage and die from neglect?

Drawing a deep breath, she batted her tears away. No time for weakness. No time for regrets. She would face her end with the dignity of her station—the daughter of an earl. The daughter of the famous Captain Merrick, a man she could never face after what she'd done. The look of shame and disappointment on his expression would be worse than hanging. Which was why she'd kept her identity to herself.

And she had prayed. Oh, how she had prayed. For forgiveness at first, and then for rescue, for help.

But heaven had been silent. The presence of God absent, no doubt pushed away by her rebellion. Her mother and father had always told her God was a God of forgiveness. But during the past four months, Gabrielle had come to believe they'd been wrong. Perhaps there was a point of wickedness past which God could not redeem.

Pop pop pop!

Pistol shots peppered the air. A shout. A foul curse. The loud crunch of wood and stone. Gabrielle was having a nightmare, a dream filled with memories of the many battles at sea she'd experienced while on her father's ship, *Redemption*. More shots, the eerie clang of swords, a cannon blast! The cot beneath her shook. Something crumbled on her face. Pebbles? Dust?

Raising her hand, she wiped her cheeks as the sound of musket shots rapped against her mind, jarring her awake. Struggling to rise, she sat, cradling her belly, breath heaving as another explosion rocked her cell. Prisoners, awakened from their slumber, rattled the iron bars of their cages, cussing and shouting.

Blinking, she tried to see what was happening, but darkness hung heavy in the fetid prison. Had she died and gone to hell? That place of eternal torment of which her parents often spoke? If so, a fitting end. But her child? Heart hammering, she wrapped arms around her extended belly and leaned forward as if she could somehow save her babe from the demons surrounding her.

A shriek split the night, the cry of death. She'd heard it before. Someone had just died, run through with a blade perhaps. Footsteps thundered. Light burst on the scene, and in marched a band of men, cutlasses drawn. Two of them carried torches.

The man in front, who must be the leader, peered into the cells across from hers. Lazy-eyed Smity uttered a yelp of joy. "Knew ye'd come, Cap'n!"

Further down, Durwin shouted with glee. "Took ye long enough!"

The leader's deep voice responded in a jovial tone. "Been a little busy." He slipped out of sight as one of the men behind him unlocked the cell doors with a set of jangling keys he'd no doubt stolen from a guard. The torches passed by Gabrielle, leaving her in darkness once again. She shrank into the shadows. Best to remain unseen, unnoticed. Quiet. Yet her heart pounded so loudly against her ribs, she was sure they would hear.

More shouts of joy rumbled through the stone walls as more demons were set free. Yet not all were released. Pleadings and beggings from left-behind prisoners were soon followed by obscenities and the damming of the captain's soul, along with the mother who bore him.

The torches reappeared. The leader or *captain* halted before Gabrielle's cell, his back to her, ordering his men to hurry. He was tall in stature, broad in shoulders, and his dark hair was tied back cavalier style.

Gabrielle held her breath and prayed for him to take no note of her.

The freed prisoners darted past him until only Durwin and Smity remained.

"That all of them?" he asked.

"Aye, 'cept ole Willard," Durwin drew his thumbnail across his neck. "Jist two days past."

The captain cursed.

"Escaped prisoners!" a shout railed from outside. Pistol shots rang through the air.

"We'd best go," the captain said.

"Ye may want to take 'er." Smity gestured toward Gabrielle.

Her breath caught in her throat. Foolishly, she glanced around her cell, seeking a place to hide. But of course there was none.

The captain swerved to face her. Durwin held up his torch.

Penetrating eyes speared her from a handsome, well-chiseled face.

"She carries Allard's brat."

The captain's eyes narrowed into spikes of hatred as they lowered to her belly. "Bring her," was all he said before he marched away.

Chapter 2

It was a fate worse than death, even death by a noose. A fate Gabrielle ne'er thought to face again in her short, calamity-stricken life. Yet here she was being dragged through the dark, misty streets of Nassau to God-only-knew-where. Though Gabrielle had a good idea. And the thought churned nausea in her belly. *Pirates.* Of course, it had to be pirates. Behind them, gunshots echoed through the night, along with shouts and heavy footfalls, accompanied by the eerie twang of an off-key violin emanating from a tavern up ahead.

The man they called captain led the way, cutlass drawn, issuing orders right and left. "Hurry!" he shouted, and the men on either side of Gabrielle squeezed her arms tighter and dashed after him.

Fast. Too fast! Pain throbbed across her belly with each jolt. She tugged, trying to free her hands in an effort to support her babe, but the men only tightened their grips. She couldn't breathe. Her swollen ankles ached. Her heart did flips in her chest. Would her baby die? He kicked as if to say, *I'm still here,* but it was a hard kick, one that nearly knocked the air from her lungs.

Oh, God, please. Please don't let my baby die. Tears blurred her vision and spilled down her cheeks.

Her legs gave out. She fell limp in the pirates' grips.

"Cap'n," one of them shouted. "Leave the wench 'ere. She can't keep up."

"Then carry her," the captain returned with authority.

Grunts and curses flooded her ears as one man shoved his shoulder under her left arm and the other under her right, and together they lifted her from the ground. The odor of sweat, gun smoke, and the sea assailed her.

Shots exploded behind her. Something whizzed past her ear, and she prayed the next one would hit her and put her out of her misery.

She must have lost consciousness for a time, for the next thing she knew, the captain and his men crossed blades with a group of soldiers. Her hands were free! She pushed from the ground where she'd been laid. Metal *clanged* through the night air, along with grunts and cries of pain. A cramp raged across her belly. Was she losing her baby?

Things went black again.

Now she was in a small boat. Oars slapped the black waters on each side. The twinkling lights from the city grew dim in the distance as she tried to make out the faces of the creatures sitting around her—creatures of the night. Nay, pirates. Same thing, she supposed. One of them slumped over, hand pressing a wound in his side. A bloodied scarf was tied about another pirate's arm. Gabrielle swallowed a knot of fear, inching off the thwart, thinking to fling herself into the harbor, but the pirates on either side shoved her back.

The small craft leapt over wavelets. Up down, up down. Nausea rose in her throat, and she slammed her hand over her mouth to keep from tossing her accounts. Water sloshed at her feet, soaking her stockings. They passed the hulls of mighty ships sleeping in the harbor like sea monsters, so close, she could reach out and touch them. A breeze, rank with the odor of unwashed men and sodden wood filled her nose, adding to her queasiness.

The boat thudded against one of the hulls. She was shoved harshly up a rope ladder and onto the deck of a ship, a brigantine, from what she could tell. With her hands finally free, she embraced her belly and the precious child within.

Blinking away her terror, she searched for a way of escape. Anything, even an early death, would be better than the future she faced.

Without so much as glancing in her direction, the captain ordered her locked below, then began spouting orders for the injured to find someone named Moses and for his crew to weigh anchor and set sail.

Lazy-eyed Smity shoved her down a ladder. Hard. Stumbling, she gripped a nearby crate to steady herself as he grabbed a lantern from a hook. Holding it above his head, he pushed her down another ladder into the hold. A stench rose to sting her nose and steal her breath. She coughed as they made their way past barrels that no doubt held salted meat, biscuits, and other foodstuffs, past an upraised platform holding bags of flour, past the shot locker and the hold-well where water sloshed with the movement of the ship. Finally, across from the copper-lined magazine where gunpowder was stored, stood an iron cage. Her new prison. He slammed the door shut in her face. The clank of metal echoed through the bowels of the ship, sealing her fate.

"Why do you hate me so? What have I ever done to you?"

He held up a lantern, the flickering light transforming the scars on his face into monstrous scales.

"Ye women are all alike. Whores, the lot o' ye." He sneered at her, then marched away, leaving her in utter darkness.

Groping behind her, she touched the bench she'd seen upon entering and lowered to sit. The babe within had gone quiet. *Please, God. Don't let him be dead.* She had no idea why she continued to pray. God had not answered her prayers in a long while. In fact, when she prayed, things usually got worse.

Oddly, she preferred the prison at Nassau to being locked in the hold of a pirate ship. She'd grown up around pirates. Most were naught but cutthroats who enacted torturous punishments on their enemies—and sometimes on their friends. Women prisoners were normally confined in small cabins or even the captain's cabin if he had evil intent. Which they all did. Then why was she in the hold? Bah, what did it matter? Perhaps 'twas for the best, for surely she would die in this cesspool sooner than were she given any comforts.

Footsteps thundered above, along with shouts and the grunts of men heaving sail. The ship lurched and began to move. Water purled against the hull, the sound oddly soothing for the memories it held, happier memories of a childhood spent upon the sea with parents who loved her. She fought back tears. Surely, after what she'd done, they no longer harbored such sentiments. Shame was likely the only feeling they bore now. But who could blame them?

The shame of the great Captain Damien Allard.

Odd that the mention of his name caused this particular pirate captain to kidnap her. How had Durwin known? She couldn't remember telling anyone who had sired the child within her. Perhaps she had cried out his name in her sleep.

Another cramp struck her belly. She leaned back against the iron bars, holding her breath to stop from screaming. The pain passed, and she gasped for air. The stench of human waste, rotten food, mold, and decay saturated her lungs. She'd sailed on tall ships her entire life, but one never grew accustomed to the putrid stink of the hold.

The thunder of sails snapped above. They must have emerged from the harbor onto the open sea.

The ship lurched, stronger this time. Gabrielle held onto the iron bars to keep from falling.

Bilge water trickled over the floor. Hefting her swollen wet feet atop the bench, she lowered her head and began to sob. She thought to pray once more, but why? God had long since abandoned her.

Captain Cadan Hayes grabbed a decanter of rum from his desk in his cabin and raised it to his lips. Taking a big gulp, he braced his feet against the heaving deck, lowered the bottle, and spun to face his quartermaster, Joseph Pell.

"I see your mission was successful, Captain." Pell cocked his head, one brow raised.

Cadan grinned. "Would you expect any less?"

Snorting, Pell glanced out the stern windows onto the dark seas, sprinkled with light from a half-moon.

Taking another sip of rum, Cadan set the bottle down on his desk. "I'd offer you some but…"

"'Cause I used to be a preacher? You know I forsook that calling years ago."

Cadan studied the man who had become a good friend over the past few years. With his stained linen shirt, colorful waistcoat, tan breeches tucked into jackboots, and cutlass at his side, no one would suspect he'd once been a man of God sent to convert the heathens on Antigua. All save for the wooden cross hanging around his neck. "Then join me in a drink, my friend." Cadan picked up the bottle again, but this time poured some into a glass.

Pell held up his hand. "I prefer to keep my wits, Captain." He slanted his lips. "As you should as well."

Cadan laughed. "When have my wits ever done me any good?" He slammed the rum to the back of his throat. "'Tis usually when I am without them that I achieve my goals."

"And was your goal to bring aboard a woman ripe with child?"

Cadan huffed. "Not at first, I admit." Movement caught his eye as Zada scrambled across the map on his desk. Picking him up, he scratched the iguana's back before placing him on the deck.

Pell shook his head and seemed about to say something when a rap thundered on the door. Best to allow the interruption before his friend gave him another of his lectures. He might not be a preacher anymore, but he sure spoke like one. "Enter."

Lazy-eyed Smity poked his head in. "She be locked up below, as ye ordered, Cap'n."

"Very good," Cadan returned, which Smity must have taken as permission to enter and give his opinion.

"Good thinkin' in lockin' 'er up, too. A wench should ne'er be trusted." He rubbed the scars on the right side of his face. "I thank ye, Cap'n, fer gettin' us out o' that hellhole."

Cadan nodded at his bosun, one of the best sailors he'd come across, but the man could be as heartless as an angry viper. Perhaps learned from his time with the famous pirate Captain Avery. Regardless, Cadan still felt a twinge of guilt whene'er he looked at the scars on his face and his wandering eye.

"The key?" Cadan held out his hand. The last thing he wanted was for the woman to be ravished without his permission.

Lamplight flickered off the single pearl in Smity's right earlobe as frowning, he fished it out of his pocket and tossed it to Cadan.

"Now, get above and keep the men in order and all canvas to the wind," he ordered, catching it.

No sooner did Smity turn to leave than Omphile shoved her way past him, a scowl on her otherwise pretty face. "What's dis I hear 'bout a woman on board? And one wit' child as well?"

Pell smiled.

Cadan released a heavy sigh and crossed arms over his chest. "'Tis none of your business, woman."

Swinging one of her long braids over her shoulder, she flattened her lips. "I thought you was a decent man, Cap'n. Not one t' take a mistress by force."

"Mistress? Scads. Nay, she is my bait."

"An' what d'you hope t' catch wit' her?" The comely middle-aged Negress planted a hand on her rounded hip.

Pell raised his brows, clearly interested in the conversation.

"That'll be all, Pell. Back to your duties."

With a huff, the quartermaster left, offering a wink to Omphile.

Cadan should not allow the woman to speak to him thus, but for some reason, she reminded him of his mother, all pluck and goodness and honesty. Something found lacking in the rest of his crew.

She stood there staring at him, her ebony skin aglow in the lantern light and her long braids swinging with the movement of the ship.

"'Tis the babe within her that will bring me the greatest prize of all, and that's all I'll say of it."

"Will it bring the same prize if it dies?"

Cadan studied her, confused.

"D'you think she an' the babe will survive in the filthy, sodden, vermin-ridden hold?" She cocked her head. "Bring her above an' allow me to tend t' her needs."

The blasted woman had a point. Females were such weak creatures. No doubt the wench would not last long below. And that wouldn't do well for his plans at all. He waved a hand through the air. "Very well. I'll have Moses set up Barnett's cabin for her." He tossed her the key, which she expertly caught with a grin. "But have him bring her to me first."

Chapter 3

When a giant, dark-skinned man appeared before Gabrielle's cage, lantern in hand, she thought her fate was sealed. But instead of a malicious look, the flickering light revealed a kind face. Holding up the lantern, he examined her more with curiosity than animosity, announced the captain wished to see her, and promptly unlocked the iron gate.

Pushing against the bench, she struggled to rise, but the ship leapt over a wave, and she fell back.

The man entered the cell and held out his hand.

Hesitant, she swallowed down a burst of fear and took it. Surely if the captain wished to see her, this man would do her no harm. His large hand engulfed hers as he gently lifted her from the seat, then immediately released her.

"Dis way," he said. Hefting the lantern, he led her through the hold, up two ladders, and onto the deck.

With heavy breath, she struggled to keep up, ignoring the ache in her belly. But soon she emerged to a blast of warm, moist air that swept away the stench of the hold and brought with it the smells of a salty sea, sodden wood, and the sweat of men—oddly comforting in their familiarity. Above her, a glorious splattering of twinkling stars spanned from horizon to horizon, displaying the handiwork of God. Or so her father had oft told her. Pirates stopped to gape at her as if she were a mermaid drawn from the sea. Salacious suggestions and untoward invitations peppered her from all directions, things no lady should hear, but she ignored them.

After all, she was no lady.

The large man escorted her down a companionway to their right, through another short hallway where he knocked on a carved oak door.

The captain's smoky voice shouted "Enter," and instantly Gabrielle was nudged into the lion's den, for what rose from behind a desk was as frightening as a beast searching for prey.

"That'll be all, Moses," he said.

The dark man left. The door shut with an ominous thud. Gabrielle lifted her shoulders and returned the man's stare with as much courage as she could muster. Which wasn't much at the moment. Still, a flash of confusion crossed those hazel eyes of his as he rounded his desk toward her. Aye, she'd noticed the color of his eyes, so striking against his tanned skin and coal black hair. A handsome beast, if she admitted it. But a beast, nonetheless.

"You may sit." He gestured toward a chair bolted to the deck toward her right. At least she thought it was a chair. Hard to tell with the piles of books, parchments, bowls, and various trinkets cluttered on the seat.

He made no move to clear it. Hence, Gabrielle swept it to the deck with one hand, ignored the clanging and thumping, and promptly slid onto the seat. If she angered the beast, what did it matter? He was clearly no gentleman.

When she dared raise her gaze to his, an odd smirk sat upon his lips. He crossed arms over his chest and studied her with an intensity that forced her to look away. *Lud.* The last thing she wanted was to cower before this pirate, to give him the power over her he so craved. But the man radiated a confidence, a strength, an intensity that filled every crack and crevice of the cabin.

A cabin that resembled a garbage heap. A lantern hooked above sent waves of golden light over waistcoats, trousers, shirts, and hats crumpled in piles where they'd no doubt been carelessly removed. Atop a bed perched against the starboard bulkhead, various quilts appeared to have fought an overnight battle. And lost. Open bottles and silver-lidded claret jugs littered the cabin on shelves, a desk, and a mahogany sideboard like statues to a foreign god. Parchments, maps, and navigation instruments covered every inch of his desk in such aimless turmoil, 'twould be hard to find any of them when needed. Weapons—flintlocks, knives in all sizes, blades, and an ax—lay casually about, within easy reach of the man, who likely wielded them expertly.

In truth, a small knife sat on the top of a chest near Gabrielle. Her eyes latched upon it for but an instant before she shifted them away.

The beast noticed and quickly moved to remove it.

His gait was strong and determined, boots of black Cordovan leather thundered on the deck. A sleeveless leather waistcoat covered an open-collared black shirt stuffed into brown breeches that clung to firm thighs. Leather braces crisscrossed a thick chest, devoid of weapons at the moment. Wavy strands of his dark hair had escaped their prison and hung about his stubbled jaw.

Her breathing came hard and fast as he approached, though she tried to hide it. A waft of spice and the sea swept over her as he grabbed the knife and strode back to the desk.

"What do you want with me, Captain?" she dared ask, hating the quiver in her voice.

He spun to face her, the slight grin on his lips fading as his eyes lowered to her belly. Instantly, his expression twisted into a dark malevolence as if a demon had suddenly possessed his thoughts.

Gabrielle covered her belly with her arms, hoping to protect her babe from whate'er dark spirits leapt from this evil man.

He pinched his right earlobe, continuing to stare at her stomach, his jaw flexing and bunching until she thought it would burst. Finally, he turned, poured a drink from an open bottle, and tossed it into his mouth.

Rum. She knew the pungent scent well.

Against her will and every effort, tears flooded her eyes. "Have we met before?" Though she was sure she'd remember such an encounter.

Snorting, he stared out the stern windows where a dark, moonlit sea swayed in and out of view with each leap of the ship.

When he faced her again, his expression had softened ever so slightly, giving her hope he wasn't the monster he seemed to be.

"Nay. Though I am quite familiar with your type."

Gabrielle raised a brow. "And what, pray, is my type?"

"From your speech," he continued, leaning back against his desk. "I perceive you to be a lady of some education and means."

The deck slanted as the ship leapt over a wave. She shifted in her seat, confusion tumbling through her. But she must not play his game. She must never show fear. Hence, she met his imperious gaze. "Indeed. I have been raised in fortunate circumstances. Is that enough to warrant your hatred?"

"Not of itself." Grabbing a bottle, he gestured with it toward her belly. "You carry the seed of the devil himself."

His words struck with the force of a cannon ball. Yet she allowed not so much as a wince to appear. Instead, she lifted her chin. "I see you are acquainted with Damien Allard."

A hint of a grin lifted one side of his lips, then disappeared as quickly as it had come. "So, you do not deny it."

"I do not deny his acquaintance."

"Or the result." He snapped back, perfidious gaze landing once again on her belly.

Fear like she'd never known swamped her, squeezing every nerve tight. "You want my child," she mumbled out as the realization hit her.

He said naught, merely stared at her with such ferocity, she nearly collapsed. *Nay*! She would not allow another pirate to harm her. Or her child. Drawing a deep breath, she sat up straight and threw back her shoulders. "I realize, Captain, that I am your prisoner and being a woman do not have the physical strength to fight you and your men, but I assure you, I will do everything in my power to save the child I'm carrying. If it comes to it, I will fight to the death and gladly die and take the babe with me to the depths of hell rather than hand him over to you."

Cadan didn't know whether to applaud the wench's performance or throw her back in the hold for her brazen insolence. Either way, he couldn't help but smile at the lunacy of her threats.

She had pluck, he'd give her that. And courage. Quite surprising in a woman who obviously hailed from nobility. Another disparaging mark against her character. Most females were not to be trusted. But those born to wealth and power were the worst of the lot, naught but sharks whose bite could sink a man to the depths.

And this particular siren shark had quite a bite.

She was a rare beauty, much like his wife had been. Another strike against her. Still, how could he keep his eyes off those golden tresses tumbling over her shoulders to her waist? Even dirty and tangled, each strand glittered in the lantern light like fine gold intertwined with pearls. High cheek bones, a chiseled nose, and lips that would drive any man wild completed the face of a goddess. But those eyes, the color of the Caribbean, one minute streaked in terror, the next covered by a determined, defiant sheen….a man could get lost in those eyes.

He was not the young fool he used to be. Nay, he would not come under her spell.

"I will excuse your impudent affront, my lady," he began, using his most imperious tone, "for you do not know me. But henceforth, I will have you thrown back in the hold should your tongue run its foolish course again."

Her pert little nose twitched. "Am I not going back there regardless?"

"Do you wish to?"

She studied him. "I wish to be off this ship."

"That will not happen. At least not until you serve your purpose."

"To bait Captain Allard?"

He shot his gaze to hers. Smart. Another quality he had not expected.

"If you think he will come for me, you are quite mistaken, Captain. Allard bears no affection for me at'll. In truth, I doubt he cares for anyone but himself."

Cadan nodded. "I quite agree, my lady. But you are not the bait."

Confusion wrinkled her face until she glanced down at her belly. "You think he cares for his child?"

Cadan arched a brow. "Does he know?"

She gently caressed her stomach as if she were comforting the child itself. What was it about women who could love a babe they had not yet seen or held? Even after they were born, they were naught but screaming, smelly creatures.

"Nay," she said. "He left me to hang for piracy ere my stomach grew." Bitterness stung in her tone as she looked up, eyes moistening. "He is a monster of the worst kind, but then, so is a man who would use a baby as bait."

"Watch your tongue, woman!" His sharp words hit their mark as the wench cowered slightly. What did this peckish minx know of his life? Of him? Grabbing the rum, he took another gulp. Out of the corner of his eye, he spotted Zada scampering over the deck toward the lady. Women were such skittish things. He should warn her. But why? 'Twould be amusing to watch her scream, run to the door, cower in disgust... He waited with anticipation.

Instead, a smile graced her lips, and she leaned to the side, swept the iguana in her hands, and brought it to her lap. "Who are you, little one?" she said as if talking to a cuddly cat. Then ever so gently, she pet the lizard on its cheek.

Zada, the traitor, turned one eye on Cadan as if to say, *I like her.*

Baffling woman. Cadan needed more rum. Instead, he called for Moses, knowing the man would be right outside.

"Lock her in Barnett's cabin."

"Aye, Aye, Cap'n." The carpenter/surgeon gestured for the woman to follow him.

Setting Zada down, she rose, balanced her feet on the shifting deck, and followed Moses. She glanced at Cadan as she passed, and he saw terror in her eyes...yet something else, strength and courage.

After Moses shut the door, Cadan grabbed his rum, moved to the stern windows and stared at the dark, riotous sea.

He'd expected a cowering female, uneducated, immoral, foul-mouthed. A wench. He'd expected her to beg for her life, or at the very least, try to seduce him into gaining her freedom.

What he'd gotten instead was a witty, educated, courageous lady who even liked his iguana. Despite that, he must remember who she once loved...

And whose child she bore.

Chapter 4

The man called Moses escorted her onto the main deck, back down a ladder, then through a narrow hallway to a cabin similar in size to the cage she'd been locked in below. Not that she was complaining, for at least there was a bunk, a small table and chair, and a chest of drawers, all bolted down, of course. A small round window nearly out of Gabrielle's reach opened to the dark sky and allowed a salty breeze to enter.

Moses hooked the lantern on the ceiling and turned to leave when a dark-skinned woman appeared in the doorway, a bowl in her hands.

Upon seeing Moses, she smiled up at the man who towered well over a foot above her.

"How are you, Moses?"

"Fine, ma'am." He shifted his feet but remained in place as if the shock of such beauty held him captive. "Good dinner you made earlier."

"I's glad you liked it." She smiled again. Several minutes passed as the couple stared at each other. "Now step aside, you big fool, so's I can tend the lady." She gestured toward Gabrielle.

Muttering, the poor man attempted to leave but kept stepping in the woman's path. "Beggin' yer pardon, ma'am." He backed into the cabin, knocking Gabrielle onto the bed.

Finally, chuckling, the woman squeezed past him and bid him farewell as he shuffled out and shut the door.

"I'm Omphile," she said, setting the bowl on the table.

Gabrielle's stomach lurched at the scent of some kind of stew. Was she to be fed or merely tortured with the smell?

"Gabrielle."

Lantern light flickered over the woman's fine ebony skin and long dark braids. Deep set eyes, a prominent nose, and full lips formed an attractive face. But there was also something in those eyes that made her even more beautiful…a light, a cheerfulness, a kindness Gabrielle would not have expected on a pirate ship. "I didn't know there were other women on board."

Water gushed against the hull as the ship tilted to larboard.

Sliding onto the chair, Omphile took the bowl and handed it to Gabrielle. "Jist me. And now you." She smiled.

Gabrielle stared at the stew, unsure whether her stomach would welcome it or toss it back into the bowl. She couldn't remember the last time she ate anything that smelled so good.

"Go on, now, eat." Omphile nodded. "I knows you're scared, but the babe needs it."

So that was it. The captain's motive for this small measure of kindness—to keep her baby alive. In that goal, she was quite in agreement. 'Twas regarding the purpose of it, on which they parted. Drawing the bowl to her lips, she slowly sipped the savory broth, cold, but a tasty brew of pork, onions, corn, and something else she couldn't place. Her stomach embraced it with a leap of pleasure.

"You are the ship's cook?" Gabrielle asked, taking another sip.

"Aye, among other duties." Rising, she opened a drawer and pulled out a small pillow and quilt. "These will do nicely for you tonight, Miss." She set them at the bottom of the bed, then gripped the bulkhead as the deck shifted slightly. "Tomorrow, we'll git you cleaned up an' in some fresh clothes." She began to hum a pleasant tune.

Fresh clothes? Clean? Suspicion rose at such kindness. "I thank you for the stew. 'Tis delicious." Gabrielle handed her the bowl, unable to finish it. In truth, her stomach was in as much turmoil as her nerves.

"You should eat more, Miss." Omphile sat again and leaned forward, studying Gabrielle with curiosity.

Gabrielle would guess the woman to be in her late thirties or early forties, though 'twas hard to tell with such glowing, rich skin. "What does the captain want with my baby?" she blurted out. "What is he going to do with me?"

Omphile's face scrunched as she waved a hand through the air. "Ah, never you worry, Miss. The captain's more bluster than bite. He'll do you no harm in de end."

Not from what Gabrielle had seen from a few minutes with the man. "Perhaps not me, but my babe." She gripped her rounded belly.

Omphile released a heavy sigh. "Never you worry. Let us see what the good Laud will do, Miss."

Gabrielle closed her eyes. Lord? Was He good? She'd been taught so, but in truth, the Almighty had been naught but cruel to her of late. The baby moved, and she opened her eyes and smiled. Still alive and kicking.

Omphile's tender gaze moved to Gabrielle's belly. "What a miracle t' feel a life growin' wit'in you."

Perhaps Gabrielle could appeal to the woman's motherly instinct. "Do you have children?"

Joy fled her face. "I was wit' child once, but…"—she moved a hand over her own flat belly— "she's wit' the Laud now."

Gabrielle didn't know what to say. Though she had not yet laid eyes upon her child, she could not imagine losing him. "I'm sorry."

Instantly, the pain on Omphile's face disappeared. "It was God's will."

God again. Odd that a pirate's whore would speak of the Almighty so fondly. "His will to kill a child?" Gabrielle said a bit too harshly.

"'Course not. To take her to heaven." She replied in a tone that brooked no doubt. "When is your birthin'?"

"Any time now, I guess." Gabrielle had given up counting the days since she discovered herself with child. Though it seemed an eternity.

Omphile reached out as if to take Gabrielle's hand, then pulled back. "Now, don't you worry, Miss. I have experience birthin' babes."

Sails snapped above, and a moist breeze coming in from the porthole swept around Gabrielle. She swallowed a lump of dread. She'd heard from her mother that labor pains were excruciating. Even so, she'd rather not bring her child into the world on board a pirate ship.

As if reading her mind, Omphile added, "De captain's a good man. You'll see."

"Of course he's kind to you." Gabrielle snorted. "You're his paramour." 'Twas a rude thing to say, but what other explanation could there be for the woman's presence on board? And a beautiful woman at that.

"Good Laud!" Instead of showing anger or insult, Omphile merely laughed. "It's not like dat, Miss. Cap'n Hayes saved me, rescued me. Found me starvin' on the streets of St. Kitts, he did. I would be deep in my grave if not for him."

Wonderful. Paramour or not, the woman was far too loyal to the captain to be of any use to Gabrielle. She'd either have to convince her of the man's evil heart or find another ally— someone who would help her escape. 'Twas her only hope.

"You'll see, Miss." Slapping her hands on her thighs, she rose, grabbed the bowl, and turned to leave. "I's best get some rest afore the sun rises. You should too, Miss. I'll come back tomorrow t' empty your chamber pot an' see to your needs. Oh" —she faced Gabrielle again— "I's lockin' the door, but not t' keep you in, if you knows what I mean." With that, she closed the door and the clank of a lock echoed through the cabin.

Gabrielle brought the pillow to her chest and squeezed it, tears flooding her eyes. Aye, she *did* know what she meant, and that didn't bode well for her future. Or her precious babe's.

Captain Cadan Hayes shoved open the door to the Slippery Eel tavern and stepped inside. Smoke and the stench of cheap perfume, sweat, and pungent spirits assailed his senses. Mobs of seaman cluttered the large room like cockroaches at a picnic, some skittered about, others gambled, some angrily drew swords, while others feasted on women and wine. Gripping the hilt of his cutlass, he forged through the mass of humanity, scanning for the vermin he sought.

Durwin, Lazy-eyed Smity, and Pell followed on his flank.

He wet his lips at the smell of rum, longing for a drink, and upon not seeing the cur in question, he approached a table occupied by three men. "Begone," he commanded with confident authority.

One of the men gazed up at him with glassy eyes, his forehead wrinkling beneath a strand of greasy hair. "What ye want, ye bloated jellyfish?"

Cadan gripped the hilt of his cutlass. "I believe I made myself clear."

The other two men finally looked up from their cups. The only one of the three who apparently had not drunken his wits into an early grave gaped at Cadan with terror.

His friend uttered a string of curses and waved Cadan away as one would an annoying gnat.

"It be Cap'n Hayes," the man who stared wide-eyed at him whispered to his friends. Rising, he yanked one of them up and tugged him aside. "Come on, Mires," he shouted to the third man who slowly rose, swaying on his feet. After casting a frightened look at Cadan, he scampered away with his friends.

Grinning, Cadan slid onto a chair.

"Proud of yourself?" Pell sat across from him, raising one eyebrow.

"Indeed." Cadan gestured for a barmaid and ordered mugs of ale. In truth he rather enjoyed the respect and fear he'd earned from the Brethren of the Coast. His reputation as an expert swordsman and skillful captain—one he'd worked hard to achieve—had its privileges. And one day he hoped it would bring him both the wealth and power he craved.

Durwin took a seat beside Pell, but before Smity could join them, Cadan waved his bosun away. "Keep your eye out for that scug One-tooth Leadwig and report back to me."

With a scowl, the man wandered away.

The barmaid returned, slamming mugs on the table and spilling foam over the rims. No doubt because her batting eyes were all over Cadan. Leaning forward, she gave him a full view of the crests of her over-sized bosoms peeking above her stays. "Can I git ye anything else, Cap'n?"

It had been a while since he'd been with a woman, a *long* while, but now was not the time. And this was not the woman, if ever there would be one again after Elyna.

Grabbing his mug, he waved her away and took a long draught.

Durwin's lusty gaze followed the barmaid as she swayed off. "I could use a bit o' *somethin' else*, if ye's know what I mean, Cap'n."

"That's not why we are here," Cadan replied.

"Remind me again, Captain." Pell sat back with an incriminating huff. "Why exactly we are here in this redeeming establishment?"

Durwin chuckled. "Ye sure talk pretty, Pell."

"He was a preacher." Cadan snorted "They all talk pretty." He glanced over the tavern, alert to any malevolent looks cast his way. One unfortunate curse of being a respected and powerful pirate captain was that someone always wanted to knock you from your throne. "We are here to set a trap, as you well know."

Across the room, shouts and curses blared over the normal clamor. A table crashed to the floor. Blades chimed, drawing a mob of ruffians toward the altercation like rats to cheese.

Durwin's right eye twitched as he shifted his gaze about anxiously.

Was the man nervous? Nay. He'd more than proven his courage in battle. Then why did he always appear as twitchy as a schoolgirl in a brothel? Perhaps 'twas his lanky figure that resembled more mast than man. Though only in his twenties, the sun had left lines upon his brow, forming a perpetual frown. That and his hawk-like nose made him appear untrustworthy, but he'd more than proven his loyalty to Cadan.

"You should eat more," Cadan shouted to the man over the violent tumult in the far corner.

In the distance, a sailor flew through the air, landed on a chair, crushing it into pieces.

Above him, a parrot squawked from the rafters, flapping its wings. "Blast me barnacles! Blast me barnacles!"

"I eat plenty, Cap'n." Durwin gulped his ale. "Thanks to ye! This be the most flesh I've had on me bones in years."

Cadan nodded. Indeed. The man had been a mere shadow when he'd found him begging for work in Jamaica. Cast off from the royal navy for continued illness, he had a difficult time convincing the captain of any ship—pirate or merchant—to bring him on board. Cadan was glad he'd given him a chance, for he'd turned out to be a worthy first mate.

Light from a lantern overhead shifted over Pell as he stared at his ale, deep in thought, oblivious to the clamor and debauchery surrounding him.

"What say you, Pell?" Cadan asked.

He slowly raised his gaze, the look in his dark eyes intense as if he were planning how to save the world.

"I say naught, Captain. Merely that I wish this night to be over." Lifting his mug, he took a sip and wiped the foam from his lip.

As if his words summoned Lazy-eyed Smity, the crotchety pirate emerged from the throng, a man in tow.

Not just any man, but One-tooth Leadwig, the most unscrupulous, dung-souled skunk ever to sail the Caribbean. The man would sell his own mother for a shot of rum.

Which is what Cadan was counting on.

Smity shoved him into a chair next to Cadan, then grabbed an empty one and straddled it backwards, gesturing for Durwin to hand him his mug.

In the corner, a pirate began banging out a tune on a harpsichord.

Leadwig smiled nervously at Cadan, his single tooth resembling a man hanging from the gallows.

"Cap'n Hayes." Headjusted his black periwig. "Didn't expect t' see ye 'ere."

Finishing off his ale, Cadan lifted his hand, snapping for the wench to bring rum, then leaned toward One-tooth. "Word is, you sail with Captain Allard on occasion."

"Aye, that be true." His shoulders rose as if he was proud to be associated with the blackguard. "One o' 'is top men, I is. Helped 'im acquire a bit o' wealth, says I. Did I ever tell ye about the St. Croix raid? Was me idea, it were, an' when we—"

"I have a message for Allard," Cadan interrupted, annoyed with the man's theatrics.

One-tooth glanced at Cadan's men. "I's be happy to tell 'im."

The barmaid returned with glasses of rum, setting one before One-tooth.

He reached for it, but Cadan stayed his hand. "There's more than rum in it for you if you do precisely what I say."

One of One-tooth's eyelids twitched as he raised his gaze to Cadan. "Like what?"

Cadan nodded at Pell, and the quartermaster reached into a pouch and tossed a velvet sack onto the table. The clinking of coins could be heard even over the curses and continuing chime of blades. A few men glanced their way.

One-tooth licked his lips, greed glimmering in his eyes, along with Durwin's, whose gaze had not left the bag.

"There's ten doubloons for you now and double that when you complete your task."

Picking up his rum, One-tooth tossed it to the back of his throat with one flick, then slammed down his glass. A wide grin split his lips, revealing that stubborn tooth yet again. "I'd cut out the man's liver an' feed it to 'is mother fer that price."

Durwin chuckled. Groaning, Pell sipped his ale.

"Perhaps another time." Cadan grinned. "But for now, tell Allard that you shared cups with one of my men right here at the Slippery Eel."

A fly landed on One-tooth's periwig, feasting on whatever scraps of food remained there. "That'll be the truth, seein' I'm wit' yer men now."

Cadan shook his head at the man's stupidity. "Indeed, but you will tell him that the man in his besotted stupor gave away the location of the cove where we will be careening the *Resolute*."

One-tooth inched his hand toward the bag of coins. "What will that be to 'im?"

"It will be everything to him when you also tell him that Captain Hayes has his mistress and unborn babe."

Chapter 5

Gabrielle ran through the ship's narrow hallway, heart pounding, splinters pricking her bare feet. The deck lurched to larboard. She crashed into the bulkhead. Pain etched up her arm. Ignoring it, she raced onward. Lanterns swayed above her, casting ghoulish specters over the walls. Sweat slid down her back. Her breath slammed against her lungs. She was nearly at the ladder! She reached to grab it, But no! It sped backward. Grabbing her skirts, she dashed toward it once again. But every time she stretched forth her hand to touch it, it retreated into the distance.

"Nay!" Stopping, she leaned against the bulkhead, tears filling her eyes.

"There you are, *ma douce.*" A voice, a familiar, repulsive voice echoed down the hallway.

Terror squeezed her throat. She couldn't breathe. Clutching her chest, she backed up slowly, her mind intent on one thing. Get as far as she could from the sound of that craven voice!

She bumped into something warm and solid.

Leaping, she spun about.

Captain Damien Allard, dressed in black silk with silver lace, cocked his head and grinned at her like a panther.

"You monster!" She raised a hand to slap him, but he caught it, tightening his grip until she begged for mercy.

He released her. She gripped her belly.

Flat. It was flat! "My baby! What have you done with my baby?" Horror pierced every nerve. She had no recollection of giving birth.

"You mean *my* son?" He sneered.

"What have you done with him!" She pounded his chest with her fists, tears pouring down her cheeks. "What have you done with him?"

Boom!

The ship quivered beneath the blast of a cannon.

Boom!

Gabrielle lurched to sit, blood racing through her veins. Darkness enveloped her. Blinking, she waited for her eyes to focus. Gray light seeping in from the porthole spilled over the chest of drawers and onto the deck. A figure stood to her left—a man. Heart seizing, she tossed off the coverlet and swept her feet to the deck.

"Who are you?" she shouted. "What do you want?"

Light from the window crept toward him, closer and closer over the deck and bulkhead, inching toward his shadow. It barely grazed his leg when he completely disappeared.

Rubbing her eyes, she steadied her breathing and dropped her head in her hands. Still dreaming. That was it.

Boom!

The deck trembled beneath her feet. *That* was no dream. Footsteps thundered above, along with shouts and commands. A battle? Were they engaging an enemy? If so, perhaps the return fire would sink them to the depths.

And put her out of her misery.

Yet…she clutched her belly. Her child had done naught to deserve such a fate. "Good morning to you, my little one."

It had been three days since she'd been imprisoned within this cabin. And aside from Omphile, she'd seen no one else. The mulatto woman had brought her a basin of water for washing and a clean gown, along with two meals a day, but she'd not had time to keep Gabrielle company. Or so she said. Gabrielle had a feeling 'twas the captain's orders.

You don't befriend the lamb set for slaughter.

The lock clanked, jarring Gabrielle from her thoughts as the door swung open and in walked Omphile, a tray of food in hand.

A glimmer of sunlight, along with a breeze ripe with salt and smoke entered along with her, sweeping aside the stale air.

The tray of food belied they were engaged in battle. "Why the cannon blasts?"

"Dems jist testin' de guns, makin' sure dey all work properly." Setting down the tray, she struck flint to steel over an oiled charcloth and lit the lantern. Light spilled over the tiny cabin, but it did naught for Gabrielle's foul mood.

"What has you lookin' so sour, Miss?" Concern creased the woman's face as she examined Gabrielle and finally took a seat beside her on the bed.

What a foolish question. Who wouldn't look sour in this predicament? But Gabrielle had learned not to complain to Omphile, for the woman always told her all would be well.

A ridiculous notion, that.

"I've been having nightmares," was all she replied.

"Ah, dems from de devil hisself."

Gabrielle huffed. "You sound like my parents."

"Dey must be good people."

More shouts filtered down from above, adding to the crash of water against the hull.

"They are." Her mother and father were the Godliest people she knew. They spent their lives and fortunes on spreading God's message of salvation to pirates and princes alike.

"Mebbe you will join dem soon."

"Nay." Gabrielle hung her head. "I'm an embarrassment. I doubt they want anything to do with me now." She caressed her belly.

Omphile snorted. "Hush now! Jist because you're wit' child?" She took her hand in hers and squeezed it…a very intimate action but one Gabrielle needed at the moment. "If we repent, de good Laud forgives all our sins, an' if your parents are good people, dey will forgive you too."

Joy and peace filled the woman's dark eyes, reminding Gabrielle of the light that always shone in her mother's eyes. "You haven't done what I've done."

"Good Laud, Miss. I's done far worse."

Shocked, Gabrielle stared at her. Then again, the woman lived on a pirate ship.

Minutes passed in silence. A thousand questions crowded Gabrielle's tongue.

"You should eat something, Miss. For de baby." Omphile started to rise, but Gabrielle held her back.

"Where is he taking me? Do you know?"

Omphile shook her head.

"We dropped anchor somewhere yesterday. Where was it?" She knew ships. Had been on them all her life, so it wasn't hard to figure out from the sounds and the movement of the ship that they'd sailed into a harbor. Not to mention the squawk of birds and the brief glimpses out the porthole she'd been able to get if she jumped high enough. Not an easy task in her condition.

"Antigua. Cap'n an' a few men went ashore for an hour or two den returned. Dat's all I knows, Miss."

Gabrielle nodded, swallowing down a burst of fear.

Omphile rose.

"Don't leave. I'm so lonely."

Kindness softened the woman's expression. "I can stay a little while. Long as you eat." She cocked a brow.

Gabrielle smiled as Omphile set the tray on her lap and slid onto a chair. The scent of buttery biscuits, eggs, and oatmeal caused Gabrielle's mouth to water. They must have gotten the fresh butter, eggs, and milk at Antigua. She bit into the biscuit, enjoying the savory taste.

"May I ask how you came to be on this pirate ship?"

Omphile drew a deep breath. "A long story, Miss. Like I said, I's done far worse deeds dan you."

"I'd still like to know," she said between mouthfuls of eggs. "If you would share."

Omphile shrugged. "I was a slave on Barbados, but I managed to escape an' joined a group of runaway slaves in de hills. Dem was angry people. Filled wit' hate. Dey raided towns, killed innocent people."

Gabrielle stared at the woman, horrified. "You?"

"I might as well have. I was wit' dem who done it." She released a sorrowful sigh, then glanced at Gabrielle. "See, you look at me different now."

"Nay, I'm sorry." Gabrielle set down her fork. "I have no right."

"Anyways, I left dat group, stowed away on a ship to St. Kitts, an' would have starved dere if I hadn't met Sir Alfred Blake, a prominent landowner who took me in as a servant an' cared for me." Her gaze drifted away as if she were remembering the man.

"What good fortune. Did he treat you well?" But even as she said it, Gabrielle had her answer by the mournful look tugging on Omphile's face.

"At first. But I shoulda figured he had other motives. Soon enough, I found out I was wit' child."

Gabrielle set down her glass of milk and moved the tray to the deck.

A lump sped down Omphile's throat even as her eyes moistened. "He beat me. I guess he worried his wife would find out, you see, 'cause she came from a wealthy family. I lost de babe."

Gabrielle's eyes burned at the woman's story. "I'm so sorry, Omphile."

"Ah, never you mind. It all worked out." Her tone instantly perked. "I found de Laud Jesus, an' Captain Hayes found me doin' laundry in de river t' survive." Her grin revealed a row of bright, white teeth, an oddity among the lower class. "He asked if I could cook, an' when I said yes, he brought me aboard."

Gabrielle shook her head. "And you trusted him? After what happened?"

"Like I said, I found the Laud, or He found me. When I asked Him, He said to go wit' de captain. I's glad I did. He's been kind to me. Never touched me or allowed any o' his crew to touch me."

To say Gabrielle was surprised would be an understatement. Not only at the captain's chaste behavior but that this woman, who'd had a terrible life, could continually give God praise. And more importantly, as it related to Gabrielle's situation, how could she reconcile the kind man Omphile described with the monster who intended to use her unborn child as bait?

Standing, Omphile bent to get the tray from the floor.

"You don't know where we are going?" Gabrielle attempted one more time.

"No. Alls I heard, Miss, is somethin' about careening de ship."

Careening? Hope dared make an appearance in Gabrielle's heart. Careening meant she'd be taken onto land, and on land she'd at least have an opportunity to escape.

"Come down. I've got you." Cadan gestured up the rope ladder for the wench. He'd been surprisingly pleased when she'd first appeared at the top of the companionway and stepped onto the main deck. Omphile had asked for permission to allow the woman to bathe, but the transformation was beyond expectations. Rays of sunlight glinted off skin as smooth as pearls and spread alabaster threads among the gold of her hair. Her gown of blue grogram, no doubt one of Omphile's, fit too perfectly over curves that would drive a preacher mad, even brimming with child as she was.

In truth, even Pell stared at her, along with every other man on deck, and even those furling sails up on the yards.

When her eyes met his, the courage he'd seen in them reappeared, along with uncertainty and a hint of fear. Swallowing, she'd raised her shoulders and moved toward him with the grace of her station, reminding him why he detested her so.

She'd halted before him, raising her chin. "Where am I to be placed as bait, Captain? On the hook of a fishing line or perhaps tied to the masthead?"

Brazen little minx. Cadan grinned. "Don't tempt me, my lady." He turned, if only to take his gaze off her. "We go ashore."

At this, a tiny smile had graced her lips, and he realized the little vixen thought to escape. He'd allow her this small measure of hope for now, if only to keep her compliant.

Now as he waited for her in the boat, she shouted from above. "Step away. I have climbed down many rope ladders before."

"Climb, then." Cadan took a step back in the wobbling craft, releasing his hold on the ladder and allowing it to flail with the wind.

To her credit, the lady made it halfway. No doubt she would have climbed down the entire thing with ease were her belly not swollen like a blowfish. As it was, her foot missed one of the rungs and despite her attempts to tighten her grip, she slipped, tumbled downward, and promptly fell into Cadan's arms.

The pirates in the boat chuckled.

She looked up at him in horror, scrambling to be free of his grip, but the babe restricted her movements. "Let me down at once, you defiled fiend!"

Her insult, shouted with such authority, brought more chortles from his crew.

He grinned, enjoying being so close to her, her every movement causing his body to react in a way it hadn't in years. Her scent of sunshine and sass with a hint of rose wafted over him, alerting every sense.

Enough of this!

Regaining his senses, he set her down, but before he could steady her against the swaying of the cockboat, she dashed from him and fell into Lazy-eyed Smity's lap. The bosun's disdain for women with loose morals revealed itself in an expression of abhorrence as he shoved the poor lady away from him. She landed on Soot, his gunner, who was more than happy to provide a seat for her on his lap beside his rabbit, Hellfire.

The woman shrieked.

Finally, Pell cast a look of castigation at Cadan, took the lady's hand and offered her his seat as Cadan gave the order to row to shore.

The woman stared over the rippling water of the hidden cove, nose lifted, eyes focused and chest heaving. He supposed women like her were used to being fondled, yet real fear quivered in her eyes. *And* disgust. She behaved like a chaste virgin, yet her belly belied that notion.

The woman was full of surprises.

The cockboat struck shore and out leapt his men to drag the bow onto the sand. Cadan stepped into the swirling surf and gestured for Pell to help her ashore. He'd had enough of her highborn audacity so reminiscent of Elyna. Besides, his body was still recovering from her closeness. Scads! Perhaps he should have accepted the barmaid's offer, after all.

He waded through the foaming waves onto shore, assessing the trees, foliage, and rocks for the best hiding places for men and weapons. *And* for a secure place to keep the woman safe from both him and his crew. Pell and Moses could help with that, the only two men he trusted with her. Not that he cared. But soiled bait would not bring the catch he desired.

Ignoring the lady's protests as Pell carried her ashore, Cadan began barking orders to his crew to remove only certain items from the *Resolute* and to begin tying lines and tackles to the mastheads. Once everything was in place, he'd have the ship tilted just enough to mimic a full careening to anyone entering the cove.

Hence, the trap would be set.

Chapter 6

Along with all the other indignities Gabrielle had suffered of late, the man named Pell hoisted her ashore as if she were a sack of rice, then ordered her to sit in the sand. The sand! Nary a chair, rock, or coverlet in sight. Not that she wasn't accustomed to sand, being raised in the Caribbean, but 'twas because she'd been raised here, she knew what was *in* the sand—all manner of fleas, crabs, bloodworms, beetles, and clams. Why she concerned herself with these things when her life lay in the balance, she couldn't say. Perhaps it kept her mind off her impending doom.

At least she'd been placed beneath the shifting shade of a palm. Pell fingered a wooden cross around his neck, gave her the oddest look, and then strode away to join his captain. Perspiration formed on her forehead and neck, and she longed for a sip of water or grog or anything wet.

Where had they anchored? Trying to avoid touching skin to the sand, she scanned the tiny cove. Turquoise waters filled a small bay deep enough for a ship to enter and yet hidden from the sea—perfect for careening. And though she'd oft helped her father careen the *Redemption*, naught was familiar about this inlet. Lud. That meant it was most likely an island and not the Spanish mainland, which meant she was just as trapped as if she remained on the ship.

Omphile finally came ashore in the last boat and headed toward Gabrielle with much-needed grog, some food, and a stretch of canvas on which she could sit. The woman was a godsend. Yet, after handing Gabrielle the supplies, she begged off to help the crew, leaving Gabrielle alone again.

Yet not alone. One of the crew, a plain looking fellow, wearing brown breeches and a checkered shirt and with sun-lightened hair that fell below his shoulders, came and stood nigh four yards from her. Folding arms over his chest, he merely stared out across the sand. Was he there to protect her or keep her in place? What did it matter? She ignored him and instead, kept her gaze on Captain Hayes, trying to assess this enigma of a man.

Gabrielle had participated in many careenings in her short life, but it didn't take her long to determine that something was not right with this one. For one thing, she noticed that several of the smaller guns offloaded from the ship were dragged with difficulty to the spit of land curling around the narrow entrance of the cove. There they were hidden among the brush. Two of the larger guns were placed on shore, also covered with foliage. Why? Surely, they'd be put to better use as ballast to aid in tipping the ship. Even so, why not position them closer to the *Resolute*, for 'twas not easy to move them about. Also, several crates and barrels were brought from the ship, yet 'twas obvious by the ease with which the crew hefted and carried them, they were empty. These also were placed on the sand close to the incoming waves.

Nothing else was brought ashore—no furniture, no supplies, no casks of gunpowder—all weighty items which would need to be removed from the ship in order to tilt and properly careen it.

Her eyes landed on Captain Hayes again as he shouted further orders which sent Durwin and Moses rowing back to the ship. Raking back his dark hair, he dabbed sweat from his forehead, then reached down and tore his shirt over his head. Sunlight glinted off his bronzed back as muscles bunched and rolled beneath his skin. Such strength. Gabrielle swallowed at the sight. But something else caught her eye. Scars, long, pink, and dimpled, stretched from his neck to his waist.

He'd been whipped. Hard.

Gabrielle cringed. Who *was* this man?

As if reading her mind, his gaze snapped to her and remained far longer than Gabrielle felt comfortable. Still, she did not turn away. She would not grant him the satisfaction.

Finally, Lazy-eyed Smity drew the captain's attention with a question she couldn't hear. Whatever his answer was, it came out loud and forceful, eliciting a frown on Smity's face and a rude gesture behind the captain's back. Typical Smity, for the man had been more than cruel to her in prison.

A welcome breeze wafted in from the sea, fingering Gabrielle's hair and cooling the perspiration on her neck. The smells of salt, fish, and earthy loam normally soothed her, but not this day.

A white rabbit hopped across the sand, heading toward the jungle. Was she seeing things? Gabrielle blinked, but it was still there, now being chased by a pirate with long, rope-like red hair and a barrel-shaped body. He gathered the rabbit in his arms and began chastising the creature for his defiance. Only then did Gabrielle remember falling on him in the boat.

What a strange crew. Swinging her gaze back to the captain, she wondered where his pet iguana was. Perhaps he left him on board with everything else. In truth, nothing of significance was brought ashore, raising Gabrielle's suspicions even further. By late afternoon, the ship's lines were tied to trees and, using tackles, the mighty craft was tilted ever so slightly on its side—not far enough to scrape the barnacles. This was no careening. It was a trap.

And she was the bait.

An hour later as the sun kissed the horizon and spread a rainbow of colors across the sea, Gabrielle found no enjoyment in the sight. In truth, an ache had formed in her legs, whirled through her belly, and stretched into her arms and neck, stiffening her spine and making it impossible to find comfort in any position. She'd removed her shoes due to feet the size of an elephant's, and the indignity of having her bare feet exposed only added to her humiliation. Sand fleas and other hopping vermin continually assaulted her, and she'd long since run out of grog.

Still, her guard remained in position beside her. Her every attempt to engage him in conversation only resulted in a silent but kind glance her way. Perhaps the man was a deaf-mute.

A fire was lit, and the smell of food nearly caused Gabrielle to faint. But instead of Omphile bringing her the evening repast, 'twas Durwin who finally strode over with a steaming bowl.

Staring at her curiously, he handed it to her and was about to leave when Gabrielle, desperate for company—obviously *any* company—attempted to engage him in conversation.

"You're the first mate, then?" She drew the bowl to her lips and took a sip. The tangy taste of fish stew filled her mouth.

"Aye. What o' it?" Removing his hat, he swept an arm over his moist forehead.

"You were kind to me in prison. Thank you."

Shock flitted across his eyes. He stood nearly as tall as Moses, but where Moses had bulk and brawn, this man was all skin and spindle. Dirty-brown hair matched a shaggy mustache and a doubloon-sized patch of beard sprouting on his chin. His beady eyes skittered about, clearly uncomfortable in her presence. The odd scent of lemons bit her nose.

"How did you come to sail with Captain Hayes?" Her father had always told her that the more you knew your enemy, the more chance you had of defeating him.

At first, the man seemed anxious to leave, but then he kicked the sand and stared at the surf. "I been sickly me whole life, Miss. Stomach pains. Can't get weight on. Kicked out o' the royal navy. Cadan, I mean Cap'n Hayes be the only one willin' t' take me on."

Gabrielle frowned. "And you have no family to come to your aid? No physician, apothecary to help you?"

He chuckled and spit to the side. "Me father were a chimney sweep an' me mother a laundress." He shook his head. "I barely survived livin' on the streets in Portsmouth 'til I were pressed into the navy."

Gabrielle took another sip, trying not to gulp the entire bowl down and make herself sick. She wanted to tell him that her mother knew about herbs and local remedies that might help him. She wanted to tell him that God could heal him like she'd seen Him do countless times. But she could never disclose the identity of her parents, and she no longer believed God rescued everyone. For He had not rescued her.

"Durwin!" The captain's shout jarred the man out of his thoughts, and he sped away.

Finishing her stew, Gabrielle set down the bowl. At least her stomach wasn't complaining anymore. The rest of her had plenty of complaints to last a lifetime.

The babe kicked. "You are enjoying the food as well, my wee one." Smiling, she pressed a hand on her belly. There it was. What felt like the heel of a tiny foot moved across her palm. Ah, the incredible miracle of forming a human within her womb! No matter the horrid conception or the deviant father, this child was meant to be here, and she would love him with every ounce of her being. In truth, she already did.

Night pulled the remainder of light over the horizon and flung glittering stars above, reducing her view of movement on shore to shifting shadows and the dancing flames from a fire.

Omphile emerged from the darkness, a lantern in one hand, and a stack of blankets in the other. She never once acknowledged Gabrielle's guard but merely plopped to the sand and exclaimed. "Laud, but all my bones ache!"

"I can imagine. From what I saw, you worked hard today and then had to cook."

The sound of a fiddle rose from the pirates' camp.

Omphile set down the lantern and reached for Gabrielle. "I's sure you need to relieve yourself by now, an' after, we can make our beds for de night."

With great effort, Gabrielle rose to her feet, pressed her hand on her aching back, and followed the mulatto a short way into the brush. Once the task was completed, they returned to find the pirates' revelry had increased as shouts accompanied the ribald ditty and off-key singing.

"What happened to the captain's back?" Gabrielle asked as Omphile shook out the blankets and spread them over the sand.

"You mean his scars?" She shook her head. "Word is he were an indentured servant on Barbados for a few years afore he took to pirating."

Gabrielle's heart shrank. "He's a criminal?"

Omphile laid two more blankets atop the others, forming a soft bed. "This'll do nice, aye?"

One of the blankets lay skewed slightly from the others, but she resisted the urge to fix it. "Yes, very. Thank you." Glancing back toward the pirates, she found the captain standing away from the revelry, staring out to sea. "What did he do to deserve such a sentence?"

"I can't say, Miss." Omphile put hands on her hips and followed Gabrielle's gaze to the man. "I hears something to do wit' a woman an' a betrayal. He don't talk about it to me. You might ask Pell. De Captain confides in him."

From the look the man had given her earlier—one of pity and disgust—she doubted he'd answer her questions.

Gabrielle longed to ask Omphile more, but the lady promptly lay down on the blankets, patted the space beside her for Gabrielle, and closed her eyes.

To Gabrielle's right, the pirate who'd been guarding her was gone. The warble of night birds joined the lap of waves on shore, bringing a soothing cadence. Or it would, if not for the noise coming from the pirate camp. "How can you sleep with all this discordant clamor?"

"Dems will quiet down soon. Best git some rest, Miss. Only de good Laud knows what tomorrow will bring."

Struggling to lower herself, Gabrielle eased beside the woman with a huff. She didn't want to be alone. She had so many questions, and talking to Omphile eased her nerves. But no matter how much she huffed and puffed and groaned, the woman soon fell fast asleep.

Not so for Gabrielle. The sounds of the debauched drunken revelry kept her awake for hours, not to mention the racing of her pulse at what awaited her on the morrow.

Cadan, one arm behind his head, lay in the sand staring up at the night sky. A myriad of stars, too many to count, winked at him as if they knew his plan and approved of it. If only that were so. If only whatever God existed beyond those stars was anything like the one his mother had espoused and worshiped. She'd said her God was worth following. But Cadan knew differently. A God worthy of worship would not have allowed his mother to die, would not have allowed the heartache and betrayal and imprisonment that happened to Cadan later on. Hence, the only conclusion he could come to was that either God did not exist or He was not worth knowing.

Which put Cadan as the master of his own destiny. In truth, he liked the sound of that anyway.

A breeze swept over him, stirring his hair and spinning the sand by his arm. The scent of the sea—all salt and fish and freedom—filled his nostrils and made him smile. He was master of this wild sea, had more than proven that as a member of the Brethren of the Coast *and* to more than one merchant ship. And soon he would prove that to the infamous Damien Allard, only infamous in the blackguard's own skewed perception.

Once that injustice was corrected, Cadan would find the long-lost treasure of Captain Dempster and with it, create a new life for himself. A life in which he would be counted among the world's nobility, those with land and wealth and hence, power. He'd long since learned that only those with wealth and power could rule their own destinies.

Snores rumbled behind him, along with the spit of dying embers from the fire. One of the pirates shouted in his sleep, but soon settled down. They were a squawky bunch of thieving barracudas, but most were faithful hands before the mast. Still, they were his to command as long as he kept them drowning in rum and gold.

Pushing himself to sit, he stared over the dark sea beyond the cove where moonlight rippled white lace over waves. Out there, Allard should be setting sail toward this cove. *If* Cadan's plan had worked. And what a surprise the man would receive.

Smiling, Cadan pushed to his feet and stretched his back against a pinching ache. He would not be sleeping tonight. Yet, no different from most of his restless nights. Would he ever find peace? His glance wandered to where Omphile and his prisoner slept, but he couldn't find them in the darkness. What he *did* see was Moses's large shadow standing before the women, keeping an eye out for intruders as Cadan had ordered.

No sense in both of them not sleeping.

"Get some rest, Moses," Cadan whispered as he approached the man.

With one quick glance at the women, Moses asked. "You sure, Cap'n?"

"Aye, get to it."

With a nod, the carpenter shuffled away. Cadan stood for a moment, waiting for the moonlight to shift between the fronds above to give him a better view. He clearly saw Omphile curled up in a ball beneath a coverlet, and not a yard beside her, Allard's wench lay still and quiet. Moving toward her, he lowered to sit in the sand on her other side. Why? He couldn't say. He supposed the woman intrigued him, even confused him. And he hated being confused.

Moonlight spread bands of silver over her as she lay on her back, hands on her belly as if she could protect her babe from all harm. Golden hair splayed about her head like a halo while her chest rose and fell with ragged breaths. Above her long lashes, her eyes moved across her lids as if she lived another life in her sleep. Her unique scent drifted to his nose, and he remembered the look of terror in her eyes earlier, along with her courage and her sharp tongue. He could see why Allard chose her. She wasn't a typical courtesan a man grew bored with after a few days.

Ugh. What was he thinking?

Shifting his gaze away, he drew a deep sigh.

"Have you come to accost me in the thick of night, Captain?"

Chapter 7

Heart thrashing, Gabrielle pushed against the ground, attempting to rise. Unable to do so, she fell back down. "Lud."

The captain gripped her arm to help her, but she slapped him away.

He chuckled. *Chuckled!*

Still, he remained, a shadow in the darkness. What did he want? Nothing good.

Finally, with difficulty she rose to sit, breathing fast. "I believe I asked your intentions for sitting so close to me whilst I sleep."

"In truth, you accused me of desiring to ravish you. Which would be quite difficult in your condition." He nodded at her belly.

"How dare you!?" She raised her hand to strike him, but he caught it in the air. Tight at first, but soon, he released the pressure and placed it gently on the blanket beside her.

"Believe me, I have no interest in Allard's castoffs."

Fury burned at the insult. But then what did she expect from a pirate? "Pray, exactly what are your intentions?" she snapped.

He paused. Even in the darkness, she felt his intense stare upon her, so sharp, so malevolent, she shuddered. A breeze spun his wild dark hair, showering her with his scent…leather and spice. Shifting his gaze, he drew his knees up and placed his arms atop them.

Fear slithered through her at his silence. "Why do you hate Allard so? What is he to you?"

"Why did you love such a beast?" he shot back, restrained fury in his tone.

"Whatever do you mean? I loathe him. He ruined me."

"Tush! What did you expect when you crawled into his bed?"

"Crawled!?" She raised her hand to strike him yet again but thought better of it. "An ugly insinuation, that. You discredit your ability to reason, Captain."

He snorted and raked back his hair. "And you discredit the feminine tongue, which is often best still."

Grinding her teeth, Gabrielle remained quiet, not to appease his insult to women but because this imperious banter served no purpose.

Picking up a handful of sand, he allowed it to sift through his fingers. Still, he made no move to leave. For what purpose did he converse with her? 'Twas like a fisherman speaking to a worm.

He was a shadow, a large, looming figure of muscle and sinew, tightly woven with an intensity, deep sorrow, and restrained savagery. This was not a normal pirate who lived for rum, women, and coin. Nay, this man's raw emotions were as deep as the sea.

"Why did you leave everything on board and only tilt the ship slightly?" she dared ask him, both to change the subject and to gather information.

"Ha, the lady knows about careening."

Gabrielle bit her lip. She must not give too much away. "I've heard of it."

"More than heard, I'd say." His gaze swept her way again, then back across the beach.

"'Tis the trap you spoke of," Gabrielle offered. "Most of the guns remain on board, along with most of the supplies. The empty crates and barrels on shore are meant to deceive Allard otherwise. The smaller guns hidden in the brush of the bay's headland will fire at his ship should he attempt to enter the cove, hopefully crippling him. If so, you and your men can easily board his ship from there. Either way, he'll not be able to navigate quickly enough to level his guns at the *Resolute* before her guns can fire at him. However," she continued, pleased she could see the full plan now, "if Allard believes it to be a trap and doesn't enter the bay, you can quickly cut the lines holding the ship, weigh anchor, raise sails, open the gun ports, and set upon the chase. The only thing is"—she drew a deep breath—"most of your crew would either have to be on board or hidden in the brush of the inlet."

He stared at her not saying a word, and she sensed she was saying too much, a bad habit of hers. "Are you quite finished, my lady?"

Thankfully, his tone was more sarcastic than angry.

"'Tis actually quite genius, Captain."

He rubbed the stubble on his chin. "You confound me."

"To my advantage or disadvantage?"

"At the moment, it matters not." He stood. "What is your name?"

"Gabrielle."

"Nay, your surname?"

She swallowed down a lump of fear. "Bolton." The lie slid easily enough from her lips, for she surely could not tell him the truth.

"Hmm."

Wind whipped hair into her face, and she snapped it aside and looked up at him. "I assure you, Captain, whatever trap you lay for Allard, 'twill not work. Whatever you wish from him in exchange for me, he will not give. As I've told you, he harbors no affection for me, and I am quite sure neither would he give a care for any child of his."

A shaft of moonlit filtered through the fronds above and lit his features. Contempt burned in his eyes, and she swallowed a burst of fear.

"I seek no exchange, my lady. The only thing I want from Allard is his dead carcass hanging from my yardarm."

Cadan left the wench more confused than ever. A condition to be expected from most women, he supposed. But this one? She knew a great deal about ships, setting traps, careening, and battles. By her speech and mannerisms, she was highborn. Then how did a noble lady learn so much about pirating? She'd explained his plan to trap Allard with precision. It made no sense. He hadn't even fully disclosed the details to Pell or Smity. But this lady, watching from afar, had figured it out. Baffling.

The night passed in a slow churn of angst and bewilderment. Cadan's heavy eyelids had barely closed when the sun christened the horizon with swaths of gray and gold. Wavelets lapped ashore accompanied by the squawk of birds and buzz of insects. He sat and rubbed his eyes.

Today would be the day he'd get his revenge. That or die trying.

Birds swooped and glided over the calm water of the bay, seeking their morning prey. Upon sighting a tasty morsel, they dove into the surf only to emerge moments later, flapping fish in their beaks.

Exactly what he was planning to do.

Struggling to rise, he brushed the sand from his shirt and breeches, grabbed his flintlock and cutlass from the ground and slid them into their scabbards. Then turning, he bellowed for his men to wake up. It took three shouts to stir the sluggards, and Cadan envied their ability to sleep so soundly.

But soon, with Pell and Durwin's help, the men grabbed their weapons and took positions. Half joined the men manning the cannons at the entrance to the cove and half climbed on board the tilted ship. A few he stationed in the surf by the hull to give the appearance of careening, while a few remained on shore near an open fire. Two men stood at the ready to slice the lines tying the ship to shore, and one man was perched high in a Manchineel tree as a lookout.

Regardless of whether Allard entered the cove or not, Cadan was ready for him. Now, to put the bait on the hook. He started for the women where Moses stood guard.

Soot limped up to him. "Cap'n. Ye seen Hellfire?"

Halting, Cadan growled at his master gunner. "You're supposed to be manning the guns at the headland," he seethed out, constraining his temper with difficulty.

The man's blue eyes skittered about the beach. "But me rabbit. She ne'er runs away."

If the man wasn't such a skilled gunner and loyal friend, Cadan would restrict his rum rations for such a ridiculous interruption. But Soot cherished that rabbit as a pirate cherished his gold. In truth, the creature seemed to soothe the gunner's nerves and settle the twitch in his eye that appeared when he was out of sorts.

A twitch that now began with urgency in his right eye.

Regardless, Cadan opened his mouth to chastise him and send him off when Soot's eyes widened, and he grinned.

Following his gaze, Cadan watched as Lady Fox—for that was the name he'd given her—waddled toward them, Hellfire snug in her arms. Moses and Omphile, her arms full of blankets, followed behind her.

She promptly stopped before Soot, glanced down at the rabbit and scratched the vermin between the ears. Then handing her to Soot, she said, "I believe she is yours?"

Soot shouted with glee. "Thank ye, Miss!" For a moment Cadan thought he'd kiss the woman. "I been lookin' fer 'er everywhere."

The rising sun glistened over her skin, transforming it to gold silk. A forest of black lashes surrounded sharp blue eyes filled with kindness as they looked at the master gunner. "She hopped into my bed sometime during the night. I'm sorry to cause you alarm."

But Cadan's eyes were on her lips, pink and plump and moist, and he suddenly wished he'd been the one who had hopped into her bed.

Scads! He shook away the thought. Still, why was she being so kind to a pirate? A feminine trick, no doubt.

"Begone, Soot. Back to your post!" He gestured to Soot as Moses and Omphile halted before him.

"Moses," Cadan ordered. "Settle Omphile on the ship and remain on board at the ready.

"Aye, Cap'n." Moses started forward, ushering both women toward the cockboat.

Cadan grabbed Lady Fox's arm. "Not her."

Hesitating, Moses glanced between Cadan and the woman.

"It'll be dangerous here, Captain." Omphile's concerned gaze landed on Gabrielle.

"Exactly." Cadan gestured with his head for them to leave. "Now do as I say!" He was growing tired of his orders being questioned.

Lady Fox raised her chin, her chest rising and falling. "Where would you like your bait to stand, Captain?"

Wind danced among her long pearly hair, waving it about like silk, and he longed to run his fingers through it. She winced slightly and placed a hand on her belly. Was she in pain? No doubt 'twas no easy task to carry a child.

"You may sit there." He gestured toward a crate perched on the sand before a mound of other crates and barrels. To the left, three of his pirates sat playing Spades in the sand.

The lady swept out her skirts and sat with difficulty on the crate. "Now what, Captain?"

"We wait."

"In the hot sun?"

"For now."

Cadan moved several yards away from the wench, but still within sight of anyone approaching the cove. She brought nothing but fluster and confusion and a physical reaction he'd not experienced in years. Best to keep his distance. If this trap worked and Allard was dead by nightfall, he'd release the woman at a port of her choosing.

An hour passed. And another. He brought the woman a flagon of water and a bowl of remaining fish from last night's repast. Thankfully, she said naught, but merely gobbled up the food as if it were her last meal. It might be.

After another hour, Cadan tore off his shirt and took to pacing the shore, dipping his bare feet in the surf. The foaming water cooled his toes, but not his temper, nor his fear that setting this trap had been for naught.

"'Tis possible Damien will not come today, Captain," the woman's voice pummeled his back. "It takes more than one day to careen a ship."

Cadan frowned and stared out over the turquoise water. Finally, he spun to face her. "Perhaps. But he has no way of knowing how long we've been here, and he would not wish to miss the opportunity."

Nodding, she brushed damp strands of hair from her forehead, clearly suffering from the sun's heat.

Guilt swelled in his gut, and he cursed himself for his weakness. He strode toward her, intending to move the lady to the shade when a shout ran out from the treetops.

"A sail! A sail!"

The man was no gentleman, leaving a woman with child in the sweltering heat and sun for hours. Those were the thoughts which flooded Gabrielle's mind as the captain swerved to face her. And she fully intended to voice those opinions when the shout of *a sail* bounced over the water of the bay.

The cloud of gloom which had enveloped the captain all day instantly blew away, replaced by a look she well knew—the determined look of a man about to go to battle.

Yet he did naught. Merely stood his ground, occasionally glancing out to sea, waiting, pacing, musing. The muscles of his bronze chest bulged in anticipation, the scars on his back cried out in pain...or was it revenge?

"It be Cap'n Allard's colors, red and blue with a sword arm and flames of fire."

She knew those colors well. 'Twas indeed Damien Allard's ship, *Nightblood*.

Tension stretched tight over the beach, a palpable unease that caused Gabrielle's heart to tighten into a knot.

She'd been in many ship battles, had watched her father and brother—and her mother—fight with both cannon and blade. But she'd never been the prize, nor the cause of such violence. Closing her eyes, she embraced her rounded belly and dared to ask the God who had repeatedly ignored her if He wouldn't mind helping her out of this predicament.

No answer came. No ship appeared at the entrance to the cove.

Instead a shout filtered down from above. "She sails t' the west, round the island!"

Chapter 8

Round the island? Cadan fisted hands at his waist and groaned. That could only mean one thing. Allard was privy to Cadan's trap. *Scads*! Yet he'd not even sailed past the cove to see if Cadan and his crew were here nor slowed at the entrance to determine if a trap existed.

Raking back his hair, he glanced at Lady Fox. Though her lips pursed in alarm, she held her chin up and shoulders back as any stalwart warrior.

Wind tore through the leaves of a grove of Island Oaks behind her. The jungle. Of course! If Allard suspected a trap, his best option would be to attack from behind. Whether they were truly careening or 'twas a trick, he would have the advantage.

Why had Cadan not thought of that?

"Kipp," Cadan shouted to one of the men playing cards. "Make haste to the headland and tell every pirate, save those manning the guns, to join me here on the beach!"

"Aye, Cap'n." Kipp took off, flinging sand in the air behind him.

"Barnett, have Rawlins and Hamo cut the careening lines."

Nodding, the short, bullish pirate darted for the other side of the ship.

Dashing into the surf, Cadan cupped his hands and shouted. "Ho there! On the ship!"

Finally, hands appeared, gripping tightly to the bulwarks and Pell's face popped over the side.

"Hang on! I'm cutting the lines!"

Before Pell could reply, the snap of twine chimed, sodden timbers groaned in rebellion, and the ship lurched and fell back into the cove, slapping the water so hard, a wave struck Cadan.

The water soaked him to the waist, cooling his heated skin as the ship righted itself.

A band of thirty of his best fighters—the ones he'd stationed at the headland—marched around the curve of the shore toward Cadan, Smity and Soot among them.

He should send his master gunner and bosun onto the ship. They'd be needed if a battle ensued. Still, if Cadan was right, he'd need their skill ashore even more.

"Draw your blades, gentlemen," he ordered. "Enter the jungle. Our enemy comes from behind."

With grunts and foul curses, the men obeyed, bloodlust in their eyes, and soon a swarm of the most violent of pirates disappeared into the foliage. Cadan smiled. 'Twould be Allard who would be surprised this day.

He glanced at the woman. He couldn't very well leave her ashore in the midst of a battle and especially not where Allard could get his hands on her. She'd be safer on board the ship.

But did he have time?

Marching toward the woman, he helped her rise, then escorted her into the frothy surf as close to the ship as he could get. The cockboat had been dragged ashore and it would take too long to retrieve it, but she might be able to climb the rope ladder.

"Can you swim?" he asked her.

She glanced down at her belly. "Aye, but—"

He growled. Of course. "Start out, then."

Frowning, Lady Fox grabbed her skirts and waded out into the calm water.

"Orders, Cap'n?" Durwin shouted from the *Resolute*.

"Send Moses to retrieve the woman," he shouted back with cupped hands. "Wait until the woman is on board and then weigh anchor and set sail for the other side of the island. If Allard is there, attack him with every gun you have."

"Aye, aye!" came Durwin's excited response, and soon Moses leapt over the railing into the bay.

Grabbing the hilt of his cutlass, Cadan spun his glance back over the jungle, listening for any shouts, shots, or any sound of battle.

He clenched his fists. The island wasn't very large. Surely his men would encounter Allard any moment.

Splashing brought his gaze back to the cove where the lady flailed like a wounded duck in the water, her wings flapping, her voice squawking, her skirts floating about her in a halo of blue. Then she disappeared beneath the waters.

Cussing, he dove after her, surfacing moments later to see Moses holding the lady's head above water.

Shots exploded like fireworks over the beach. *Pop pop pop*! At least two of Allard's men emerged from the greenery, flintlocks in one hand, blades in the other. Cadan glanced at Moses and then at his ship. They'd never make it on board without getting shot.

Grinding his teeth, he shouted for Moses to bring the lady ashore. What was he to do with her now? He must join his men in the battle.

With one glance up at Pell, who reappeared at the bulwarks, he waved his hand toward the sea, ordering the man without words to go after Allard. He hated not being in command of his ship, especially during battle, but he trusted Pell. He'd seen him in action. He was a leader of men and more than capable.

Pistol shots rang through the air.

Ducking, he took the sodden woman from Moses and rushed over the sand, diving behind a group of barrels just as more shots struck the ground and flung sand in the air beside them.

Gripping her belly, Lady Fox leaned over with a groan of pain as Cadan dared peek above the barrels at their advancing enemy. Where were his men?

Surely they had not all been defeated! Alarm ignited every nerve.

The sounds of sailcloth fluttering and the anchor chain chiming resounded behind him. Good. The *Resolute* would soon give chase.

Two pirates advanced upon their hiding place.

"We's see ye, ye half-masted cockle. Come out an' fight like a man."

Rising, Cadan stepped away from the barrel. "Come and get me."

One of the pirates, a squat man with bulbous nose and bright red scarf around his neck leveled his flintlock straight at Cadan…

And fired.

Were all pirates fools? Of a note, they called it courage. But placing oneself in the direct line of a flintlock, Gabrielle called utterly mad. Yet she suddenly wondered what would happen to her should the captain meet his demise. Not that his death mattered, but she'd certainly be in no better hands with his crew, perhaps worse. Nor would she be safe back in Allard's evil grip.

She was trapped either way.

Heart pounding, she stared up at Captain Hayes, standing casually, one hand lounging over the hilt of his cutlass and a smile on his face. A fool, aye.

The gun fired. Her heart stopped beating. She waited for the captain to fall, but instead, he drew his blade with an eerie chime and said, "Come meet your fate."

Rising from her other side, Moses also drew his blade and the two of them advanced upon Allard's men.

With difficulty, Gabrielle got on her knees and peered between the barrels.

Tossing down his smoking flintlock, the pirate drew his own cutlass and met the captain's swift strike with a jarring clang that sent him stumbling backward. Moses engaged the other man, hacking and slicing with his blade so ferociously the man retreated.

Gabrielle had witnessed many a sword fight in her life, had even seen men cleaved with those vile blades, but it didn't take long to discover that the captain's skills far surpassed most she'd seen.

He swooped upon his enemy with confidence, thrusting his sword this way and that so fast, the poor pirate could hardly keep up. As it was, his eyes grew wide, and beads of sweat broke out on his forehead. Their blades rang together yet again, and with expert speed and precision, Captain Hayes cleaved downward and sliced the man's side.

Cursing, the pirate pressed a hand to the bloody wound, a desperate realization crowding his features. He charged Captain Hayes, blade aloft in one last attempt to defeat him.

Muscles rolled and bunched on the captain's bare chest as he raised his cutlass and brought it down upon the man in one final swoop.

Behind them more of Allard's men approached, at least ten by her count. The captain was skilled to be sure, but he could not be victorious over so many. Gabrielle scanned the shore. To her left, the jungle was only yards away. If no one paid her any mind, she could easily make a run for it—or a waddle—and find shelter there. No matter who won this battle, perhaps she could seek out a hiding place and eventually the pirates would give up their search.

Lud. The pirate who'd guarded her yesterday stood to her right as still as a statue watching the battle. He didn't blink, didn't move, didn't engage the enemy. Gabrielle had no time to consider the oddity as musket shot pummeled the air. Shouts and a cacophony of chiming swords caused her to once again peek over the barrels. Captain Hayes' pirates had finally arrived and were parrying with Allard's men.

One glance at the captain told her he had dispatched his opponent and was taking on two more with ease.

Perfect. Keeping an eye on the pirate guard, she pushed from the sand, rose, grabbed her skirts, and moved as fast as she could to the brush, shoving aside vines and branches as she entered. One glance over her shoulder told her the guard pirate had not moved. Warm moisture kissed her face, and she proceeded, drawing in a deep breath of air that smelled like tropical flowers, life, and earthy loam. Beneath her feet, twigs and dead leaves crunched as she made her way deeper into the greenery, hoping to put as much distance between her and the madness on the beach.

Spears of sunlight stabbed the thick canopy above, casting a magical aura onto the trees, vines, and bushes. Her feet ached already, but there was naught to be done for it. Better to risk dying alone on this island with her babe in her arms than die at the hand of cruel pirates.

Birds chirped, insects buzzed. Perspiration slid down her back. Coming upon a large boulder, she sat to catch her breath and dabbed her forehead and neck with her sleeve, laughing at how unladylike that was. Her mother hailed from nobility. Her father was an earl. She'd been raised to behave with composure and dignity, though she had to admit her sister Reena had not learned those lessons. She smiled. She missed her sister, her parents, her strong brother, Alex. Her smile faded. What they must think of her now. No doubt they had given up searching for such an embarrassment to the family.

So engrossed in her thoughts, she didn't hear bootsteps approaching. Didn't smell the lavender musk cologne, not until a blade cut into the skin at her throat.

"Together again at last, *ma douce*."

Cadan drew his bloody blade from his opponent and scanned the shore for another. But all Allard's men were engaged with his pirates, and from the looks of things, his men were winning. He spotted Smity, Soot, and Moses battling their opponents without difficulty.

Good time to check on the woman.

She wasn't there.

Cursing, he glanced at the jungle.

Half-witted lady. Did she really think she'd escape him on an island?

After one glance at the battle to ensure he wasn't needed, he dove into the foliage. She couldn't have gotten too far in her condition. In truth, 'twas quite easy to find her trail of flattened leaves and broken branches.

Voices filtered his way. A male voice, a *familiar* voice that caused every ounce of Cadan to tighten in fury. He halted, breathing deeply of the humid jungle air, listening, seething, hating. He pulled the knife from his belt, clutched it tightly in one hand and inched forward.

There. The snake had a knife to the woman's throat and was whispering in her ear.

The snake he hadn't seen since their sword fight seven years ago. A palpable pain seared his missing earlobe, and he touched it absently.

The snake who had ruined his marriage and his life.

The snake who would pay with his own.

Allard must have heard him for he looked up, scanned the brush, and drew the knife closer to Lady Fox's throat.

Cadan, blade drawn, stepped into the clearing.

An insolent grin lifted the cur's lips. Ever the popinjay, he wore a purple doublet, slashed and paned, with great sleeves slit to show stitched linen beneath. The red cashmere sash about his waist matched the ostrich plume in his cocked hat, and the ruby drop earbob dangling from his ear. "Ah, Cadan. Or should I say *Captain* Hayes," he said in a slight French accent. He snapped back a strand of his long hair and grinned. "Captain of a ship? Who would have guessed such an achievement from someone so baseborn. Alas, I heard you were on this island. But you look different somehow." He cocked his head, a petulant look on his sharp features.

Terror streaked across the lady's eyes.

"I am not the naive boy you dared attack all those years ago," Cadan hissed.

"Attack?" Allard chortled. "'Twas you who attacked me. Without provocation, I might add."

Rage ignited every inch of Cadan, prompting him to silence the snake once and for all. But he could not risk harming the lady. He must get her out of the way, so he could *then* squeeze every drop of blood from Allard's wretched body.

"I told you I'd leave your wife's bed. All you had do was ask."

He was baiting Cadan, just as he had done all those years ago. Baiting him to fight, which unfortunately Cadan had done, and with very limited skill, he'd been easily defeated.

Not this time. Nay. He'd honed his skills these past two years as a pirate, making a name for himself as a ruthless and expert swordsman.

"Release the lady and let us end this man to man," Cadan commanded with authority.

"The lady you say?" He laughed. "Has she bewitched you as well? Though I do thank you for informing me of my child." With the knife still at Lady Fox's throat, he glanced down affectionately at her belly.

So, the man *did* care for his offspring. "If you kill her, your child dies with her."

Allard blew out a huff. "I have no intention of harming the strumpet, not at least until my child is born. Hence, allow me to leave with the woman, and I'll call my men off and not sink your ship to the depths."

"A grand boast, that. But then you always bore no doubt of your own omnipotence."

Allard grinned. "Have I not caused you enough pain that you wish me to put you in the grave as well?"

Cadan snorted. "The grave awaits one of us. Let us not delay in finding out which."

A parrot flapped above them, squawking in protest.

Allard glanced up and Lady Fox, taking the opportunity, kicked him backward in the groin. The knife flew from his hand as he yelled in pain, blinking and cursing. Grabbing the blade, the woman dashed to the side as Allard let out a growl of fury and drew his rapier.

Chapter 9

In one swift move, Cadan tossed his knife and drew his cutlass, ready to meet Allard's attack. Nay, he was more than ready, for this was the moment he'd waited for, trained for, for years.

A thunderous roar boomed, sending a quiver through the thick humid air.

Allard halted, his blue eyes seething with hatred, his jaw tight, his blade raised high.

Another blast sent a flock of birds flying from their perch above.

Cadan smiled, gesturing with his fingers for Allard to approach. "What are you waiting for, Damien? Your blood will spill on the ground whilst your ship sinks to the bottom of the sea. Both fitting judgments for your crimes."

Lady Fox's anxious gaze snapped between the two men, yet she remained, knife in her hand, as if she could somehow defeat them both.

Allard lifted his aquiline nose. "How do you know it is not your ship being attacked?"

Cadan smiled. "Because you were not expecting my ship, and because I know my men."

A rare fear swirled in Allard's eyes—a glorious site Cadan had longed to see.

Another cannon blast pounded the jungle, and a defiant frown creased his lips. There was no denying it now. His ship was under attack.

Taking a step back, he leveled his blade at Cadan, then snapped his gaze to the lady. "Come with me now, Gabrielle."

The woman stared at him, perplexed. Her chest rose and fell.

"You carry my child. I will do you no harm." His voice softened into the gentle hiss of a lover…*or* a venomous snake.

"Enough of this!" Cadan finally had Allard in his grasp, and he would not allow him to slither away. Raising his cutlass, he stormed forward and swept it down upon the demon. Allard met his thrust with his own blade and a hardened grunt.

Cadan was about to bring his cutlass around from the left in a move he'd perfected when a pistol fired and a shot sped by his ear so close, he felt the stirring of air.

A pirate stormed into the clearing, tossing down a smoking flintlock and plucking another from his belt. He pointed it straight at Cadan. One-tooth Leadwig, minus the wig, but Cadan would recognize him anywhere. The traitor. He seethed. That's how Allard knew 'twas a trap.

"Cap'n," he addressed Allard. "*Nightblood*'s under attack."

Allard, blade still leveled at Cadan, turned to the lady. "Come with me. I can assure your safety more than this muckrake."

Every inch of Cadan longed to thrust the blackguard through, but the flintlock pointed at his chest restrained him. He would not die at this man's hand. True, One-tooth might miss, but from the look in his eye, Cadan best not take that chance.

Still, how could he let Allard go? After all these years? And his bait with him!

Cadan glanced at the lady. Her wide eyes flitted between him and Allard, uncertainty and terror running rampant over them.

"I will go with neither of you!" she finally shouted.

Another cannon blast thundered, quivering the leaves on the trees.

"Now!" Allard stormed toward her to grab her, but she swept her knife out, striking him across his arm.

A red line of blood appeared on his shirt.

The Quiet Flame

Book One of The Oathfire Saga

By Willow A. McDowell

ISBN (paperback): 979-8-218-74580-6
ISBN (eBook): 979-8-218-74581-3

Editing: Sian Morgan
Proofreading: Laë Proofreading
Cover Design: The BookVeil
Interior Formatting: Willow A. McDowell

Printed in the United States of America
First Edition

To everyone who believed I had a story worth telling,
your encouragement kept me writing.

And for those who are no longer here,
but who I know would've bought fifteen copies
just to hand them out to strangers.

I carry your love on every page.

Contents

Chapter One

Wynessa

Morning dawned, calm and golden, moving through the shrubs then setting softly atop the garden dividers, dreamlike rather than upon waking. I liked it best this way, when the palace still slept, and the world hadn't remembered how to be sharp yet.

I knelt in the rosemary patch with my skirts bunched around my legs, fingers dyed green and damp from dew. Here, a small, plump thrush, with plumage the color of faded autumn leaves, lay nestled in my palms; its wing twisted at an odd angle, fluttering against the twine I'd knotted into a tiny splint.

"Steady now," I hushed, my voice barely a breeze. "I know it hurts. But you're braver than you look."

The bird blinked up at me, its chest rising and falling so rapidly that the flutter was perceptible against my skin.

I smiled, brushing a stray strand of strawberry-gold hair behind my ear.

"You're fortunate," I whispered. "You fly when loads grow too heavy."

The bird gave a faint twitch in reply. I was unable to determine whether it was in agreement or protest.

I'd found her beneath the balcony garden, half-buried in a bed of violets, her wing caught in the thorny grip of a rose briar. I hadn't even intended to go out this morning, yet something allured me here. The garden often did. Only here, could I truly breathe. Here, fear didn't earn a scolding. Smiles didn't need to be forced, and the weight of a kingdom I barely understood didn't have to be shouldered. The herbs didn't care that I stammered in court, and the bees never asked about my lineage. I was myself here.

They just desired gentleness, plus perhaps some sunlight.

I opened my hands.

"There. Go on. You're free now." I smiled gently.

The thrush hesitated, tiny talons digging into my skin.

Then, with a sudden, breathless flutter, she launched from my fingers, wings wobbling slightly, but determined to fly. She soared past the rosemary and thyme, through the dappled light and over the stone wall, her speckled breast soaring as she disappeared into a blur of soft feathers and silent flight.

I sat back on my heels, watching the sky swallow her. My heart ached with envy.

A memory from a summer long ago came to mind, before the crown was a heavy burden, before I understood what it meant to be watched at all hours, evaluated like a crop before harvest. Alaric and I had crept out here barefoot, racing across the lawn with wildflower crowns sliding off our heads. The grass had reached our knees then, and we'd pretended it was a sea. I was a sailor, and he was the sea monster dragging me under.

A faint, almost imperceptible smile played on my lips as our laughter echoed in my ears. We'd gotten in trouble for tracking mud back into the marble halls, but I didn't care. That day, I laughed so hard that I cried.

Later, our nursemaid, with hands smelling of earth and woodsmoke, showed us how to steep valerian root and hang dried yarrow for warding off evil spirits. She'd told us tales of the gods who once walked Wildervale, their very steps painting the land with vibrant gardens. In those days, and in the magic she taught, I believed love could overcome anything.

But now I know better. The world was not made of magic; it was made of rules. And I possessed no talent for rule-following.

Sometimes I wondered if there was a place beyond the borders of Elyrien. Where the high courts and walled gardens didn't define me, where the silver threads of dirt, woven into each breath, loosened their grip. A place where I could be Wyn, and not Princess Wynessa of the Grainlands, a name that felt less like an honor and more like a heavy cloak.

Elyrien, cradle of harvests. The softest kingdom on the continent of Aetherra. A place of rolling sun, gilded hills, fields that hummed with unseen life. Vineyards that spread like emerald tapestries across the slopes, their leaves trembling like whispers in the breeze, while ancient temples stood bathed in a soft, honeyed light that seemed to pulse with a quiet magic.

But beneath the abundance lay roots bound too tightly by ancient treaties and political debts. My existence felt no different: merely a field's produce, destined to be harvested or worse, planted as a seed in their soil.

The sharp clip of boots on stone shattered the morning hush.

"Princess Wynessa?"

The voice startled me gently, like a ripple across still water. I turned to see a young page standing at the edge of the hedged path – Davien. He was barely older than thirteen, all elbows and sunburns, but he bowed with more grace than most men twice his age.

"My lady," he said again, cheeks pink with embarrassment, "you're summoned to the throne hall. The King and Queen request your presence."

Of course they did.

Still, I offered him a warm smile, despite the urge to run in the opposite direction. "Thank you, Davien."

He looked surprised to be called by name. "I'll walk you there if you like." He beams.

"Please."

I rose, brushing soil from my skirts, and fell into step beside him. The palace loomed beyond the garden, all pale stone and gold-veined marble, beautiful and cold. As we walked, I traced my fingers over the ivy trailing the walls.

Davien bowed again at the carved double doors and scurried off, leaving me alone beneath the high arch.

Two guards swung open the throne room doors with a creak that echoed too loudly. I stepped inside.

The hall was not vast, but it was tall, with columns rising like pillars of judgment around me. Sunlight streamed through stained glass in gentle shades of rose and sea foam, casting a wash of color across marble and gilded archways, softening the edges of the hall, but never quite dispelling its chill.

My mother, Queen Elenya Elira, stood in her usual place, one gloved hand resting atop her carved ivory staff. Her pale hair, the color of spun moonlight, was drawn back from her face and meticulously coiled into an intricate knot at the crown of her head, with not a strand out of place. Her expression was carved from ice, like the face of a statue in a perpetual winter. Her silks were the color of frost-kissed lavender, and she wore them like armor.

Beside her, my father, King Thalen Elira, occupied the silverwood throne. He was older now, his beard entirely white, his posture stiff from old battle wounds, but his eyes were warm when they found me. Tired, perhaps. But not cruel. Not like her.

"Wynessa," he whispered, gesturing me forward. "Come."

I trod softly on the stone floor, the sound of my slippers echoing fainter than my perception of myself. When I reached the podium, I curtsy with lowered eyes. My mother did not bid me to rise.

"Wynessa," she said, crisp as frost. "Why are you covered in soil again?"

I stood quickly and tucked my herb-stained hands behind my back. "There was an injured bird. I was helping."

She narrowed her eyes at me, still just as cold. "And that deserved your attention, did it?"

Her eyes were like twin magnets, pulling me down, and I could feel my body shrinking beneath the crushing weight of her judgment. "I thought so," I said, timidly. The moment the words left my lips, I instantly regretted it.

Her eyes only seemed to grow colder at my response, making a chill run down my spine.

"We've come to a decision," my mother announced, raising her head to the court, her voice smooth as if it were polished bone. "The matter of Caerthaine must be resolved. They have drawn a treaty. You will marry Prince Kaelen before the next moon wanes."

Each word fell like a stone into a bottomless well, sinking into me with cold, unforgiving finality.

"But—" My voice cracked, thin against the vaulted ceiling. "I haven't even met him."

"There is no need. He is young, wealthy, and politically valuable. That is all that matters." She stepped closer; rosewater and iron filled my lungs. "This marriage will keep Elyrien safe from Vireth's ambitions. That is your role, Wynessa." Her words pressed the air tighter around me, until even the stones seemed to lean in, reminding me that my desires were shadows against duty.

"My lady," I tried carefully, "surely there are other ways to secure an alliance."

Her eyes narrowed like frost closing in. "There are not."

My father shifted in his seat, discomfort clear in the angle of his shoulders. "We have delayed this as long as we can, little star," he said, using the name he once gave me when I was small and clumsy in the orchard. "We are not simply choosing a husband. We are choosing survival. Elyrien feeds half the kingdoms in this quadrant of Aetherra, but we are farmers and villagers, not soldiers. If Vireth marched tomorrow, our armies would not hold. And Caerthaine has already tied itself to Vireth. Together, their strength would crush us."

He exhaled slowly. "Caerthaine's fields are salt and stone. They cannot feed their people. They need Elyrien's grain as much as we need their ships. This union ensures we both endure."

Mother's gaze sharpened, a blade hidden in silk. "It is not a question of if you will sign the treaty, Wynessa. You will. That is what is expected of you."

I swallowed hard, my throat aching. "So, it is my choice only in ink."

Her lips curved, thin and unyielding. "Your father and I were an arranged match, and we are fine. You will learn to be fine too."

The silence that followed felt like a door closing, leaving no air behind it.

The urge to scream clawed at my throat, to run until my lungs burned, tear off the restricting slippers glued to me and escape over the garden wall barefoot, without looking back.

"You've always been delicate," she said coldly, and somehow, it was the cruelest thing she could've picked. "Softness is not a virtue for a crown."

My father cleared his throat, his voice roughened with regret. "You'll leave tomorrow at first light. You'll travel by horse to Caerthaine. Captain Gideon and Erindor of the guard will accompany you. They're the best swordsmen I can spare." His gaze flicked briefly to my mother, then returned to me. "I would have sent your ladies, but the queen believed…distractions would only make things harder." He lowered his head like a submissive puppy, avoiding my gaze.

My shoulders slumped, and a heavy sigh escaped me, a defeated whisper into the suddenly cavernous silence. What more was there to say?

My mother turned toward the steward and started issuing instructions to him.

I curtsied again—though it was like bowing to a noose—and walked calmly from the room. My steps were quiet, but I could sense the pressure building behind my ribs, a tide of grief I did not know how to name.

The hall sealed itself behind me like the lid of a coffin.

I walked quickly at first. Not fast enough to draw attention, but fast enough that no one dared stop me. I briefly looked over my shoulder—no sign of any guards. I let out a small sigh.

No stewards appeared with scrolls or itineraries. The message had been delivered, and the deal had been sealed. I had become just one more pawn in their intricate game of appearances and expectations. A familiar tightening landed in my stomach. It was the same feeling I'd had as a child whenever my parents arranged a playdate with someone they deemed 'suitable.'

Two maids rounded the corner near the archway, arms full of linen and sweet-scented sachets. I knew them; Mira and Lina. They had worked in the palace since I was a child and had long since stopped being surprised when I addressed them.

"Good morning," I murmured as we passed.

"Morning, Princess," Lina said with a soft smile. Mira added, "We saved the last honey cakes for your tray."

Their voices were gentle, familiar. I gave them a grateful nod.

I kept walking. Down the long corridor, past the portrait hall, past the window alcoves where Alaric and I used to sneak peach tarts, past the tapestry of the First Queen holding out a blade to the sea.

The familiar marble floors, once polished to a mirror shine, now seemed to absorb the light, their intricate patterns lost beneath a film of dust that shimmered faintly, like a layer of forgotten dreams.

I reached my chambers and closed the door quietly behind me.

The sunlight that had spilled so warmly across the stone earlier was fading now, retreating up the wall like it, too, was unwilling to stay.

I didn't change. I didn't wash. Instead, I sat down at the edge of my bed and stared at nothing.

They had decided.

Not asked. Not warned.

I would be sent to Caerthaine to wed a stranger. A prince known more for his perfect etiquette and glacial court than anything resembling warmth. His lands worshipped the god of water, Kaelor, whose temples were quiet, silver, and still. His priests never smiled. The new place would be a hollow drum, lacking the vibrant heartbeat of affection found here within these walls. A long, slow exhale escaped, laden with the weight of the day and what would become of my future.

They said Caerthaine held back Vireth's ambition. And it was the only thread holding back the tide of war.

But now, apparently, I was what stood between Caerthaine and betrayal.

I rubbed my thumb across the palm of my hand, grounding myself. The skin was still stained with rosemary, still faintly fragrant with earth.

My mother called me delicate, as if it were an accusation.

Maybe I was delicate, but fragility differed from frailty. Flowers bloomed in ash. Kindness thrived where cruelty expected silence. What did my mother know about kindness? She never gave it.

I looked toward the lavender sprig on my nightstand. I harvested it last summer, dried it carefully, and bound it with a blue ribbon. I remembered laughing as I gathered it. How it stained my slippers and made my hair smell like comfort.

But I had no desire to laugh right now.

I lay back slowly on my soft, peaceful mattress, my skirts still rumpled, hands clasped on my chest like I was waiting to be buried. Stars and ships adorned the ceiling above, a mural from when an astronomer-princess had owned the royal chambers generations ago. I used to trace constellations in the dark.

Now, as I stared at them, I wondered how many other girls had been promised away under the same painted sky.

I closed my eyes and tried not to imagine the sea.

Chapter Two

Wynessa

It was strange, the things we remembered.

The sound of silk folding. Floral oil's scent. The way the light pooled on the floor of my chamber like a spill no one dared to mop up. The morning sunlight, usually taken for granted, now felt like a final embrace on my skin, each golden ray a fragile gift soon to be lost.

Jasira was elbow-deep in my traveling wardrobe, muttering curses at a stubborn ribbon. She piled her dark curls on her head with a strip of mint-green silk. Jasira hummed under her breath, folding a pale cream chemise with unnecessary precision. She consistently acted in that manner when she lacked something to state—methodically, quietly, gently. Though only one year older than me, she carried herself with the calmness of someone twice our age.

"If I ever meet the tailor who thought rose-gold satin and floor-length skirts were sensible for a diplomatic journey, I would personally feed him to a goat," Jasira grumbled.

"I think someone has already fed him to the court fashion council," I said absently, combing through the tangles in my hair.

The room smelled of orange and lemon oil, the kind Jasira always rubbed into the wood of the wardrobe drawers. My lavender cloak lay draped across the end of the bed; its edges embroidered with trailing vines and stars. It was too fine for riding. And too heavy for summer.

"You'll charm him, I think." The words came tumbling out of Jasira, her eyes fixed on her task at hand. "Unless he's allergic to flowers and hates the gardens. In which case, we may have a problem."

That earned a brief laugh from me. "With my luck, he will be, won't he?"

She glanced at me, her soulful brown eyes full of mischief. Jasira was sunshine wrapped in sarcasm and strength, and was also the only friend I could speak plainly with.

Jasira paused, then turned to me with arms crossed. "Do you want to bring your journal?"

I blinked. "Do you think I'll have time to write?"

"You'll make time." She glanced out the window. "It'll remind you who you are."

I hesitated before walking over to the shelf and running my hand over the worn spine. It was green with gold-pressed leaves on the cover—pages marked with pressed petals, sketched leaves, and half-finished thoughts.

I slipped it into my satchel, nestled amongst my scrolls and herbs.

"I packed your lavender soap," she added, placing it beside my cloak. "In case Caerthaine has forgotten what civility smells like."

"Thank you." I smiled weakly.

I stared at my reflection in the mirror. My bare feet were tucked beneath my nightgown, while my hair cascaded loosely around my hunched shoulders.

My eyes looked far too much like my mother's when I was quiet, except mine always gave too much away.

"Do you think he'll like me?" I asked, the silence becoming a little too unbearable for me to withstand.

Jasira looked at me through the mirror. "If he doesn't, he's a blind fool. And if he is a blind fool, I'll happily trip him into the harbor."

Before I could reply, the door burst open in a theatrical sweep.

"By the heavens, I hate silk," said Alaric, striding in like he owned not just the castle but the sky above it. His hair was a lighter blonde than mine, sun-swept and always tousled like he'd escaped a duel or a lover's bed. His tunic was half-buttoned, and his sword belt hung crooked at his hip.

Behind him stood a massive warhound, dark gray and thick-furred, its amber eyes alert but unbothered. It moved with the grace of a wolf and the weight of a storm.

"Is that your new tactic?" Jasira teased. "Seduce the enemy into surrender?"

"I'll have you understand, this shirt costs more than your entire wardrobe," he mentioned, turning to me and dropping to one knee with exaggerated solemnity. "Dearest sister. Flower of Elyrien. Don't marry the snake prince."

I snorted. "Get up."

But he pressed his forehead against my stomach, wrapping his arms around my waist like a child clinging to safety.

"Wynnie," he murmured, his voice dipping lower, "don't go."

I stiffened. He was always the dramatic one, but this felt different. I rested my hands on his shoulders, silent.

"I did try," he said, his eyes widening with a silent plea. "I presented my argument. I raised my voice. I threw a goblet. Mother said it was unbecoming of a future king." He leaned back and offered a wry smile. "So, I threw another."

"Did Father say anything?" I asked softly.

Alaric hesitated. "Only that we do what we must to keep our people safe. He said he trusts you to make the people love Elyrien."

My throat tightened.

Jasira gave him a look. "That is both touching and infuriating."

Alaric stood, brushing imaginary dust from his knee. The warhound sat beside him, ever still. Bran, as people called him, embodied shadow and steel; his ears twitched at every sound, always alert. Loyal beyond reason, he had followed Alaric onto battlefields and into ballroom halls with equal poise.

"If anything happens, Wyn—"

"I'll have Gideon to guard me," I said. "And Erindor."

He raised an eyebrow. "The quiet one?"

I nodded. "Apparently."

"Good. Quiet men are harder to bribe."

He reached into his sleeve and pulled out a pressed red poppy. "For courage," he said, tucking it into the palm of my hand. "And memory." He looked at me with an understanding gaze.

I accepted gratefully, gently closing my fingers over it. "I'm not small."

He kissed my forehead. "Not where it matters."

I knelt, and Bran padded forward, resting his massive head in my lap.

"Oh, you sweet boy," I murmured, burying my fingers in the thick fur behind his ears. He gave a low huff of approval, his tail thumping once on the rug.

Ignoring the slobber already soaking into my nightgown, I continued to scratch him under his chin. "I'll miss you the most," I exclaimed, enough for Alaric to hear.

Alaric gasped in mock betrayal. "Bran, how could you?"

"He's clearly the better brother," Jasira added dryly, grinning.

Bran snorted and nuzzled closer. I rested my cheek against the side of his head, breathing him in.

"Take care of him for me," I whispered. Bran made a soft sound, almost like a promise.

Alaric pivoted, halting near the door, and as he left, he plucked his old lute from its usual spot by the doorframe, strumming a soft, wistful chord as he walked away. "It won't be the same without you here, Wynnie." Alaric sighed before closing the door behind him.

His departure hung in the air long after he was gone.

I lingered a while longer, sitting back against the edge of my bed, watching the light shift across the floor in bands of honey and dust. It all seemed so final.

"Do you remember when we used to pretend we were priestesses?" I asked Jasira quietly, still staring at the sunlit dust.

She looked up from tying the last ribbon on my cloak. "You mean the time you made a crown from garden weeds and declared yourself 'Wynessa the Merciful'?"

"You called yourself Jasira the Blasphemer."

"Because you made me sacrifice my hairbrush to the bees."

The sound that emerged was a mere whisper of a laugh, thin and fragile, as if it might shatter at any moment.

"I wish we'd stayed in that game," I said. That world seemed so much simpler.

Jasira crossed over to me and took my hand. "It was easier. It was ours."

I squeezed her fingers. "Promise me you'll take care of Alaric. And Bran. And the garden."

"Only if you promise to come back with stories."

...

That night, the castle exhaled into silence.

I left my chambers wrapped in a gray cloak, soft-soled shoes whispering against marble. The moon was a waning crescent, a silver eyelash drifting across a velvet sky. No one stopped me. No one ever did. A princess is invisible when she wants to be.

The garden shrine was no longer truly a shrine. Instead, an alcove hidden behind a veil of ivy and moonflowers, once devoted to Cireth, the Bloomfather— God of rebirth, balance, and green things. No priest lit incense here. No offerings lay at his feet. Vines had overtaken the altar, curling around a cracked stone bowl etched with his symbol: a flame inside a blooming flower.

Most had forgotten him and his shrine. That made it mine. I knelt in the moss, the earth cool beneath my knees, the sky aching above me. My hands folded, not because I believed it helped, but because it seemed like a necessary response to the longing in my chest.

"I am unsure if you're listening," I whispered. "I don't even have proof that you're still there."

Then, without warning, the wind veered, whipping hair across my eyes and tugging at my clothes.

"But if you are," I continued. "If there's a god who still remembers the quiet ones, the ones who smile through duty and ache under silk, then please, please see me."

I bowed my head lower, fingers trembling against the hem of my cloak.

"I don't want to be bartered like grain in a shipment ledger. I desire to be more than a bride to a stranger with icy hands. I want to walk through Wildervale without fear. I want to heal things. Grow things. Be something more than just soft and silent."

A breeze stirred the chapel garden, soft and sudden. It slipped through the clover, kissed my cheek, and rustled the petals of a pale lavender bloom beside me.

"I want to mean something."

I held my breath.

It was the wind.

But for an instant, it felt as if something had noticed me.

A hush. Like something was listening.

And then, it was gone.

I opened my eyes slowly, and the moonflowers swayed as if exhaling. My palms were damp with earth, my knees sore from stone, but I didn't rise.

My eyes traced the weathered carvings in the shrine's stone, the remnants of Cireth's sigil, half-erased by time and moss. The air seized in my lungs, refusing to move.

I reached to brush the vines aside, but a thorn snagged my wrist—sharp, sudden, almost deliberate.

A bead of blood welled up on my skin.

I remained fixed on it, half-expecting it to burn or shimmer or speak. But it didn't. Yet, something within me shifted. A quiet tension tightened, drawing inward like a held breath deep within the marrow. I pressed my palm over my heart.

And in this moment, I was a girl again, kneeling in a forgotten chapel, with moss clinging to my hem with a poppy tucked behind my ear.

The last of the candlelight clung to the chapel walls, soft and stubborn. I traced my fingers along the stone as I rose. My knees were aching from kneeling too long, but I wasn't ready to return. Not yet.

Outside, the stillness of the garden descended once more, a quiet that made the world seem remote.

I sat on the bench beneath the arbor, my breath plumed before my lips, a fleeting ghost in the frosty air, each exhale a miniature cloud that vanished as quickly as it appeared. The moon was rising, silver and whole. From the pouch at my hip, I pulled the little leather-bound green journal I hadn't written in since summer. I ran my fingers over it, hesitating.

And then, slowly, I opened the next blank page:

I used to think the garden chapel was the quietest place in the world. But tonight, it seemed loud, like every hope I've ever whispered there came echoing back, unanswered.

We have packed everything. My room is bare. I keep telling myself I'm ready, but I'm not sure I even grasp what that signifies anymore.

They say it's my duty to go, that peace depends on it, that I'm the bridge between Elyrien and Caerthaine. But no one's ever asked what I want. It could be because it's insignificant? Perhaps that is the essence of royalty. You trade your voice for a crown and your name for a signature on treaties.

Still...I'm not courageous.

Alaric says I am. But I realize they're only saying it so I don't fall apart.

I have no idea what sort of princess I'll become out there.

But I hope to remember who I was before this began.

-W

Chapter Three

Erindor

The sun hung low over the southern training yard, casting the stone walls of the barracks in copper and fire. Bells tolled faintly from the temple towers, a deep, mournful sound that seemed to carry the weight of centuries beyond the courtyard walls. Crows circled above in the bruised twilight, their dark silhouettes looping lazily as if they were waiting for the moment when they could swoop down and claim whatever remained, hungry for the promise of a feast yet to come.

Dust rose with every strike, painting the air with the smell of sweat, steel, and scorched leather.

I rolled my shoulders and shifted my grip on the practice blade, my fingers wrapped firmly around the worn leather. Across from me, Sir Crowen grinned the way a dog might when it believes it has cornered something smaller.

"Ready to lose, commoner?" he sneered, tossing his sword in a flashy spin that made the gathered onlookers murmur.

I didn't answer. His fingers drummed a restless rhythm against the handle. A slight, cheeky grin tugged at my lips. My silence annoyed him. It always did.

Crowen fought like a peacock; all flourish and no weight behind his wings. Yet, I knew his sort. He fought to be seen. Each strike, each parry angled toward the balcony where nobles gathered to sip and judge.

I fought to end things.

He lunged first, as expected. The motion happened with speed, aiming for the shoulder, intended and daring. I stepped aside. My blade flicked upward, catching his mid-thrust and twisting him off balance.

Still no applause. Only the hush of those waiting for one of us to bleed.

"You fight like an ill-nourished inchworm," Crowen spat between breaths. "It's not surprising that a woman's never called out your name in pleasure."

Laughter rippled through the onlookers—all squires, stable hands, one or two drunk veterans leaning against the fence.

The urge to retort flared and died. I'd learned young that silence is a blade of its own.

He advanced again, chest puffed out, pressing harder this time, sweat glistening on his brow. I allowed him to feel like he was driving me to my place. Let him believe he was in control. I watched as his movements grew bolder.

Then I turned. Stepped into his swing. And with a clean movement, one born not of pride but precision, knocked the blade from his hand.

It clattered onto the dirt before us.

Gasps and surprised chuckles reached my ears.

I met his eyes. "Losing to an inchworm must sting."

His face darkened. He attacked without thinking, but I had already shifted. My foot swept low, catching his ankle. He stumbled and fell to the ground with a resounding thud. I stopped short of planting my blade in his throat.

The commander's voice cut through the moment like a hammer on stone. "Enough! Stand down."

Crowen seethed. I bowed, small and sharp, then returned the blade to the rack. I'll leave them to their whispers. To their wonder.

As I passed the weapons rack, I sensed a mutter behind me.

Another snorted. "He's too quiet. Even the commander flinches when he walks in."

They weren't wrong. I was quiet. And that silence unsettled people more than violence. It made them imagine things that weren't there. Or worse, things that were.

"Erindor, haul your damned carcass in here!" Commander Harven bellowed from across the yard.

Located over the forge, the commander's tower office remained warm, permeated by the aroma of oil, chain-mail, and aged parchment. I stepped down the corridor to Harven's office, every crack in the stone of the corridor seemed to hold a whispered echo of past battles. The faded banners, hanging like tattered ghosts, serving a silent reminder of the border fights that had shaped this place. Dust clung to the corners, and the sconces along the walls burned low. I'd walked down this path a dozen times; each one the same, each one lonelier. Once upon a time, a shield had been hung crookedly on the wall. Before someone had decided to take it down. Now gazing at the wall, I wasn't sure if that made the place better or worse.

"By the black breath of Tharn, get in here now, boy," he growled loudly

I took a breath, straightening my back as I walked through the door, and stood at attention.

Harven remained oblivious to my entrance, his fingers dancing a furious rhythm on the scroll, hammering out a beat that resonated like a war drum. Broad-shouldered with a thick middle, his once dark beard, now streaked with gray strands. A long scar cut across one temple and disappeared into his hairline; a souvenir from a campaign he never talked about. His armor hung from hooks behind him, dented and worn, like it had been through too many winters and not enough polish.

"You've been assigned to escort Princess Wynessa to Caerthaine," he said finally.

My brows didn't move, though something in my chest did.

"Remove that expression from your face," Harven snapped. "This isn't a cushioned parade. You'll pass through Wildervale and several worse places. You keep her alive, understood?"

I nodded in agreement.

Harven leaned over the map spread across the table, the lines of his scar deepening as he scowled. "The southern road's half-flooded from the autumn storms. Bridge at Deymarch is gone. You won't be able to take a wagon across, not with the rivers this high."

He rapped his knuckles against the pass etched in faint ink near Wildervale. "There's the ridge path, but no one with sense goes that way. Too many stories. Too many bodies. Stick to the lowlands and keep ahead of the cold-season rains. If you time it right, you'll reach Caerthaine dry."

He leaned forward, elbows on the desk. "And don't get attached. She's not for the likes of you. She has a prince to marry."

The pause stretched, thick as smoke.

"Understood Sir. I'll guard her with my life," I said.

"That's all you're here to do," he muttered, before flicking his fingers at me. "You're dismissed, Sir Erindor."

I stepped back, then raised my right fist over my heart, fingers curled tight; the old salute of Elyrien's royal guard. A vow of silence, service, and steel.

He didn't reciprocate.

I turned and left without another word.

. . .

The wind changed when night fell. The courtyard emptied of voices, but not of ghosts, their mournful whispers carried the wind that rustled the withered leaves clinging to the ancient stone walls.

I sat alone on the old stone bench that faced the withering apple tree near the edge of the barracks yard. Its branches stretched out like fingers grasping at the stars. Leaves murmured secrets to the wind, brittle from the end of summer.

A basin of water sat beside me, half full from my earlier training. I dipped my hands into it and rinsed the dirt and sweat from my palms, watching the ripples catch the faint light of the torch.

Everything seemed peaceful when people weren't looking. That was the danger of stillness; it gave you back your thoughts.

I leaned back and stared up. The sky above the barracks stretched wide, bruised and star-choked, a scatter of quiet fires. My mother used to say each held the memory of a soul. Lights that watched. Lights that remembered.

She believed in stories, but I wasn't sure if I ever had.

Still, I found myself searching for them anyway.

The scent of mint came unbidden. Simply a memory.

She'd taught me to read storms by the scent of the wind, to tell which herbs numbed pain and which ones called dreams. She never carried a blade, but she didn't need to. I remembered the way men flinched from her gaze.

I closed my eyes and tried to forget the ache in my shoulder. The day's training had gone on long. Too long. Tomorrow, I was to ride alongside a princess. I'd never spoken to a girl spun from silk and hopes.

Would she speak in honeyed words and walk as if on glass? Would she scream at the sight of blood? I remained unsure, and I didn't take the time to speculate.

It was apparent to me that I was meant to guard her, and I had never failed a post. So, that would have to be enough.

. . .

By the time dawn broke, I was already at the stables. A dull gray-violet defined the sky, and the air held the burden of an approaching storm, though clouds hadn't gathered. Horses shifted in their stalls, snorting into the cold, while leather creaked beneath my hands as I tightened Flora's girth strap.

Boots scuffed against stone behind me. They sounded like light and careful steps. I turned.

It was Princess Wynessa and her personal lady.

She looked delicate, not in the noble sense of ornament and poise, but like someone still learning how to stand up in a world that had pressed too hard. Her cloak snagged briefly on the stirrup as she passed. She waved off the guard who moved to help and tugged it free herself, though her hands trembled.

Her hair caught the early light, a glint of copper and gold. Her posture was straight, too straight, the kind of stiffness that came from trying not to fold. Her eyes swept the yard as if she expected someone to call her out for being here. I moved closer toward her; she hardly reached my shoulder, and I wasn't a large person by any measure. A solid foot separated us, enough to make her look like she'd drown in a borrowed saddle.

She looked at me. I held her gaze long enough to nod.

"Thank you," she said softly. "For…coming." She cleared her throat. "On this journey. I mean."

A pause.

"I'm Wynessa, by the way," she added quickly, like she'd only just remembered how introductions worked. "But…I suppose you knew that."

I gave a low grunt in acknowledgment. Little could be voiced.

She and her lady stepped back a few paces, just out of arm's reach, their voices lowering to a whisper. They probably thought I couldn't hear.

Wynessa turned toward the other woman beside her; Jasira, if I remembered correctly. Dark curls pinned back in a twist of green silk. She had a grounded look about her, with strong arms and a solid posture. Not a guard, but someone who'd learned how to protect things, anyway.

"I think he hates me," the Princess murmured.

Jasira huffed. "He doesn't hate you. He looks like he was sculpted by someone who's never laughed."

Wynessa gave a quiet, breathless laugh.

I looked away, pretending not to have heard.

She turned her attention from Jasira and stepped closer to a nearby stable hand who was no older than fifteen, with hay in his hair and a saddle strap clutched in his calloused hands. I'd seen him once or twice around the barracks but never bothered to learn his name.

"Good morning, Talen," she said gently. "Thank you for readying the horse."

The boy blinked, wide-eyed. "Y-you're welcome, Princess," he stammered, his cheeks going crimson.

Wynessa smiled like she meant it. "This one's yours, isn't it?" She reached to pet the nose of the chestnut gelding. "He's beautiful."

Talen nodded mutely.

I clenched my jaw. Of course, she knew his name. Of course, she asked after the horse as if it mattered. She had no idea what the road ahead held, and she was wasting her attention on stables and pleasantries.

Then, to my horror, she added, "I've never really ridden before. Do you have any advice?"

Talen's mouth opened and closed like a fish. "Oh, uh, don't— don't grip too tight with your knees. Let the horse move under you."

"Like dancing?" she suggested, with a hopeful tilt.

"Sort of?" he stuttered, clearly overwhelmed by her questions.

I turned away, biting back a sigh.

She was going to die.

Not by my hand. But by the road. She'd fall from the saddle before we cleared the foothills, twist her ankle on a rock, and offer honey to a bandit. She seemed the type of girl that smiled at a wolf and expected it to wag its tail.

And I was bound to her. Responsible for that smile. For those fragile and foolish questions.

I wanted to resent her. I told myself I did.

But deep beneath the irritation, something else stirred. Not pity. Not admiration. Just the uncomfortable sense that softness like hers wasn't meant to last, and if it died out here, I'd have to carry the ashes.

How was I going to manage this task?

Chapter Four

Wynessa

Lilac and gold were bleeding together in the sky like watercolors left out in the rain. The travel cloak clung to my shoulders, a familiar burden. Yet, a colder, heavier dread, born of the coming storm, settled deep within me as I surveyed the imposing palace courtyard.

Stone steps gleamed beneath the dawn. The air was cool, edged in the quiet hush of servants watching from balconies, guards posted like statues. This was no longer my home. It was a gilded stage for goodbyes.

My mother stood at the top of the marble steps, dressed in a pale silver gown. As ever, she swept her hair into a high, immaculate twist. She looked down at me, her eyes cold, like those of a gardener critiquing a hedge, assessing my every detail: trimmed, sculpted, and merely *useful.*

"You will make a good impression," she said, her face remaining carefully blank. "You will speak with grace." She stepped forward and fastened my brooch—a sunburst wrought in gold and garnet, glinting too brightly for the gray morning, to my collar. Her fingers were like slivers of frozen glass against my neck.

"You are not only a daughter." Her words emerged in a calm, precise monotone. "You are a promise."

"I understand," I said, though my voice was barely a whisper.

She lingered a moment longer, studying me like a statue she wasn't quite proud of. "Keep your shoulders back. Chin high. Do not babble when spoken to. And for mercy's sake, keep your hands still. You fidget like a child." She shook her head disapprovingly.

I clenched my hands at my sides, every muscle straining against the urge to fidget.

My father, King Theron, stepped forward next, reaching out to me with his hands. His beard was white as winter ash, eyes shadowed with weariness. His grasp, unexpectedly gentle, seemed to transmit a quiet warmth, a silent offering of comfort as his fingers closed over mine.

"Trust your instincts, little star," he mumbled. "They've always been kinder than mine."

His touch lingered. Then, as always, duty called him away before his comfort settled enough to take hold.

Footsteps rang on the stone, louder, more dramatic, and then: "What, no goodbye for your favorite brother?"

Alaric walked toward me with a swagger; his copper-blond hair was windswept, and his fitted riding leathers looked more suited for a parade than a journey. Bran padded beside him, his tail flicking lazily.

My heart leaped with joy. "You're coming?"

He threw his arms wide. "Of course, I'm coming! What kind of big brother lets his little sister waltz off to enemy territory with nothing but her plants for company?"

I laughed, throwing my arms around him. He pulled me close and rested his chin on my head with exaggerated tenderness.

"You're not allowed to cry," he warned. "That's my job. I'm the dramatic one."

"You're the reckless one."

"Reckless, charming, and essential. I'll be serving as your 'advisor,' which is a formal way of saying I'll argue with every noble who so much as frowns at you. Also, I've decided the most important diplomatic tool I'm bringing is my lute."

"You didn't?" My grin felt like it might split my face.

"I absolutely did. Can't represent Elyrien properly without a serenade or two. Might even charm a duke," he joked while wiggling his eyebrows.

"You'll charm someone, alright."

Jasira appeared beside us, adjusting the satchel on her hip. Despite pulling her dark curls back behind her ear, a few strands had already escaped to frame her face. She wore a soft green tunic embroidered at the cuffs, which was both practical and pretty. She smiled when she saw me and reached out to squeeze my hand.

"You're doing better than I thought you would," she whispered.

"I'm just pretending not to be terrified."

"That counts as better. Do they have my horse ready yet?"

I blinked, surprised. "Wait…you're coming with us too?"

Jasira gave me a look. "Of course I am. Did you think I was going to let you travel halfway across the continent with nothing but guards and your brother for company?"

"But you said nothing!"

"You were already worrying yourself breathless," she said with a shrug. "Besides, someone has to make sure Alaric doesn't insult the wrong kingdom, and you don't fall off a horse."

The cobbled path led us to the looming gates, where the small company had already assembled.

Three guards awaited us: Corren, an older man with sharp blue eyes and a weathered face. He looked like he'd survived more battles than were countable. Lark, barely older than me. His fingers constantly adjusting his grip on the reins, his hands never quite still. Tyren was tall and silent, with a jagged scar stretching from his jaw to his ear. He looked like he'd seen one or two things I'd rather not imagine.

Then there was Sir Gideon.

He had a lopsided grin, armor slightly mismatched, and a dent in one pauldron like it had seen more tavern stools than swords. His skin was rich brown, and his eyes sparkled with warmth and mischief beneath a head of cropped black curls.

He bowed with exaggerated flair. "Sir Gideon, at your service. Hero of one tavern brawl, three broken chairs, and at least five unintentional insults to nobility. But I ride true and fall with flair."

Jasira raised her eyebrow. "That's...oddly reassuring." A smile tugged at the corners of my lips, surprising even me. "I'm glad you're coming."

"Prepared and ready for the journey, my lady," he said brightly. "Though I should warn you, my horse bites." I was unsure whether that was meant to be a joke. Either way, I would stay clear.

A sliver of light caught the polished edge of a dark mare's saddle, then brightened, *insistent*, demanding attention.

Only then did I see him.

Erindor. He stood beside his black mare, armor catching the sunrise like old bronze. His hair curled slightly around his ears, wind-tossed and unbothered. He looked carved from storm clouds and silence, with broad shoulders, a strong jaw, and a sword at his hip that looked like it had never left him. There was something about the way he stood, still and steady, that made everyone else seem to fade into the background. I had seen him before, of course. Quiet in the corridors. Sharp at council practice sparring. He was always on the edge of things, like a shadow that obeyed light but never belonged to it. But I'd never spoken to him.

Now, facing him in the unfiltered daylight, a knot tightened in my stomach, stealing my breath.

A flush crept up my neck, scorching my cheeks with the raw memory of my humiliation in the stables just moments before.

When our eyes locked, for just a heartbeat, a single, sharp nod came from him. I forced myself to swallow, the gesture rough against my dry throat, and in an instant tore my gaze away, the heat in my face burning.

Bran trotted over to me, distracting me from myself. He nudged my hand, and I gratefully scratched behind his ears.

"At least someone likes me."

Lark unfurled a folding map across the low stone bench near the gates and held it in place with a dagger and a crust of bread. Gideon crouched over it, brow furrowed in an expression far more serious than I expected from someone who had bragged about tavern chairs.

"So," he said, pointing with the dagger, "we'll follow the Eastwood trail into the Emberwood, then pass through the market village of Graymere. From there we'll cut into the southern edge of Wildervale before reaching Caerthaine. That keeps us on the lowland route—safer, and past the flooded roads."

The blade traced a line through the patch marked with clawed script and faint burn marks. "Avoiding Thorncross Ravine entirely. Last I heard, wolves nested too close to the pass. We'll ride hard until Graymere, resupply there, and keep moving."

Gideon leaned forward, tapping a finger to a jagged crease of the map. "There's another way. Narrower path through the ridge—faster, but not one you'd take unless you had no choice. Landslides, old ruins, things in the rock that don't like to be disturbed."

Erindor's mouth tightened. "We've both taken it before. Once was enough. If the rains don't cut us off, we stick to the lowlands."

Alaric leaned over his shoulder. "Tell me we've had scouts take this route recently. Any chance we're not the first poor fools to ride into Wildervale this season?"

Gideon didn't miss a beat. "Scouts passed through last month. No signs of ambush, but there've been murmurs of bandits trailing the outer reaches of the Emberwood. Nothing confirmed, but I'd rather we keep watch in shifts once we make camp. It's safer to treat rumors like warnings."

I stepped closer, studying the map. The road ahead twisted like a vein across the skin of a continent. I had little experience with maps, though not completely. Some names resonated with me. Emberwood, Graymere, and Wildervale, I had seen them written in the margins of old maps and scribbled in the pages of dusty histories. I'd read about them beneath the garden arbor in the fading light, envisioning what it would be like to walk the paths of those stories.

Now I was going to live these stories.

"Wildervale," I whispered, eyes on the shaded green stretch that dominated the center. "I've always wanted to go there. Is it peaceful?"

Gideon gave a short laugh. "Only if you think whispering trees and forgotten gods are peaceful. Stay sharp when we cross it."

He looked up and grinned at me, then tapped the next mark north. "One step at a time, Princess. We'll get you to Caerthaine with your limbs intact, your dignity mostly preserved, and, if the gods are kind, your humor sharpened."

I smiled, a faint, almost involuntary gesture. The solid black line of the path in ink provided an anchor of sorts, though the true landscape remained shrouded in doubt.

When it came time to mount, I paused beside the unfamiliar mare they'd brought for me. The saddle looked impossibly high. I reached for the stirrup and nearly tipped backward.

Alaric chuckled. "Need help, Wynnie?"

"I've never ridden before," I admitted, the words tasting like ash.

Before he could move, Erindor appeared beside me.

He didn't speak, just offered his ungloved hand. His calloused palm felt steady. I placed my hand in his, and he lifted me easily, effortlessly, into the saddle.

For one moment, our eyes met, and something passed between us. Not heat, not lightning, but something quieter. Like the hush between two heartbeats.

"Thank you," I gasped out, feeling the tell-tale flush creep up my neck from the unexpected kindness.

He said nothing.

And with that, the gates opened. The road stretched like a ribbon of uncertainty ahead of us.

As we rode out, I clutched my journal tightly and looked back at the garden balcony one last time. The roses there were already beginning to close for the season.

Above us, a single dove cut across the morning sky.

I gripped the reins tighter and shifted my gaze forward. Behind me were duty, silence, and the shape of a life not chosen. Before me stood a prince I did not love, a war unseen, and something within me I had not yet grasped.

Something that might one day burn.

. . .

The sun climbed higher as the road narrowed beyond the outer walls of the palace, winding into the scrub and shade of the Eastwood trail. For a while, I tried to focus on the rhythm of hoofbeats, the sound of birds hidden in the trees, and the occasional creak of saddle leather. But it was impossible to ignore how uncomfortable I was in the saddle. Each rut in the road sent a jolt up my spine, jarring every bone. A dull throb settled in my lower back, and my knees, already stiff from the journey, locked up. I shifted for the third time in five minutes, hoping no one would notice. Unfortunately, someone did.

"You ride like you're trying not to touch the horse," Gideon said beside me, his voice low and amused.

"I'm trying not to fall off," I scolded.

He grinned. "That's fair. But you'll want to relax your legs a bit. Let the movement carry through your hips. Right now, you're bracing every time the horse shifts, and that's only going to make it worse."

I tried adjusting, but it only made me slide sideways in the saddle.

Jasira trotted up beside us with far more ease than I expected. She looked perfectly at home on her horse, her posture relaxed and confident. *How is she doing that?*

I stared at her. "What's your riding experience?"

She gave me a crooked smile. "Just because I like embroidery doesn't mean I've never left the palace, Wyn. I grew up on a vineyard. Horses are easy."

I blinked. "That actually explains a lot."

"You should see me with a crossbow," she chirped, and then kicked her horse ahead to join Alaric up front.

"Here," Gideon chimed, and guided his horse a little closer. "Watch me. See how my hands stay light? Let the horse find its rhythm. You're not steering a cart. It's a conversation."

I watched, trying to mirror the way he moved. How his legs and back flowed with the horse instead of fighting it. But it was more difficult than it looked.

"Better," he said after a moment. "You'll have it by Graymere."

"That's days away."

"Well, then we'll either arrive with you riding like a proper scout, or I'll carry you across the border myself."

A burst of laughter escaped me, shaking my shoulders. The pain in my spine, while still present, seemed to recede, a manageable throb now.

We pressed on beneath the trees; the road stretching ahead in dappled light and dust. Behind me, the palace had vanished into the haze. Before me, the world waited.

Chapter Five

Erindor

Three days into the journey, we passed a landmark known as the Whispering Spire. A single jagged stone jutted from the forest floor like the tooth of some ancient god. Faint carvings spiraled around it, half-lost to moss and time. Someone had stacked three smooth river stones at its base, which was either a silent offering or a stark warning.

Wynessa gasped softly when she saw it, reining her horse to a halt. "I've read about this," she murmured, more to herself than to anyone else. "The Spire marks the place where the gods last spoke before the silence. It was a place of oaths. Of unmaking."

Gideon raised an eyebrow. "Charming. That's exactly where I hoped to pass the morning."

No one laughed.

Even the birds had gone quiet.

Wynessa remained still for a moment longer, sketching the stone's outline into her journal before nudging her horse onward, her expression heavy with an unspoken thought.

"Were you aware marrowgrass only grows in places where the veil between life and death is thin?" she said moments later.

I glanced at her.

"No."

That was all.

She'd turned back in her saddle, clearly trying to pretend she hadn't hoped for more.

By midday, the forest changed before us.

The path narrowed as we approached a rotted blackwood bridge arched over a chasm so narrow it looked like a wound in the earth. Jagged stone teeth jutted from the sides below, partially hidden by rising mist. Charred handrails leaned precariously, and half the planks groaned under our weight.

Alaric peered down. "If that drop doesn't kill you, the embarrassment will."

"It's said that a company of Caerthaine soldiers disappeared crossing this very spot," Jasira said, her voice low. "Some say the forest swallowed them. Others say they turned on each other."

Wyn tilted her head. "It's likely someone misled them. Someone omitted checking a map?"

She smiled subtly, but her gaze lingered on the trees, as if searching for something unseen.

The shadows on the other side of the bridge were deeper. The trees grew denser with every step, their branches knitting together overhead as if the forest itself had been waiting for us to cross.

And we did. One by one. Without breathing a single word.

It began with the trees. Gradually, towering giants replaced pale-trunked birches and sleepy elms, and their bark flaked in red and black, like something had scorched them and left them to bleed. The leaves hung in thick clusters overhead, colored crimson, copper, and ember-gold. The wind moved through them in fits, sending the rustle of dry paper across our path like a whisper that didn't want to be caught.

The horses' ears started twitching, their hooves scuffing nervously along the ash-dusted path. The forest was strangely muted. No birds chirped. No breath of a breeze stirred the crimson canopy. Instead, an oppressive stillness reigned, the forest not welcoming them, but *watching*.

They called this place Emberwood.

Beside me, Wynessa scribbled in her journal again, oblivious to the crunch of poison-bramble underfoot. She rode with both legs side-saddled today, her boots tucked neatly under the pale lavender riding skirt, which was utterly impractical. Her hands moved like a painter's, sketching the shapes of moss or lichen, as if they were worthy of a crown.

We were riding through a forest that had eaten whole patrols. And she was writing poetry about vines. Silly girl.

"Why is it called the Emberwood?" she asked aloud, turning in her saddle to glance at Gideon.

He perked up like a bard on cue. "Because it looks like it's perpetually on fire," he chirped, gesturing at the trees. "And sometimes it tries to eat you."

She laughed. Light, high, like something unafraid. "Eat me?"

"Carnivorous moss," he said, deadpan. "Hangs from trees like lace. Pretty, until it isn't."

She squinted upward. "You're joking?"

He paused for a moment. "I am," he said. "Well, mostly."

I didn't correct him.

This forest had killed men. Not only with teeth but with silence. With wrong turns, with half-remembered paths, with spores that paralyzed and vines that waited. The monsters weren't the ones who initially got you; it was what you couldn't see or hear.

Ahead of me, Wyn reined in and her gaze caught sight of something in the undergrowth. I watched it with her. A cluster of low ferns, their fronds tipped with pale lavender blossoms.

Until suddenly, she slipped from her saddle before I could call out.

Her boots hit the earth softly. She crouched beside the flowers, inching closer to sketch their shape in her little notebook, her silken strands tumbled from beneath her hood, catching the dappled light filtering through the canopy. It gleamed, a vibrant spill of color like captured firelight.

She looked like she'd wandered into the wrong story.

I leapt from my horse, my boots landing with a soft thud into the soil. The air ahead had grown unnaturally still, the silence pressing down, heavy and wrong.

"Stop," I said, sharper than I meant to.

Wyn jumped, her head snapping up to meet my gaze. "What?"

I closed the gap between us in swift strides. I dropped my voice low, "What are you doing?"

She glanced down at the blossoms. "I've never seen these before," she said. "They looked like some kind of fern, but with open faces. Like asters, almost. I thought—"

"Poisonbramble," I said, cutting her off. "Don't step in it unless you want to hallucinate your own ancestors."

Her head snapped back, eyes wide, as she recoiled

"You might attempt walking if you do not want to survive this forest," I grumbled.

She looked at me for a long moment, narrowing her eyes, expression unreadable. Then she stepped around me without a word and went back to her horse.

I almost let it pass, but as I watched her fingers quiver as she lifted the reins, the knot of impatience in my gut tightened one more.

She acted as if kindness were a weapon, as if smiling at strangers and scribbling flower names into a book would protect her. Maybe she thought it made her brave. Perhaps she thought it made her likable. Who knew what went on in that poor girl's head?

But places like this did not suit her. Not for silence that devoured sound or forests that buried names. She didn't understand the rules. And people who didn't understand the regulations usually died before revising them.

So, I said nothing.

. . .

Before dusk, a low rustling reached our ears, too heavy for wind. It moved against the trees, then vanished. We paused, listening. Nothing followed. But we kept our hands near our blades and our voices low.

We made camp soon after, in a clearing edged by blackbark trees. Shadows danced long between the roots. As the others unpacked and began settling around the fire, Alaric dropped beside me, offering a wineskin I didn't take.

"You're quiet," he remarked, his voice a casual murmur that belied the sharpness of his gaze. "Even for someone whose profession is observation."

I didn't answer. Silence usually did the work for me.

He leaned forward, resting his arms on his knees. "You served in the border campaigns, didn't you? The skirmishes with the Eastline raiders."

I nodded once.

"And yet here you are, babysitting a girl who thinks poisonbramble is decorative."

That earned the slightest twitch of my brow.

"I need to understand something," Alaric continued, quieter now. "Can you keep her safe? I don't mean in the 'stand-in-front-of-a-sword' way. I mean, out here. In this kind of place."

I looked over at Wyn, who sat laughing beside Jasira, her cloak tangled around her ankles and her journal open again in her lap.

"She's not ready for this," I said flatly.

"I understand," Alaric replied. "That's why I'm asking if you are."

We didn't speak after that, but when he stood to join the others, I watched the way he looked at her as if she were still that small girl climbing garden walls barefoot.

A chill prickled under my skin, a cold dread of an understanding I desperately wished to ignore. Shadows danced long between the roots. I sat a few paces back, blade in hand, dragging a whetstone slowly along its edge. A quiet rhythm. Familiar. Clean.

Gideon reigned from his perch by the fire, legs comfortably crossed, the flames dancing in his eyes as he began, "So, there I was," he said, "with a bottle of cherry wine, one sock, and a duck under my arm." Wynessa snorted. "Why a duck?"

"Because the goose bit me first."

Laughter erupted, Jasira bubbled the loudest, Alaric wheezing, clutching his stomach behind his arm. Even the hardened guards cracked genuine smiles. It was a foolish, carefree moment, the kind people only truly appreciated once it had vanished. Gideon had a rhythm of his own. Bright-eyed, always grinning, always easing the worst moments with something absurd. I'd seen him put his body between a bandit's blade and a stranger without blinking. He was the real deal.

Jasira laughed. "No, seriously. Why did you become a knight in the first place, Gideon?"

He blinked, then grinned slowly. "Because it paid better than starving. Plus, I look good on a horse."

When the others chuckled, he added more quietly,

"My father," he said, poking the fire, "used to call me a waste of good shoes. Died in a bar fight he didn't start. And instead of crying, I picked up his sword, left home, and tried to laugh more than he ever did."

Wyn's voice was quiet as she leaned forward. "I think you've done that beautifully."

Gideon shrugged, but there was something fragile in the smile he gave her. "Not bad for a fool with a fondness for pastries and bad luck."

She touched his sleeve with a brief, tentative gesture, as if testing whether comfort could be offered without words to him. Her fingers lingered just long enough to transmit warmth through the worn fabric, bridging the quiet gap between them. After the others had drifted toward sleep, I kept to my post near the fire, still cleaning the edge of my dagger. My shoulder ached from the day's ride, though I didn't let it show. I'd taken a jolt earlier that afternoon when my mare stumbled on a root along the ridge, wrenching something that hadn't quite healed from a sparring match days before.

Wynessa came to me carrying a small tin cup. "Balmleaf," she said. "For the shoulder you keep pretending doesn't hurt."

I looked at the cup, then at her. Her fingers were dirt-stained, and her hair had waved slightly toward the tips, brushing past her shoulders as she leaned down.

"Is it poisoned?" I asked.

"Only if you insult my brewing," she retorted, a playful glint in her eye.

Her face was pink from the firelight, her cloak dusted with leaf bits, and there was soil beneath her fingernails. She smelled of lavender, thyme, and something wilder. Whatever root she'd crushed last. Her beauty wasn't the sculpted perfection favored in courtly halls.

She was…fierce. Like an unexpected grace of a wildflower forcing its way through solid stone. Ethereal yet undeniably wild. Her eyes, the color of deep forest moss, held a light that was both ancient and untamed.

I accepted the cup, our fingers brushing briefly. "Thank you," I said, surprising us both.

She tilted her head. "Oh, I get a thank you instead of a grunt? Are you warming up to me, or are you grateful I haven't fallen off my horse yet?"

"You almost did."

"And yet"—she beamed—"here I stand." She opened up her arms playfully.

I didn't smile, but she grinned anyway, causing my heart to forget how to beat for only a second.

I watched as she floated away. My mouth forgetting to speak. I watched as she returned to Jasira and curled up beneath a cloak of clover-dyed wool.

Before sleep took me, I caught her whispering something to her friend.

"I think he does have a heart," she said. "It's buried under thirty layers of steel."

She didn't know the half of it.

Chapter Six

Wynessa

It crept in slow and soundless, veiled in mist thick enough to choke on.

Emberwood felt like it was holding its breath.

The air was colder than yesterday, the damp clinging to skin and bone. Even the horses were restless, hooves shifting, heads tossing at shadows that hadn't moved. Bran let out a low growl and stared into the trees, fur raised along his back.

Something was out there. Not moving, not approaching. Just…watching.

I ran my fingers along the spine of my journal, but didn't open it. Not this morning.

Jasira moved with deliberate care, her hands steady but her eyes scanning everything.
Tyren rubbed his thumb over the hilt of his sword, again and again, like it might vanish if he stopped.

"I don't like this," he muttered as he fastened the last strap on his pack. His voice cut through the dense fog, unnervingly clear, almost jarring in the muffled silence. "Good," Gideon said, slinging his cloak over one shoulder. "Fear means you're alive. Or smart. Or both."

He paused, sniffing the air. "If I drop dead from ghost mold spores, avenge me with poetry."

We were nearly ready to move when a raw, desperate scream tore through the silent trees. High-pitched. Panicked. A boy's voice, too young to belong to anyone in our group. It was a sound that instantly froze my blood. Everyone moved at once. Steel hissed from sheaths. Hooves pounded through the fog. I chased the noise without thinking.

A small caravan had taken shelter ahead in a grove of cypress. There were tipped wagons, canvas half-collapsed, and smoke that still rose from a dying cookfire. A boy no older than thirteen limped backward in the clearing, a red gash seeping down his leg. His eyes were wide with terror.

Three raiders surrounded him. Mountain-born, by the look of them. They were broad-shouldered and weather-beaten, their cloaks sewn from patchwork fur and bark fiber, teeth stained from root rot. One bore the sigil of a Caerthaine trade house, burned into a stolen pauldron. Another wore a child's ribbon tied around his wrist like a trophy.

The moment their eyes locked with ours, a clatter of steel filled the air as they snatched their weapons free. Behind them, my eyes were wide with horror at the shattered remnants of the caravan, which told their own story. An overturned and burnt wagon; a child's doll blackened in the mud beside a broken wheel. A woman lay half-covered by a torn canopy, throat cut, her hand still curled around a wooden spoon. Another figure, perhaps the boy's father, slumped unmoving beside the fire pit. Something jagged and cruel had opened his chest.

The boy hadn't run from danger. He had run from death.

"Down!" Erindor's voice cut through the morning like a blade.

And then he was a blade.

He lunged forward, low and fast, slicing one raider cleanly across the gut. The man staggered, clutching his belly as crimson soaked his tunic, but Erindor was already moving. Another raider roared and charged at him with a rusted axe. Erindor ducked under the swing, rolled through the slick earth, and came up behind him. His blade cut clean across the back of the man's knees, sending him down with a cry. Without pausing, Erindor plunged his sword through the man's ribs and yanked it free with a grim twist, blood spraying in an arc that vanished into the mist.

Alaric and Tyren were not far behind, steel flashing in the half-light. Bran leaped into action and bit into the nearest raider's leg, mangling it. Lark took a hit to the shoulder and stumbled, but recovered when Corren came to his defense. A dagger streaked toward him, but Gideon's shield swung up, shunting it aside. Without pause, he lashed back with a stone. It hit the raider square in the nose.

"You picked the wrong fog to lurk in, you tree-moss bastard!" he yelled.

My muscles locked, a sudden, primal clench that bolted me to the spot. My legs trembled, the tremor a silent scream before my mind could even process the danger before me.

But the boy. Gods, the boy.

I ran. Branches clawed at my cloak as I pushed through the underbrush, thorns snagging at my sleeves.

I dropped to my knees beside him, the cold from the soil seeping into my skirts. Blood spilled from his thigh, dark and fast. His face was pale beneath the grime; his lips were blue at the edges.

"Hold still," I whispered, my voice trembling. "You're safe now. You're safe."

But he wasn't, far from it. Nevertheless, I needed him to believe it.

I pulled herbs from the pouch at my belt: yarrow, crushed comfrey, a thick salve of beeswax, and lavender. My fingers pressed into the wound to slow the flow, ignoring the warmth, the smell, and the way my hands shook. Jasira appeared beside me, helping to unroll the bandages as my fingers became tangled in the cotton.

"Breathe, Wyn," she whispered. "You're here. He's here. Breathe."

"I'm trying," I rasped, blinking against the sting in my eyes. "I'm trying."

When I looked up, the raiders were dead. One guard was wounded. Erindor stood still in the mist, blood dripping from his blade, his breathing measured. He looked like something carved from stone and fury.

The boy stirred. Alive. His lashes flickered—a breath caught in his throat. Then he sagged against the earth, slipping into a dark unconsciousness.

I sat there, frozen in a paralysis that defied the will to flee, his blood drying into a sticky film beneath my nails.

Jasira stayed beside me, gently taking my hands and wiping them clean with a strip of linen. "You're alright," she said softly. "You did well."

I whispered, "I was breathless."

"But you didn't run. You stayed. That matters."

I looked across the clearing.

Erindor stood apart, shoulders squared, sword still in hand. He wasn't looking at anyone. Not at the boy. Not at me. But at the trees. The way someone looks when they've already seen this too many times.

He didn't speak. He simply wiped the blade clean and walked back into the mist.

· · ·

We traveled more slowly after that.

The boy named Kellen now rode with Lark, barely awake, his leg bound and stiff. He had woken only once, just long enough to whisper his name before slipping under again. He would heal, but only if we found him a proper shelter soon. By mid-afternoon, we sought refuge in a patch of sun-dappled clearing, where the light broke through the canopy in golden shafts. The mist had thinned, but tension lingered in the branches.

Jasira unpacked a small satchel of dried fruit and broke it into portions, handing pieces to anyone who passed. Alaric reclined with one arm behind his head and the other tossing twigs into the low firepit. Despite the risk, we built a small, smoky fire, tucked low into a ring of stones, for the sake of the boy. Kellen needed warmth and something hot in his belly. The twigs crackled softly beneath the pot, the flame of their fire barely more than a flicker, but it was enough to boil water for soup.

Gideon was crouched nearby, fiddling with a half-bent buckle on his armor and telling Tyren an embellished story about a cursed heirloom that made its owner fall in love with frogs. His laughter was a mere echo of its usual boisterous self, a soft breath of sound almost swallowed by the quiet. Tyren, bruised and winded from the morning's fight, didn't join in, but did appear to be listening intently.

Corren sharpened his blade with careful, practiced strokes, his eyes constantly flicking toward the treeline. Lark sat with Kellen propped against him, dozing. He hummed softly under his breath, some lullaby that sounded older than the kingdoms.

I sat cross-legged with my journal, Bran's head resting heavily in my lap. I tried to write something, anything wise or comforting, but the words wouldn't come. My hands still smelled faintly of iron and moss. I looked down at my palms, the persistent aroma, a strange blend of raw iron and the cool, damp breath of moss, still clung to them.

"Princess."

I looked up.

Erindor stood over me, a dagger in his hand.

"You froze," he said. His voice gave away nothing.

I took the statement slowly. "I acted."

"Badly."

I bristled. "Why are you here? To shame me?"

"No," he said, stepping forward slowly toward me. He held something out for me to take. I hesitated, peering out to see what it was. A dagger. Its polished bone hilt, intricately carved, was aimed directly at me. "To teach you," he said softly, his eyes gazing at mine, waiting for my reaction.

I stared at the dagger. "I'm not helpless."

He nodded once. "Then learn."

He led me away from the others, down a narrow deer path that curled toward the edge of camp. The trees grew denser here, their branches weaving the sunlight into thin ribbons of gold.

We had been walking in silence for a couple of minutes when I spun around expecting an empty space, but instead I nearly collided with Erindor. There he stood. Far closer than I expected, silent as a shadow, and somehow more solid than anything else in the world.

I fumbled a step back, my heart jumping. "You move like a ghost," I muttered.

He didn't respond. Just tilted his head slightly, eyes unreadable.

I turned away again, trying to focus. My fingers fumbled with the dagger, already painfully aware of how awkward I must look. My palms were sweaty. My skirts kept catching on the underbrush. I briefly looked over my shoulder. Erindor continued to stand behind me like a statue. Unbothered. Unmovable.

Then suddenly, in an instant, he filled the world, every detail of him pressing into my senses. The low, vibrating rumble of his voice, a faint, intriguing scar etching his wrist, the subtle prickle of stubble along his jawline. The primal scent of iron, pine, and woodsmoke enveloped me.

His closeness stole the air from my lungs, as my heart hammered against my ribs, a desperate drumbeat against the overwhelming intimacy of his presence. I could barely contain the tension and unsettling steadiness that had come over me. He was close, closer than anyone had been before. The men at court always seemed untrustworthy to me—all smiles and empty flattery, perfumed and polished but hollow. Erindor was the opposite—all rough edges, calloused hands, and a silence that said more than most men's oaths.

He tapped my wrist. "Too tight."

"I don't want to drop it."

"You'll drop it faster if your hand goes numb."

Obeying, I loosened my grip.

He stepped closer behind me, close enough that I could feel his warmth at my back. One of his hands hovered just over my shoulder, the other adjusting my grip.

"Here," he said quietly. "The dagger isn't about force. It's about precision. Keep your wrist loose but not flimsy. Like this."

He guided my arm forward in a short arc, the blade slicing through the air.

"Don't swing wide. Short. Fast. You're not trying to impress anyone. You're trying to stop them from killing you."

I swallowed hard. "Comforting."

"Truth isn't meant to comfort. It's meant to keep you alive."

I nodded, fighting to concentrate, my pulse skipping like a stone on water beneath the weight of his presence at my back.

"Now try it again," he said, stepping back. "Yourself this time."

I exhaled, reset my grip, and swung. Too stiff and too slow. The blade wobbled at the end of the motion like it wasn't sure where to land.

Erindor's expression didn't change.

"No," he said simply.

Heat rushed to my cheeks. "I'm trying."

"I know," he said, and gestured for me to do it again.

He nudged my shin with his boot. "Feet apart."

After a pause, he moved in front of me.

"Try to hit me."

I blinked. "What?"

"Come at me. Keep your balance."

"I'll lose."

"I know."

I narrowed my eyes and lunged. He sidestepped easily, catching my wrist as I stumbled into him. His other hand shot out to steady me.

Gods, he was solid, not like the courtiers who wore armor as decoration. No, they built him for battle, for carrying weight. Lean muscle, hard lines, and unwavering control.

My breath caught. The warmth of his body soaked through every layer between us. My pulse betrayed me, fluttering high and unsteady.

"I told you to keep your balance," he said, keeping his voice low.

His hands, still resting on my skin, were a static charge that bypassed my thoughts, leaving only a chaotic hum where focus should have been. He looked down at me, and his eyes weren't only steel. There was something beneath the surface. Something quieter, more curious?

"You don't blink when you're afraid," he murmured.

"I blink plenty."

"Not when it matters."

A lump formed in my throat, dry and insistent. "Why are you teaching me?"

"Because next time," he said softly, "I might not be there."

He stepped back, and a wave of longing, sharp and unexpected, washed through me as his heat vanished.

I hated how obvious I must've been. My face burned, my breath catching in my throat as though I had raced through the courtyard. This wasn't infatuation, I told myself. That wasn't possible. It was a mix of gratitude, admiration, and embarrassment all tangled together.

He didn't seem to notice. It's possible he did, and he was thoughtful enough to omit mentioning it.

I lunged again. Faster this time with more determination. My arm extended, feet pushing off the earth with more control.

He shifted just enough. Turned his body, caught my wrist, and redirected my weight past him. Not harshly, just enough to remind me how easily he could.

I stumbled two steps and caught myself.

"Better," he said. "But don't lean forward like that. You'll lose your footing, Princess."

"I'm not meant to stab people," I muttered.

He raised an eyebrow. "Then let's hope they never try to stab you."

I shifted, but a root in my way caught my boot. I lurched forward, off balance enough to crash into him.

His hands came up instinctively, catching me around the waist. I landed hard against his chest, breath shallow. His grip steadied me, unflinching, and then lingered for a beat too long.

He set me upright as if I weighed nothing.

"You alright?"

"Don't stop on my account," came Gideon's voice from behind a tree. His arms crossed, grinning. "I was rooting for you to stab him."

Erindor stepped back fast. I lowered the dagger, mortified.

"Are we interrupting?" Jasira asked, smiling far too knowingly.

"No," I said too quickly.

"Yes," Gideon replied at the same time.

I spun on my heel and rushed back toward the clearing.

Jasira fell in step beside me. "You're glowing."

"It's the firelight," I muttered.

"There's no fire over here," she said, smirking.

I almost dropped the dagger.

. . .

That night, sleep evaded me.

Kellen whimpered softly near Lark, who stayed beside him like a quiet anchor. Tyren and Corren took watch while the others tucked themselves in beside blankets or saddle rolls. The forest pulsed with slow tension, like it hadn't quite forgiven us for surviving the morning.

I lay curled beneath my cloak, my gaze lifted upwards through the canopy at slivers of sky, too faint to hold the distant sparkle of stars. Jasira shifted beside me, turning to me and propping herself on an elbow. "You're quiet."

"I'm thinking."

She gave me a knowing look. "Dangerous pastime."

"Do you think I'm foolish?" I asked softly.

Jasira didn't answer immediately. Then she said, "No. I think you're brave enough to be kind in a world that punishes kindness. That's not foolish. That's rare."

I swallowed, my throat tight.

Somewhere across camp, the steady scrape of a blade met stone. I didn't need to look to know it was Erindor.

"Do you think he heard?" I whispered.

Jasira offered a hesitant reply. "Perhaps, but I believe he was already aware."

I turned on my side, Bran's warmth tucked against my back, and I listened to the rhythm of the whetstone. Even in sleep, the forest watched.

I closed my eyes, but the weight of the day still clung to my skin. All the blood, the fear, the way his hands had steadied mine. Today, I held a life in my hands, and I stood toe-to-toe with someone made of storms.

And tomorrow, I will try again.

I curled my cloak tighter around my shoulders; the fire had long since been reduced to coal. The others were asleep: Jasira, finally resting after tending to the boy; Gideon snoring softly nearby; Alaric murmuring something in his sleep, Bran twitching beside him. Erindor stood beyond the firelight, his back to us, watchful as ever.

My fingers ached from clutching the dagger too tightly. I was still conscious of its weight even now, long after he'd sheathed it for me.

With sleep evading me, I reached into my satchel, pulling free the leather-bound book tucked between sprigs of dried peppermint and crushed willowbark. The familiar scrape of charcoal against parchment steadied my breath.

I don't think I'll sleep tonight.

Every time I close my eyes, I see his face—the boy from the road. Blood pouring from his leg, his eyes full of fear. We saved him. I saved him. But it wasn't clean. That moment was not an insignificant one, like the ones in my old healer's books. It was real. It was messy. And it was terrifying.

I keep wondering what would've happened if I'd hesitated longer. If the others hadn't fought so fast. If Erindor hadn't…been who he is.

He taught me how to hold a dagger today. Told me to stab him.

I couldn't.

Not because I didn't want to learn, but because part of me still clings to the idea that I'm not a warrior.

There was something in his eyes afterward. Not judgment. Something quieter.

I don't think I'll ever be a fighter.

But I could learn to stand tall despite things.

-W

I closed the book with trembling fingers and tucked it beneath my cloak. Across the clearing, Erindor turned slightly, enough for me to realize he'd heard the parchment shift. He didn't speak. Neither did I.

But I sensed a companionship between us.

Tired, and still breathing.

I decided that tonight was enough.

My eyes finally closed.

Chapter Seven

Wynessa

Emberwood breathed around us, but not the way a forest should. It didn't speak in birdsong or rustles of leaves. It murmured in pulses of pressure and silence, a hush that lived beneath the bark. Not dead but dreaming, watching, and waiting.

We should've kept riding.

But the fire betrayed us.

I should have known better. I'd read the old texts, written by moss-fingered scholars who warned never to light a fire beneath an amber canopy. But knowing and remembering are not the same thing.

The sun had barely kissed the horizon, casting the sky in watercolor gold and purples. We meant to rest only for an hour. My fingers were stiff. I tossed a twig into the flames, and something in the smoke caught my eye. A spark leapt upward and touched the mossy carpet.

For one suspended heartbeat, nothing happened.

Then the world lit.

Not in violence, but in a sudden curtain of shimmering orange, like the forest had exhaled flames. These spores. I'd read about them. Ember Veil Spores: flammable as oil, invisible until touched by heat. They shimmered through the air like fireflies, drifting upward and vanishing into dawn.

We stomped it out quickly, the flare only a gasp of light, but the damage had been done. Spores drifted like burning silk, igniting midair and vanishing. The horses panicked. Hooves pounded. One guard nearly fell to the ground. My mare screamed next to me, wild-eyed, and bolted into the brush.

"Wynessa!" Alaric's voice cracked sharply and loudly. He shoved through the smoke toward me.

I lunged for the reins, gripping them tight, murmuring whatever calming words came to mind.

She jerked back hard as I held on too tight.

For a few wild steps, she dragged me through the leaf-littered clearing, the reins burning through my hands as I stumbled after her.

Then she tugged the reins out of my hands, and I hit the ground hard, the breath slammed from my lungs, as the saddle blanket vanished into the trees.

When I rose to my knees, my horse was gone.

So was my pride.

Alaric cursed under his breath. Gideon muttered something about keeping matches away from royalty. Erindor offered his hand.

"We'll find her," he said. But he spoke in a clipped, tight tone. "Next time, leave the fire to us, Princess."

Next time.

His words stung sharper than they should have. I brushed his hand aside and stood on my own.

"I'm fine."

"If you say so," he muttered, clearly unconvinced. His eyes lingered on mine for a moment longer before flicking away.

I turned away before he could see how right he was.

I didn't sit.

It was impossible.

. . .

I walked. Alone.

No one noticed, not right away. The morning's chaos had left the camp in disarray. Gideon was helping Tyren to his feet, muttering something about bruised ribs. Jasira knelt by Kellen, checking the bindings on his leg. Someone had gathered the scattered supplies. Somewhere behind me, Erindor gave orders in a raised voice.

It was easy, really. One step. Then another. Then gone.

A silly thought, certainly, but I was unable to stand the idea of my terrified mare alone in this blazing forest. The mist was thinning, but the sun only made the wrongness more vivid—the silence too sharp, the trees too watchful.

She had bolted because of fear. And part of me understood that all too well.

With every step, guilt gnawed deeper. I should've remembered the spores and the warnings about them. The pages I had studied for hours on end, whilst bent over my desk with ink-stained fingers and just candlelight, were now useless. How did I miss something so basic, so critical?

Under my breath, self-directed curses formed an endless loop. My cheeks burned, not just from the cold, but from a flush of embarrassment. How foolish I was. How reckless.

I pictured their expressions: Erindor's tight-lipped disapproval, Alaric's forced calm masking worry, Jasira's concern morphing into unspoken judgment. Out here was not where I belonged. I never had. And now I had proven it to everyone.

The mist thickened the deeper I went, swallowing the path behind me. The trees loomed taller here, closer together, their trunks dark and slick with dew. It was as if the forest had drawn a breath and forgotten how to let it go.

My boots sank deeper into the moss, muffling every step. A branch cracked nearby, and I spun, heart thudding, but nothing moved. Shadows clung to everything. I imagined claws in the dark, eyes watching from the hollow of every tree.

Still, I didn't turn back.

There was a pull now, subtle but sure. Not panic. Not instinct. Something quieter. A thread wound through the trees, tugging gently at my ribs, not quite commanding, yet pleading to be followed.

So, I walked on.

Beyond where the moss grew thick enough to drink sound, the hush deepened into something reverent. The world slowed. Every breath was loud. Every heartbeat, magnified.

Then it registered with me—a rustle too pained to be wind.

I parted the ferns with cautious fingers and saw it.

A stag.

The stag lay half-curled in a nest of twisted barbed wire and rusted iron teeth, a trap more fitting for war than wilderness. Blood seeped into the moss beneath it, dark and slow, pooling like ink in the fading light. The trap mangled one leg so severely that it was beyond recognition, with bones jutting where fur should've been.

Its sides heaved with shallow, rapid breaths. A visible tremor running through its weak frame.

And yet, even broken, it was beautiful. Its antlers rose like a crown, wide and sharp, catching what little light filtered through the trees.

But it didn't thrash.

Instead, it watched me.

Its eyes, great liquid mirrors, held no fear. Only pain. And patience.

I stepped forward carefully, my boots meeting the earth with a slow, deliberate pressure, sinking into the saturated moss with a soft, sucking sound. The air grew dense, pressing against my skin, thick with an unspoken weight that defied description, yet felt utterly real. The stag didn't move or flinch.

My throat tightened. My fingers trembled at my sides. I was no threat, and it seemed to know that.

A wave of raw emotion, sharp as any physical blow, stole my breath as I fell to my knees. Something ancient hummed through the ground beneath me— older than gods, older than names. Smelling iron and bark, the bitter rot of old blood, mingled with a sharp wildness, like lightning before it struck.

"Shhh…It's all right," I whispered, though my voice cracked. "I'm here."

I was unable to tell if my words existed for the stag or myself.

Beneath my knees, the soaked moss felt warm. The snare bit into my fingers the moment I touched it. I winced but didn't let go. Slowly, I uncoiled the rusted wire, wincing with every metallic snap. My palms *shredded*, mingling my warm blood with the cold, dark stains already coating the stag. It didn't move.

"Almost there," I breathed, tears slipping down my cheeks. "A little longer."

The trap gave a final creak, and I eased it open. The stag let out a groan that reverberated in my chest.

I dug into my pouch, fingers frantic. Balmleaf. Marrowroot. Silk wrap. I crushed and mixed them with water from my flask, grinding the salve against a flat stone with the heel of my palm. Then I pressed the mixture gently into the wound, whispering apologies under my breath.

Through the haze of pain and blood, the stag's gaze held mine, liquid and impossibly mournful, a silent accusation.

And I sensed something observing through it.

Its gaze was too still, too ancient. I experienced no fear, only pressure. Like the forest itself was breathing with me. Like my blood pulsed to its rhythm. I had read once that the gods sent stags to those who had lost their way. Or perhaps it was the stag who chose the lost. I could never recall which, but I believed it now.

The air shimmered faintly around us. The moss near the wound curled slightly as I pressed my hands down firmly, almost like it recognized me.

It didn't see a princess. It didn't see a pawn.

It saw me. Wyn.

I moved slowly, speaking in a whisper even I couldn't understand, as I reached into my satchel. My hands worked on instinct, cleansing the wound as best I could, packing the worst of it with poultice, and wrapping the leg in linen strips soaked in sap and tincture.

The stag didn't fight me; only breathed. Watched. Trusted.

When I finished, I sat collapsed onto my heels, my breath shallow, a hollowness echoing the tightness in my chest. Blood and resin glued my hands together, a gritty, cold mess. The damp moss clinging to my knees, offering no prisoners.

The stag rose.

It moved slowly with deliberate grace and stood despite the wound. Its legs trembled, but it held. It shouldn't have been able to, and yet, there it was. Alive and enduring.

A hard lump formed in my throat, burning with the bitter realization of its suffering. I hated that the world could hurt something so beautiful without hesitation. It deserved to remain untouched in the wild. It deserved more than rusted teeth and silence.

Its gaze stayed on mine.

Then it bowed.

The motion was deliberate, slow. One leg folded beneath it, head dipping in a movement too graceful to be a coincidence, as if in recognition.

My heart thudded once, hard. I didn't breathe, as if I'd forgotten how to for a moment.

Then the stag turned, limped to the edge of the glade, and vanished into the trees.

I remained frozen in place. What did it mean, that bow? Why me? I wasn't brave. No one chose me. I was a girl who stumbled through every expectation placed on her. The Stag hadn't feared me, hadn't fled. It had seen something and honored it, but I didn't know what. And that terrified me more than anything.

A warm breeze brushed my cheek.

Yet, nothing stirred the leaves.

I returned to the camp dazed. Blood and moss streaked and tore my skirts. My hands trembled as I peeled them open, raw with scratches. My knees ached, and my scalp itched where twigs and leaf litter had tangled in my loose hair. Strands clung to my face, damp with sweat and forest air.

I smelled of smoke, loam, and crushed herbs, like something newly unearthed.

But it was as if...

I was weightless.

Inside, I sensed a change. Something had settled.

"Wyn," Jasira said, standing. She thrust a waterskin at me, brow knit with worry. "Where the hell were you?"

"Eat something," Gideon called. "Or I'll feed you myself."

Alaric glanced up from polishing his blade, froze, then tossed it aside and hurried toward me, his expression twisting between relief and exasperation.

"Wyn, are you hurt?" he asked, eyes scanning me from head to toe.

Before I responded, Erindor rose.

"Someone could have killed you," he snapped, stepping forward. "This isn't a garden, Princess. You don't wander off."

I flinched at the heat in his voice.

"I was fine."

"You were gone for an hour," he said through gritted teeth. "We thought someone had taken you." His jaw was tight, a silent tension of anger in his shoulders. It was a controlled storm, simmering beneath the surface, a bitter tang of scolding laced with a surprising thread of worry.

I didn't answer. I didn't have the words.

He stepped closer, and for a moment, the tension held. Then, something in his eyes shifted. The hard lines in his brow softened slightly as he took in the dirt on my skirt, the dried blood, the scratches on my hands. He exhaled quietly and long, as if releasing a breath held captive for far too long. His gaze flicked to mine, expecting another retort. But I didn't speak. I didn't have the energy to.

That's when he saw it, really saw it. I wasn't the disobedient princess or the reckless girl, but a trembling body in borrowed strength that was barely holding it together. His mouth tightened, then released.

"You're not fine," he breathed quietly, like it hurt to admit it. "Sit," he said gently. "Rest. We'll sort it out."

I didn't meet his eyes.

I couldn't

Something in me was too raw. Too bright.

I sat near the fire, it burned low and cautiously now. There were no sparks or warmth beyond its borders. But enough light to keep the dark from swallowing us. Jasira acted at once; she knelt beside me and wrapped a blanket around my shoulders.

"You scared us," she whispered. "Next time you decide to do something foolish, at least take me with you; that way, we can do it together."

A shaky breath left me. I didn't trust my voice not to crack, not yet.

Erindor's gaze stayed steady.

I thought of the stag. Of the blood and the way it bowed in front of me.

I thought of the warmth still humming beneath my skin like golden light.

And I thought—

Even in the stag's wounded state, he still fought to live. Why shouldn't I?

. . .

Far above, almost impossible to see, a pale owl watched from the branches. Its feathers shimmered like mist in moonlight, eyes reflecting not the fire but the girl beside it.

It only observed, still as bark, old as the hush between heartbeats.

He had watched many pass beneath his perch; knights, wanderers, wild things with teeth and flame. But no one like her.

The glade had seen many things, but it had not seen this.

Not a spell. Not a prophecy.

Only a beginning.

The seed of fire the owl had long waited for began, at last, to glow.

Chapter Eight

Erindor

Graymere emerged from the mist as we left Emberwood behind us.

Wyn shifted in front of me, her slight frame pressed against my entire front. Every time her hand brushed my thigh or adjusted her balance, it sent a jolt of heat through my skin, leaving a phantom sizzle where she'd touched. I gripped the reins harder, swallowing hard.

It wasn't supposed to be like this.

Her horse had vanished into the woods after the flare. We searched and whistled, but we had no choice. She had to ride with me.

She was quiet about it. Blushing, yes, her voice a murmur when she asked, "Is it all right?" But no complaints. Just her soft intake of breath when I pulled her up and settled her down before me.

Now she sat within my arms, and every movement of the horse shifted her closer. Her hair brushed my jaw, and her back pressed against my chest.

She fitted perfectly.

And that was the problem.

I told myself it was nothing, that it had been a long time since I'd ridden with anyone like this. Since I'd touched anyone with any softness to them. That the heat I experienced wasn't from her, but from the proximity. Just the cold of the Emberwood wearing off.

But I knew better.

I wasn't supposed to notice the way her shoulders tensed when she was nervous, or how her breath hitched slightly whenever the horse stumbled.

And yet.

There she was, all stubborn and warm.

Too close in every way that mattered.

Graymere crouched at the edge of the Emberwood, a town half-swallowed by its own decay. Worn stone and crooked roofs leaned into one another like drunkards clinging to old stories. The muddy road narrowed as we entered, flanked by shuttered houses with sagging porches and broken steps.

Lanterns burned low behind cloudy windows, their glow casting long shadows through the mist. Doors opened only an inch, long enough for someone to fetch water or chase a chicken, before slamming back into place with a sharp thud.

It was nearing midday, but the damp and haze made it feel like twilight.

At the town's center, a cobbled square pulsed with movement. Crates of root vegetables and smoked fish crowded the market, and hawkers shouted half-hearted deals under drooping canvas tarps. The clatter of carts and clang of pans echoed in the stillness of surrounding streets, as though the town permitted joy only in one small corner.

Everywhere else looked starved of warmth, color, and hope.

I'd been here once before, years ago. It hadn't been this cold. Or maybe I just hadn't felt it then.

"Strange place," Jasira said lightly as we passed a crumbling shrine covered in moss. "Does anyone else think a disappointed librarian is watching us?"

Wyn laughed softly.

The sound curled against my ribs like warmth that didn't belong.

Alaric, ever the performer, raised his arms with a flourish. "Graymere!" he declared. "Land of ghosts, goblets, and goats. Bran, let's find something cursed to sniff."

The warhound barked once and padded ahead, tail high.

We followed, turning down a narrower street near the square, where an old inn leaned at a tired angle beneath a creaking sign that read *The Hollow Hearth*.

I dismounted first, boots splashing into the mud. Then I moved to help Wyn down, drawing out the moment longer than I needed to. Her hand found mine. She didn't meet my eyes, but she lingered for a second too long.

We left the horses at the inn's stables. Alaric took Bran and wandered off toward the market's far end. A cacophony of good-natured negotiation began to swell, a clear indication that the day's commerce was well underway. Lark took Kellen inside the inn for proper warmth and to find him a place to settle before we continued our trip at dawn the next day. That left Wyn and me alone. Together.

We wandered from stall to stall, her steps hesitant but growing bolder with each stride. Wyn pressed closer to me as we entered the fray. I could feel the tension in her as she hooked her arm around mine, fingers tight against my sleeve.

"Too many people," she breathed, her voice barely audible above the insistent murmur of the crowd. "Too many eyes."

I leaned slightly so she could distinguish my voice over the noise. "Then look at me."

Her gaze, previously diffused by the swirling crowd, suddenly snapped into focus, locking with mine with an almost palpable force.

"Good, now breathe."

She obliged willingly. For a breathless moment, the crowd faded. The noise, the smoke, the strange tension hanging in the air—now gone. All that remained were her wide, storm-soft eyes fixed on mine and the fragile trust in them.

Her hand didn't leave my arm after that.

A current of nervous energy, like a faint electric hum, flowed from her fingertips, but her eyes lit with curiosity. She asked thoughtful questions about herbs, cloth dyes, and the meanings behind the little bone charms sold in bundles. I watched in awe as each answer steadied her.

Nearby, Alaric had gathered a cluster of village children and was strumming his lute with theatrical flair, weaving a song about a heroic hound and a goose that bit back. The children clapped along, shrieking with laughter whenever Bran barked in rhythm.

Close to him, Jasira and Gideon stood at a produce stall, mid-argument with a vendor over the price of dried pears. Gideon insisted on a lower price and, after a few increasingly theatrical gestures, accepted a trade that left him holding a single, comically large root vegetable. Jasira laughed herself hoarse, bent double with mirth as he held it aloft like a trophy.

The market briefly seemed safe. Almost normal.

A vendor with honeyed eyes waved us over, offering candied nuts and pastries dusted with cinnamon sugar, and Wyn's face brightened.

"I'm getting you one," she said, already fishing coins from her pouch. "For saving me from a crowd-induced spiral back there. And because you look like you haven't smiled in years."

"That's unnecessary—"

She pressed a honey-glazed cake into my hand before I could finish. Its warmth immediately radiating through my palm. The air around me seemed to thicken with the sweet, spicy promise of cloves and the delicate perfume of orange blossoms. I took one bite. Then another. And another.

Wyn giggled. Quiet at first, then louder as I devoured the rest in three quick mouthfuls.

"You have a sweet tooth," she teased.

"I do not," I muttered, licking honey from my thumb, savoring the taste.

"Uh-huh." She grinned, already buying more.

She handed me another and walked beside me for a beat in companionable silence. Her fingers brushed mine as she pressed another honeyed cake into my hand.

Then she was there.

Beside me with the quiet woven of a comfortable closeness that needed no words.

"Was that your first proper meal today?" she asked.

"Depends on what you count as 'real.'"

"You count battlefield rations as cuisine, don't you?" she said, a prim line to her lips that barely masked the glint of mischief in her eyes.

I didn't answer.

"You've done this before," she added. "Escorting people. Was that your job?"

"For a while."

"What about before that?"

I looked straight ahead. "Different work."

She didn't push. Merley nodded, as if that answer still told her something.

We drifted onward. Near the edge of the square, a low wall curved behind a cluster of wooden booths. Children had scrawled it with chalk pictures of flowers, animals, and looping shapes. Wyn reached out to touch a crude sketch of an herb sprig. Then we both saw it.

One figure stood apart. Drawn in black.

Its limbs were too long. A sword slashed across its back. And where the face should've been, two white circles stared out like empty moons.

In the depths of those eyes, there was no spark, no reflection. Just empty ash.

I stopped, the air around me suddenly felt starved of oxygen, thin and biting.

Wyn followed my gaze and tilted her head. "Erindor?"

I gave a quick submissive shrug. "A child's drawing."

A cold dread had already begun its insidious crawl, seizing my heart and numbing my entire body.

She didn't press. I didn't elaborate. She might have already known I wouldn't tell her, even if she had questioned me.

She lingered by the wall a moment longer, back at the black figure.

"I don't require that information," she whispered, lost in thought. "But I'll listen if you ever decide to tell."

Somehow, that struck harder than any demand would have.

I motioned for us to move on.

At a weapons cart near the back of the square, Wyn lingered over a rack of polished daggers. She frowned thoughtfully, fingers grazing the hilt.

"I should carry something," she said. "Just in case."

The merchant handed her a slim, silver-hilted blade. It was narrow and light enough to conceal beneath her cloak. She assessed the grip, then tucked it into her belt with quiet resolve.

Then, a moment later, a sharp, sudden yelp tore through the quiet, making us both jump.

The blade had shifted, jabbing her in the thigh.

"Blast—"

She tried to fix it, flustered, tugging at the strap with one hand.

I couldn't watch any longer. "Here," I said, stepping in. I knelt and adjusted the belt, tightening the leather until it sat flush.

"Still dangerous," I murmured, "though not to your enemies."

A flush of pink rose to her ears, and she smacked my arm. But left the blade as it was.

We continued to walk. Wyn's fingers curled back around my arm, saying nothing.

And neither did I.

We returned to the inn before sunset. The place was old and drafty; the floorboards creaking beneath every step like old bones groaning in their sockets. They had hung dried lavender, mint, and yarrow as herbs above the lintels, seemingly to ward off mildew or misfortune. The hearth crackled low, throwing flickers of gold against the scarred walls. Travelers hunched over chipped bowls of stew, muttering in low voices, eyes flicking toward the windows with a kind of habitual dread.

Near the fire, Kellen was curled beneath a woolen blanket, a faint sheen of sweat still clinging to his brow. Jasira sat beside him, brushing damp hair from his forehead. She had coaxed a few spoonfuls of broth into him, though he mainly remained quiet. The boy had spoken little since the attack. I wasn't sure if it was the pain in his leg or the terror at losing his family in the way he did. His kin slaughtered beyond the trees, their wagon ransacked and left to the crows. Sometimes grief was louder than fear.

A bard sang near the hearth, voice low and lilting.

"Ash for eyes, a blade for breath—He walks where whispers feed on death. Beware the man with a bloodless grin, for where he treads, the end begins..."

My stomach sank. I didn't need to ask who the song was about.

Wyn glanced at me, her expression pale. Wary. "That song…"

"Rumors," I said quickly, in a bid to comfort her, before looking away.

…

Night fell like wet wool.

I took a walk to clear my head. The fog curled through the streets like smoke. Lanterns glowed faintly behind shuttered windows.

Then I saw him across the square.

A man in a dark cloak. A bone-hilted blade strapped casually over one shoulder like it belonged there, like it had always been there. His hood was low, but I would have recognized him anywhere.

Riven.

He didn't move. Didn't blink. He stood there in the mist, as if he'd been waiting for my arrival.

Our eyes met. And though he stood yards away, I sensed it. The familiarity, the challenge, the memory of ash and ruin.

The corner of his mouth twitched. Not a grin, but the promise of one.

And then—

He was gone.

Like smoke, or memory, a whisper of something that had never truly existed outside of my mind.

But he did.

And he wasn't finished with me yet.

Chapter Nine

Wynessa

We rode out of Greymere on the same horse, my back pressed lightly against Erindor's chest, the rhythmic sway of the mare keeping us in an uneasy but constant closeness. His arms bracketed me on either side as he held the reins, silent and steady. Every time our knees bumped, or his breath brushed my hair, the warmth didn't just settle. It spread, a slow burn igniting something nameless and new inside me. The storm washed the sky above; the fog swallowed the village's crooked rooftops behind us. Silence pressed close as the forest swallowed us once more. Not a peaceful hush, but something that waited, watched.

The boy we rescued in the Emberwood days before, Kellen, was not with us. We had left him, safe and warm, in the innkeeper's care in Greymere, promising to return when we had a workable opportunity. I thought of his quiet eyes and wondered if he was dreaming of forests now, or if he, too, still saw the shadows behind the trees.

I adjusted myself in the saddle and let my gaze drift to the underbrush. Brambles twisted beneath the trees like tangled fingers, and among them grew a line of pale-stemmed flowers, their silvery-blue thistles glinting faintly with dew.

"Lunethistle," I murmured, more to myself than anyone else. "Used to make sleeping draughts."

Erindor's voice came from behind, low and wry. "You're also acquainted with poisons?"

A tingling sensation spread across my cheek. "Only the sleepy kind."

A pause. Then: "Good. I'd hate to find out you've been plotting my demise with flower petals."

I smiled despite myself. "Well…not lately."

I didn't turn around, but I heard the breath he released, almost a laugh if he ever allowed himself one. The warmth lingered like the last glow of embers across my neck.

"This one's fireleaf," I explained gently, pointing beside us. "It only grows in scorched places. Some plants flower only post-fire."

Erindor hummed in acknowledgment. Not stopping the tangent.

Then, in an instant, the woods shifted. The trees grew tighter, the air thinner. I couldn't say when the change occurred, only that I felt it instantly. We were not alone.

Emerging into a clearing, a pale glade veined with moss and brittle leaves appeared, the sunlight filtering in through the branches above, thin and hollow.

And then came the whistle of arrows.

Erindor's shout ripped through the stillness. "Down!"

Chaos erupted.

I barely had time to register the hiss of air before the first arrow buried itself in the tree beside me. Horses screamed, rearing in panic. Hooves tore through the brittle leaves. The soldiers drew blades, and steel rang. I hit the ground hard; the impact knocking the breath from my lungs. Dirt and bark gouged my palms as I stumbled. The second arrow thudded into the ground, missing my shoulder by moments. Then a third arrow flew past, this time close enough that I felt the wind of it brush my cheek.

From the treeline, five figures stormed into view. Their clothes were a patchwork of hide and stolen cloth, their faces smeared with soot and painted with crude war symbols. One wore a necklace of teeth. Another had scars carved into his arms like tally marks. They bore mismatched swords, axes, and curved daggers. Marauders. Mercenaries. Killers.

One of them spotted me. He was tall, lean, his eyes hollow with desperation. He sprinted forward, dagger raised, a snarl ripping from his throat.

A leaden weight seemed to root me to the spot. My limbs were like waterlogged stone, impossibly heavy, refusing to obey.

And just as the man reached me, Erindor was suddenly there. Slamming into him with terrifying speed.

Their blades met in a clash of sparks. Erindor spun, fluid and precise, catching the man's wrist and driving his sword deep into the space beneath his ribs. The man gasped once, then crumpled.

Erindor stood over him, breath tearing from his lungs in ragged gasps. "You don't touch her," he growled, the words forced past clenched teeth, a primal warning.

Another enemy tried to circle him. Erindor pivoted without hesitation, parrying high and driving his boot into the attacker's chest. The man flew back into the underbrush with a choked wheeze.

He didn't glance back at me.

He didn't have to.

Alaric met another attacker head-on, his blade gleaming with clean precision. Bran, wild with fury, lunged for the man attempting to flank Gideon and sank his teeth into the raider's thigh.

Gideon laughed mid-strike, his shield ringing as he blocked a blow.

Corren fought beside him with the grim calm of a veteran, his sword flashing in clean, efficient arcs as he cut down an attacker aiming for our flank. Tyren moved like a ghost through the trees, intercepting a raider who had broken off toward Alaric and cutting him down with a single, silent stroke. Lark stumbled early, his blade knocked from his hand, but he rolled free and scrambled for a spare dagger, as Jasira threw one to him from across the field with deadly aim.

She landed beside me with a dagger already in hand and a curse on her lips. "Stay down, Wyn!"

But past the fray, one mercenary stumbled, gravely wounded. Blood darkened his tunic, seeping through his fingers. He crawled away from the fight, gasping, dragging himself through the leaves like a wounded animal seeking refuge, before finally hauling himself against a tree trunk, spent. He wouldn't live without help.

My heart pounded. My satchel shifted against my hip.

I didn't think. I moved.

Jasira cursed again, reaching for me, but I slipped through the fray, hands low, breath quick.

The man groaned as I knelt beside him, eyes fluttering open, blood coating his palms. He reached for a dagger, but it slipped from his fingers and landed near my knee.

I picked it up by the hilt—slick, stained, and still warm—and grimaced. The weight of it felt wrong and mean in my hand.

With a shudder, I flung it into the trees. It vanished into the underbrush with a satisfying thud.

"Absolutely not," I muttered. "You don't get that back."

Pressing my hand to the wound, I hissed. "Stay still."

His skin was cold beneath my touch, but I worked fast, my fingers trembling yet certain.

This kind of bleeding, this rhythm of life slipping away, was familiar to me. I smeared lunethistle paste along the wound to dull the pain, then packed it with moss and balsamroot, whispering half-formed prayers to any god who might still be listening.

He spat near my foot, but I didn't flinch.

"You heal your enemies now?" he rasped, his voice rough and bitter. "What kind of fool are you?"

"The kind that doesn't want another body in the dirt," I whispered, pressing his hand over the dressing. "You're still a person, and that matters to me."

His breath shuddered. But he didn't fight anymore.

And then, just like that, the battle was over.

The last two mercenaries had fled. Three lay dead among the brambles. The fifth, the one I had saved, remained against the tree, pale and sweaty, but alive.

They argued about what to do with him.

Alaric, arms crossed and eyes sharp, wanted to strip him of weapons and dignity, leave him bleeding in the dirt with a warning in his ear.

Tyren, still raw from the fight, offered to end it quickly. "He'd do the same to any of us," he said flatly.

But I stepped between them.

"He won't," I said, more confidently than I really felt. "Not today."

Alaric raised an eyebrow. "You think a little mercy will change a man like that?"

"No," I replied. "But killing him won't change *us* either."

They hesitated. The silence stretched.

"If he can walk, he walks away," I said, voice steady. "We don't stoop to blood for blood. Not today."

In the end, Corren left him with a waterskin and some rations. I watched as he crawled to the edge of the clearing, each strained movement a vivid portrait of his suffering. He didn't thank us. And he didn't look back.

I stood watching, breath shallow, hands sticky with blood and salve once again.

Then Erindor's shadow fell over me.

"What the hell were you thinking?"

His voice was low, furious, not like the heat of battle, but colder, sharper, more personal. His eyes blazed down at me, and I turned slowly to face him.

"He was dying," I insisted, lifting my chin. An act of defiance despite the tremor that rattled my voice. "He's human."

"So are you." He stepped closer, tension drawn tight across his shoulders like a bowstring. His voice was low, roughened by restraint. "You could have died, Princess. And then—" He stopped.

There was more in his eyes than anger, frustration, and fear. Something unspoken. And then he said it.

"This isn't some fairy tale. You show mercy like that again, and you're going to get yourself killed and the kingdom with you."

For a breath, I couldn't speak. A gasp stole the breath, voice simply vanishing, trapped behind a sudden, solid wall of disbelief.

The words hit harder than the battle.

We stood there with the trees pressing in. I saw the regret in his eyes the instant after he said it and the way his shoulders tensed, how his mouth opened slightly, then shut.

But the damage had already been done.

Before I found my voice again, Alaric stepped between us. His posture was firm and protective.

"That's enough," he said to Erindor, his voice cool and even. "We've all had enough death for one morning."

Erindor's eyes flicked to him, unreadable, then back to me. Whatever storm had risen in him was now buried deep.

He turned without another word.

I watched as he trudged away, each step heavy, his figure growing smaller with every purposeful step.

. . .

We rode in silence for hours, the forest pressing close on either side of the narrow trail. No one spoke of the fight. No one spoke at all, really. The mist returned as the sun sank, curling low around the hooves of the horses, brushing the hems of our cloaks like it was meant to follow us all the way to sleep.

By the time we found a clearing large enough to make camp, dusk had bled into near dark. The light was dim, silver, and strange, like the forest had forgotten how to be warm.

We made camp under the limbs of an old cedar tree. The mist still clung to the edges of the clearing, curling over the forest floor like smoke. The air was thick with everything unsaid.

Gideon built the fire with more force than finesse, stabbing kindling into the pile like the flames had offended him. Alaric sat with his back against a stump, one leg stretched out, absently running a whetstone over his sword while Bran dozed at his feet. Corren checked the perimeter twice before finally resting.

Lark busied himself mending a torn satchel with trembling fingers, and Tyren watched the dark with his usual, unsettling calm.

Jasira stirred the stewpot with slow, methodical motions, humming a soft tune I didn't recognize, her eyes occasionally flicking to me as if she wanted to speak, but never quite did.

Erindor sat apart.

I could feel his gaze on me.

I sipped my tea, pretending not to notice, cheeks still warm with the ghost of that argument.

His words echoed in my mind, a relentless clamor that drowned out all other senses. They circled, an endless, tormenting loop: *Do you think any of this will mean anything if you're dead?*

Perhaps he was correct. It was possibly reckless rushing in like that. But how could I have left someone to die when I had the means to help?

Still, his words struck something deeper than frustration. Not because they were cruel, but because they weren't. He hadn't been only angry.

He had been telling the truth.

That shook me more than his anger.

My fingers traced the rim of my mug; the tea within lay inert and cold, a mirror to the chill that had settled in my bones. No matter how much I'd scrubbed my hands earlier, the scent of iron-rich blood and the sweetness of the salve still clung to my skin, stubborn as a stain. I was aware of the wounded man's pulse beneath my hands. The flash of fear in his eyes, the resignation. No one else would have helped him.

But I had.

What did that make me? Brave? Or foolish?

I didn't know.

Jasira leaned in, voice low and full of amusement. "He's still watching you," she whispered. "Either he's planning your execution, or he's completely bewitched."

I choked on my tea, coughing hard as I turned a shade that would've made an apple proud.

Gideon looked up from his bowl. "Did I miss something? Should I be blushing, too?"

Jasira grinned but said nothing.

I dared a glance at Erindor.

His eyes, no longer shadowed by rage, instead held a quiet, steady flame that ignited a warmth deep within. A warmth that drew me in closer.

. . .

That night, the dream opened in silence.

I stood barefoot in a field of wildflowers beneath a sky without stars. All around me, the earth glowed faintly, as if lit from within.

A pale-gold fire flickered at the center of it all, breathing slowly and steadily like a heartbeat. There was no smoke. No heat. Only light. It swayed with the rhythm of the wildflowers, casting long shadows over stone and root.

I walked toward it. Every pace became a deliberate, leaden effort, the weight of sudden recognition pressing down with each footfall. As if my body remembered this place, even if my mind did not.

The fire leaned toward me.

I knelt, uncertain. My hand trembled as I reached out.

When my fingers touched the flame, it wrapped around them like silk. It didn't burn; it welcomed. It pulsed against my skin with purpose, as if it recognized me.

A whisper stirred the air, soft as breath.

"Speak it. And be worthy."

But I was uncertain of what response to give. My throat closed. I wanted to name something, anything, but the truth lodged behind my ribs.

The wind rose, curling through my hair, through the petals at my feet. The fire flowed into my hands, tracing the lines of my palms, as if reading a story I hadn't yet written.

And at that moment, I felt—

Seen. Entirely.

Not for who I pretended to be. Not for the girl fumbling through diplomacy or the healer trying not to shake when holding a blade.

But for something buried deeper.

It felt as if the very fabric of the world drew tight, as though it had paused, waiting for me to name what I feared most: that I wanted to matter. To burn bright without breaking.

Until suddenly, I woke with a gasp.

The fire had burned low and the forest was still.

I pressed a trembling hand to my chest. The warmth of my dream lingered beneath my skin.

Like something ancient had stirred.

And it was waiting.

I sat near the edge of the trees, knees drawn to my chest, cloak tugged tight. The others were sleeping, or pretending to be. Even Jasira had left me alone tonight.

I deserved it.

I opened my satchel and pulled out the little leather-bound journal. Although the charcoal nub wore nearly flat, it would do.

I made a mistake.

I thought I was doing the right thing. The bandit was bleeding out. He was human; scared, dying, alone. I saw a person, not an enemy. So, I moved toward him. I wanted to help. Like I always do.

But I forgot something important.

I'm not just a healer anymore.

I'm a target. A symbol. A liability, if I forget the world we're walking through.

Erindor yelled at me. He's never yelled like that before. His voice was sharp, wounded. I think I scared him because I didn't think it through. I think…he expected me to be wiser.

Or, I expected that of myself.

He didn't speak to me again after that. He kept pacing the perimeter, jaw tight, cloak snapping behind him like it was angry too.

I hated that I hadn't listened.

I don't want him to think I'm reckless.

But I'm unsure how to end my desire to help, even if it proves deadly.

-W

I shut the book and pressed it against my chest, eyes stinging. Somewhere behind me, I heard the faint crunch of boots on frostbitten grass—soft and deliberate. Erindor, circling the camp again.

I didn't look at him or move either.

Tomorrow, I'd try again.

Chapter Ten

Erindor

The rain began as a hush against the leaves. It was soft, steady, almost gentle as we slipped into the forest.

The Wildervale did not welcome us.

The others sensed it too. Alaric pulled his cloak tighter and glanced over his shoulder more than once, his usual banter silenced by the weight of the air. Jasira muttered something under her breath about the silence being too loud, her hand drifting toward the dagger at her hip. Gideon, trying to lighten the mood, cracked a joke about ghost squirrels planning an ambush, but no one laughed. Not even he, really. The three additional guards, Corren, Lark, and Tyren, rode in uneasy silence. Corren made a quiet blessing motion with two fingers over his chest, and Lark kept fiddling with his reins like they might suddenly snap free. Tyren muttered a silent prayer in a tongue I didn't recognize.

We all felt it.

Like the Wildervale had opened its mouth and swallowed the sound whole.

The towering, enigmatic forest embraced the narrow trail, its air a dense, damp veil rich with the scent of moss and wet bark, underpinned by a subtle, almost melancholic floral hint, like crushed violets slowly fading into the earth. The silence wasn't true silence, but a layered hush filled with distant drips of rain through branches and the soft rustle of unseen creatures moving in the underbrush. Every hoofbeat felt louder here, swallowed not by space but by something older, something listening. The chill of Wildervale was not only in the air, but in the way the light moved, reluctant and fragmented, as if it were trespassing. Its trees were impossibly old; their trunks split with time and slick with moss that shimmered faintly in the mist. Vines hung like braided ropes from crooked branches, some trailing into the underbrush as if they had minds of their own. The light barely touched the forest floor; what sunlight broke through the canopy came in filtered shards, painting the path in watery gold and green. Here and there, crumbled stones jutted from the earth, the remains of something ancient, half-swallowed by vine and root.

Wyn sat in front of me again in the saddle, her cloak damp and clinging to her shoulders, her posture quiet. Her mare still hadn't turned up, and no one argued when I helped her onto my horse again that morning. Least of all, me.

She didn't speak. Neither did I.

And yet, I was too aware of her. Too aware of every breath she took.

I told myself it was duty. Just vigilance. She was a princess, and I was her shield. Nothing more.

She wasn't a woman to whom I was drawn to. Too trusting. Too easily hurt.

But no court lady I'd guarded had ever sketched flowers with such a quiet purpose. No noblewoman I'd trained beside had ever looked at the world like it could be both beautiful and broken.

She was different. Not because she was royalty.

She looked at the moss-covered stones and tried to understand their language.

And that terrified me more than any blade ever could.

Every shift of her weight.

Every time her back pressed a little more into my chest with the rhythm of the ride, I had to fight the instinct to close my arms around her. To keep her safe. To have a sense of stability in an unstable world.

She had said little all morning. Her steps had been careful when we broke camp; her eyes distant. I told myself it was exhaustion, but I knew better.

She was still thinking about the day before.

So was I.

I cleared my throat. "Wynessa."

She startled slightly. Her head turned, her eyes meeting mine—wide, wary, and searching.

"I...about yesterday," I said. The words came harder than I expected. "I didn't mean what I said. Not all of it."

Her gaze held mine for a breathless eternity, plumbing the depths of my fear. Until finally, a slow, knowing nod followed. "I know. You were worried," her voice soft with empathy.

"I still am."

A breath escaped her. Her voice was softer this time. "Me too."

I hesitated. She sounded more than tired...Hollowed out perhaps.

And I didn't understand why.

I shifted in the saddle behind her. "You don't have to be," I offered awkwardly. "We're through the worst of it. No more raiders. No more storms. This forest might be cursed, but even curses eventually run out of energy."

She gave a faint smile but didn't turn around. "That's not why I'm worried."

I didn't press her. We left it to rest there and rode in a comfortable quietness together.

By the time the temple revealed itself through the trees, half-swallowed by moss and time, the rain had deepened, soaking through my cloak and dripping steadily from the brim of my hood. Alaric rode ahead, sword drawn, scanning the perimeter like he expected the stones themselves to rise and challenge us. He didn't speak. None of us did.

The temple appeared ancient. Not dangerous. Old in a way that demanded silence. I'd heard rumors about places like this. Temples left behind by the godmarked, where the veil between worlds was thin and spirits wandered, still waiting for prayers that never came. I'd never put much stock in stories. But standing before the vine-choked stone, I suddenly didn't feel like a soldier, but an intruder instead.

There were markings carved into the stone that didn't match any language I knew. Twisting symbols and spiral suns that made the back of my neck prickle. One statue stood intact near the entrance, a tall, hooded figure with antlers rising like blackened branches. His eyes gouged out.

Corren took one look at it and muttered a curse. He refused to sleep with his back to the altar and set up his bedroll facing the entrance, blade within arm's reach.

I found no fault with him.

We cleared a dry patch under one of the larger arches and set up to rest. As we unpacked, Gideon muttered something about stopping for 'an hour or two' to dry out and shake the rain from our bones. Alaric agreed, saying we wouldn't make it far, soaked to the skin and with visibility like a drawn curtain. Bran flopped at Alaric's feet with a groan, already half-asleep. Jasira shook out her cloak and began unpacking rations.

Gideon climbed atop a cracked statue and declared himself "high priest of the conveniently dry pedestal," which earned him a sharp look from Jasira and a muttered, "You're going to fall and chip your other shoulder."

Despite the tension, a fragile chuckle broke through, a little strained, yet undeniably welcome, softening the sharp edges of the moment.

I didn't join in.

I kept my eyes on Wyn.

She sat alone on a low stone near the fire, her legs tucked beneath her, sketchbook open. Her fingers moved with the practiced ease of someone who had done this a thousand times. She was tracing the carvings on the walls—the old spirals, rivers, beasts made of wind and flames. Her brows furrowed in concentration. A smudge of charcoal streaked her face.

I didn't think. I crossed the space between us.

"Hold still," I said.

Her head snapped up, eyes widening in a sudden jolt of surprise.

I crouched beside her and brushed the smudge gently from her cheek with my thumb. The fire painted her skin with a rosy, warm hue. She stilled under my touch.

"Th-thank you," she murmured.

Her voice was barely there.

I sat down beside her, forcing my attention away from the ache in my chest. Her head lowered again, and she returned to her drawing. For a moment, we sat in silence, warm and still. I didn't know what to say. So, I said nothing at all.

I looked up and caught Alaric by the fire, watching me with a furrow between his brows that didn't ease. He wasn't subtle. He never was. But the way his gaze lingered when I brushed the mark from Wyn's cheek made my spine stiffen.

Jasira didn't miss it either. As I stepped back from Wyn and sat beside her, Jasira's eyes caught mine across the fire. Her silence was punctuated only by the slow, deliberate arch of one eyebrow, a gesture that spoke volumes and seemed to peel back my own unspoken thoughts. Then she looked at Wyn with something like concern, or curiosity, or maybe a warning. I couldn't be sure. Nonetheless, it made my chest tighten.

Then Wyn passed the page to me.

Before I could speak, she gestured to the carvings on the wall.

"That symbol there," she whispered, pointing, "is a sun spiral." It's old—pre-God wars, probably. I think it means rebirth, or maybe convergence. This one with the teeth might be a warning symbol. Some texts suggest people used them in marking boundaries between sacred and forbidden spaces.

I blinked. "How do you know all this?"

She flushed. "I spent a lot of time in the castle library. Reading. Mostly when I didn't want to be seen. Books don't care if you're too quiet or too much of something else."

I didn't know what to say. So, I looked back down at the page.

I stared at it longer than I should have. Her lines were clean, careful. The carvings had come to life under her hand.

"This is incredible. You're not only clever," I said, not looking at her. "You notice things others don't."

She didn't answer immediately. Her fingers worried at the stitching of her dress like she needed somewhere to put the nervous energy.

"I just pay attention," she said at last.

"That's rarer than you think, Princess."

The corners of her lips softened into a slow, gentle curve that reached her eyes, crinkling them at the edges. It wasn't the polite smile she wore in court, or the brave one she showed her guards. It was unguarded. Fragile. And for the first time, I wanted to be the reason she smiled again.

I held out her journal for her to take.

She extended her hand, and our fingers touched. Just barely. A brush of skin, warm and fleeting, but enough to make my pulse stumble. She hesitated a heartbeat too long before taking it, as if the space between us wasn't so easily bridged.

"Thank you," she murmured, her eyes not quite meeting mine. But I saw the faint flush along her throat, the quickening of her breath.

I could've stayed there longer. Watching her. Letting the firelight paint her shoulders in gold and shadow, tracing every line of her face until I could memorize it. Letting myself imagine what it would be like if duty didn't bind my hands.

The ache in my chest pulled tighter, dangerous.

"You should rest," I said finally, though my voice was lower, rougher than I intended.

She glanced sideways. "I'm afraid I'll miss something."

"You won't," I said. "Not while I'm breathing."

She didn't answer, but she stayed beside me.

For a while, neither of us moved. The fire snapped softly. The temple walls whispered things in languages long lost.

Then she smiled at me.

Quiet. Real. Like something rare and unsought.

She stood, brushing her hands over her skirts, and walked back to the others to sit down and eat—tucking herself into the circle of warmth and conversation like she'd never left.

But I stayed where I was.

I watched her laugh at something Gideon said, her head tilted just slightly, her hair catching the firelight. I watched the way her shoulders finally loosened, like a weight had slipped from them without her noticing.

She walked as if the world was something to be healed.

And I followed her as if it might save me.

I remained where she drew, sharpening my blade out of habit more than need. The scrape of stone against metal steadied my breathing, gave my hands something to do while my thoughts refused to still.

A sound stirred in the trees.

Soft. Too soft for the wind.

I paused mid-motion.

Possibly an owl. Or not. I couldn't be sure. The Wildervale held more than animals in its boughs.

I looked toward where the trees thickened into something impenetrable and was aware of something watching.

The blade in my hand stilled.

And though the fire behind me crackled warmly, I couldn't shake the chill pressing at my spine.

Chapter Eleven

Erindor

We had left the forest floor behind just before dawn, climbing until the trees thinned and the cliffs loomed overhead like ancient teeth. The trail narrowed to a ribbon of stone with mud-slick switchbacks and knife-thin ledges that would have sent even the surest mount over the edge.

It wasn't merely a matter of caution. It was survival.

We couldn't bring the horses. Not up there.

"We tie them and come back," Tyren said, glancing toward the hollow below where grass still grew and a thin stream whispered through the rock.

"You tie them," Gideon mumbled, "it's like offering them up on a silver platter. Predators will smell them by nightfall."

"So we just let them go?" Tyren frowned. "And hope they find their way back?"

Alaric stood between them, hands on his hips. "Horses know the land better than we do. They'll follow the stream. With luck, circle back to Graymere or farther."

There was no correct answer. But we didn't have the time—or the trail—for debate.

One by one, we removed their tack and packs, smoothing their necks, whispering old words into twitching ears.

Alaric tied blessing knots into each mane, not bridle this time—loose and worn, but deliberate. Elyrien superstition. A ward against wolves and worse.

I pressed my forehead against the horse's flank for a moment. She huffed warm breath into my shoulder and turned, disappearing into the trees with the rest.

We watched them go, hooves muffled in moss and pine needles.

Then we turned to the cliffs.

If the trail held.

If *we* did.

There had been talk of circling the ridge entirely, following the river low and looping around the far side of the vale. But time wasn't a luxury we had. The southern pass had succumbed to the rain's fury, leaving the northern route as their only hope of crossing the treacherous Wildervale Mountains before the inevitable deluge transformed everything into an impassable swamp. It was Alaric who'd first spotted the old stair-cut ascent leading upward, a route chiseled into the side of the cliffs, half-lost to time and lichen.

With every upward step, the world opened to a terrifying duality: one side plunged into an abyss of mist and nothingness, while the other clawed skyward in a defiant wall of jagged rock and rain-slick shale. We moved into a single file. Steadying my boots with each movement. Up ahead, Alaric's armor clanked faintly in the distance.

Gideon walked ahead, humming something tuneless to break the silence. Jasira followed close behind him, one hand gripping the back of his belt for balance, her other hand braced lightly against the cliff whenever possible. It wasn't fear, just practicality. The ledge didn't allow for pride.

She was quiet and focused. Every step counted.

Wyn followed behind me, her breath shallow and her eyes distant. She had spoken little since we had left the forest floor. She was paler than usual, though she tried to hide it. I turned back to watch the way her fingers trembled as she adjusted her cloak.

"You're cold," I breathed.

She shook her head. "I'm not sure it's only the cold."

We stopped to catch our breath beneath a rocky outcropping. The rain had started again, fine and silver-like threads unraveling from the sky. Wyn pressed her back against the unyielding stone, forcing herself to slow the frantic pace of her breathing. A whisper of fear could be seen in her eyes as they drifted to the twisted pine silhouettes half-eaten by fog.

"Something's wrong with this place," she whispered. "Even the animals won't look at us."

"It's Wildervale," I said. "Wrong is its natural state."

She hesitated, then looked up at me. "Do you know what it used to be?"

I blinked. "Only stories."

She leaned her head back against the stone and let the rain speckle her cheeks. "I found a book once. Hidden in the castle library. Dusty and half-eaten by moths. It said that this valley was once sacred. Before the wars, before the gods turned on each other."

My brow creased in thought. "Sacred how?"

"All the gods lived here. Or so the myths said. Each one had a temple: fire, wind, earth, water, light, and dark. Their magic flowed together, balanced, and whole. Wildervale was once different from its twisted state. People revered it. The heart of their realm."

She peered back into the swirling mist, her eyes clouded with unspoken worries. "Vireya, the goddess of flame, believed she was above the others. Brighter. Purer. She began the war. And when it ended…the rest of them left. Or died. And Wildervale rotted in their absence."

I knelt beside her, listening more carefully now.

She looked down at her hands. "The trees warped. The winds grew strange. People stopped returning from pilgrimages. And now all that's left are ruins and curses."

I glanced at the curling mist, its slow crawl over the trees. "And we're the lucky fools walking through it."

She gave me a weak smile. "You're not afraid?"

I hesitated, then said, "Fear's not the enemy. It's what you do with it."

A faint color flushed her cheeks. Before she could reply, Alaric signaled our departure.

We continued the climb in silence. The trail narrowed further as we ascended, only a ribbon of stone cutting across the ridge. Mist clung to our boots, and the wind rose. It was soft at first, then sharp enough to bite through our cloaks. The drop beside us grew more treacherous with every step, a chasm of fog and crag where even echoes dared not linger.

Jasira pulled her hood tighter and muttered something about cursed air. Gideon tried to break the tension with a joke about cliffside taverns. Alaric glanced behind us more often than ahead, hand near his sword hilt. The guards exchanged wary looks, their fingers brushing the charms they wore beneath their collars.

Wyn said nothing more, but I could feel the unease rolling off her like static. Whatever weight she carried from the forest, it hadn't eased here.

And neither had mine.

We rounded a jagged bend where the wind howled louder, funneling between the stone like a living thing. The ridge ahead sharpened into a ledge no wider than two paces. On the left, cloudless sky dominated the horizon. On the right, a steep rise of wet rock, jagged as shattered glass.

Wyn's steps grew increasingly hesitant. I saw it in the way her shoulders hunched inward, how her hand clutched the edge of her cloak like a lifeline. Her breath came quickly and shallow, the kind that preceded panic.

I'd seen it before in new recruits facing their first real drop. That brittle, wide-eyed silence. When their bodies betrayed the effort to seem composed.

She was trying to be brave. Pretending.

But the tremble in her fingers gave her away.

I slowed my pace as far as possible without breaking the line. I couldn't reach her—not without endangering the others—but I turned just enough to catch her eye over my shoulder.

"Princess," I whispered, not wanting to startle her. "Wyn. Look at me."

She reluctantly did. Her eyes widened, caught between the terror of falling and the shame of revealing her fear.

"Tell me something," I said. "Something you know. Something interesting. Doesn't matter what."

She frowned. Then, after a moment, she said, "Nightbloom asters only open when the moon is full. They close again before sunrise, no matter what."

Her voice steadied slightly with each word, her steps evening out.

I nodded. "Good. Another."

"Um…bees don't like the color red. They prefer blues and purples."

Her tone was firmer now, less breathless. And the panic had eased from her posture.

"Keep going."

She did.

The ridge curved again, widening a bit as it arced around a jut of stone. I felt the shift in the air before I saw it, like something sucked the wind backward into the mountain's lungs. My hand went instinctively to the hilt on my belt.

And then I heard it.

A sharp gasp.

I turned in time to see Corren, two paces behind us, frozen in place. Something was wrong. His body had gone rigid. And then I saw the shape behind him. A shadow uncoiled from the stone, tall and lean and too close.

A blade arced forward, slicing across Corren's throat with terrifying silence. No crying, no chance to move. Just the wet gurgling snap of breath and blood. He fell to his knees first, clutching at his neck as a spray of red fanned across the stone. For a heartbeat, he knelt there, shaking, eyes wide with shock, before his body crumpled and pitched sideways off the cliff's edge, vanishing into the mist below.

Wyn let out a terrifying gasp, a raw, involuntary sound, as if the air itself was trying to escape her lungs in sheer panic.

The shadow straightened itself.

Riven.

His silhouette emerged from the mist. Dark leather, scarred hands, a long blade still dripping red. His eyes flickered with something not wholly human, something cold and lit from within.

Lark shouted, panic flaring across his features. He rushed forward, sword raised, but he didn't see that Riven was ready. A dagger flashed and drove deep into his abdomen with a sickening crunch. Blood poured instantly, soaking the front of his tunic in a grotesque bloom. He gasped, a high, broken sound, and staggered back a step, then another. His sword slipped from his grip. He looked down, hands trembling as they pressed uselessly to the wound. More blood welled up between his fingers. Then his knees buckled, and he collapsed beside Corren's still-warm trail, gasping like a fish on dry stone.

Gideon was already moving, blade drawn and angled low. "We've got company!" he barked. Alaric raised his sword.

"Hold the edge!" I shouted. "He's driving us toward the drop." I grasped Wyn's hand in mine.

Riven smiled, raising one hand. "That one," he said, eyes sliding to where Wyn had stood, who was now in front of me, "you weren't supposed to make it this far."

The words crawled over my spine like ice. I clenched my jaw. Of course, it would be this. I'd seen him do it before—twisting earth like it was clay. I saw the magic take hold. Veins of light, how raw and fractured it was as it crawled up his forearms, pulsing just beneath the skin. His fingers twitched, and the ground answered. He was rock-gifted, born of Tarnak's domain. The air went tight around us, pressure rolling in like a wave.

The cliff responded as if familiar with his voice. Cracks split beneath our boots like lightning etched in stone; slow, deliberate, and lethal. Shards trembled loose from the ledge's edge. I saw the magic crawling through the rock itself, glowing faintly. A sickly, unnatural green pulsing into jagged veins. The cliff began to cry out a low, building rumble, escalating into a growl that vibrated through the air.

Then everything shifted.

The stone beneath our feet lurched with a violent crack, like ribs splitting under pressure. A deafening groan echoed through the cliffs as the ledge buckled and split. Chunks of shale exploded outward, clattering down the ravine like shattered bone. I just about threw myself sideways as the earth dropped out beneath us. I tried to hold on tight to Wyn in an attempt to pull her with me, but her fingers slipped through mine. "Wyn!" I called, eyes snapping to the spot where she'd been moments ago.

But she was gone.

I turned in time to see her silhouette vanish along with the crumbling edge, her cloak flaring like a dying flame. She fell, tumbled, skidded, and scraped down a steep slope of stone and brambles before disappearing entirely into the mist below.

A scream followed. A single, sharp cry of terror that cut through the chaos like a blade. It wasn't loud, but it struck something primal in me. Something cold and profound. It wasn't fear; it was knowing, being aware that she was falling. Knowing I couldn't see her. Knowing I might never again.

It hit me harder than it should have.

And it terrified me more than the drop itself.

"No!"

I didn't think. I ran.

Branches clawed at my arms as I tore through the underbrush, boots skidding over rain-slick roots and tangled brambles. My breath sawed in and out of my chest, each gasp a spike of panic. The world narrowed to sound and motion, the slapping rush of leaves, the distant roar of water growing louder with every step.

She had fallen. Gods, she had fallen.

The ravine opened up in front of me like a wound in the world. Jagged rocks lined the river's edge, and down below, the current surged, white-capped and violent, snarling like a thing alive. My boots hit wet stone, and I skidded to a halt in time to see her.

A blur in the water. A pale smear of lavender cloak. Arms flailing.

"Wynessa!"

Her head broke the surface. "Erin!" she screamed, voice raw with terror.

Then she went under.

I tore off my cloak, yanked the buckles of my chest armor so hard they nearly tore loose. The metal hit the rocks behind me with a thud. My sword belt went next. I didn't care. She was in the river. And I would not let her die.

I crashed down the embankment, slipping on slick moss and jagged stone. My foot caught on a root. I fell, rolled, and hit the edge hard, but I had to keep going. The river loomed, a churning beast.

I dove.

The biting cold blasted me like a wall, numbing fingers and toes instantly. This was no ordinary water. It was ice, a living, furious entity that devoured me whole. The current seized me instantly, spinning me, pulling me under. My shoulder slammed into a submerged boulder, sending a jolt of pain through my body. The coppery taste of blood filled my mouth. I ignored it, fighting on as I kicked and struggled against the current. Where was she?

My eyes burned. My lungs screamed. I came up for air and there, out of the corner of my eye, was a flash of lavender.

Her cloak.

She surfaced again, choking. Her mouth opened, and she said my name. A gurgled plea. Then the river dragged her back down.

No.

I forced my arms forward, slicing through the water. A shape. A hand.

I caught it.

Her skin. Cold. Slipping.

I locked my grip around her wrist and pulled her to me. Her body hit mine; slack, breathless, but not gone. I wrapped her against me and kicked as hard as I could for the bank.

It took everything I had.

The current tore at us, trying to claim her back, but I held fast.

Until finally, we hit the shallows hard.

I surfaced with a gasp, already reaching for her. She was right beside me, sputtering, struggling to find a footing on the slick stone. Together, we scrambled up the embankment, climbing onto a flat slab just above the waterline.

I collapsed onto my back, soaked and heaving. She dropped beside me, coughing, her chest rising and falling in sharp, uneven bursts. For a few breaths, neither of us moved; we just lay there, side by side, the world spinning above us.

Then I sat up, chest still tight, and leaned over her. Her lips had a blue tinge. Her eyes fluttered open, dazed. Wet hair clung to her cheeks like riverweed.

I cupped her face. Still gasping for breath, I forced out the words "You're safe. You're all right. I've got you."

She blinked at me. "You…you came after me…"

"Of course I did." My voice was a ragged whisper.

She gave a weak laugh.

"Is now a bad time to tell you I can't swim?" she puffed out.

I stared at her.

Then I laughed. Broken. Real.

She smiled.

The remainder of the group caught up to us after we made camp beneath the crooked skeleton of an ancient tree that had collapsed into the ravine wall. The roots twisted like the fingers of a dead god, forming a hollow deep enough to block the wind.

Jasira reached us first, hair wild, eyes frantic. She dropped beside Wyn and wrapped her arms around her tightly. "You're alive," she breathed. "Saints above, you're alive."

"I'm all right," Wyn whispered. "Erindor found me."

Alaric was next; his face had gone pale beneath streaks of mud. "Don't you ever do that again," he muttered, voice choking. "Don't you dare disappear on me, Wynnie."

Wyn reached out; her hand was cold but steady. Alaric grabbed her and kissed her forehead, pulling her close.

"I thought—"

"I know," she mumbled.

Gideon knelt at the fire, eyes scanning the darkness. "No sign of Riven. He's gone for now. But that bastard won't stay gone forever."

"We lost Corren and Lark." Alaric's voice was a monotone drone, a stark contrast to the storm of grief brewing behind his eyes.

The silence that followed was a crushing weight, a silent testament to the grief and shock that filled the camp.

The fire crackled softly, a small comfort against the sudden fury of the storm that finally broke overhead, pattering against the tree roots and soaking the mossy floor. We wrapped ourselves in cloaks and silence. Each of us was too grateful, too raw, and too shaken to say anything else. As the others drifted toward sleep, Wyn shifted beside me and reached into her pocket.

"I picked this…before the attack and the fall," she whispered.

In her hand, an impossible thing: a small, frost-pink flower, its delicate petals unmarred despite its journey over a raging cliff and through the churning rapids

She placed it in my palm. Her fingers grazed mine, sending sparks of heat through my arm despite the cold.

She gave me a gentle smile that took the breath from my lungs, then turned to sleep, curling beside the fire.

I didn't speak. I just stared at the bloom in my hand—fragile, improbable, still clinging to beauty after everything it had endured.

I turned it over gently, memorizing the color, the curve of each petal, and the faint scent like snow and wild honey.

Then, carefully, I folded it into a strip of cloth and tucked it into my armor.

Close to my heart, where it wouldn't break.

Safe.

As I sat there, drenched and motionless, the only sound I could hear was the frantic thrumming of my own blood in my ears, gaze fixed on her. The image of her slipping away, a terrifying ghost, still clawing at my mind.

The subtle curve of her lips, a smile she wore with innocent obliviousness, totally unaware of her impact on everyone around her.

Each time it flashed, a jolt of something akin to a mortal wound pierced me.

Chapter Twelve

Wynessa

The rain had finally eased, but the damp clung to everything. The moss, the bark, the hair at the nape of my neck. Fog drifted like low-lying breath between the trees, and the fire crackled weakly, struggling to stay alive in the heavy air. The others slept in bundles of cloaks and blankets, their faces shadowed and still.

The night had remained quiet. But too many unknowns still lingered in the Wildervale for it to be peaceful for good.

That was when I heard it.

Jasira's breath was too fast. I knew the sound before I even opened my eyes, the stuttering pull of lungs fighting against heat. Fever. I rolled over and reached for her instinctively, brushing her cheek. Her skin was hot, damp, and flushed far beyond what it should've been.

"Jasi," I whispered, trying not to wake the others. "Can you hear me?"

She stirred, lips parched, murmuring something broken. Despite the thick blankets, a tremor shook her body, a shiver that seemed born of the stormy night and the dampness still clinging to her cloak. And now the cold had seeped in, beneath her skin, deeper than any blanket could reach. Panic rose in my throat, but I forced it down. I couldn't risk losing control. Not now. Not with her depending on me.

I'd felt this kind of fear only once before, when the apothecary's son fell ill from tainted river water, and nothing I did was enough. I remembered the heavy feeling of the mother's stare, how her hope vanished behind her lips when I gave an uncertain answer.

That helplessness had hollowed me out.

I was determined to prevent its recurrence.

I was already moving, slipping from my bedroll and kneeling beside her with my satchel. I checked her pulse, too fast, and her breathing, shallow and sharp.

The fever wasn't the worst I'd seen, not yet, but I knew that could turn quickly. I tried to remember every page I'd ever read, every note I'd scribbled in margins late at night while the castle slept. I had learned about healing long before I'd ever picked up an herb knife. Books had been my first teachers, and in this moment, I clung to that knowledge like it was the only real thing in the world.

"I need feverroot," I muttered to myself, my fingers scrambling around my satchel. "Pine bark, sun leaf. Something to heal her from the inside."

"Tell me what to do," came Erindor's voice, low and steady at my shoulder. He didn't flinch at my urgency and didn't ask questions. Just listened.

"I need shelter, genuine warmth. Something dry to cover her. And I need time."

He nodded and was gone in an instant.

Alaric stirred and was instinctively on his feet, eyes sharp. When I told him what was happening, he moved without hesitation. Gideon joined him. Together, they cleared a better path up the slope toward the shallow rock overhang we had passed the day before. It was a space that promised shelter from the worst of the rain. "It's not perfect," Alaric muttered, "but it'll do."

Gideon didn't wait. He crouched beside Jasira and, with a soft grunt of effort, lifted her into his arms. "I've got you, sweetheart," he whispered, careful not to jostle her too much. "Let's get you somewhere dry."

Every step beside them felt like an eternity. My heart hammered against my ribs, a frantic rhythm of utter helplessness.

The new shelter, though cramped and barely large enough for all of us, was much better than our previous spot. The stone above created a sloped ceiling that let the water slide off in thin rivulets. Erindor returned with his own cloak, several long branches, and a bundle of oilcloth from Gideon's pack. Alaric and Gideon helped anchor the coverings, creating a makeshift tent that sealed out the worst of the damp and allowed us to build the fire higher.

Tyren stood outside the shelter's lip, his sword unsheathed and resting across his knees as he kept a quiet watch. His eyes scanned the dark tree line without pause. Occasionally, he muttered a low prayer to one of the old gods, fingers brushing the carved token around his neck. As we settled Jasira under the layers of blankets, he stepped forward, knelt briefly, and placed the small wooden charm near her side, an offering of luck. Then he resumed his post.

Only when the heat gathered around her cheeks again did I let myself exhale.

"Thank you," I murmured, glancing up at Erindor.

His gaze, usually so guarded, lingered for a beat too long, a silent question in the depths of his unreadable eyes. Yet, his mere presence was a steadying anchor against the rush of my racing pulse.

I gathered what I needed quickly: a sun leaf, a strip of pine bark, a brittle twist of root I prayed was feverroot. My hands moved automatically, sorting, preparing. My breath hitched with each painful throb, a desperate struggle for composure as fear clamped its icy tendrils tighter around my chest.

The fire burned low in the center of the shelter, casting gold and amber light across the stone walls. I dropped to my knees beside it, arranging the herbs on a flat rock, and began grinding them together with the butt of my knife. The scent was sharp, bitter, and piney, with the faint sweetness of sun leaf.

I poured water into the blackened tin kettle and set it over the fire. As it warmed up, I scraped the herb paste into the bottom of a cup. The bark needed longer, so I added it to the boiling water first, letting the scent fill the air.

Oily steam enveloped my face, its humid warmth a sticky caress that promised the slow burn of healing. I closed my eyes and tried to focus on the rhythm, the careful measure of each motion, the ancient practice of tending to someone you love.

From behind, a choked sound tore from Jasira's throat, a tiny, broken noise that barely reached the ears over the wind.

When the tea was finally ready, I knelt beside her again. Her lips were parted, skin slick with sweat, but her lashes fluttered as I touched her shoulder.

"Jasi," I whispered, gently sliding an arm beneath her shoulders. She was burning. "Try and take small sips," I said softly as I propped her against me, tilting the cup to her lips.

Her throat worked slowly. She didn't swallow easily, but she drank.

I whispered to her while she did; nonsense things, comforting things, stories about when we were little, about garden games and secret rooms behind the library shelves. The first time we tried to make soup without help, we nearly burned down the kitchen as a result.

She smiled weakly and lopsidedly.

"I remember," she mumbled.

"So do I," I whispered, brushing damp curls from her temple. "Stay with me, Jasi."

Her eyes, clouded with pain, fluttered to stay open. "I'm trying," she rasped,

And, gods help me, she was.

. . .

The shelter had gone still. Jasira's breathing had settled. Alaric dozed beside Bran, and Gideon's soft snores filtered in from the far side of the fire. The smoke drifted in soft spirals.

I sat curled against the stone wall, wrapped in my blanket, but sleep would not come.

Across the fire, Erindor sat quietly, his sword across his knees. His eyes flicked to mine briefly, then away.

I hesitated, then reached into my satchel and pulled out a small bit of honey bread I'd kept hidden since Greymere. I crossed the fire and held it out to him.

"Thanks." He looked surprised but took it with a nod, murmuring, "Are you alright?"

"I couldn't sleep," I said.

He nodded again. "Me neither."

We sat like that for a while, two shadows in the firelight. Then he spoke, voice low.

He turned the bread over in his hands, then broke it in half and held a piece out to me. I took it without hesitation, grateful for the gesture.

"My mother used to make sweet rolls like this," he said, his voice softer now, almost distant. "She'd use whatever she had: dried cherries, flower syrup, even crushed mint once. She claimed sweetness mattered more when the world turned bitter."

There was something raw in his voice. I didn't press, but I didn't leave it either.

"She sounds kind," I whispered.

"She was."

He stared into the flames, as if each flickering dance was a silent echo of a forgotten past.

"She was brave," he added, almost as if the words tumbled out before he could stop himself. "Not the sword kind. She never touched a blade. But when I was ten, she stood in front of a man once, armed and angry, with nothing in her hands but a wooden spoon. And she told him to leave." He paused. "She did it for me." His eyes lingered over the fire once more.

My lungs refused to expand, suspended in a moment of utter stillness.

"She died protecting me." His voice cracked. "And I stood there. Too young. Too slow."

I didn't move or dare to take a breath.

His voice, quiet and blunt, hit me with the force of a punch, and my chest constricted.

He wasn't the type to talk to fill the silence. Every word cost him as if he were carving it out of stone.

As he stared into the fire, jaw clenched tight, posture rigid, the truth of his revelation hit me.

He screamed not loss, but a crushing weight of self-blame.

Erin sat as if he were still ten years old. As if he had never left that moment, like part of him still believed he should've done something, anything.

And I hated that. A suffocating weight pressed down on me, every muscle tense, knowing I was utterly incapable of changing the past for him.

The boy he was should have known no such burden, yet the shadow of the shield clung to him. Even as a man, its spectral weight bent his shoulders

I wanted to reach for his hand and tell him he wasn't alone.

But I whispered the only truth I could find. "You didn't forget her," I said. "That matters."

His gaze locked onto mine, and for a moment the world contracted to nothing but the sudden intensity in his eyes. "You remind me of her," he said.

I blinked. "Because of bread?"

He huffed, a ghost of a laugh. "Because you care. Because you didn't flinch when she needed help."

The sound of his voice, low and rough with memory, threaded straight through me. Something in my chest swelled until it was too big for my ribs to hold, an ache so fierce it stole the air from my lungs. It was tender, but sharp, like something blooming in a place it shouldn't be able to grow. Like fire sprouting roots.

"She asked me to keep something alive. To still plant something, even after..." His fingers twitched, curling tight as if he was holding onto her ghost. "You do that. You plant things. Even in people like me."

The words hollowed me out and filled me in the same breath. I wanted—gods, I wanted—to reach for him, to press my hand against his and tell him he wasn't as ruined as he believed. The urge was terrifying in its strength, dangerous in the way it threatened everything I had been taught to want.

Instead, I sat frozen, my throat tight, the ache inside me burning bright and unbearable.

He went quiet again, and I let him. The silence between us was companionable. And when he finally glanced at me again, I knew he was remembering more than he said.

Whatever storm still lived in him, I hoped briefly that I could be a quiet place where it passed.

Chapter Thirteen

Wynessa

The path was gone.

Seraph Arch had washed out overnight, reduced to a churning mire of broken stone and white water. The roar of the river below was louder now, more aggressive—as if the land itself was angry. Mist rose from the shattered gorge in damp curls, and the morning sun did little to cut through it. Alaric looked uncertain as he stared at the collapsed ridge, his jaw tight with the silence that meant calculation was underway.

"We could cross it," Alaric said finally, gesturing to where jagged stone and crumbling ledges still jutted out across the chasm. "If we're careful, we might climb down to the waterline and ford across."

Gideon barked a short laugh. "And drown halfway through? That current could snap a horse in half. You saw what it did to the bridge."

"We're losing time," Alaric shot back, eyes narrowing. "We'll have to go around the entire ridge to reach the high trail. That's a full day, maybe more. And we already lost a full day. I'm sorry, Jasi, but it's true."

"I'd rather lose a day than a life," Erindor said evenly, his voice cutting through the rising tension like steel. "If we go down there, we won't all make it."

Tyren grunted in agreement, turning to me. "The river's too fast, Your Highness. And too deep. It would wash us off the rocks before we found footing."

Alaric exhaled sharply, running a hand through his rain-damp hair. He didn't argue again, but the frustration in his stance said enough.

Jasira slumped against my shoulder, a fragile balance of weakness and stubborn will. Even on her own feet, her weight felt like a dead load, pressing down on me. Erindor turned his gaze eastward, toward the tangle of shadowed forest past the broken trail. "There's another way. In the old groves, we passed an entrance earlier, barely visible from the main path. If we follow the groves, we can meet the road again after the cliffs. It'll take time, but it's safer than trying to cross that."

It was settled.

We turned off the main trail shortly after dawn, heading east into a grove no one recognized.

I felt it the moment we passed under the first arch of trees.

The air changed.

There wasn't a temperature shift, but a palpable switch in the very fabric of the air, as if the world itself had slowed to a crawl, its breath held in a heavy silence. The wind was still. The scent of damp moss became sweeter, and twisted trees arched toward each other like hands folded in prayer, leaning in strange, deliberate ways.

We moved beneath them like trespassers in a cathedral. Each step seemed heavier, but not with dread. The deeper we walked, the more the hush pressed in. Not oppressive. Just watchful.

My heartbeat slowed here, or maybe the gentle pace of everything else made it seem as if time stood still. My fingers twitched at my sides, not out of fear, but from the weight of something unspoken. The stories I'd read in the castle library—the old ones, barely preserved, spoke of places like this. Sacred groves, thinned from mortal memory, where gods once whispered through bark and breeze. The membrane that separated the living world from the echoes of the past was gossamer-thin, almost transparent, as if it threatened to tear at any moment. I glanced at Erindor. His hand lingered near the hilt of his sword, but did not draw it. Alaric said nothing. None of us did. Jasira continued to lean against me, still struggling to balance herself as we walked. So, I adjusted my steps to match hers.

I wanted to say something. Anything. But every word I thought of felt too loud for this place.

Then, the animals appeared.

A fox, sleek, russet-furred, its paws silent on the moss. Eyes bright and tail flicking, it stepped from the brush as if we were unwelcome visitors in a forest that clearly belonged to them. It didn't run. It merely observed.

I stopped walking. Something stirred in the back of my mind—a page from a book I'd once read, its corners torn and its ink faded with time. Not all creatures in Wildervale were simply beasts. Some were signs.

"Messenger beast," I murmured softly, not really meaning to say it aloud. "They say foxes walk closest to the old gods. They appear only when the divine is paying attention."

Jasira's breath caught beside me. I didn't need to look to know she'd remembered the same stories.

Then, a red-breasted bird landed on a branch above my head and chirped once, softly and clearly.

And then a deer with velveted antlers and moss-touched, one of its eyes glowing faintly blue. It stood across the grove, perfectly still, gazing not at the group but at me.

I stopped walking.

Wynessa.

The name whispered across my spine like wind without breath. My mind wrestled with the sound, unable to classify the creature as real or an illusion. The fox swiveled, its eyes holding a lingering spark before it began to prowl away, its steps silent and unhurried.

Suddenly, I noticed my friends weren't following.

Alaric, Jasira, Gideon, Tyren, and Erindor all stood still, frozen in place mid-step or mid-turn. Not rigid with fear, but paused. It was as if someone had stopped time for them.

But the animals were still moving.

Ahead, the fox walked. The bird shifted on its branch. The deer's breath steamed faintly in the air.

"Wynessa," my name was called again.

I stepped forward toward the voice with Bran padding quietly after me.

He didn't hesitate. The massive hound followed each of my steps as if the pull of the place beckoned him too. When we reached the edge of the deeper grove, he gave a small chuff and pressed his body against my leg. Then, without prompting, he trotted ahead.

I followed.

The grove deepened, the trees forming high arches overhead, so perfectly curved it appeared to be a place designed by thought, not nature. The light was golden and dappled, filtering through leaves that shimmered with a faint silver tint.

The fox led me to a small clearing, at the center of which stood a moss-draped shrine.

Stone cracked and leaned. Vines crawled up its sides, thick with golden blossoms I didn't recognize. The scent was warm, floral, and strange.

Behind the shrine, nestled in the dappled green, was a small cabin.

Its roof blossomed with wild herbs and tiny white flowers, a vibrant contrast to the walls of weathered wood, furrowed by age and carpeted in moss. Plants spilled from every windowsill with long-stemmed blooms, curling ferns, and potted vegetables that looked recently tended.

A narrow footpath led around toward the back, where a garden bloomed in quiet defiance of the wild. Rows of medicinal herbs, flowering vines, even a gnarled fruit tree heavy with pale gold pears. It smelled of earth and rain and sun-warmed leaves.

It was a haven, a place so ancient its age was a physical comfort, a deep-rooted security felt to its roots. The weight of countless seasons settled there, a soothing blanket woven from centuries of quiet stillness.

And in front of it, standing calmly as if he'd always been there—

A man.

His presence was ageless, like river stone or old roots. He was tall, broad-shouldered, with hair the color of dark honey and a well-kept beard. Cloaked in faded green and brown, his clothing seemed a part of the forest itself. When he turned toward me, his pale eyes seemed to skim over me, not truly seeing, but perceiving something more profound, as if his vision didn't require the need to look.

Bran bounded up to him, wagging his tail. The man crouched with a soft laugh and scratched behind his ears as though he were greeting an old friend.

"Oh, you're here!" he exclaimed, practically bouncing on the balls of his feet. "I've been waiting for you," he added, clapping his hands together, as if continuing a conversation we'd already started. A wave of paralysis swept through me, seizing my limbs and tightening my chest.

Light filtered in through the trees above in long, golden shafts, casting a radiant glow over the clearing. Bees hummed lazily among the flowers. The air here seemed softer, thicker, like something divine had kissed it. Peace spread through me like a slow, warming tide. Even Bran, usually so alert, rolled onto his side near the shrine and let the man rub his belly, tongue lolling in delight.

I blinked, hesitant. My voice came out small. "Why aren't they moving? My friends…what did you do to them?"

He glanced up with warmth in his eyes. "Nothing they won't wake from. The grove holds time differently. Only those who are called move forward."

"Called by what? By whom?"

His smile deepened, and for a moment, he looked impossibly old. "Secrets, my dear! Besides, you already know. Deep down. You wouldn't be here otherwise."

He reached beside him and plucked a sprig of golden root from a bundle. "Here, this is for you." He held it out for me, his gaze fixed on a point just past my shoulder. "It's out of fear. You carry too much of it in your ribs."

With my breath hitched, a silent battle raged within as my body was forced to move forward. I stepped closer, my legs felt like water, but they slowly moved one foot in front of the other. The tremors began in the hands, a visible quake as I reached for his offering. The sprig settled into my palm, radiating an unexpected warmth that seemed to steady the tremor in my fingers.

The fox let out a slight sound, a sharp, pained yip, and I turned to see it limping slightly, favoring its paw. Instinct took over. I knelt, drawing it close. It didn't fight me.

A thorn had snagged the foot.

I worked gently, humming under my breath. My fingers moved almost of their own accord, pulling herbs from my pouch and wrapping a bit of linen. The fox licked my wrist once as I'd finished, then bounded off toward its friend.

"You do not need a flame to burn," the man said.

My gaze lifted. His pale eyes fixed on mine, his attention unwavering

"Gentleness," he murmured, "can be the sharpest blade."

I swallowed hard.

"The flame within you will not burn," he added, "until you believe it won't destroy."

Something fractured open in my chest, a truth too raw to accept acknowledgment.

"Who are you?" I whispered.

"You must get back to your friends." He smiled faintly, avoiding my question.

Still in shock and unsure what to do, I turned to go. He reached out and brushed the back of his hand across my arm.

I flinched; however, there was no pain. Only warmth.

Pure and golden, like sunlight pressing against my skin.

It wasn't a warmth like fire, but something older, like the patient memory of something ancient finally recognizing a kin spirit. This warmth permeated my skin, seeping into the very marrow, filling my lungs with a soft, steady rhythm.

I gasped softly.

Suddenly, my forearm started to glow.

A flower mark, intricate and delicate, shimmered to life on my skin. It wasn't etched, carved, or burned, but it was there as if it had been awoken from beneath the surface.

Gold light curled inward like a seed turning in soil, delicate and pulsing. It moved faintly, tuning in to my breathing.

My knees wobbled, threatening to give way beneath the sudden onslaught of emotions.

I clutched my arm, not in pain but in awe, in some nameless knowing. The mark pulsed once more, and then faded, leaving only the memory of its light and the faintest warmth, like a heartbeat echoing beneath the skin.

I looked back up, eyes wide.

But the man had already pivoted, a jaunty whistle erupting as if to dismiss the entire encounter. He glided back toward his cottage with casual, unbothered steps. Bran nudged my side gently. I turned, and together we began walking back toward the trail. The trees closed around us, familiar and real, but something tugged at me—soft and insistent.

I paused. Glanced back over my shoulder.

The man, the cottage, and the garden were all gone. The clearing had unraveled behind me like a dream. Just trees now. Ordinary. Undisturbed. No shrine. No blossoms. No trace of wild pears or golden flowers.

Only birdsong and forest.

I rejoined the group as the light shifted again. The air grew thinner and colder. The bird flew off. At the edge of the path, the deer stood still and surveyed me. It bowed its head once, slowly and solemnly.

Then it turned and vanished into the trees.

Jasira let out a shaky breath. "Wyn…when you left, none of us could move."

I shifted to face her fully. Her brow plowed a deeper furrow between her widened eyes. "I tried to speak," she whispered. "To call for you. But it was like my voice…froze."

"I felt it too," Alaric muttered, jaw tight. "Something held us still. Something magical."

Gideon rubbed his arms. "It was like the forest itself told us to wait."

I glanced at Erindor, expecting doubt, but he was staring at the trees where the deer had disappeared, his gaze dark and unwavering.

Erindor pulled his eyes away and stepped beside me. "Are you alright?"

I nodded slowly. "I feel…lighter."

I glanced back down the grove one last time. The air shimmered faintly at its edge. Just beyond the trees, far in the distance, I caught a last glimpse of the fox.

It stood perfectly still. Observing me from a distance.

A quiet thread of understanding passed between us, unspoken but sure. I raised my hand slightly.

The fox blinked once and vanished into the brush.

No one spoke as we left the grove.

But something had changed.

In me.

In the air.

And somewhere beneath my skin, something had glowed.

Chapter Fourteen

Erindor

By the time we made camp that evening, the sun was already low, casting long golden slants through the trees. We spent the better part of the day winding through Wildervale's quiet groves. The light shifted with a deliberate slowness, as the forest breathed around us. Thoughts of her consumed my mind.

Wyn.

She had said little after the grove and the fox.

She had vanished from our sight and returned an entirely different person. A newfound radiance clung to her, a brightness that shimmered around her like a halo. Something in her eyes had shifted, like someone had lifted a weight I hadn't even known she was carrying.

Even the animals noticed.

Bran, normally so selective, followed at her heel like a knight sworn. Birds landed near her as she walked. A white moth clung to her hair for over an hour. It was subtle at first and easy to dismiss, but I saw it.

So did the trees.

We made camp beside a shallow bend in the river where moss grew thick between the roots of weeping willows. Their branches hung in veils, shifting enough in the wind to hide or reveal. It was quiet here, the quiet that left you alone with your thoughts.

And mine lately were a mess. All I could think of was her.

She was crouched now by the edge of the water, sleeves rolled, rinsing herbs she'd gathered. The sunlight touched her hair in strands of amber and rose. Every so often, she would glance back to check on Jasira or murmur something to the hound curled beside her. It was a quiet sort of care. The kind you didn't always notice until you couldn't stop seeing it.

She caught me watching and smiled tenderly. My eyes darted away, desperately searching for a distraction.

Alaric had pulled out his lute and was quietly tuning it, plucking a few soft notes that floated over the camp like smoke. Tyren sat nearby, carefully oiling his armor with a cloth. He'd placed a small carved token near Jasira's bedroll earlier, one of his "luck pieces," he'd claimed, warding off evil spirits. None of us mocked him for it, not after everything we'd seen.

Later, after the others had eaten and Jasira was dozing again, Wyn approached me while I was checking the edges of my blade.

"Would you show me again?"

"What?"

"How to use this," she asked, holding out her dagger.

I blinked. "You want to train?"

She nodded, fingers intertwined in front of her. "If that's alright."

I hunched my shoulders. It wasn't because I didn't want to. Gods, no. It was because I did. Too much.

Something inside me pulled taut at the request. It wasn't the way she looked at me, eyes wide and hopeful, or the way her fingers fidgeted with the hem of her sleeve. It was what it meant. That she trusted me, wanted to learn from me, and wanted to be near me.

An insistent pulse screamed of things I wanted but were forbidden. The truth lodged like a shard in my throat: this shouldn't matter. Her safety was the only thing that was allowed to be consumed in my thoughts. Nothing more.

Still, I nodded. "Come on."

We moved a short distance into the clearing, far enough from camp to be out of direct view. The air was cooler here, the grass soft underfoot. She took out the small dagger she'd bought at the market, the one I'd sharpened while she slept.

"Try to stay light on your feet. Don't think about fighting, think about surviving," I said softly.

She nodded and positioned herself in the stance I had shown her. I stepped behind her to adjust her, my hands brushing lightly over her shoulder, elbow, and wrist.

A subtle catch in her breath, almost imperceptible, was sensed whenever my fingers grazed her side to guide her posture. Her skin warmed beneath my touch, a transparent veil barely concealing the subtle tremors that betrayed her.

I tried not to think about how close she was. She moved like sunlight, quiet, warm, and always a little beyond my reach. She was beautiful, yes. Anyone with eyes could see that. But it was more than her face. It was the way she watched the world, as if it were still worth saving.

That gave me a bone-deep dread that surpassed every other fear I had combined.

I didn't have feelings for her.

It wasn't like that.

It couldn't be.

"She's your duty," I told myself as I moved in front of her, "not your possibility."

She lunged. Sloppy, but improving. I stepped into her space, catching her wrist, guiding the blade aside.

We were close. Closer than we should've been. Her breath stirred the air between us. Her skin was warm beneath my fingers.

I leaned in, closing the space between us, my voice dropping to a murmur meant only for her ears.

"If you're that close," I murmured, "it's not about strength. It's about conviction."

She swallowed hard. "Right. Conviction."

I circled her slowly, eyes like a hawk's, dissecting her every detail. "You hesitate. Don't. The blade doesn't care how kind you are. You move, or you bleed. Alright, Princess, again."

She took a breath, reset her stance, then struck. I blocked, twisted, and nudged her off balance.

She growled softly. "You make it look easy."

"It's not. I've learned how to make the hard parts look graceful."

Repeatedly, we ran the sequence. Each time, she got a little faster. Closer, her breath growing more ragged. Her hair clung to her neck. The torture was a steady thrum in my ears.

She spun too quickly, too committed, and her heel caught mine as her dagger arm swept low.

We went down in a blur of motion and breath.

She landed on top of me with a startled gasp, her palms splayed on my chest, my hand still wrapped instinctively around her waist. Her knees braced against my thighs, and the heat of her pressed close.

Her hair fell around us like a silk curtain. Her eyes, wide and shining, met mine.

Neither of us moved.

I sensed her pulse at her wrist; it was fast, like my own.

She looked at my lips.

Gods, she was beautiful.

But that couldn't mean anything.

Not to me.

Not like that.

"I'm sorry—" she whispered.

"Don't be," I said hoarsely.

The moment pulled tight, a thread of something unspeakable trembling between us. She looked at me as if I could be something better. I didn't know how to carry that, but I wanted to.

Her breath, a soft whisper of warmth, ghosted my cheek, sending a shiver through me. Her fingers, a feather-light touch, curled slightly against my chest, creating a spark that radiated through my core.

A low huff broke the spell.

Bran sat nearby beneath a willow tree, head on his paws but eyes alert, watching us like a chaperone. His tail thumped once in judgment.

Beside him, I caught a glimpse of Gideon standing at the edge of the trees.

Gideon grinned. "Shhh, Bran, I'll wait ten more seconds."

But Bran's second huff was louder this time.

"Oh, am I interrupting something steamy?" came Gideon's voice, bright and amused. "Should I pretend to have gone blind?"

Wyn let out a squeak and scrambled off me. I rolled away, swearing softly.

Gideon stood at the edge of the trees, tossing an apple into the air with a smirk that belonged in a tavern.

"We're done," I muttered, brushing off my shirt and walking back to camp.

Wyn didn't follow right away.

. . .

Later that night, the fire was low, and the group had fallen into one of those rare, meandering conversations that happened only when the world was quiet enough to make room for them.

Gideon was comparing the court dances of Tharnhal, "so stiff even their bowing has a curtsy," to the wild music of the coast.

Jasira snorted. "You like the coast because people there wear less."

Gideon grinned. "Yes, but I also appreciate people who are proficient with a drum."

Alaric leaned forward, plucking softly at his lute. "What about Vireth? Or Caerthaine? I've heard rumors of magic in their courts. Actual elemental gifts."

"Rare," Jasira said, suddenly more serious. "But not impossible."

Wyn stirred. Her fingers twisted around her mug as she spoke, knuckles tight. "It's said that gods give those gifts. They choose whom they bless based on their values. And even that kind of grace has a cost."

The firelight flickered over her face. I noticed the faint line between her brows.

"The old texts say it feeds on the soul if wielded without balance. And some gifts...aren't gifts at all."

"False gifts?" Tyren asked, rubbing his hands together.

Wyn's head dipped, her gaze carefully fixed on the ground. "Magic born of grief, blood, or blasphemy. Power taken instead of given. There's extraordinarily little written about them."

A profound stillness descended, swallowing the chatter, leaving only the echo of what had just been said.

Alaric frowned. "So, it's not only a tool?"

"It's never just a tool," I said.

They all turned to look at me.

I rarely spoke during these talks. Never felt like I had anything worth adding.

But Wyn met my gaze, quietly curious. And that was enough.

"If you shape wind or earth, fire or water, it shapes you back," I said. "Even the strongest get hollow if they don't know who they are."

Gideon blinked. Jasira tilted her head. Wyn smiled.

"You read?" Alaric asked, half-mocking, half-impressed.

"Sometimes," I muttered, before returning to sharpen my blade.

Jasira leaned forward, stirring the fire with a stick. "Caerthaine hides its magic behind gilded walls. All jeweled marble and velvet politics, but you bleed the same even if it's on silk."

Alaric added softly, "They may glitter, but they're Vireth's puppets now. Their power's not in magic; it's in appearances."

Gideon chuckled. "And Elyrien? That place grows bread like it breathes. Not fancy, but they'd starve us out if we lost their alliance."

"Elyria's fields are sacred," Wyn murmured. "They say the gods still touch the soil there."

One of Alaric's eyebrows arched in a silent challenge, the curve sharp and pointed, "And Tharnhal?"

"Cold," I stated. "But solid. They've got a fortress carved into the cliffs and a library older than any crown. They speak slowly and hit hard."

"Sounds like my kind of people," Gideon muttered.

Everyone laughed lightly. For a moment, the weight of the night lifted.

The fire crackled low. Alaric strummed a tune as Jasira began humming. I didn't recognize this song. Tyren tossed another twig into the coals and leaned back with a sigh.

And then, Bran lifted his head in alert.

His ears tilted toward the trees.

We all followed his stare.

The laughter faded, and everyone quieted.

Somewhere beyond the veil of willow branches, something moved. Something not far enough for comfort. A rustle. The sound of weight shifting through the brush.

"Could be a deer," Alaric offered, though his voice lacked confidence.

I stood slowly, brushing the hilt of my sword. Wyn rose too, one hand instinctively reaching toward the dagger at her belt. I noticed the way she scanned the dark with more awareness than ever before.

The rustling stopped.

Bran let out a quiet growl. Just once.

Then the forest returned to stillness.

We waited for a few moments longer, but nothing happened.

"I'll take first watch," Tyren muttered, already rolling his shoulders.

No one disagreed.

Wildervale might let you laugh, but it never truly enabled you to forget where you were.

Whatever was out there, it didn't scare me.

Chapter Fifteen

Wynessa

The first snow stole into the world like an unbidden secret whispered from the sky. It settled, soft and sudden, muffling the edges of the day.

I woke in the dim light before dawn, my breath clouding the air inside my tent. A hush had fallen over the woods, broken only by the distant burble of the river and the soft rustle of canvas as the others stirred in sleep. I sat up slowly, tugging my cloak tighter around my shoulders, and peeked outside.

The world had changed overnight. A fine layer of powdery snow blanketed the earth, turning the gnarled roots and twisted bramble of Wildervale into something briefly beautiful. Frost clung to leaves like delicate silver veins.

I slipped out quietly with my satchel and sketchbook, boots crunching softly in the snow. The cold bit at my cheeks as I crouched beside a cluster of frost-kissed flowers growing along the bank of the river. I reached out, gently brushing snow from the petals of a sleepvine bloom, blue-white and trembling in the wind. One could gather the shimmering frost from its leaves, a whispered secret for crafting calming draughts. A draught Jasira desperately needed, for she had been thrashing through the long night, unable to find peace.

I plucked a few petals and uncapped a small glass vial. As I worked, I heard footsteps, light but sure, and froze.

A heavy cloak settled over my shoulders.

"You're going to freeze to death over a flower, Princess," Erindor murmured behind me.

I flinched, muscles locking instantly, then my head snapped up, my breath a sharp gasp. He was there, closer than could have been imagined, closer than he should be. The chill air turned his breath to mist, and there was a softness in his expression I hadn't seen before. He knelt beside me.

"It's for Jasira," I said, recovering. "Sleepvines can help with dreams."

He didn't reply immediately. Then, surprisingly, he smiled, a faint, rare curve of his lips.

His hands moved to adjust the cloak, which had slipped too far to one side. Fingers steady and sure, he tugged it snug around my shoulders, brushing snowflakes from my collar. His touch lingered longer than it needed to.

"You tied it wrong," he murmured.

I blinked. "I didn't tie it at all."

"Exactly."

He carefully fastened the clasp under my chin. Time seemed to slow, every heartbeat echoing in the hush between us. I was acutely aware of the warmth radiating from his body, the gentle firmness of his touch. He was so close, so careful, as though he was afraid to shatter something fragile and precious between us. The world faded until there was only him, only this moment suspended in the crystalline morning air.

The silence between us felt fragile and full.

"There," he said, stepping back, but only slightly. "Better."

We stood together in the morning hush, strolling along the frozen bank. The snow silenced the world, giving the impression that we were the only two awake.

"I used to do this in the garden back home," I said. "Sketch plants. Take notes. My mother said it wasn't proper for a princess to have dirt on her knees."

"She sounds delightful," Erindor said dryly.

I laughed softly. "She was...practical."

He was quiet for a moment. Then I felt him glance at me again.

"Erindor," I said, stopping beneath a tree heavy with frost. "You don't always have to protect me, you know."

"Yes," he said. "I do."

I turned toward him, heart thudding. I felt my cheeks flush, and not only from the cold. Snowflakes dusted my eyelashes.

He reached out without thinking and brushed one off my cheek. His fingers lingered for a breath.

"I—" I began, but a voice rang out from the trees.

"Breakfast, snow fairies!" Gideon called. "Come get it before it freezes solid!"

We pulled apart, a silent, almost reluctant severance. My eyes closed briefly before opening to blink back the present. Then, with a heavy heart, I turned toward the smell of the camp.

As we walked back together, he looked over at me and asked, "Is that why you can't swim?"

I blinked. "What?"

"Because it's not 'princess-like'?"

I stared at him, cheeks flushing again. "Perhaps. I always had tutors for music, diplomacy, and lineage. No one ever thought of throwing me into a river."

He grunted. "Might've done you some good."

While saying, "Not all of us were raised by wolves," I playfully glared at him.

"Not wolves," he said. "Worse."

He didn't elaborate any further.

I rubbed my hands together and glanced down. A strange warmth pulsed in my palm.

I opened my hand.

There, glowing faintly against my skin, was a single ember, no larger than a spark from the fire. It flickered once. Then faded.

But it didn't burn.

It had felt like a single, reverberating heartbeat, slow and profound, stretching out of time.

I closed my fingers over the spot and said nothing.

At breakfast, Jasira gave me a long, sly look over her steaming tea.

"You're blushing like a girl who got wrapped in a hero's cloak and didn't hate it," she said, voice low and teasing. "What did he do—whisper something noble while fixing your buttons?"

A sudden heat crept up my neck, stealing my breath and making my face feel strangely tight. Fingers trembled, struggling to maintain a grip on my cup, rattling the delicate ceramic against the plate. "I didn't—he didn't—it wasn't like that."

She laughed and leaned in. "Wyn, you're allowed to want." Her voice was low and gentle. "You've lived your whole life being what others needed. Let yourself desire something that seems like it belongs to you."

Hesitation washed over me, holding me captive. Guilt, raw and bitter, climbed into my throat, a slow, suffocating burn that mimicked my own pulse.

"It…feels like something I shouldn't want. I'm promised to someone else. I shouldn't be thinking about anyone else, much less feeling…"

"You're only human," Jasira advised. "You're not betraying a duty by feeling it, Wyn. And you have done nothing wrong."

I nodded, eyes low. "It still feels like I'm breaking something."

Jasira's teasing smile softened, melting into something so tender it made my throat tighten. "It's not wrong to want something gentle. Something that looks at you like you're worth protecting."

I looked down. My eyes fell to the sprig in my palm. "Do you ever feel that way?"

Jasira was quiet for a moment, then her voice dropped slightly. "Gideon sometimes. He makes everything loud, but when he's kind, it's like the world listens. It surprises me. And I think that's why I noticed it."

Our shared silence spoke louder than words.

I glanced at her then, and for a heartbeat I forgot we were nearly the same age. She laughed like we were still girls, but her eyes…her eyes always seemed older than mine.

I looked at her. She looked at me.

And then we both choked on silent laughter, breathless and giddy, like children with a secret too big to hold.

The sound bubbled up between us, cutting through the tension of the day like sunlight through mist.

The soundless mirth frothed between us, cleaving the day's tension like a sunbeam cleaves through morning mist.

That afternoon, as we moved deeper into Wildervale, the air shifted. The wind shifted, sighing through the branches, but a strange undercurrent hummed within it.

. . .

The deeper we went, the more unnatural the forest became. Tree trunks bowed in on themselves like bones trying to curl inward. Moss crept too far up the bark, clutching branches like fingers. And though snow clung to the earth, the air had a wet, stagnant feel that didn't match the cold. Like something unseen was breathing under the surface. I was the first to feel it. A prickling sensation at the back of my neck, like we were being watched.

My pace slackened, a growing unease making me drag my feet. Finally, I stiffened, unable to move a muscle.

"Did you hear that?" I asked Erindor.

He turned toward me sharply. "What did you hear?"

"My voice," I whispered, pointing my finger. "Calling from the trees over there."

A moment later, my voice echoed again. Exactly. A perfect mimicry, but wrong in cadence. Cold. Mocking.

Erindor didn't hesitate. He moved between me and the voice, blade in hand.

Then I saw them, half-shadowed figures in the boughs, revealing them—gaunt, stooped figures, their forms draped in whispering leaves, like ancient, emaciated apes. Their faces were wrong. Smooth white masks, too large for their heads, carved with smiling lips and wide, empty eyes. But their faces—those were the true horror. Smooth, oversized masks of bleached white, the lips stretched in an eternal, sickening grin, the eyes wide and devoid of all feeling.

One, balanced on a precarious limb, cocked its head with a jerky, unnatural motion. Then, came a chilling echo of him, mimicking my earlier words, perfectly mirrored, issued from its frozen grin. "Did you hear that?"

Another giggled, light and mischievous, before it launched itself with fluid grace to the neighboring tree.

They spoke again—snippets of the group's voices.

"Help me!" it cried in Jasira's tone.

"Wait! Over here!" in Gideon's laughter.

Then my voice: "Please…don't leave me."

Their tone curdled into something both cruel and infantile, a chilling childlike sing-song that raised the hair on my arms.

"Wynessa," one cooed. "Come play. Come play."

"They don't want you," said another, in a deadpan version of Erindor's voice. "Only we do."

"They're Mimics," Erindor hissed. "Don't listen to them. Don't speak."

The entire group had slowed, tense and silent.

"They lure travelers off the path," he added, low. "With voices and memories. Then they…take something."

"What?" I asked, my eyes fixed on them in fear.

"Your heart. If they can reach it."

A cold tremor ran down my spine, raising goosebumps. Then came more. Dozens of them.

The forest bloomed with pale masks. The trees above us shimmered with movement—thin limbs hanging, crawling, and clutching at bark. Their heads tilted in unison. Mocking laughter echoed.

"Pretty girl," one rasped. "Soft heart. Break it. Drink it."

"Take her smile," another hissed.

"They're all liars. Give her to us."

They slithered down the trees in a silent, sinuous crawl, their forms coalescing within the deepening shadows.

Erindor stepped forward, jaw tight. "Run," he announced, his voice carrying to each of us.

Hard. Blind. A desperate plea for air scorched my lungs, while my heartbeat exploded in my ears, eclipsing the bellowing shouts that were a chilling reminder of the proximity of the mimickers behind me.

As I stumbled through the forest as fast as my feet could carry me, roots clawed at my boots. Thorns tore at my sleeves. The forest began to blur—just shadows and speed.

Behind us, I heard someone cry out. A crash. More laughter.

They were closer.

I pushed harder, tumbling through brambles, my breath ragged—

Then, my skirts tangled around my legs, and I went down. Hard.

The impact knocked the air from my lungs as the snow slammed into my ribs. Pain burst up my side.

Mud streaked my hands, and stones etched into my palms.

"Damn these skirts," I hissed, kicking at the fabric. "Who in all the gods' names thought this was practical?"

The howls grew louder.

I scrambled to rise.

And then suddenly something slammed into me from the side.

It hit like a boulder, knocking me flat onto my back. A weight pressed against my chest, heavy and reeking of rot. Fingers not quite human, clawed at my arms.

A Mimic.

Its face shifted—too smooth, too close to mine, its mouth twisted into a mockery of a smile, disturbing and unnatural.

I screamed, wriggling my body in an attempt to free myself, I drove my elbow as hard as I could into where its ribs should've been. It snarled, flinching backward, and I used the moment to wrench myself free, shoving it off with everything I had.

I scrambled to my knees, gasping—

But then it was back, knocking into me with brutal force.

Faster this time, its claws gouging into my cloak, hauling me back down with brutal force.

And then it was back on top of me.

A scream tore from my throat as the Mimic lunged toward my face. Its mask split at the jaw as it shrieked, teeth glinting beneath porcelain. It pinned me, claws digging into my arms. Its breath was hot and sour.

I screamed again, kicking with every ounce of might I had. Without thinking, my dagger came up. I slashed, shallow, but enough to make it reel back—

And then Erindor was there. He struck with brutal force, his blade cleaving straight through the Mimic's neck. Blood, black and slick, sprayed across the snow. The mask shattered as the body twitched, then stilled.

Erindor moved with a sudden, decisive urgency. One arm snaked around my waist, the other hooked beneath my legs, and I was heaved onto his shoulder in one fluid motion.

"Hold on," he growled.

My arms locked around his waist, my knuckles white, as I desperately held onto him. My heart thundering against his back, a frantic drumbeat against his warmth.

We tore through the woods. *Were the others ahead of or behind us?* I couldn't tell. Mimics shrieked all around us.

Then, the sound changed.

We slammed into a creek, the icy current lashing at our waists. Erindor didn't falter; he drove forward, heedless, his boots churning the freezing water with powerful, loud splashes.

And then suddenly the shrieks disappeared.

I turned and lifted my head behind me. The Mimics stood on the other side, masks tilted. Watching.

But none crossed. I gave a small sigh of relief.

Erindor set me down slowly. A beat longer than necessary, his arms stayed on my waist. His chest heaved with breath. His dark eyes seemed to hold me captive.

"You alright?"

I nodded, tears stinging. "Yes."

We scrambled to the edge of the creek, boots skidding in the mud, lungs dragging in ragged breaths.

Everyone was breathing hard, Jasira clutching a stitch in her side, Alaric doubled over, Gideon muttering a prayer between gasps. Even Tyren's calm had cracked, his shoulders heaving as he stared into the distant trees behind us.

Bran stood at the edge of the water, hackles raised, teeth bared in a low, guttural growl that never stopped.

Across the creek, shadows shifted.

The Mimics emerged slowly, unnaturally still, their forms flickering at the edges like smoke trying to be solid. Some wore our faces. Some didn't bother. One had eyes that opened too wide. Another's mouth stretched too far, a grin carved into something that should not grin at all.

Alaric spat, grabbed a stone from the riverbed, and hurled it across the water.
"Cowards," he snapped. "Come try me, you bastard patchwork sons of—"

The rock vanished into the mist behind The Mimics. They didn't flinch.

They just watched.

He stepped back. His words hung in the air: "They don't cross running water."

Wildervale, I realized, had rules.

Old ones.

Deadly ones.

But I was still alive.

Because we ran.

Because he came back.

And carried me out.

· · ·

After resting and catching our breath, we continued to walk. However, my legs still trembled from the adrenaline. My fall caused pain in my side, and the river water soaked and weighed down the hem of my skirts.

"I'm sorry," I murmured, breathless. "I shouldn't have tripped, I wasn't watching, I—these skirts are awful."

Erindor halted, turning to look at me. His eyes scanned down the length of me, making my cheeks burn under his scrutiny. Suddenly, he dropped to one knee and unsheathed a small knife.

I blinked. "What are you doing?"

He didn't answer right away. With a few swift motions, he cut the skirt below my ankles, straight and clean. The fabric fluttered to the snow, lighter, freer.

As he worked, my thoughts scrambled. I placed my hands lightly on his shoulders to steady myself, the heat of him rising through my palms. A heat of a different kind stirred low in my belly; sharp, unexpected, impossible to ignore.

He glanced up at me. "Hold still, Princess," he murmured.

My head dipped in agreement, trying to keep my breathing even.

After he finished, he straightened himself, his gaze locking onto mine, unwavering and direct. The intensity stole my breath, leaving me frozen in stunned silence.

"Better?" he asked simply.

I nodded, too flustered to speak. My face flamed. My heart tried to climb into my throat.

Erindor glanced to my side. His eyes narrowed.

"Are you hurt? You've been holding your side as we walked."

The words caught in my throat, held captive by the intensity of his gaze. "No—I mean—just bruised, I think," they came out in a rush, a scramble to regain composure.

He stepped closer, reaching a hand out me, brow furrowing. "I can take a look, if you want."

"No!" I blurted, a little too loudly, and slapped his hand away. Then softer, mortified at my initial response, "I mean, no thank you. Exceedingly kind, but I'm fine. Yes. Thank you."

He raised an eyebrow. "You're the worst liar I've ever met."

"I'm also very modest," I muttered, clutching my satchel tighter.

His mouth twitched, but not quite a smile. "As you wish, your modest highness."

And then, mercifully, he walked ahead again, giving me space.

I exhaled slowly, my face burning so hot it could've melted the snow.

. . .

That night, I had a dream of a garden I had never seen.

The snow was gone, replaced by ash, but nothing burned. Flowers rose from scorched earth: golden blossoms curled like tongues of flame, glowing at their edges. A warm breeze stirred the air, fragrant with smoke and something sweet, like honeyed moss.

A figure moved between the trees, cloaked, faceless, watching. Not threatening. Not human.

"You lit the dark," it whispered, "but the fire is not yours until you believe it is."

I turned, and the flowers turned with me. Each pedal flickered. Each stem leaned toward my breath. The sky overhead shimmered with violet light, a veil of dancing flame like a second dawn.

In my hand, I held nothing.

Until suddenly a spark appeared.

Small. Steady. Alive!

Warmth bloomed through me, not fire but hands. Erindor's hands, calloused and careful, adjusted my cloak, brushing snow from my cheek. Within the dream, the essence of him was felt more than seen, a steadfast presence that solidified through the ethereal haze. That anchoring feeling was then embraced and ignited by the curling flames of the dreamscape.

Not dangerous.

Not fear.

But they wanted to be known. To be seen and not flinch.

The spark pulsed.

When I woke up, my palm was warm.

Chapter Sixteen

Erindor

The cliffs fell away behind us.

We had descended from Stonespine Crossing in tense silence; the sun rising pale and uncertain through low clouds. A light frost still clung to the rocks in places, catching the morning light in sharp glints. Wildervale opened again below us in a vast hush. It was less jagged here, but no less strange.

The trail snaked deeper into a forest that predated the very mountains themselves, where ancient trees with trunks like weathered monuments stood in silent, watchful ranks, barked like cracked stone, and moss hung from their branches like faded banners. The air smelled of damp earth and crushed lichen, with a faint trace of old smoke that lingered low in the underbrush.

We walked with more precision today, keeping our voices hushed.

The mimics had shaken us more than anyone would say aloud. Jasira walked beside Wyn, steady but pale, still recovering from her sickness. Alaric led up front with Bran pacing ahead, ears alert. Gideon was behind him, though, looking back at the Princess and her friend more often than not. Tyren flanked us loosely. I took the rear.

It let me watch them.

Let me watch her.

Wyn had spoken little since we broke camp. But her eyes flicked to the tree line often, her fingers brushing the hilt of her dagger every so frequently, like she needed to be reminded it was there. I couldn't blame her. The memory of the river, raw and unforgiving, haunted her waking thoughts as it did mine. There was something about her walk today. It was more measured, cautious, and sure. She loosely braided her hair, and strands escaped, brushing the collar of her cloak with each step. She walked like someone waiting to be called back by something unseen but still choosing to move forward. It wasn't a strength I recognized in her initially. It was persistence. And I admired it more than I knew how to say.

She didn't look back at me, but I watched the way the sunlight struck her. The way animals moved slightly toward her. Bran lingered closer when she spoke. A sparrow had landed on her shoulder earlier and stayed there for a moment longer than made sense. Wildervale was paying attention to her.

And so was I.

It was midday when we decided to take a break. We found a clearing ringed with old stone pillars, worn down to stumps and lichen-crusted. Something about them felt purposeful. Some had fallen sideways or cracked in half, but a few still stood, leaning slightly as if bowed by time. Vines coiled at their bases, and faint carvings marked their surfaces: weathered spirals, sunbursts, and long-faded glyphs. The moss underfoot was thick and springy, and the filtered light fell in long gold shafts like columns, striking only the stones. It was a silence that felt like breath held.

The clearing felt inhabited by history. A place where the earth itself recalled names no longer spoken. The hush of moss and memory. The light slanted through the trees in shafts like columns, touching only the stone as if nature itself dared not intrude.

Tyren passed through the ring first and muttered, "Creepy place," under his breath. He didn't stop moving, but he gave the pillars a wide berth.

Unpacking was a silent ritual, each item placed with care, every offering food with a wordless acknowledgment. Wyn settled against the cool stone, carefully unrolling a small parcel of dried fruit, and Bran instinctively curled close, a silent testament to the fragile intimacy of the moment. I didn't sit. I couldn't.

My eyes stayed on the woods.

Eventually, Wyn rose and walked to me leisurely. "You haven't eaten."

"I'm not hungry."

She raised a brow and held out a slice of pear.

I shifted my weight for a moment, then took it. Our fingers brushed. Her touch didn't linger, but my awareness of it did.

"I've always wanted to come to Wildervale," she said softly. "It feels like the world's thinning."

I glanced around. "It is. The gods lived here once. Places like this, they remember."

She turned to look at me. "Do you?"

"Do I what?"

"Remember."

Her voice held no accusation, only a tender curiosity that frayed my defenses. The air became too thick, too revealing, and my gaze darted away, unable to meet hers.

"I remember the things that matter."

She stepped closer. "And what matters now?"

My jaw flexed. "Getting you to Caerthaine alive, Princess."

She didn't argue.

But she didn't leave either.

Beside me, she remained, a soft, insistent warmth that sparked both comfort and a frustrating ache for more. I felt a sensation of being both filled and left wanting more at the same time.

She wandered along the ring of ancient pillars. Her fingers brushed one and paused. "There's a mark here," she murmured.

I stepped forward. Someone had scorched a spiral into the face of the old and distinctive stone. The pillar itself leaned slightly toward the riverbank, its surface marred with soot and ancient fire scoring that had blackened the glyphs into ghostly relief. Moss and faint golden lichen framed the spiral, as though nature itself remembered its shape.

Wyn traced it lightly. "I read about this in one of the temple records," she spoke softly. "It's called the Flamebite Mark. Supposedly left by Vireya's chosen when they fled the god's wrath. It only appears before a death."

Her voice dropped lower, her fingers trembling against the scorched stone.

"I told no one I read Vireya's lore," she added. "People called it dangerous nonsense. Said I was wasting time with stories meant to frighten children. But the texts didn't feel like warnings. They felt like memories someone didn't want forgotten. I think she was the first to break. And everyone else called her dangerous because she didn't stay small."

My eyes widened, and my muscles suddenly locked, a stiffness seizing at my limbs.

I knew that mark. I'd seen it before. On a cliff. In fire. Burned beneath Riven's feet.

Smoke. Screams. Blood. Riven's eyes light with something not entirely human.

My grip on the hilt of my sword tightened.

"Where did you say you read that?" I asked too sharply.

She looked at me, startled. "A temple text in Elyrien. Why?"

I shook my head, forcing calm. "Doesn't matter."

But it did. Gods, it did. I stared at the spiral again, my stomach knotting. Knowing what this meant didn't require me to believe in every myth. I'd seen the mark appear before someone died. I'd seen it glow.

I looked at Wyn's face; earnest, curious, unaware. She didn't know any of it. She didn't understand what Riven was. What I used to be.

She turned back to the stone, thoughtful. "We weren't supposed to study Wildervale lore. They deemed it too speculative. But I always found myself drawn to it. The pieces scattered throughout the old temple archives felt like secrets left behind intentionally. Even after exile."

"You studied more than they intended you to? " I asked.

She gave me a small smile. "Books were easier to face than most people. And the gods…" She paused, searching the trees. "The gods never asked me to be anything I wasn't."

Something in me tugged at that. The way she said it. Like it meant more than she was letting on.

I said nothing for a long moment. Then, surprising myself, I muttered, "I never had access to temple texts. Or any library."

Wyn's gaze found mine, a bewildered crease appearing between her brows. "Never?" The word was a bare whisper, loaded with disbelief.

I shook my head. "I used to sneak to the edge of the scribe's hall in the city, to hear lessons. But I'd get kicked out. Too dirty. Wrong clothes. Wrong everything."

She didn't speak for a moment. Then, quietly, "I'm sorry."

"Don't be," I said. "You didn't build the walls. You walked through them."

We stood there in the hush of ancient stone and soft wind.

A breeze stirred, and a leaf caught in her hair. I reached forward before I thought twice and gently pulled it free.

She looked up, surprised, lips parting slightly. Her eyes locked on mine.

I opened my hand to show her the leaf, then let it drift away.

A beat of silence stretched between us, thick with unspoken things, before she finally uttered, "Goodnight."

Her voice was soft as dusk.

She turned and walked back toward the others.

I didn't follow.

My chest felt as though it was caught in an invisible vise, a suffocating grip of emotions too new and too potent to be easily labeled. Whatever left that mark, I thought, we'd be ready.

But I wasn't sure if I meant the gods or myself.

The more I watched her, the way she looked at the world, the way she touched it with courage, the more I wanted to believe in things I'd buried long ago.

The gods weren't what scared me.

It was the quiet ache of wanting something gentle.

It was hope.

And I didn't know how to survive that.

As the camp settled into quiet and the fire burned low, I noticed Gideon helping Jasira adjust her blanket. She grumbled something at him but didn't push him away. He nudged her flask toward her with the toe of his boot.

"Drink it. You'll sleep better."

"Only if you promise not to snore again."

Gideon grinned. "No promises."

Their banter was low but familiar. They seemed to fall into a rhythm of it effortlessly.

I turned slightly and caught Alaric watching me.

He raised an eyebrow and smirked. "I've seen you, you know. Careful," he murmured. "She's promised to another."

I grunted and turned away, jaw tight.

Alaric's tone softened. "Don't let your guard down, Erindor. You're here to keep her safe. That's all." He paused for a moment before uttering. "I'm sorry."

I nodded, but the words sat heavy.

Was I sure that's all I wanted to do?

Chapter Seventeen

Erindor

The Hollow Watcher's Glen was silent in the same way a grave was. Trees rose like petrified bones, their bark blackened and flaking with age, and their limbs tangled in a canopy so thick the daylight barely touched the ground. Fog moved across the soil in low sheets, curling around our boots like grasping hands. Every sound, every breath, every creak of leather seemed muffled. Swallowed.

The air was cold; this chill lived deeper, in the marrow. It clung to us like a second skin, heavy and wet. The scent of rot lingered beneath the moss and soil, as if something had died an extraordinarily long time ago and still remembered how to fester.

Everything in this place felt old, but not in a way that earned admiration. It was forgotten. Abandoned. Trees wept black resin like sap that had soured, and fungal growths bloomed pale and trembling along the trunks. Stones, half-buried and slick with slime, jutted like teeth from the ground. This was not a place where things lived. This was a place where things were forgotten to die.

We were in the dead heart of Wildervale now, where even the gods no longer looked. The center of the forest. The cursed middle.

The river had narrowed into a sluggish vein of dark water beside us, barely making a sound. Even our footsteps were too loud. Each one echoed back from the trees like a warning.

Wyn's steps faltered beside me. She whispered, "It feels like we're being watched."

I nodded. She wasn't wrong.

I raised my hand to signal for silence. Alaric came up behind me, his jaw was a hard line. "This forest swallows patrols whole," he muttered. Bran padded closer to his heels, growling low.

Gideon tried to lighten the mood. "Don't worry, Princess. If we're cursed, at least it's scenic."

Wyn didn't smile. Her knuckles whitened around her satchel. Tyren hummed softly, a shaky tune to fill the oppressive quiet.

Then everything exploded.

Shadows moved like water as creatures poured from the underbrush, sleek and wrong, like the forest had birthed nightmares.

Vorrhounds.

They emerged from the fog like phantoms, their bodies shifting in and out of focus. The edges were forever blurring, a ghost of form that writhed like mist but moved with the deliberate grace of something alive. Taller than wolves, thinner than panthers, their limbs moved with a boneless, slithering grace. Their hides were the color of coal, pulsing faintly with veins of red light like magma under cracked earth.

Their heads were narrow, eyeless, but glowing slits burned across their skulls like open wounds, and from the gaps in their ribcages, you could glimpse something writhing, like shadows alive inside them.

Worst of all were the sounds. They didn't bark. They whispered. A thousand voices rasped from their open jaws, some of them human, some of them not. Fragments of sentences. Names. Begging. Laughter. Screams from forgotten battles and lullabies sung in broken tones. Each word was a needle. Each whispers a memory.

Vorrhounds weren't beasts. But leftovers from something much older and crueler that had bled into Wildervale and never left.

The fog split, and one launched straight at Wyn.

I moved without thinking, throwing my body between her and the beast. My sword flashed in the dim light, meeting the Vorrhound mid-air with a jarring crash of bone and steel. We both hit the ground hard, rolling in the mud and leaves. Its claws raked across my shoulder, the heat sharp and hot. I growled, planting my boot against its ribs and kicking it away. My blade slashed across its throat, and black smoke hissed from the wound instead of blood.

Another howl tore through the mist. Tyren screamed and fought.

He raised his blade in time to parry the snap of one Vorrhound's jaws, its teeth clamping down on steel. He grunted, twisting and stabbing the creature through the side, smoke pouring from the wound. Another Vorrhound tackled him from behind. Tyren let out a roar, shoving the dying beast off and swinging again. He struck a third time, cutting deep into a flank, but he was tiring.

A third beast came.

It slammed him against a tree, claws raking across his chest. He bellowed in pain and tried to swing again, but the Vorrhound lunged low, jaws locking around his thigh and dragging him down.

A strangled shriek ripped from his throat, a sound filled with the desperate terror of a creature cornered and in agony.

The other Vorrhound returned and sank its teeth into his shoulder. Flesh tore. Blood sprayed across the moss in thick ropes. Tyren stabbed wildly, blade glancing off bone, but there were too many. One clawed into his stomach and ripped. He choked, breath gurgling with blood.

His last sound wasn't a scream; it was a gasp.

Then he went still.

"Form up!" Alaric roared. He and Bran surged forward. Bran tore into a Vorrhound's back leg with a snarl, dragging it down as Alaric's sword pierced straight into the hollow beneath its ribs. It howled, a burst of shrieking voices that sounded like a family screaming.

Jasira yanked Wyn behind a tree, hurling a dagger with fierce precision. It struck a Vorrhound in the eye-slit. It shrieked and writhed, smoke pouring from its maw. Another lunged at her. She rolled aside, her second blade sweeping low and biting into its hindquarters. Gore and smoke sprayed across the roots.

Wyn turned, breath ragged, in time to see another Vorrhound stalking Jasira. She leapt in front of her friend, dagger in hand, trembling. The creature lunged. She screamed and stabbed, meeting its hide, sliding off, but cutting enough to halt its momentum. Jasira rose and shoved the beast back with her shoulder.

The Vorrhound hissed, circling again.

Gideon roared as he charged, blood streaking down one arm, his blade raised. "Back off, you smoky bastard!" He slammed the blade into its spine. The Vorrhound convulsed, black limbs thrashing. "This is why I'm more of a cat person!"

Another Vorrhound broke from the trees and slammed into Alaric, who blocked the strike with his shield. Bran lunged up, tearing into its side, dragging the beast down. Alaric skewered it through its mouth, silencing its many voices at once.

I wheeled back into the fray, blade flashing. One Vorrhound lunged, and my sword caught it mid-throat, splitting it open in a gout of smoke and heat. Another lunged from behind. I pivoted, slashing deep through its shoulder and kicking it away. A third beast dove low, trying to flank me. I dodged, swept my blade across its belly, and watched it crumple.

I was breathing hard, blood coated my armor, but I didn't stop. Not while they were near her. Not while Wynessa was still in danger.

Then, claws ripped across my back.

I staggered, my sword knocked free. I collapsed beneath the weight of another Vorrhound. Its breath reeked of rot and sulfur. It pinned me down, its maw opening wide over my face.

Wyn saw.

And something in her broke.

"NO!"

Her voice cracked like thunder.

Light surged from her chest; brilliant, wild, alive. Not just fire, but something more profound. Elemental truth wrapped in gold.

It exploded out of her in a wave. There was no flame, no heat, but the memory of both. It shimmered like sunlight on armor, like truth made visible.

Every Vorrhound froze. The whispers stopped.

Then the light struck them.

The closest Vorrhound howled as its shadow-flesh peeled back like smoke torn by wind. Others burst apart mid-lunge, their ribcages splintering with the force of it. One tried to flee, but it dissolved in an instant as the light touched it. Wyn stood in the center, her eyes wide, her mouth parted in silent awe and terror. Her cloak whipped around her like agitated wings. Her frame trembled violently, the residual power of her summons rippling through her.

And then, as the danger had evaporated, the fire in her dimmed.

The light collapsed inward, returning to her chest with one final pulse— like a heartbeat.

She swayed, her eyes flickering, but I was already moving.

The moment her knees buckled, I was there, crossing the space between us in three fast strides, catching her before she hit the ground.

Her weight sagged into my arms, light and shaking. She was warm and still.

I cradled her gently, one hand behind her head, lowering her to the earth like she might shatter.

Her hands were ice, her face pale, but her eyes were wide.

She looked at me. "What…what did I just do?"

I couldn't answer. I didn't know.

So, I held her.

Alaric slowly approached, his expression guarded. "What the hell was that?"

"She saved us," Jasira said hoarsely. "Gods above…she saved us."

Gideon sat down hard on a log, rubbing his ribs. "If that's what she does when she's angry, I'll never flirt with her again."

I didn't laugh. I couldn't.

Because I was still staring at her. At the place where the light had come from.

The ground beneath seemed to tilt, a dizzying sensation of being out of control. *What was she now capable of?*

Alaric dropped beside Tyren's body, silent. Bran whined low beside him, pressing his muzzle to the torn leather of Tyren's boot. Wyn pressed her hand to her mouth, her eyes glassy. Gideon swore under his breath, rubbing his eyes. Jasira crouched nearby, tucking a torn bit of Tyren's cloak over his face.

He wasn't simply a guard. He'd been one of us.

"He used to sing when he stood watch," Jasira murmured. "Badly. But it helped me sleep."

"We should bury him," Wyn whispered. "He deserves more than to be left in this place."

Alaric stood, nodding grimly. "We'll do it right."

We dug as deep as we could into the damp earth. When we were done, Wyn placed a small bundle of herbs over the grave: sleepvine and bloodmoss. The same ones she used to help calm her dreams.

"We shouldn't forget him," she said. "Not here. Not like this."

"He won't be," I promised.

We stood in silence for a while. No one rushed to get moving. The moment hung like thick, unmoving fog. Bran let out a low whimper and nudged the dirt with his nose before returning to Alaric's side.

Wyn stood a little apart from the others, arms wrapped around herself, her breathing still unsteady. I moved toward her slowly. She didn't look up when I approached.

"Wyn," I said softly.

She turned to me, her eyes rimmed with unshed tears. Her face was pale, though a faint glow still lingered on her skin. Her hands were trembling.

"I didn't mean to—" she began, her voice cracked.

"I know," I said. "It wasn't your fault. You saved us."

She shook her head. "But it felt like I became something else. Like I wasn't myself."

I reached out and placed a hand on her shoulder. "You were more yourself than I've ever seen."

Her gaze, wide and startled, shot up to meet mine. The words, soft and trembling, were barely audible. "I'm scared," she whimpered.

"I know."

The silence between us pulsed with warmth, and was alive with something that neither of us could name. I could still feel the echo of the fire she'd unleashed deep inside myself as if part of her had reached into the hollow places inside me and lit a spark there.

"I'm here," I said. "You're not alone, Princess."

Her eyes brimmed again, but she nodded. "Thank you."

And for a moment, she leaned against me, the weight of her fear and fire settling into the space between our hearts.

It was a welcoming comfort.

Chapter Eighteen

Wynessa

The Vorrhounds haunted my thoughts. Their snarling mouths, the way they moved like smoke, like nightmares, stitched to the shadows. I still heard their echoing cries and the memory of Erindor falling. My scream. Forcing something else to take over.

A light. A golden blaze not born from firewood or spell. It had burst from me like a heartbeat—warm, immense, and terrifying. But it had driven them away, saving us.

But what was it?

I glanced at my hands, they were pale and trembling in the morning light. They looked like they always had, but I no longer trusted them. That light hadn't burned me, but instead, empowered me. Jasira sat beside me now, carefully rinsing the blood from my fingers with water from a canteen. Her own hands were shaking.

"They would've killed us all if you hadn't. Whatever that was, it saved us."

I stared at the minor cuts along my knuckles. "But it didn't save Tyren."

Jasira stilled. I could feel her pause, see her mouth open and close like she wanted to deny it, but couldn't.

"You didn't know it would happen," she said softly.

"But what if I had? What if I could've done something sooner? Maybe if I'd felt it earlier, or—"

"Wyn."

Her voice was firmer now. She took the cloth and gently pressed it to my palm.

"You don't get to blame yourself for not knowing how to be a miracle."

My eyes met hers, my voice, raw with a confession barely understood, fractured. "It came from inside me, Jasi. That power wasn't something I cast or conjured. It was there somehow. Waiting. Watching. I don't know what it means."

Jasira's eyes searched mine. "I don't either. But I know this—when the world gave you something terrifying, you used it to protect us. Not yourself. Us. That's what matters."

My throat closed. I wanted to believe her. I wanted to believe I hadn't failed. A constriction seized my throat, making it difficult to swallow past the sudden lump. Every fiber yearned to trust the words, to banish the gnawing fear that I had not failed.

A tremor ran through my hand as I wiped at my face, attempting to scrub away the sickening emptiness that filled them. Every breath felt shallow, the heart aching with a regret that whispered, "I wish it hadn't come too late."

Jasira said nothing for a moment. Then she reached out and took my hand in hers, steady and warm.

"Then use it now. Use it to keep the rest of us alive. That's what Tyren would've wanted."

Across the camp, the silence was brittle.

Gideon paced near the fire, muttering under his breath. "Didn't even see it coming. One blink, and he was gone."

Alaric sat nearby, sharpening his blade with steady, violent strokes, the motion too fast, too harsh, his knuckles white around the hilt.

No one responded. There was nothing to say.

Jasira stood and trudged back toward her bedroll, but not before exchanging a glance with Erindor. They both knew I was different now, something more.

That night, as the last light faded, and we made camp in the haunting forest, the sky came alive.

I found Erindor standing at the edge of the camp, alone on the cliff's edge, watching the night like it might crumble.

Veilfire.

It began with a small shimmer. The stars blinked out, one by one, veiled by something brighter. Curtains of light unfurled from the heavens in undulating waves—violet, crimson, gold. It was something old and holy. It twisted and flowed like ink dropped into water, painting the sky in colors that didn't belong to the world of men.

I had read about it once in an ancient text with pages that crackled at the touch—Veilfire, the ghostlight of the gods. They say it appears only when someone has awakened a divine tether, when the realm beyond ours leans too close.

It was beautiful. But it also terrified me.

The trees stood still beneath it, every branch silver-edged in its glow. The wind didn't move. Even the fire in our camp dimmed, as if bowing to a more ancient flame. I stood, feet fixed firmly to the ground, watching the sky breathe.

Something inside me responded, a thread pulled tight, a presence stirring beneath my ribs. I felt seen by something otherworldly and vast.

Erindor said nothing when it appeared. Even when the strange light painted his shirtless back with violet fire. He was crouched in silence, shadows moving down the muscles of his back like something sacred. His body was marred, yet he had beautiful, broad shoulders that tapered into lean muscles and long scars. I shouldn't have stared, but I did.

I knelt behind him and unwrapped a clean bandage, then unscrewed the lid of the salve I'd made that afternoon. "Let me," I said softly.

He didn't respond, but he didn't stop me either.

I gently peeled back the bloodstained wrapping. His back tensed under my hands. The old scar stretched white and smooth, like lightning carved across the skin, but the fresh wound from the Vorrhound was angry, deep, with edges that were red and hot to touch. I cleaned it carefully, then dabbed the salve over the worst of it.

He hissed softly. "You don't have to do that."

"I want to."

Stillness lingered. Then, quietly: "You've got a terrible habit of looking after people who don't deserve it."

"You've got a terrible habit of believing you don't."

A new kind of silence unfurled, deeper than before, filled with an awareness that hummed in the air.

My eyes were drawn to him. I reached out gently, my fingers dislodging a leaf tangled in his dark silk hair.

He turned toward me, shadows flickering across his face.

"Your scar…" I said softly. "How did you get it?"

At first, I thought he wouldn't answer. The moment his eyes truly met mine, a jolt went through me. He didn't just see the surface; his eyes delved deeper, and under that relentless scrutiny, the carefully constructed walls around his heart seemed to tremble, threatening to crumble.

"I was ten," he whispered. "The raider. The one who slaughtered my mother in front of me. I didn't even think after she fell. After I was too late. I picked up a kitchen knife and put it to his throat. Not before he nicked me with his sword. That was the day I stopped being a child. The sword came first after that. Always."

The familiar ache of held-back tears prickled in my throat.

"You are more than a sword, Erindor. I see it every day."

He didn't look at me. But he didn't move away when I touched his shoulder again.

My hand lingered, fingertips brushing the edge of the scar. I watched the muscles shift beneath his skin, the subtle rise and fall of his breath.

The Veilfire above cast shifting color over his face, reds and violets bleeding into gold. I watched him through my lashes, heart stuttering. A strange silence pulsed between us.

He glanced at me then, shadows in his eyes. "You're staring."

My eyes, unwilling to linger, darted away as a wave of heat washed over my face. "Sorry. I…I've seen nothing like that scar. Or…you. Like this."

"Like what?"

"Human," I whispered.

He blinked. "Most days I forget I am."

I shook my head. "You're more human than anyone I've ever met. You're just buried under armor."

His voice dropped. "And you see through it?"

"Sometimes," I admitted. "Not always. But when I do, I like what I find."

He inclined his head, his eyes, dark pools of unknown depths, finding mine. My hand remained, a silent anchor, fingers tracing the ridges above his scar. Every breath brought a new awareness of him: the sharp tang of pine, the subtle metallic hint of steel, and, most powerfully, his inherent, captivating warmth.

"If you keep touching me like that, Princess..." he said, voice husky, "...I might forget I'm not allowed to want you."

And for the briefest second, I felt it again.

A flicker of heat deep in my chest. Not like blush or embarrassment, but something steady. Quiet. A warmth that unfurled beneath my ribs like the hush before a storm. My fingers twitched where they touched him, and from the corner of my eye, the mark on my forearm pulsed faintly; gold, soft, and gone again.

I sucked in a breath. No one else saw.

Did he feel it too?

A sudden chill seized me, freezing me in place. My lungs refused to draw air, and the fingers recoiled as if burned. My eyes flew to him, then the sky, then anywhere but his mouth.

Heat rushed to my face like fire beneath my skin, my pounding heart echoing in my ears. He looked so solid beside me, so strong, wounded, and real. It wasn't fair that he made me feel unsteady by breathing.

Then he blinked hard, the spell breaking. "Sorry," he said quickly, looking away. "I didn't mean—That wasn't—gods, that came out wrong."

"No, I—" I stammered. "I just—I wasn't expecting—"

He ran a hand through his hair, turning further from me, clearly flustered. "Forget I said anything."

But I couldn't.

He stood and stepped away from the ledge, posture stiff. I caught one last glimpse of the scar trailing down his back before the shadows swallowed him.

And I stayed where I was, the light of the Veilfire catching in my eyes, wondering what it was I had awakened inside myself.

What exactly had he awakened in me?

I drew my knees to my chest, curling under the shadow of a half-fallen pine, the veilfire flickering through the gaps above me. A dormant part of me ignited, a vibrant spark of life that hadn't burned so brightly in years, or perhaps ever. I had spent my whole life within stone walls. Being quiet. Proper. Small. Measured in silks and curtsies, in whispered obligations and words I never said aloud. I'd once watched a noblewoman scold a servant for crying and been told, "Feelings are for peasants."

I practiced curtsies while dreaming of running barefoot through trees; something that now feels so close, so true.

But out here, in the dirt and ash and sacred flames, I was louder. Wilder. Real.

And I realized I didn't want to go back to who I had been.

Not if it meant losing who I was becoming.

So, I stayed curled in the quiet hush of the flame-streaked sky, the mark on my arm still warm, as I whispered to the night, *"Please...let this be real."*

Chapter Nineteen

Wynessa

The forest widened into a yawning canyon, its smooth boulders draped in moss and dappled with gold-touched mist. Wind whispered low between the stone crevices, weaving a melody that tugged at my bones. Jasira called it the Singing Stones.

We weren't camping again; we were pausing for a rest, though no one said as much. The path ahead still sloped down into the canyon's belly, but the way behind was too steep to climb back. The Vorrhounds and Mimics were gone, but the memories still stalked me. Every shadow held a shape. Every breeze felt like a breath on my neck. The air, though fresh, still carried the weight of something watching, as if the new land we'd trampled on had not yet decided if we were welcome.

Tension hummed within our group like a second wind song. Gideon muttered under his breath about cursed echoes and ghost rocks. Jasira busied herself with her tea satchel, but her hands trembled when she thought no one was watching. Even Bran growled low at nothing. We were all on edge, and the Singing Stones seemed to listen.

Alaric inspected the perimeter with half-tired caution, reinforcing what little defense we could manage. Erindor was on the river's edge, cleaning his hands in the water.

I watched him from the shadows of the canyon wall. He didn't move with the usual tension he carried, didn't pace or glare into the trees. Instead, he knelt by a patch of wild thistle near the bank, fingers brushing the petals without picking them. For a man who could end a life with one blow, he was oddly gentle with small, defenseless things.

I needed space. Air. Silence. Something else.

So, I wandered.

Alone, I followed a narrow ledge deeper into the canyon, where moss softened the stone, and the wind's song grew louder, humming like a lullaby beneath my skin. The ground felt alive, every footfall stirring echoes not from rock but from somewhere deeper, older. People didn't name the Singing Stones simply for their sound. They were a place of memory, and beneath our feet, the ground thrummed with a resonance of long-gone footsteps.

Suddenly, a jagged edge of the landscape revealed a sight that stopped me in my tracks. It was a boulder torn in half, its face carved with strange fire-marked symbols. They shimmered faintly, like the last embers of a dying flame. The shapes were not of any language I knew. More like memories burned into the rock, etched by a hand that didn't need tools.

I held my breath as I reached out.

The surface pulsed warm under my palm.

A flicker of light danced at my fingertips, a golden flame, delicate as lace. It curled and vanished. A frantic rhythm began, as if a blacksmith was suddenly at work within my chest, striking steel with each pounding beat.

Then I noticed another stone nearby, smaller and weathered by time but unmistakably carved with the image of a fox. The lines were simple yet elegant; its eyes were formed from smooth insets of glinting amber. It sat as if waiting, its tail curled, its head tilted toward the canyon's deeper reaches.

The divine messenger.

I crouched and traced the image with my fingers, awed with quiet wonder.

Had it been following me? Or was I following it? I didn't know. But something about the way its image lingered here, carved into stone as old as the gods, made my pulse stutter. This was no mere coincidence; foxes never appeared twice without a purpose, especially not like this. I sensed movement behind me, familiar. The hair on the back of my neck didn't rise, and something in my chest settled.

"Alaric?" I called softly over my shoulder.

He appeared moments later, arms crossed, gaze already on the stone. "You found it, too."

"I've seen the fox before," I whispered. "Near the glade. And now here."

He nodded. "It's one of the oldest symbols left behind. Some say the fox is the one who guided the chosen to safety when the gods fell to war. Others believe it's the only creature the fire goddess feared. Too clever to be caught and too quick to be burned."

"What's it doing here?"

"Watching," he said simply. "Maybe waiting."

He closed the distance between us, his hand a warm weight on my shoulder. His voice dropped to a conspiratorial whisper, saying, "They say the canyon remembers old powers. People come here to seek answers, but it gives them riddles."

"What riddles?" I asked.

"Questions that sound like answers. Echoes that feel like your own voice." He stepped closer, his face solemn. "They say this place, the Singing Stones, is one of the oldest remnants of the gods' first breath. Before they fractured and fled. Before Vireya scorched the world. Some say the ancestors come here to listen. Or to wait."

I glanced down at the fox again, its eyes glinting in the canyon light.

"Did they love each other, our parents?" I asked softly.

His eyes fluttered open, a momentary confusion clouding his features. The unexpected question seemed to catch in his throat, and after a beat, a soft, almost reluctant 'Yes' emerged. "In their own way. Duty bounds them, but I remember the way Father looked at Mother when she wasn't watching. Like he'd die before letting her fall. That kind of love doesn't need poems. Even if she is terribly strict."

I smiled a little; the memory softening my chest. "You were always good at sneaking me things when Mother was cross. Do you remember when she locked me out of the library wing?"

Alaric grinned. "You mean the time she found you reading that scandalous romance hidden in a history tome?"

"I was studying!" I protested.

"With characters named after herbs and kissing behind waterfalls?"

Heat rushed to my cheeks. I let out a laugh and immediately buried my face in my hands. "Oh gods. Stop. I'm never going to live that down, am I?"

Alaric chuckled harder, and I peeked at him through my fingers, still blushing.

He laughed, heartily and genuinely. "I snuck you pastries that night, remember? Hid them behind the curtains so she wouldn't see. And that book."

"You did," I said warmly. "You always looked out for me."

"I still do and always will." He grew quiet again. "Even when you scare me half to death."

We sat in silence after that. The kind that settles between two people who don't need to fill every space with sound.

"Do you think…do you think the prince and I will fall in love?"

Alaric didn't answer right away. "I think you could. But only if he earns it."

"And if I don't?"

"Then don't pretend you did, Wynnie."

I looked down at the ground, twiddling my fingers. "And what if I already feel something for someone else?"

He looked at me carefully. "Then be careful. And be honest with yourself first. You've always had a soft heart, but that doesn't mean it's fragile."

I looked up at him, searching his face.

"Alaric," I said, twisting my hands together, "have you ever been in love?"

He raised a brow, smirking. "What, now you're asking the older brother for romance advice?"

"Be serious," I pleaded.

Something shifted in his expression. The teasing fell away.

He sighed. "No. Not yet. But I'd like to be one day."

I tilted my head. "How will you know?"

He looked back at the canyon. "When I choose them over purpose. Over duty. In every life. That's how I'll know."

"What if love makes me lose control? What if I'm dangerous?" I whispered. I wasn't sure I wanted to say the thought aloud until I already had.

Alaric stepped even closer and pulled me into a gentle yet firm embrace. He kissed the top of my forehead. "You're not dangerous, Wyn. You're the only one of us brave enough to feel everything fully."

The light thinned as we walked back to camp together. When we arrived, Alaric glanced at the group huddled around the fire and smiled sideways at me.

"Do you want me to play you something? Like when we were little?"

My eyes widened. "You still remember the lullabies?"

He gave a mock gasp of offense. "Wynnie. Please. I'm a man of many talents." He grinned, putting his hand across his chest.

He pulled out his lute and strummed softly. The moment the tune started, everyone groaned.

"Oh no, not this again," Jasira muttered.

Gideon groaned dramatically, flinging himself backward. "Have mercy!"

Then he lobbed a small stick at Alaric's head.

Alaric ducked and pointed the lute at him like a weapon. "Ungrateful! All of you!"

I burst out laughing, warm and genuine.

Erindor, sharpening his blade a short distance from the others, let out a long breath through his nose. He didn't look up, but the movement of his hand slowed for a moment.

"Of course," he muttered to himself. "The lute."

But when Alaric struck a softer note, the kind that lingered in the air like a memory, Erindor's sharpening resumed, rhythmic and steady. As if he were pretending he wasn't listening to every note.

The wind whispered and sighed through the canyon, winding between stone teeth and hollow chimes. The song that rose was soft, haunting, and somehow familiar. I felt it in my ribs, in my spine, like a memory I hadn't lived yet. My voice seemed to echo inside the hum.

One must give it freely.

One must believe it.

I curled tighter in my blankets, the warmth in my palm pulsing once more before fading. In my dreams, the golden fire returned, not to burn but to bloom. Like a promise. Like a choice.

And for the first time, I wasn't running from it. I was walking toward it, even if I stumbled.

Chapter Twenty

Erindor

Suddenly, we stepped forward and the forest changed.

One moment, the trees still bore the last bruises of winter. Next, we entered a silence so profound, it seemed to actively swallow the air, leaving a strange pressure in its wake. Even our boots seemed hesitant to disturb the moss-padded ground.

The trees here were different; stripped of bark and color, trunks as pale as old ash and smooth as bone. Their branches twisted skyward like brittle fingers. Light filtered through them in a sickly, washed-out haze. The air felt thinner. Pressed.

Gideon slowed his pace, muttering something under his breath.

"What is this place?" Jasira asked quietly, eyes scanning the skeletal canopy.

"The Bone Orchard," he said after a pause. "Or so the maps call it."

Alaric turned. "That does not give me any comfort."

Gideon didn't smile. "It's not meant to be. Locals claim that a great battle took place here during the Forgotten Wars. Thousands fell, but no one buried them. The war moved on, and they left the dead behind."

He studied the trees.

"They say the roots drank deep. Took the flesh, the blood, the memory. That's why the trees grow so pale. Like they're full of ghosts."

Jasira shivered. "That's a bit morbid."

"That's Wildervale," I muttered.

The name fits. There was something wrong with this place. Not in the way of traps or predators, but in how everything still was, like the forest had gone hollow. Waiting for something to return.

Wyn said nothing. She slid between the bleached trunks, her hair swaying gently as she walked ahead of the group. I only wished I could read her expression.

I'd been watching her more closely since the light.

Something was changing in her. Untouchable almost. Like the gods had taken notice, and now she belonged to them more than to us.

Alaric veered off to scout the path ahead with Bran. Gideon stayed near Jasira. I lingered a few paces behind Wyn, keeping my hand on my blade even though nothing stirred.

She dropped to her knees suddenly, fingers brushing the moss near the base of one of the taller trees.

"What is it?" I asked, stepping closer.

A line creased her brow as she exhumed a glint of metal from the moss. It wasn't lost debris or a forgotten trinket; instead, it was a pendant. Elegant in its simplicity, shaped like a teardrop of blackened silver, cool and ancient. The chain had long since worn thin, but the pendant itself gleamed faintly despite the misty light.

On its surface, spun in lines so delicate they seemed to shimmer, was a wildflower whose petals curled upward like flames.

She turned it over in her palm. "It's warm," she whispered, raising her eyebrows.

I stepped forward, drawn inexplicably toward it. Like I'd seen it before in a dream I hadn't known was mine.

She startled when I reached for it and let it fall into the moss. I crouched and picked it up. The warmth wasn't sunlight—it was deeper. Like breath caught in metal. Like something old, and grieving, and waiting.

A sudden surge of adrenaline made the blood rush through my veins.

Cireth. A name rose in my thoughts like a whisper, unbidden.

I didn't know how or why, but this piece of the past had been waiting for me.

Wyn stepped back, her voice shaky. "It sees us."

I looked at the pendant in my palm, the faint warmth pulsing through the metal like a second heartbeat.

"No," I said softly. "It remembers us."

Her eyes blinked open in a flash of surprise.

I couldn't explain it, but I sensed it. The pendant wasn't just reacting to her. It had been waiting for me, too, sent here like a thread in a story we hadn't told. The thread only made sense when the two pieces came together.

When flame met earth. When memory found purpose.

Her eyes flickered, but she said nothing more. She just watched my hand, where the pendant rested.

And though I was unsure why, I already knew its intended use.

Not as a weapon. Not even as a ward.

As a promise.

I slid the pendant into my satchel before I could think twice.

We moved on in silence, but the Bone Orchard felt different now. It had seen us and chosen not to interfere.

Far behind us, underneath the twisted roots and whispers of long-dead memory, an ancient power continued to radiate a faint, unsettling glow.

We collapsed into camp, most of us seeing proper rest as a distant, forgotten luxury. The campfire remained unlit, a flickering hearth of comfort denied. The weary silence between us was unbroken, each of us lost in our own shadowed thoughts.

The bone-white trees stood like silent sentinels, and no one dared speak above a whisper. Even the breeze here was brittle, threatening to shatter if we moved too quickly.

The ground was too hard for proper tents, and too soft for comfort; slick with moss and brittle roots. Gideon muttered while unrolling his blanket, calling the place "cursed deadwood" and giving every pale tree a sideways glance like it might breathe.

Wyn sat beneath the tree with her knees drawn up, staring into the distance. The last rays of the sun skimmed the edge of her hair, making it glow faintly gold against the sickly white backdrop. She possessed an otherworldly beauty, seemingly crafted from a dream, delicate yet vibrant with suppressed energy. I touched the pendant nestled in my pocket.

It was still warm.

Then I turned my attention back to camp.

"What the hell are you doing?" Alaric's voice came low but sharp, breaking the silence like a splinter under the skin.

I looked up to see him marching over, his jaw a rigid line. "You didn't scout the ridge like we agreed," he snipped. "We were able to push farther today, to make it past the orchard. Instead, we're wasting time."

"We're resting," I replied evenly, standing with my arms crossed. "You think your sister can keep walking on sheer will alone?"

His eyes flicked to Wyn. "She's stronger than you think."

Alaric's jaw clenched, a muscle twitching near his temple

"You're not her commander, Erindor," he said. "You're her guard."

"And you're not a general," I snapped back. "You're a prince with no map and too much pride. I've crossed this stretch twice before; you haven't. You want to run us into a trap? Be my guest, but don't pretend you know this land."

Alaric took a half-step closer, closing in on my face. But I didn't move.

"Don't forget your place," he hissed.

I met his stare. "I haven't. I just know when to speak, and when I should keep my mouth shut."

He opened his mouth to respond, but I interrupted him before he could say anything further.

"Wyn's doing her best, but she's not trained for this. She's exhausted, and it's showing—she hasn't said a word in an hour, and she's barely keeping pace. And Jasira just recovered from being sick. You want to run us harder, that's fine, but know who you're running with."

"Enough," Jasira's voice broke in. She stood with her arms crossed, glaring at both of us. "You two want to swing your egos around, do it when we're not sleeping next to death trees, alright?"

Alaric exhaled hard through his nose and stomped away in the opposite direction.

I didn't follow.

Instead, I sat down on the edge of the clearing, back against a pale root.

Alaric's words pressed on my chest. Not because he was right, but because I hated that it was coming to this. With every step we took away from the palace, civility frayed. We were unraveling slowly but surely.

The pendant was still in my palm, faintly pulsing. I stared at it in the dying light.

And yet, it had drawn me to it.

What is happening to you, Wynessa?

The fire, animals, and dreams. Her eyes seemed to glow when she forgot anyone was watching. The way the Veilfire had flickered when she stood beneath. The burden would have crushed most, let alone her, yet she carried it with a quiet fortitude, possessing a grace for which there seemed no name. And I had absolutely no idea how to protect her from it.

I closed my eyes and the slow breath of the forest filled the silence again. Instead of the usual sound of wind, it was replaced with voices pressed between bark, as if it were waiting for a name.

Something ancient, possibly.

And *her*. Right in the middle of it all.

I looked over at the small pouch tied to my belt. Inside, the frostbloom that she'd given me days ago remained pressed between folds of cloth. I hadn't looked at it since. Now I opened it slowly, letting the folded petals catch the pale light. Even wilted, it was still beautiful. For a long moment, I stared at it, feeling the tightness in my chest ease, not gone, but quieter. I closed the pouch gently and patted it once,

Darkness descended, heavy and absolute, swallowing the sky without a single star.

We took shifts through the night. Gideon paced the edges of the grove like a caged beast. Alaric sat apart from the group, arms crossed over his chest, eyes fixed on nothing, Bran at his side. Even Jasira had grown quiet, rubbing her thumb in circles over a worn pendant of her own, not magical, just a treasured gift her mother had given her.

And Wyn lay with her back to the group, curled beneath her cloak like a question that hadn't yet found its words.

I wanted to say something. Just to her. To tell her again that she wasn't alone in whatever was happening to her, that I, too, felt the shifting ground beneath my feet.

But the words stayed where they always did, buried beneath duty, beneath doubt. So, I stayed near. Not beside her, but within a heartbeat's reach, ready to respond should she stir.

I was close enough to hear when she cried out.

A fragile breath, barely audible, escaped her lips, but I was on my feet before she moved again. Her sleeping face was etched with a deep furrow in her brow, her limbs tense. Her lips moved as if she were whispering to an unseen entity.

Then: a full-body jolt, and a scream.

She bolted upright, gasping, hair clinging to her face, eyes wide with fire and fear.

I was at her side.

In the dark, her hands scrambled aimlessly for something. Her skin glowed faintly in the moonlight, with sweat and fear. Her eyes didn't see me at first. They saw something else. Something far away.

"Wyn." I kept my voice low. Gentle. "It's alright. You're safe."

She blinked rapidly, then focused on me. "Erindor?" Her voice quavered, each word thin and unsteady.

"I'm here," I said, crouching down closer to her. "You're alright."

"No," she breathed, gripping her cloak like it might fly from her shoulders. "I saw…gods, I saw fire. A throne of flames. And a crown that was black and burning. It—it was on my head, Erindor."

Her final words shattered into a raw sound in her throat. She wrenched her head, as though trying to erase what she'd just recalled. One hand clamped onto her temple. My hand hovered over her shoulder, unsure, then settled gently. She didn't flinch. "You were dreaming."

"It didn't feel like a dream." Her voice was small now.

We sat in silence, while the others were still sleeping. I brushed a strand of damp hair from her face, letting my knuckles linger a fraction of a second longer than I should have. "You don't have to face any of this alone, you know."

Her eyes met mine, wide with fear. "I don't know what's happening to me," she whispered. "The fire, the mark, the animals. And now this? A crown made of ash? What does it mean?"

I hesitated before answering her. Not because I didn't believe her, but because I had no answers. Only worry and a gut-wound ache that deepened every time she looked scared.

"I don't know," I said at last. "But I believe you."

A moment passed between us, quiet and threaded with something unspoken. I let it settle, didn't run from it. Didn't lean into it either. I was too good at walls for that.

Wyn's breathing slowed. Her shoulders slumped, losing their stiff posture.

"Will you stay here for a while?" she asked. "Until I fall asleep again."

"I'm not going anywhere," I murmured.

She shifted slightly, then leaned into me, resting her head against my shoulder.

The contact was gentle. Natural. But it sent something sharp and indefinable straight through my chest.

I stayed still, barely daring to breathe, afraid I might ruin it somehow. Her warmth soaked through my sleeve. Her hair smelled like rain and crushed herbs.

She was asleep within minutes.

I stayed by her side long after her eyes closed, watching the moonlight shift across her face. She looked peaceful. Touched with fear but resting now despite it.

And gods help me, I didn't want to move.

The silence was absolute; the grove stood breathless, every rustle hushed.

Wyn stirred beside me, her forehead knitted, with a visible sign of her concern, but she hadn't cried out again. No more whispers, no more visions, simply the steady rise and fall of her chest beneath her cloak. I stood before her, brushing dirt from my knees and quietly tucking the pendant back into my belt.

Around camp, the others emerged from restless half-sleep. Gideon muttered about curses and morning stiffness, his jokes thin and brittle. Jasira brewed tea with fingers still pink from the cold. Bran pawed at the dirt, agitated. The bone-pale trees cast long shadows, and none of us spoke much.

Alaric paced. He always paced when he didn't want to show how shaken he was.

"We should have crossed the river," he said eventually, not looking at me. "Back where the bridge collapsed."

I didn't argue. He wasn't wrong. We should have. Yet, a chilling unease clung to the river, whispering of a price far greater than any toll. "We'll make better time today," I said instead. "There's an open trail ahead. If we keep east, we'll clear the ridge before nightfall."

Suddenly, Wyn woke up, rising with her cloak wrapped tightly around her, eyes shaded but steady.

"I'm ready," she declared, her voice firm and unwavering.

We moved as one, boots crunching over brittle moss, breath steaming in the cold. No one looked back at the trees. In the Bone Orchard, there were no farewells.

Chapter Twenty-One

Wynessa

We continued through the Bone Orchard, but the forest was no longer familiar. It had shifted, taking on a new, unsettling aura than the last.

Where once the trees grew tall and skeletal, here, they curled inwards, their gnarled trunks and branches fusing into a grotesque, organic dome. Above, the sky was a distant rumor, barely visible through the choked foliage. The path ahead was not merely overgrown; it was entombed beneath a writhing mass of thorn-laced vines that pierced the ground like insistent claws.

"It's called the Thorn Maze," Gideon rasped, a tight grimace pulling his lips into a thin line. "Not exactly subtle."

I glanced at Erindor, clearly chafing under the unwanted burden of leading the way.

"Alaric insisted," he muttered, arms crossed. "Said we'd make better time if we cut through instead of circling the ridge."

At that, Alaric, already sweating, shrugged dramatically. "And I still say we could. Unless you'd like to climb back up that hill we just slid down on our backsides."

"It's cursed," Jasira said, voice flat.

"It's efficient," Alaric replied with a mock cheer.

Erindor studied him.

Alaric grinned. But no one else laughed.

The silence was heavy, broken only by the creak of thorns shifting in the breeze.

"I've heard stories," Gideon muttered, staring at the curling vines. "Which say someone summoned this maze instead of growing it. Ages ago, a priestess of Vireya built it to catch souls. To give them to the flame." He glanced at me briefly, then turned away.

Jasira crossed her arms. "Fantastic. A soul-trapping hedge maze."

"It's not just thorns," Gideon added. "It pulls memories. Feelings. If you've got something buried inside, it'll find it."

We stood silently for a moment.

"I still believe we could get there faster," Alaric said again, with less confidence.

We all knew this was a bad idea, but no one wanted to argue anymore. The days had worn us down. Our group moved like tired ghosts now; wary, bruised, and half-afraid to hope for peace.

I hesitated at the threshold. The vines covered not only the ground; they arched above us, forming a dense tunnel. A maze made not of hedges but of bramble, ancient and unnatural. Somewhere within, I thought I heard something moving.

"Stay close," Erindor said quietly, adjusting his grip on his blade.

I fell beside him. "You don't think this is a terrible idea?"

He glanced at me, almost as if apologetic. "Every idea has been terrible lately."

And so, we stepped in.

We walked single file, since the path was too narrow for anything else. The thorn walls rose high on either side, woven too tightly to see through, too jagged to force our way back. The brambles pulsed faintly green, and the leaves didn't rustle like normal ones; they hissed.

The further we went, the more unsettling it felt.

The air grew thick, sticking to the back of my throat like smoke. Light filtered oddly here, bending at strange angles as if the maze itself didn't follow the rules of the sun. Sometimes the light came from above. Sometimes it seemed to come from the ground.

A curve. Then another. The turns came too frequently, too sharply. There were no landmarks. No sky. No birdsong. Only the wet scrape of boots, the breath, and the hissing of leaves.

The thorns didn't stay still. They shifted. Not enough to notice right away, but I felt it in my bones—the way they leaned inward, the way they seemed to breathe. Roots curled shyly away from our feet. Vines moved along the walls like veins.

The quiet around us felt both sacred and cursed. We should have only been walking for minutes, but my throat was already dry, and sweat coated my back. Time didn't seem real here, as if something had swallowed it.

That was the moment I heard my name.

"Wynessa…"

I froze, a primal instinct locking me into place as my heart hammered a frantic rhythm. "Did someone say something?"

Erindor, ahead, turned his head slightly. "No one's talking."

I shook my head, forcing a laugh that barely escaped. "Must've been the wind."

Alaric, farther ahead, muttered something, but I didn't catch it. Another bend in the path and—

A faint, dry scraping sound heralded the movement of the thorns. It was subtle, almost elegant. A whisper of motion that shouldn't have been possible. The vines on either side of me twisted inward, knitting together like closing eyes. The way behind me sealed in seconds, then the space ahead constricted too, cutting me off. Isolating me.

"Alaric?" I called, stepping forward. "Erindor? Jasira?"

Nothing.

Then, muffled: "Wyn!"

Erindor's voice, faint through the hedge.

"I'm here! I'm—It closed! The path closed!"

"Stay right there! We're coming to find you!"

I stepped toward the wall of thorns that had separated us and pressed a trembling hand against it. It pulsed faintly beneath my palm, like it had a heartbeat of its own.

"Don't move!" Alaric's voice now, distant but urgent. "Wyn, just—keep talking. We're close."

I opened my mouth to speak, to answer, but the hedge rustled violently, and their voices vanished.

The silence was absolute, the kind that pressed against your ears and made you hear your own blood moving. My pulse was too loud. Too fast.

I spun in a circle. The path behind me was gone. Only thorns remained.

I took a shaky breath. My heartbeat thundered in my chest. My palms were sweaty, and my knees felt weak. I had never felt so utterly skin-pricklingly alone.

Then the voices started.

"You'll break them."

My stomach clenched and twisted as I spun around in circles, trying to catch the voice.

A new one, this time far colder and familiar in the worst way. My mother.

"Softness is a liability, child. You were born wrong for a crown."

"No," I whispered. "You're not here."

"You can't even lift a sword without trembling."

"You'll lose them all."

"No," I yelled.

"You'll die, along with everyone else."

I pressed my hands to my ears, but it was as if the voices came from inside my bones. They vibrated in my ribs, behind my eyes.

"You're pathetic."

"You don't deserve the crown."

"He won't ever love you. He won't ever feel for you."

A dozen whispers now, overlapping fragments of fear, pieces of old doubts. My mind spun. I staggered forward and tripped, hitting the mossy path on my hands and knees.

Tears stung my eyes, and my chest was rising and falling rapidly. I couldn't breathe. My throat clenched like a fist. My thoughts raced—panicked, chaotic, sharp-edged. I wasn't enough. I'd never be enough. What if they were right? What if I wasn't meant for all of this?

"I don't know who I am anymore," I whispered, the words trembling from my lips like a secret I'd never dared say aloud.

Then a fresh voice broke through, rough and achingly kind.

"You don't have to be sure. Keep going."

It was Erindor's voice.

But it couldn't be. He wasn't here. It was only what I wanted to hear.

Still, my heart held onto it.

I closed my eyes, trying to breathe, but even that wasn't easy. The maze twisted the air, thickening it with thorns and sorrow.

A cold dread seized me, making me tremble uncontrollably.

I wasn't a warrior. I wasn't brave.

I was a girl with blood on her hands and a fire she couldn't understand.

And I was all alone.

"You're not alone."

The whisper didn't originate from my memory this time. It came from here. From the maze itself or the thing inside it. A voice that carried something older than language.

I opened my eyes.

A luminous moth hovered just inches from my face, pulsing with gentle golden light.

Then another emerged from the thorns.

Then another one.

They moved ahead, not quickly or frantically, but as if waiting for me.

"Wait—where are you…?" I stumbled upright, catching my breath.

The moths fluttered once and flitted forward.

With my heart pounding, I followed.

The moths led me to a hollow in the earth, narrow and deep. A natural basin sat beneath the woven canopy of the thorn maze, where moonlight barely reached, but something older thrummed beneath the surface.

The brambles pulled away as I approached, though they kept watching. Roots like ribs overgrown in the clearing, all tangled and cracked.

At the center stood a stone altar.

Covered in moss and clawed vines, it looked older than anything I had ever seen—older than Wildervale itself. Its surface bore the same fire-etched markings I'd seen on the canyon stone. They faintly glowed when I stepped close, pulsing like embers beneath ash.

Something called out to me.

I trembled. My fingers curled at my sides. A sudden weakness buckled the knees, an involuntary tremor that echoed the frantic tightening of the fingers at the sides.

"I don't want this," a desperate whisper escaped, aimed at the empty air or perhaps the unseen force that had delivered me here. "I didn't ask for power. I didn't ask for voices or visions."

The thorn-covered altar pulsed once beneath my feet.

The air grew sultry.

Then I remembered the dream, the one I'd had after the Singing Stones. The fire curled around my hands. The words whispered like a secret prayer: You must give it freely. One must believe it.

My gaze shifted to my palm. I opened my hand. But it was empty.

Was that the price?

I stepped forward and placed my hand on the altar.

It burned cold.

A gust of wind twisted around me, and then the thorns shifted. Tighter coils, curling inward like claws. They didn't block the path; they just watched, waiting.

"You want truth," I breathed. "Fine."

My voice shook.

"I'm terrified. I don't understand what's inside me. I don't want to carry it. I want to go home. I want my life back. I want my mother to love me and my kingdom to be safe and…" My throat tightened, a tear forming in my eyelid. "And I want Erindor to look at me like I'm not a crown waiting to be given away."

Silence.

"I don't know if I'm strong enough," I said, tears slipping freely now. "But I'll try. Even if it breaks me."

The words left me like a blade drawn too fast, sharp, and painful.

And then—

The altar lit.

Golden fire bloomed from beneath my palm, soft and alive. The flames didn't burn me.

They held me.

Cradled me.

The vines sighed as they drew back like curtains. The thorn-covered roots curled upward as if bowing in retreat.

And the path ahead unfolded, it revealed a straight exit, lined with glimmering moss and light.

My breath came fast, ragged.

I looked down. The scratches along my arms glowed faintly in the firelight.

The glowing moths floated ahead once more.

So, I pressed my hand to my chest, feeling the warmth that lingered like a heartbeat that wasn't my own.

The moment I stepped through the last arch of thorns, the world felt louder.

The wind exhaled, and the trees appeared to lean closer. The air tingled with the scent of crushed moss and copper, sharp and clean. I blinked against the light—soft gold clung to my skin like morning mist, fading but not gone.

They were all waiting.

Alaric stormed over, his jaw tight, his eyes blazing.

"Princess Wynessa of Elyrien, what in the gods' names—" His voice broke off as he took a complete look at me.

Jasira covered her mouth. Gideon dropped the satchel he'd been packing.

Erindor didn't move.

I glanced down at my arms. The scratches were still there, but something shimmered around them, faint golden traces where the fire had touched me. The light hadn't vanished completely. It lingered beneath the surface, as if it had made a home there.

No one spoke.

I shifted awkwardly. "I…I found a way out."

Finally, Jasira cleared her throat and stepped forward. "It closed behind us after you vanished. I tried to follow, but the path folded back on itself. I shouted until my voice cracked."

A tight grimace etched Alaric's face as he nodded. "I tried cutting through it. The vines bled. Then they regrew twice as fast. Bran panicked. Gideon threw rocks."

"I threw one rock," Gideon muttered. "Maybe two."

Jasira ignored him. "We each ended up walking in circles. Different circles. It was like the maze split us apart, made sure none of us could reach you."

"It wasn't built for escape," Erindor stated, not turning around. His voice was tight. "It wanted to break us apart first. But you made it out."

His words dropped like stones into the quiet.

I wanted to ask how they'd found their way again. How they'd made it back to this point at all. But something in the way Erindor stood, stiff and distant, told me the answers wouldn't come easily.

Instead, I whispered, "I'm glad you did."

And though he didn't respond, I saw his hand curl into a fist at his side, a small, silent motion that told me more than any words could.

Erindor stepped forward at last. His voice was low. "What happened to you in there?"

I opened my mouth, then closed it. What could I say? I gave the fire my fear, and it offered me truth? I confessed I was broken, and the confession revealed a path.

Instead, I said, "They didn't make the maze to trap anyone." They built it to test.

He stared at me, his eyes difficult to read.

Jasira was the one who finally broke the silence.

"You're glowing," she said softly. "You were glowing when you stepped through. Not just a flicker. Like the sun came to see you off."

Gideon gave a nervous laugh, rubbing the back of his neck. "So, we're pretending this is normal now? God's trials and golden skin?"

"No one's pretending," Alaric said, his tone tight. "We're trying to understand."

"I don't understand," I said, more harshly than I meant to. My hands trembled. "I don't know what it is. Or what it wants from me. I followed what felt right."

Erindor was still watching me.

His eyes flicked to my hands, then to my face.

"You heard something, didn't you?" he asked quietly.

I nodded. "Voices. One of them sounded like mine. It said, 'You must give it freely.' One must believe it. I heard the same thing at the canyon. The Singing Stones."

The silence returned, heavier this time, not with judgment, but with reckoning.

Erindor looked away, jaw tightening.

Alaric stepped beside me and gently brushed a piece of vine from my hair. His voice when it came was quieter than I'd ever heard it.

"Whatever this is, Wyn, we'll face it with you."

His words settled something deep inside me.

But when I looked at Erindor, he was steadily shrinking in the distance.

Chapter Twenty-Two

Erindor

We emerged from the thorn maze bleeding, silent, and splintered.

The air had changed, as it always does in this cursed forest. Gone was the thick green canopy, replaced now by an eerie stillness, sharp like the breath before a scream. The sky above us boiled with gray-blue clouds laced with pale lightning, yet no thunder followed. Only a sickly silence.

The trail led us to the edge of a jagged ridge veined with crystal. The stone beneath our boots shimmered faintly, catching every flicker of cloud light like polished glass. Pale quartz and fractured obsidian glinted from the cliff sides, their edges jagged as broken dreams. This was Stormglass Ridge; I remembered the name now. A cursed place, according to campfire tales. A place where the land didn't echo your footsteps, but your fears.

Wyn stumbled once, catching herself on a nearby rock outcropping. Her fingers glowed faintly, as if the magic in her blood responded to something. She didn't speak. None of us did.

Even Bran, Alaric's hound, pressed close to the group.

A freezing wind howled between the stone fangs. When it blew across the crystal seams in the rock, the sound changed—faint whispers, scattered syllables. I couldn't tell whether they came from outside or inside.

The ridge ahead constricted, a stony bottleneck forcing the path to dwindle.

"I don't like this," Jasira muttered, breaking the silence.

"This place watches everyone. And sometimes, it shows you what it sees," Gideon said grimly.

We all looked at him.

"There's a story," he said, scanning the terrain. "During the old wars, a mage tried to trap her enemy's nightmares in stone. Thought it would drive him mad. Instead, it bound every fear she ever had into the ridge itself. And now it leaks. Into anyone who crosses it."

Wyn's voice was soft. "And no one destroyed it?"

Gideon shrugged. "How do you destroy fear?"

I said nothing. My hand rested on the hilt of my blade to ground myself. Steel was real. The feel and weight of it. The sound it made as it sliced through the air. Fear couldn't take that from me.

But as we moved forward, a chill sensation crept over me, like the feeling of stepping into a stream and finding it was far colder and deeper than anticipated.

The crystal walls rose around us like jagged glass teeth, catching the faintest light and bending it until it fractured. The narrow path twisted like a serpent's spine, carved from a mirrored stone that reflected us too closely—every blink, every breath, echoed back at odd angles.

Each step felt like venturing deeper into the mouth of something ancient.

We moved in quietly. Boots scraped over stone. The sound echoed longer than it should have. The deeper we went, the heavier the air became—not with heat or cold, but with memory. A weight behind the eyes. A pressure in the chest.

At every turn, the reflection shifted. Sometimes they showed us as we were. Sometimes…they didn't.

My reflection paused when I didn't. Smiled when I wasn't.

Gideon suddenly stopped, freezing mid-step, one hand twitching near the hilt of his blade.

I moved next to him. His face had gone pale, drawn tight around the mouth.

"Gideon?"

His lips parted. The words came like breath pulled from a wound.

"I'm back," he whispered. "Northfield. Siege of Almarrow. The fires…" His voice cracked. "Gods. I hear them screaming again."

He wasn't looking at the ridge anymore. He was staring through it, into something I couldn't see. His eyes were wide, not with fear—but with recognition. Memory. A battlefield carved into bone.

"They're burning. I smell the oil." His voice cracked, the words choked out as though the smoke still filled his lungs. "The barricade fell—no, no, I got them out, I did—" His hands curled into fists, shaking.

"Gideon." Jasira grabbed his shoulder, firm. "It's not real. You're here. With us. Look at me."

He blinked. Once. Twice. Then nodded—short, fast—but didn't speak again. His jaw tightened as he forced himself to take a step forward, then another.

We kept moving.

But the ridge observed us.

And we stared right back.

The next bend in the path narrowed, barely wide enough for one at a time. Glass spires jutted from the cliff like ribs, catching the light in sharp, unnatural ways. I heard someone behind me whisper, but when I turned, no one had spoken.

And then I saw her.

Wynessa.

Standing at the far edge of the ridge, haloed in flickering firelight. Her dress torn. Blood streaked down her arms, her face, her chest—drenched in it. I couldn't tell if it was hers. I knew it didn't belong where it was.

Her eyes *seared* into mine across the mirrored stone.

Burning. Accusing.

"You didn't help me," she whispered.

A ragged gasp tore out of my chest, and before thoughts could catch up, my legs *lunged* forward, driven by instinct more than reason. Each stride *pounded* the stone, a relentless surge toward her.

"You were too late."

The words shattered from the crystal, echoed across the vast sky, and reverberated through my sternum—a deep, bone-rattling tremor that hollowed me out.

I *reeled* back, bile *surging* up my throat.

She was dead. And somehow, it was because of me.

The ground tilted. My heel caught on a shard of crystal. I went down, hands scraping raw across the stone.

Pain flared, but I barely felt it.

The vision shimmered and then fractured, breaking apart like ice underfoot.

And a hand touched my shoulder.

Warm. Real. Steady.

Her voice followed, low and real and full of breath.

"Erindor?"

I looked up.

Wyn lowered herself beside me, her eyes wide with worry. "You saw something."

"I…No, it's fine." I looked down, realizing I'd cut my palm on the glassy stone. Blood welled slowly from the gash.

She reached into her satchel and began pulling out a small cloth and some dried herbs.

"You don't have to—"

"Shut up and give me your hand," she gestured, her hand outstretched.

I obeyed.

Her fingers were gentle. Too gentle. I didn't deserve it. I didn't deserve her.

She wrapped the cloth with precision, but her touch lingered. I watched her lips part slightly in concentration. A rose-colored dust coated her cheeks. The wind pulled a few wisps of her hair free, and they danced like silk threads in the frigid air.

And then the words slipped from me before I could stop them.

"You're…not just beautiful, you know. You're…good. All the way through."

Her hands stilled. She looked up, stunned.

I coughed. "I mean—I meant—Forget I said that."

"No," she breathed, the single word a quiet vow. "I won't."

Silence stretched between us. I could feel my face burning.

She returned to wrapping my hand, this time more slowly.

I watched her.

She glowed, not with magic, but with something older. Truer.

"Well, well," Alaric drawled, leaning against a crystal outcrop like it was a stage prop. "And here I thought you were allergic to compliments, Erindor. Was that…praise? In the wild?"

Gideon let out a low whistle. "Quick, someone writes it down before he takes it back."

I stiffened. "You lot have nothing better to do than eavesdrop?"

Alaric grinned. "Not when you're providing the entertainment. Honestly, I was half-convinced you were going to explode before saying something honest."

Wyn buried her face in her hands.

"I hate all of you," I muttered.

"Aw," Alaric said, clapping me on the back as he passed. "He's blushing. This is the best day I've had since we left the capital."

· · ·

I scrubbed my palms against my cloak as we moved away from the ridge's edge, the sting of the cut across my hand grounding me more than it should have. The others murmured in uneasy tones, glancing at the glass now and then as if it might blink.

Alaric was the first to speak. Of course, he was.

"You alright, shadow boy?" he asked, brows raised with mock concern. "Looked like you saw your own funeral back there."

I tried to reply, but my throat seized, a knot of silence where words should have been. Wyn walked ahead of me, completely unaware that I'd watched her die.

Gideon gave a low whistle. "This place feels worse than that one tavern in Greymere. And that place had a murder harpist."

"No one was murdered," Jasira muttered, adjusting her pack. "Just…emotionally scalded."

"I'll take scalding over mirrored death wishes," Gideon replied, glancing warily at the ridge.

Wyn looked back, catching my eye. Her smile was faint, tentative, the kind she gave when she wasn't sure whether to be brave or quiet. I nodded once to reassure her. Lying with my eyes, I've always been good at that.

We set up camp at the base of the ridge, where the ground leveled out in a hollow of shale and dry moss. The wind had picked up, ruffling cloaks and hair, but none of us spoke of what we'd seen. Some wounds didn't want salt or curiosity.

I kept to myself, tending the fire, letting the others arrange bedrolls and shift nervously in the growing dark. Wyn crouched beside Jasira, whispering about food stocks. Alaric was nearby, polishing the hilt of his blade as if it had offended him.

I felt the heavy silence stretch between us.

Eventually, she came to sit near me.

"Hey," she said softly. "How's the hand?"

I held it up. The cut was thin, but deep. Red blended into purple around the scrape. "It's fine."

She reached into her satchel and pulled out a salve, unscrewing the tin with practiced fingers. "Let me see."

"I said it's fine, Princess."

"I heard you, but I'm choosing to ignore it."

Before I could object again, she took my hand gently into hers. Her fingers were small and soft but steady, sure, like someone who'd spent her life learning how to heal the broken things others left behind.

She didn't speak, just uncorked the small tin of balm with one hand and dipped her fingers in. The scent of crushed herbs and pine resin rose into the air, clean and sharp.

Then she touched me.

Not the way most people did. Her fingers moved with care—all slow, deliberate, and tender. She smoothed the balm over the gash, working it in with a touch that didn't just treat pain, but noticed it. I acknowledged it.

Pain flared from the raw flesh, but the instant her hand brushed my skin, a soothing calm washed over the area.

It was warm. Not from the ointment, but from her. From whatever lived inside her now. Whatever had whispered to her in the thorn maze. Whatever made her skin glow in the firelight, even when she didn't realize it.

That warmth moved through her fingers into mine, slowly, like a promise I didn't know how to name.

And I gazed at her face. A soft furrow was visible between her brows. How her eyelashes glimmered in the light. The gentle press of her lips as she focused.

I didn't pull away.

I couldn't, even if I'd wanted to.

A deep sadness tinged her murmur. "You flinch as if no one has ever cared for you."

I tore my gaze away. "I haven't."

She was quiet for a long moment, then said, "You're good at hiding it."

"And you're not good at hiding it," I said without thinking.

She blinked, surprised. "Hiding what?"

"That you're the strongest one here."

That silenced her. She looked down at my shoulder, at the spot where the Vorrhound wound was still healing. She placed her gentle hands there. Her thumb brushed near it, not quite touching.

"That's not true," she whispered. "I'm surviving."

I turned to her then. Her face was close, too close, and every inch of me wanted to memorize it. The way her hair curled slightly near its ends, the freckles beneath her eyes, the way her bottom lip trembled when she was uncertain.

"You survive like a flame survives a storm," I said before I could stop myself. "You shouldn't still be burning...but you are."

She gulped in a slow, trembling breath, fighting for control. Her eyes glistened with a fragile vulnerability, a shimmering veil holding back a storm.

Erindor, you fool.

I looked away, then cleared my throat. "That's...not what I meant to say."

"No?" Her voice was barely above a whisper.

"No. I mean, yes. But not like that." I cursed myself silently. "I'm bad at this."

"At compliments?"

"At—" I gestured vaguely. "People."

She smiled faintly but didn't let go of my hand. "You're not as bad as you think."

I opened my mouth to argue, but her fingers brushed the back of mine again, and the words dried up.

Our eyes locked, a connection forged deeper than mere sight.

In our depths, a steady warmth pulsed, a quiet promise that I wasn't prepared to confront.

The fire crackled between us, but it wasn't the heat I felt. It was her.

Behind us, Alaric coughed pointedly. "Well, I, for one, feel blessed by this emotionally stunning moment. Gideon, fetch the lute."

"Do not fetch the lute," I snapped, half rising.

Wyn giggled. The sound scraped the bottom of my chest and left something tender in its wake.

I sat back down.

I didn't look at her again, but her presence filled the quiet.

That night, the others slept.

Gideon snored in short bursts. Jasira rolled over, murmuring something about rabbits. Alaric had somehow fallen asleep with his lute balanced awkwardly across his lap, one arm slung protectively over Bran. The warhound's massive head was resting against his ribs, both snoring in different registers like a mismatched duet. I almost smiled. Almost.

But I didn't sleep.

I couldn't.

The ridge wind chafed against the mirrored stone, a dry whisper that clung to the memory. Wyn, consumed by a fiery throne, wearing a crown that blazed with unbearable heat. Her eyes condemning.

The words echoed. "You didn't help me. You were too late."

I clenched my jaw and pressed my hand to my chest, reminding myself. It was a vision. Just the glass playing tricks. But that didn't stop my bones from freezing when I saw her covered in blood. It didn't stop me from believing her.

I'd failed before. What made me think I wouldn't again?

I stood and drifted toward the edge of the firelight, not too far but enough for the wind to find me.

The stars were veiled; the moon thin. The ridge shimmered faintly in the dark, each crystal catching what little light remained and fracturing it like fragile memories. It was like standing in the breath between worlds, neither awake nor dreaming.

Behind me, the fire popped.

I turned.

Wyn shifted in her bedroll, her hands twitching, possibly grasping for something unseen.

Then I saw it.

A thread of golden light curled from her palm.

It was soft at first, like dawn's first glimmer on still water. Then it grew, delicate ribbons of flame that didn't burn, but shimmered.

My mouth dropped open, transfixed.

It licked gently up her wrist, a shy flicker, before fading again. Her breathing evened out, and her face settled into a peaceful expression.

I exhaled.

She didn't know how much she glowed. Literally and otherwise.

Closing the space, my posture shifted into a silent vigil beside her. The fire inside her was not like mine. It wasn't rage or destruction. It was a belief.

She wasn't dangerous in the way a weapon was, but in the way she ignited a spark of something far grander than anyone ever imagined was possible. The feeling that I could rise beyond the known limits was both intoxicating and terrifying.

She turned slightly, the blanket slipping from her shoulder. Her cheek rested on her arm; her lips parted a little.

She looked…

"Don't say it," I muttered to myself.

But it came anyway. The word. The thought I kept swallowing back.

She wasn't beautiful—no, that word felt too shallow, too fragile for what she was. She was luminous. Like something forged from kindness and wildfire, soft and steady, but dangerous to look at too long if you hoped to keep your footing.

I raked a hand through my hair, then muttered under my breath, "You're not supposed to matter this much."

She stirred again, murmuring something I couldn't catch.

I stood and backed away slowly, returning to the fire. But I didn't sit. I didn't close my eyes.

I stood there watching her and wondering what it would feel like to matter back.

Chapter Twenty-Three

Erindor

The trail thinned beneath our boots as morning broke over the lower ridges. A gray veil clung to the rocks, stirred by the wind like breath over cooling embers. The trees here grew sparse, bark dark as charcoal, limbs like reaching fingers. We had been climbing for hours, the slope gentle but steady. The kind of terrain that crept into your legs and made them ache without you realizing it.

Alaric walked ahead, humming absently under his breath. His lute was lazily slung over his shoulder, despite the incline, and Bran padded faithfully at his side. Jasira and Gideon followed closely behind, whispering to each other about the rock formations, some of which resembled half-melted pillars or ancient statues overtaken by stone.

Wynessa walked beside me, quiet. She had pulled her hood low, wisps of her hair escaped in the breeze, her hands clutching the leather strap of her satchel. Every so often, her eyes would lift; not to the path, but to the ridges, searching. Perhaps it was the dream still clinging to her. As ever since her fire tore a path through the thorn maze, she had spoken very little.

She kept her distance this morning. I tried not to notice, but failed miserably.

"So," Gideon called out, loud enough to break the hush, "we're heading toward the place locals call the 'mouth of the mountain,' yeah?"

Alaric snorted. "Only if you want to get swallowed."

Jasira glanced over her shoulder. "There's an old collapsed temple near here, isn't there? One records don't name?"

"There's always a temple the records don't name," Alaric replied.

"Sounds like a perfect place to poke around," Gideon muttered. "Significant history, maybe a deadly trap or two."

"I'd bet on both," I said.

A crooked grin touched Wyn's lips, and the glimpse, barely caught, was enshrined in a quiet chamber.

A few more minutes of careful descent brought the structure into view: half-buried beneath a rockslide, its once-grand columns snapped like bones, its frieze worn bare by time. The stone bore the markings of a temple once dedicated to the gods. A familiar crescent pattern across its broken lintel suggested it had honored Tharn before it fell.

But something was wrong.

"It doesn't look like this collapsed naturally," I said, stepping closer. My voice lowered on instinct. "See the clean edges? It's like someone shaped the rock."

Wyn stooped down, brushing moss from one of the fallen columns. Her fingers lingered. "These symbols are unique. Not decorative. They're functional. Protective runes, maybe?"

The wind shifted. Gideon turned in a slow circle. "What delights have been encountered now?"

Bran barked once, low and uncertain.

That's when we saw the sigil.

Painted in dark ink, not old nor ancient, smeared fresh on a nearby stone: a jagged mountain over a broken chain. My breath hitched.

Blackreach.

I stepped in front of Wyn without thinking.

Alaric drew his sword halfway. "That's not just old mercenary work."

"No," I whispered. "That's something worse."

The silence thickened.

Then, from deeper in the ruins, came the unmistakable sound of boots scuffing stone.

We weren't alone.

The air snapped. A sharp gust, followed by the barest scrape of leather against stone.

"Incoming!" Alaric barked.

An arrow screamed through the air and shattered on the stone floor where Wyn had been standing a heartbeat before. Shards skittered past her boots as she dove behind a fallen column.

They descended like carrion birds through the ruined arches, shadows in rusted iron and piecemeal mail, cloth wrapped tightly around their faces. Four of them, or more, moving like trained predators. There was no shouting or flourish, only the low rustle of boots on moss and the sound of drawn steel.

"Mercenaries!" Gideon roared, blade clearing his back with a snarl of metal.

The clash happened quickly, without warning.

Gideon slammed into the first one like a battering ram, blade raised high. His sword met flesh with a wet crunch, the bone splitting. The man screamed, clutching the ruin of his shoulder, before Gideon twisted the blade free and drove it into his throat. Blood sprayed in a hot arc across the stones.

Alaric was already mid-duel with a second. His movements were sharper, more elegant, with years of drills behind each of his swings. He feinted, then spun low, his blade slicing through the back of the man's knee. The mercenary collapsed with a shriek, and Alaric's sword punched through his spine with a sound like breaking bark. He did not scream again.

A knife whipped past my ear.

I turned to see Jasira clutching her forearm, blood leaking through her fingers.

"Get back!" I growled, stepping in front as another figure rushed toward her.

Wyn was already moving. She dragged Jasira behind a crumbling altar and tossed a pouch from her satchel. It hit the ground and burst with a sharp crack, golden powder erupting like fireflies. The mercenary staggered, eyes seared blind. Wyn didn't hesitate. She slashed upward with her dagger, catching the man across the arm.

I lunged forward, intercepting another man mid-swing. His axe whistled inches from my ribs. I dropped low and drove my blade into his thigh. He screamed, and I twisted. Blood poured down his leg, gushing onto my boots. He stumbled, still howling, so I rammed my hilt into his jaw. His teeth cracked audibly. He dropped with a choke.

A blur to my right; young, fast, reckless.

I turned too late. His short sword raked across my arm. The pain flared hot, but I welcomed it.

I gritted my teeth, slammed my boot into his gut, and grabbed his arm before he could recover. I pulled hard and drove my elbow into his nose; it crunched inward with a fountain of blood. His scream never came; I grabbed the back of his head and slammed it into the hard stone before him. Then twice over, and he went limp.

The ruin echoed with shouts, heaving breathing, and the wet clang of steel finding bodies.

Alaric let out a sharp breath, his blade now slick to the hilt. Bran had one of them pinned, jaws buried in his side, tearing. Flesh gave up with a sickening rip. The mercenary shrieked, gurgled, then was silent.

Three bodies lay motionless across the broken floor. Blood pooled thickly around the base of the altar, already soaking into the moss.

Only one remained.

He backed toward a broken column, panting, his eyes wide above the blood-smeared wrap on his face. His sword hung loosely, blood dripping from a shallow cut along his thigh.

"Don't move," I snarled, stepping over a dead mercenary.

The man raised his hands, trembling. He turned as if he was about to run.

But I was faster.

I slammed him into the pillar, blade pressed to his throat. His head cracked hard against the stone.

"Erindor—" Wyn's voice behind me was shaky, pleading.

"Alive," I snapped. "I need him alive."

The mercenary stared up at me, eyes wide, lips bloody. And then, recognition flickered.

He knew me.

And I knew now without a doubt, this wasn't simply a hired ambush.

This was the beginning of something worse.

Alaric muttered a curse and tossed me a coil of rope.

I personally took charge of the captured mercenary and tied the rope across his hands myself.

My fingers weren't steady, and that was how I knew I was angry. It wasn't the shouting kind of anger or the kind that quickly passed. It was the kind that simmered and boiled.

The kind I learned in blood-soaked camps long before anyone called me a protector.

The others gathered slowly, remaining silent. Even Gideon said nothing. Jasira clutched her arm. Wyn, a silent figure a step behind, gave nothing away with her expression, but her eyes burned into mine.

The only sounds were Bran's low growl and the drip of blood from the temple stones.

The man I had caught was young, barely out of boyhood. His breathing was hard, and blood soaked his ribs. But he was smirking.

"What's your name?" I asked.

He spat at my feet.

I struck him with a closed-fist strike to the side of his face. His head snapped back against the stone. A tooth flung across the floor.

He grinned through broken teeth, red leaking from his mouth.

Wyn flinched from behind me.

"You're not a mercenary," I said, voice flat. "You're a maggot. A leftover from a place that fed boys to blades and called it training."

He sneered, lips split. "You're one to talk."

I slowly crouched in front of him, deliberately, drawing my smaller knife.

"I was never in Blackreach," I said softly. "But I trained with people who belonged there."

I pressed the knife into the soft meat beneath his knee. "One chance. Who sent you?"

He smiled.

"The one who's coming."

I pressed down. Skin split. He hissed through his teeth but didn't cry out.

"Name." The word cut through the air like a sliver of ice.

"Riven," he whispered.

The name hammered into me, a blaze erupting where the sound landed. My lungs seized, and the edges of sight blurred to a void.

Stone walls. Firelight. Chains rattling. A boy on his knees with a knife in his hand and a voice in his ear:

"Earn it."

I had. Gods, I had.

Inside, something gave, the soundless shatter of bone under unbearable weight.

I dragged the knife down into his thigh.

The man howled. Blood poured.

"Erindor!" someone barked. Alaric, maybe.

I didn't stop.

Not yet.

"You're one of his," I hissed. "He trained you like he trained me. Bleed out the weakness. Stitch in the rage."

The man smiled through broken teeth. "You were always his favorite. He said if anyone could be worse than him, it'd be you."

I grabbed the merc's tunic and yanked him up enough to meet my eyes.

"You think this is pain?" I growled. "Try starving under a butcher's tent. Try watching your mother die for a sack of coin because the man who led us said mercy was for the weak."

His breath caught.

"You think you know Riven?" My voice barely stirred the air. "Because I do. I know the way he smiled after a kill. The way he told me I'd be nothing more than a shadow. You think I won't gut you like he taught me to?"

I drove the knife into his shoulder, not deep enough to kill, but deep enough to make him scream again.

"Do it." He gasped. "You've done worse."

I reached for his other arm.

"Erindor."

Her voice.

Wyn.

Soft but firm. Cutting through the noise like a bell in a blizzard.

My hand trembled. The blade hovered, slick and shaking.

Then I felt her fingers on my wrist.

To remind me.

Of who I am now, of who she saw when she looked at me.

I blinked.

The blood blurred.

I stood still.

The merc was sobbing now. Quietly. His mouth was red; his body slumped.

I turned away from him, meeting Wyn's eyes. They were wide and worried but not afraid.

Not of me.

"He's not worth it," she whispered.

But he was.

He knew the name. He'd said it like a vow.

"Leave him tied," I said, my voice raw. "We are moving soon."

And for a long moment, no one spoke.

Wynessa

His hands weren't shaking.

That was what terrified me most.

Blood dripped from his knuckles. It ran in slow rivulets down his forearms, pooling at the edge of one sleeve before soaking into the fabric. Some of it had dried already, smeared like old paint across the side of his neck. His blade was still in his hand.

He hadn't even bothered to clean it.

I had never seen Erindor like that before. Not even during the Vorrhound ambush. Not even when the raiders charged at us with blades drawn and murder in their eyes. Then, he'd been swift. Focused. Protective.

But this…this wasn't protection.

This was punishment.

He had hurt that man not to save us. Not to stop a threat, but because he wanted to. He needed answers, and he knew exactly how to make a body scream them out.

The name 'Riven' seared him, a sudden, sharp pain that made him react with rage.

It broke him. Or maybe that broken part slipped free again.

He walked away from the ruins as if nothing had happened. Like he hadn't tortured someone in front of us. Like his boots weren't trailing red behind him.

I followed.

He didn't slow when I caught up. He didn't glance at me. Just kept moving with long, rigid strides, jaw locked tight.

"Erindor," I said, quietly at first. "What was that?"

No answer.

"You knew him," I pressed. "Or the name. Riven."

Still nothing. Only the crunch of leaves underfoot and the sticky sound of drying blood flaking off leather.

"Tell me, please."

"I said we're moving," he snapped, finally turning his head enough for me to see the flash of cold rage in his eyes. "Don't push this right now, Princess."

I stopped in my tracks, stunned by the bite in his voice. He never called me by name like that.

A pause. He must have felt it too, because he stopped walking.

His shoulders heaved once. Then again.

"Do you really want to know?" he asked, still not looking at me. "Because once I tell you, it will not fit into whatever neat, noble idea you've built of me."

I swallowed hard. "I'm not afraid."

"You should be," he growled, whipping around to face me.

The sight of him stopped my breath.

Blood painted his neck. His jaw. His hands. Some of it had splattered across his chest like a second crest. There was dirt smudged beneath his eyes, and something darker behind them.

Not anger.

History.

"So, you believe this is me?" The words were barely breathed, laced with a chilling certainty. "A broken blade, always seeking flesh? Well, you'd be right."

"No," I refuted, my head shaking a silent denial as my heart struggled against its confines.

His laugh was short and bitter. "You didn't see what I wanted to do to him. You stopped me. If you hadn't stopped me…"

I stepped closer, even though my legs screamed not to. Even though I didn't recognize this version of him, his furious, blood-soaked echo of the boy I trusted.

"You think I don't see you?" I whispered. "But I do. I see all of you, Erindor. And that's what scares me."

He flinched as if I'd struck him.

And then, he turned and strolled away from me.

Deep down, past the fear, past the ache in my chest, something even more dangerous stirred within him.

A part of me understood that kind of rage. The bone-deep grief that makes you want to hurt the world before it can hurt you again.

And that terrified me most of all.

That night, I opened my journal. My hands still smelled faintly of blood and lavender oil.

I don't know what scared me more—what he did to that man, or how familiar it felt watching it.

Erindor's hands didn't shake. His voice didn't rise. But I saw something in him fracture open, and I didn't look away.

I should have.

But I didn't. And that means something.

Maybe because I understood. Not all of it, but enough. Enough to know there's a kind of pain that turns your skin into armor. That hollows you out so you don't have to feel the next blow. Rage isn't always chaos. Sometimes it's memory sharpened to a blade.

And I wonder if that's what I'm becoming, too. Someone who would burn the world down to keep one person breathing.

I used to think mercy was my greatest strength. But now I'm starting to wonder if I ever meant the fire in me to be kind.

I still trust him. But part of me is afraid that we're both becoming people we won't recognize when this ends. And gods help me…Part of me doesn't mind.

-W

Chapter Twenty-Four

Wynessa

The climb had grown sharper; the ground shifting from soft moss and forest loam into brittle, cracking shale. Grass no longer grew here. Roots gave way to stone, and the trees had thinned into gnarled silhouettes; stunted, wind-bent figures that clung to the mountain like half-forgotten thoughts.

Each step felt like an unanswered question.

The air grew thinner, and yet it didn't feel clean. It stung the back of the throat, laced with the strange, sour tang of mineral steam rising from deep within the earth. Sulfur. Salt. The smell of something long buried emerging to the surface.

Patches of mist slithered between the rocks, not heavy enough to hide us, but enough to blur the edges of the world. It made the horizon shift, giving distorted distances. The muffled sounds echoed around the mountain as we walked cautiously.

Ahead, the ocean shimmered beyond the ridge. Distant and unreachable. A strip of ghost-blue against the jagged edge of the sky.

No birds. No beasts. Just the wind and the brittle crunch of our boots on fractured stone.

Erindor walked at the front, shoulders tight, and head lowered. He wasn't scanning for threats, but carrying them. I recognized that posture now. That stiff, coiled gait meant his thoughts were loud and clear. He moved only like that when he was building walls inside himself.

And judging by the weight in the surrounding air, they were high.

I hated those walls.

"Wyn?" Jasira's voice came from behind, soft and careful.

"I need a minute," I said, already veering off the trail a little.

I didn't wait for permission. Just angled away from the others toward a narrow, crumbling outcrop that jutted from the ridgeline. Not far, but far enough to feel alone. A place where I could breathe. Or try to. The wind hit harder there, sweeping in from the distant sea, tugging at my cloak like it wanted me to fly or fall.

I didn't look back, but I sensed her pause. Jasira's soft intake of breath. Then a nod.

The others kept walking, their footsteps crunching against loose stone.

Except for him.

I felt him pause without even looking. Heard the hitch in his step, the shift of his boots as he stopped at the fork in the path, uncertain. The silence between us buzzed like static. I waited. Maybe he'd stay with them for once. Perhaps he'd listen.

"Do you want—"

"No." The word came out sharper than I intended, but I didn't take it back. Didn't soften it.

"I want you to keep walking, Princess."

Silence. For a moment, I thought I'd pushed him too far. But then the sound of his footsteps drew nearer.

He could never leave me alone. Not when it mattered.

"What is it?" he questioned, his voice dropping, almost swallowed by the sudden tension.

I turned slowly to face him, and it hurt to look, not because he'd done anything unforgivable, but because he hadn't trusted me enough to do anything else.

"What is it?" I echoed, arms folding over my chest. "You tell me."

He said nothing.

"I'm not a child, Erindor."

"I never said you were."

"No, but you act like I'll shatter if you tell me the truth." My throat was tight. "You shut me out again. After everything."

His brows pinched, and his arms stayed at his sides, tense. I knew that expression was the struggle between silence and confession. Silence always won.

"I am trying to protect you," he said finally, his jaw clenched.

"From what?" I snapped. "From you? From what you used to be?"

A flinch; subtle, but there.

"You think I can't handle it? That I'm too soft or too naïve?" I took a step forward, trembling. "You don't get to decide that for me."

His gaze dropped. His shoulders curled inward a little. No words came.

I felt my breath catch.

"Why do you even stay near me?" I whispered. "Because you care, or because it's your duty?"

He looked up at that. Fast. Like the question cut deeper than I meant it to.

"That's not what this is," he said, voice low.

"Then what is it?" I asked, my voice breaking.

His expression shifted, mouth parting only to snap shut. His eyes, a brewing tempest, a palpable darkness swirled, holding thoughts too potent for release.

That silence was the answer I didn't want.

"I saw your face when he said Riven's name," I murmured. "You looked like the world fell out from under you. And then you looked at me like I was something you'd already lost."

Still, he said nothing.

"I trust you," I whispered. "Even when it hurts. Even when I don't understand. And you—" My voice cracked again. "You treat me like I'm fragile. Like you're waiting for me to break."

He took a slow breath, but it caught halfway. He clenched his hands at his sides now, not in anger, but in restraint. I saw the tightness in his throat, the ache behind his eyes. He looked like he was begging himself not to reach for me.

I hated how much I wanted him to lose that battle.

"I'm not asking for everything," I said. "Just something. Let me carry a piece of this with you. You're not alone. No matter how much you try to be."

His voice, when it came, was almost a whisper. "If I give you even a piece, it'll change how you see me."

"Maybe," I said. "But it won't change how I care."

"You can be quite suffocating, you know that?" he muttered and turned. "I'll be nearby."

I wanted to scream. To throw the nearest rock straight at his back and make him bleed like he made me bleed with every withheld truth. Instead, I said the cruelest thing I could:

"Of course you will. That's all you ever are."

He stopped. Stiffened. But he didn't look back.

And then he left me there, standing in mist and silence and my own broken hope.

. . .

I didn't know where to go, but I couldn't stay there. I needed a moment, a breath away from everyone else, to clear my head.

The cliffs narrowed fast, the path fraying into jagged stone and patches of brittle grass scorched gold by unseen heat. Steam hissed up from the cracks, curling around my legs, weighing me down. My boots slid on the slick edges, but I didn't stop.

Let it crumble. Let the world tilt. Let me fall, if it wants to.

I was so tired of being a symbol. So tired of being the fragile one people whispered about, the one who needed protecting, needed guiding, needed deciding for.

Tired of fire blooming in my chest every time I got too close to anger, fear, or something else…a fire I didn't ask for. A fire that made me feel like a weapon disguised in soft skin. A fire that lit up when I was most afraid and then left me hollow in its glow.

I was tired of people telling me I was destined, chosen, sacred, as if that would make bearing the nightmares easier.

Tired of my mother's silence, sharper than knives. Of her eyes that never quite softened, her voice that measured me in disappointment. As if I were already failing a crown I hadn't even worn yet.

Tired of always pretending the weight didn't hurt when it did.

The ledge sloped toward a crag where the view opened wide; the ocean to the east, endless trees behind. Below, somewhere in the smoke and fog, the ground fell away into nothing. An endless hush of sky and stone.

And for one aching heartbeat, I wondered what it would feel like to let go.

To let the wind take me. To stop clinging to the shape of a girl I no longer recognized.

If I fell, I wasn't sure I'd even care.

Because what remained of me that still felt like mine?

But I wouldn't. And, gods help me, I couldn't.

Too much relied on me, no matter how much I hated it.

Too many eyes, too many hopes, and too many lives hanging in the balance of a girl who had never wanted to carry any of this.

My breath became shallow. My fingers curled around the edge of the rock until they ached.

Even here, at the edge of everything, the fire inside me pulsed. Stubborn and still burning.

With a growl, I yanked the rock from the ground and hurled it as hard as I could. It sailed only a few pitiful feet before plunking into the dirt.

Heat flushed my cheeks—part anger, part embarrassment. "Truly a weapon of war," I muttered.

"Wynessa!"

His voice.

He was back.

I didn't turn. "Go away, Erindor."

Footsteps. "Are you out of your mind?"

"Probably." I let out a laugh, sharp and thin. "You should like that. Easier to manage."

I heard him behind me, boots scraping as he stopped short. "What the hell are you doing out here alone?"

"Getting some air. Since apparently I suffocate everyone."

"You could've died." He scoffed.

"Maybe that would've been better," I snapped, spinning to face him. "At least then you'd stop looking at me like I'm a responsibility you didn't ask for."

A sudden paralysis claimed him.

My heart gave a violent lurch, then pounded a frantic rhythm in my chest.

"Don't say things like that," he said, voice low, strained.

"Why not?" I hurled the words.

"I protect you."

"It's your duty."

"I've saved your life more times than I can count."

"Then maybe stop. Maybe next time, leave me to the mimics."

His hands clenched into fists. "You're not being fair."

"Neither are you! I bled myself raw trying to earn your trust, and you shut down and glare and pretend I'm some wide-eyed child who can't manage shadows!"

His jaw flexed. "Because I've seen what shadows do, Princess!"

"And I've seen what silence does!"

We were both shouting now, and I didn't care if the others heard. Let them. Let the trees hear too.

"Gods," he hissed. "Do you always have to argue like it's a duel?"

"Do you always have to retreat like a coward?"

His eyes blazed. "I'm not a coward."

"You fear me."

"I'm scared for you!"

"Same thing!"

"You drive me insane!"

"You make me feel like nothing I do is ever enough!"

"You hum like a godsdamn beehive when you're thinking!"

"You breathe like you're judging the air!"

"You stomp like a bear!"

"You smell like—like pine!"

He blinked. "That's not even—"

I gasped. "That is not an insult."

"No," he said, stunned. "I don't think it is."

Silence fell between us; wild, messy, and far too full.

And then the ground beneath me shifted.

At first, it was just a shiver underfoot, a faint crack like glass under pressure, then the stone gave way with a hollow snap. My boot plunged through loose shale, the edge crumbling outward in a sudden spray of dust and rock.

One leg dangled in the open air. My weight pitched forward, with nothing solid beneath me. The void yawned below, black and endless.

I clawed at the edge, but my fingers only scraped shards of crystal. My balance tipped. My stomach dropped.

I screamed.

And then—he was there.

A flash of movement, and his hand slammed around my wrist with bruising force. My shoulder wrenched under the sudden stop, the rest of me still sliding toward the drop. Pebbles rattled away into the mist.

"I've got you," he gritted, his arm trembling with the effort as he heaved me upward. My chest scraped hard against the ridge, knees buckling under until we both lost our footing and tumbled backward.

I landed half on him, half sprawled on the cold stone, my heart hammering so violently I could taste metal. Air burned in my lungs, coming in ragged gasps.

He crushed me against his chest, his arms locking around me like iron bands. His hands were still shaking, fingers flexing against my back like he couldn't quite let go. His breath was harsh against my ear; his body still braced like we were hanging over the edge instead of lying on solid ground.

For a moment, neither of us moved, too stunned to trust the stone beneath us.

"You're not allowed to die," he rasped.

I couldn't breathe. "You caught me."

"Of course I did." He pulled back enough to look at me, his face pale, eyes wide, voice trembling. "Do you think I'd ever let you fall?"

Tears blurred my vision. "You let me go every day."

He shut his eyes for a brief moment.

"I don't know how to do this," he whispered. "To care for someone without ruining it. I wasn't taught how to hold things that matter. Only how to survive."

I curled my hands into his tunic. "Then you learn."

We sat there trembling, tangled, and stupid, with my head against his shoulder and the entire world steaming around us.

Finally, he muttered, voice cracking: "You smell like crushed herbs and panic, Princess."

I laughed through the tears.

For a long time, neither of us moved.

His arms were still around me, not in panic now, but something quieter.

My face was against his chest, and for the first time, I realized how fast his heart raced. Not the rhythm of battle or rage but something vulnerable. Something like fear.

I leaned back far enough to look at him.

His brow furrowed; his mouth parted slightly like he couldn't quite catch his breath. The bruises under his eyes were worse up close, exhaustion blooming like shadow petals under his lashes. He looked like someone who hadn't slept in days.

No…someone who hadn't rested in years.

"You meant it," I said softly.

His eyes flicked to mine. "Meant what?"

"What you said. About not knowing how to hold things that matter."

He looked away, jaw tight. "Yes."

I shook my head. "So…I matter? To you?"

A muscle in his cheek twitched. He was still trying to stay armored, even here, even now, but he wasn't built for armor. He was built for silence. For stillness. For the edge of a blade.

And yet at this moment, he wasn't holding a weapon. He was holding me.

"Yes," he breathed.

I reached up, brushing the edge of a scrape on his temple. "You don't have to do this alone."

"I've always done it alone."

"You don't have to keep choosing that."

His gaze finally returned to mine, and it hurt; how raw it was. Like he'd let no one look that deep before.

"Why do you keep trying?" he asked. "Why me?"

"I don't know," I said truthfully. "Maybe because I see something in you that's good. Even when you don't."

He swallowed hard, throat working. "You're too soft."

"You're too stubborn."

"You're reckless."

"You're terrifying."

"You're infuriating."

"You're…beautiful," I breathed, before I could stop myself.

He went still.

I clapped a hand to my mouth. "I meant—I mean, not—I meant your soul—like, the metaphor, not your—not that you're not also—"

He blinked slowly. "You're stuttering."

"I am not."

"You're doing that thing where your ears go pink."

"They do not."

"They do," he murmured, and something in his expression shifted; gentler, unguarded. Like something had cracked open, and he wasn't rushing to shut it.

"I don't think anyone's ever called my soul beautiful before," he added shyly.

"Then they were fools," I whispered.

Silence claimed him once more, not the rigid stillness of calculation, but the sudden, breathtaking blankness of shock. His stare held the speaker, raw and exposed, as if I had reached through his chest and found a pulse he'd long forgotten.

And then, our hands touched.

Bare skin, palm to palm.

It was innocent. Accidental, even. But something happened.

Warmth stirred beneath my skin, starting low and soft like the curl of a candlewick before it bloomed into flame. A golden flicker danced between our joined hands—delicate, weightless, like a fire without heat.

I gasped.

He didn't let go.

The unburning fire shimmered. Not bright. Not wild. But alive. It rose like breath, twining between our fingers, and for a moment, it felt like I was touching not just him, but something eternal.

"What is that?" he whispered.

I could barely speak. "I think it's me."

The fire pulsed once, gently, then faded, leaving only the memory of its warmth on my skin.

We stared at our hands. Then at each other.

"I didn't mean to—" I began.

"I know," he said.

Neither of us moved.

But he didn't pull away.

And I didn't want him to.

. . .

Eventually, we walked back slowly.

The path looked different now. The air was still thick with steam and sulfur, but the sharpness had dulled, or maybe it was me. Something had shifted in the way I held my weight.

Erindor walked beside me in silence, his hand brushing mine once before slipping away again. He didn't offer any words or explain what had happened.

He didn't need to.

Something had bloomed between us. Not a confession, not a promise, but the space where both of us could one day live.

The camp came into view beyond the slope, a dim cluster of figures outlined by firelight. Gideon was poking the cookpot, muttering about cinder-tinted soup. Jasira sat wrapped in her cloak with Bran curled at her feet. Alaric lay sprawled on his back with his lute cradled against his chest, fast asleep, a smear of drool across one cheek.

No one noticed our return, not really, though Jasira glanced up once, eyes flicking between us and then narrowing with a knowing look. She said nothing as she smiled faintly and returned to her tea.

I settled near the fire, drawing my cloak tight around my shoulders. My palm still tingled faintly where the fire had kissed my skin. I opened my hand beneath the shadow of my cloak, half-expecting to see it again.

But nothing. Only skin and the glowing memory of what was just there.

Across the fire, Erindor sat a little apart. Not distant. Not watching the trees for danger.

Watching me.

Like I was something he didn't yet understand but wanted to.

He didn't look away.

And neither did I.

Something shifted in his expression, and then his gaze dropped for a breath. His hand drifted to his pocket, fingers brushing against it like a reflex. A slow, unconscious movement.

He let his palm linger there for a moment, then curled it back into his lap as if it had meant nothing.

But it had.

Whatever he cupped to his chest remained hidden, yet his touch, delivered with an unsettling gaze fixed on mine.

And for reasons I couldn't explain, it left me momentarily breathless.

Chapter Twenty-Five

Wynessa

"Tell me again why we're marching through a mountain that smells like boiled eggs and poor decisions?" Gideon muttered, swiping a sleeve across his brow. A fresh hiss of steam burst from a crack in the stone beside him, curling around his legs like a hungry ghost.

"Because it's faster," Alaric answered, voice flat. "And every day we spend out here is another day Kaelen tightens his grip on the coast."

"And because you voted for this route," Jasira added sweetly, her curls damp from the mist. "You said, and I quote, 'How bad can a little heat be?'"

"Lies," Gideon said. "Slander. I never say things that get me killed."

Bran snorted as if he agreed.

Despite the heat, I kept my cloak close, the thick humidity clinging like a second skin. Every surface here beaded with moisture, moss that glistened and curled away from vent cracks, and air that seemed to shimmer. It should have been winter. Just days ago, we were trudging through frost and collecting snowflower petals.

But here, the cold had fled.

We kept moving, winding through a narrow ridge carved by wind and time and something older. The wind had long gone quiet. The only sounds were the hiss of steam and the dull echo of our boots against wet stone.

But it didn't feel like we were alone.

Erindor walked to the front, his sword still sheathed, but his shoulders tense,

I could almost feel it too, like the cliffs themselves were leaning in closer to hear us breathe.

"We're almost there," he said finally, voice low. "A crevice opens to the left, ahead. I passed it once during a patrol. We can pass through there."

"Crevices," Alaric grumbled. "Love a good ominous crack in the mountain. Nothing ever jumps out of those."

We rounded a bend where the ridge dipped sharply, and the stone ahead darkened, not from shade, but from soot. Veins of scorched rock crossed the path, and steam rose steadily from a crack in the mountainside.

"There." Erindor pointed.

The crack was too symmetrical to be natural, half-veiled by hanging moss and the shimmer of heat. Alaric stepped forward first, ducking through it. Jasira followed with Bran on her heels.

As I passed beneath the moss curtain, the shift in air hit me like a pulse.

It was warmer inside, yet hollow.

The narrow passage gave way to a cavernous corridor, shaped more by hands than by nature. The walls were smooth, almost polished, and carved in sweeping flame-like spirals that curled around symbols I didn't recognize. Some glowed faintly beneath a crust of soot. Someone clawed or broke others a long time ago.

I reached out, brushing my fingers across one spiral.

"The design…" I whispered. "It's Vireyan. One of the oldest fire-script dialects. The flame spirals were used to mark sacred places—shrines, sanctuaries, even temples."

Jasira stepped beside me. "You can read this?"

"Not fluently. But I've seen diagrams. These symbols"—I pointed to a trio carved near the base—"they represent sacrifice, sovereignty, and rebirth. The cycle of fire, according to her oldest sects."

Erindor's gaze flicked toward the symbols. "You said 'sects.' As in more than one."

I nodded. "There were many. Some peace. Some not."

We continued down the corridor.

The light changed again.

Ahead, the narrow hallway opened into a cavern of obsidian and ash. A statue stood at its heart, regal, towering, and cracked down the center. Her arms were outstretched. Her face scorched, and someone gouged the stone where her eyes should have been.

She was both magnificent and terrifying.

"Vireya," I whispered, as though saying her name louder might wake something better left sleeping.

The space felt charged, not like magic in motion, but like a storm gathering in the bones of the world. Heat shimmered from vents beneath the statue's pedestal, and the floor surrounding her bore the darkened outlines of runes, ritual burn marks etched in soot.

But what caught me most was what lay at her feet.

A small arrangement of dried flowers. Brittle, but carefully placed. Thistle and ashbloom. Star-grass and a single stem of flamebell, its crimson petals gracefully curved like a prayer. They didn't look ancient. And they hadn't been there long.

Someone had walked into this place and brought her a gift.

Jasira's voice came softly. "Is this a shrine?"

"More than that," I said, my breath caught in my throat. "This is a throne room. A seat. The Vireyan scriptures stated that some devoted people carved temples into the earth itself, allowing its power to sleep beneath them. They weren't just places of worship; they were channels."

The heat enveloped me, a tangible weight against my skin.

The flowers trembled slightly in the rising steam.

And suddenly, I wasn't sure they had abandoned this place at all.

Bran growled low. The hair on his back stood up.

The mark on my forearm, the one from the glade, flared under my sleeve. It was a light throb, warm and faint.

Only I could see it.

The others had already begun moving again, passing the statue carefully, reverently, their footsteps light.

I lingered, rooted in the space as if something had wound itself around my ribs and refused to let go.

Vireya loomed above me, half-broken and crowned in scorched marble, her expression long weathered into something unreadable. The soot-stained runes at her feet glimmered faintly beneath the rising steam. If the others had heard whispers here, they didn't say.

I did. But not words.

That feeling I had back in the glade, like a presence curled beneath the surface of the world, watching, waiting.

I turned my head and caught the curve of another chamber branching off from the main path. This one was smaller, more intimate, and hidden from view.

Pulsing.

I stepped in alone.

The air in the alcove felt heavier. Dust moved slowly through the heat, lingering in the still air, and the walls here bore older carvings than those outside. Someone had burned the symbols into the rock so deeply that they looked melted. A fresco stretched along the inner wall. Cracked with age, but the paint still clung in patches of crimson, gold, and soot-black.

I moved closer, my heart rising in my throat.

It showed a woman robed in flame and crowned in light—Vireya, unmistakably. Her arms stretched out atop a pyre in glory. Fire bloomed from her spine like wings as she tilted her head back. Around her, carved runes spiraled like solar flares—the old language for ascend, devour, become.

Beside her, a second figure was kneeling: a man robed in dark threads of moss and silver, his hands pressed to the earth, as if anchoring something she'd abandoned. Someone had carefully etched his eyes in pale gemstone, but now deep gouges blackened and scraped them out. As if someone had tried to erase him entirely.

His face, too, had been marred by intent.

Someone had clawed it away.

At the mural's edge, the last image stopped me cold.

A dying god, draped in fractured silver and broken light, knelt at the base of a shattered altar. The woman stood beside him again, but she wasn't weeping. She wasn't reaching back. She was rising.

Not mourning…but ascending.

Her flames curled toward the heavens. His roots curled around the cracked foundation. One had chosen fire. The other had stayed behind.

And between them, a divide no carving could heal.

She rose in flame while the god withered into dust.

My hand trembled as I reached up to trace the spiral mark carved beneath her feet.

It matched the one on my arm.

"I don't think we were meant to see this," came a voice behind me.

I flinched and turned to find Erindor in the doorway.

He didn't enter fully. Merley stood there, arms crossed, eyes sharp beneath the torchlight.

"I thought you left," I said softly.

"I waited for you."

Of course, he had.

He stepped closer, slowly and quietly. His gaze flicked to the mural. "What do you think it means?"

I shook my head. "The scrolls always said Vireya was one of the oldest gods. Fire was her domain, yes, but also a source of transformation, ambition, love, and loss. Once, people revered her as a gentle goddess. Until she demanded to be worshiped as the only one."

He was quiet for a long moment.

"What about the others?"

"They fled. Or fell. Or were forgotten."

"And this shrine?"

"Could have been one of her last," I whispered. "Before she was driven underground."

His gaze dropped to the mark on my arm. "It glowed back there. In front of the statue."

He stepped closer, voice low. "What does that mean, Wyn?"

"I don't know." I looked back at the mural, heart fluttering. "But I don't think it's random."

The silence settled, oppressive as the air grew dense once more, radiating a heavy warmth that seeped from the depths.

He looked at me then, truly gazed. "You remind me of something."

I blinked. "What?"

"An old story." His voice was barely above a whisper. "Of a woman born with fire in her blood, not to destroy, but to awaken the divine. They called her the quiet flame."

He wasn't teasing. He wasn't even afraid.

The torchlight danced in his eyes as he added, "They said she'd walk among ruins, and the gods would stir in their sleep. That her flame wouldn't burn until she believed it wouldn't consume her."

I looked down at my hands, trembling slightly, but still mine.

No fire. Not yet.

But the warmth was there.

By the time we stepped out of the alcove, the others had already moved ahead, their shapes fading into the misty glow of the tunnel's next bend. The walls here still radiated warmth, but not like fire, more like a gentle breath.

Erindor said nothing as we walked. I could still feel his gaze flick toward me now and then.

We caught up to the group where the corridor narrowed into a sloped descent, the stone beneath our boots darker, ash-veined, and cracked in spirals. Soot streaked the walls, fresh enough to smear when brushed.

"I don't like this," Gideon muttered. "Shrines don't stay warm centuries after being abandoned. That thing is still breathing."

"Some gods sleep in stone," Jasira said quietly. "Some don't."

"You're a little too calm about that," he said

She gave a tight shrug. "I've read too much to be surprised anymore. Besides, some of them only wake when they're called."

Gideon grunted. "Let's not call them then."

Alaric, who had been quiet for too long, finally spoke. "What do you remember about the fire goddess, Wyn?"

I raised an eyebrow, surprised. "From the old texts?"

He nodded.

I slowed slightly, reaching back into memory, not only from the palace archives, but from the forbidden corners. The footnotes. The half-torn pages I wasn't supposed to read.

"Vireya wasn't born a god of destruction. That came later. She was once the Flame of Becoming, fire as transformation, not ruin. Her light comforted others, not consumed them."

Jasira traced a scorch mark near the base of the mural. "Then what happened?"

"They started worshipping the wrong part of her," I said. "The fire, not the warmth. The power, not the purpose. They stopped asking what she wanted and started deciding what she meant."

Gideon's brow drew together in a troubled line. "That's a dangerous devotion."

"Fanaticism always is," I murmured.

Erindor's voice was quiet, but sharp like a flint. "This wasn't worship. It was control. Fire was a leash. A measure. You didn't pass their trials by praying. You passed by surviving."

We all turned to him.

He wasn't looking at us. He fixed his eyes on the soot-dark ring scorched into the stone floor.

"I've seen marks like that before," he continued, voice flat. "Carved beneath a temple where screams echoed for days. They burned offerings at first. Then the sinners. Then, anyone who hesitated."

Jasira swallowed. "That's not devotion. That's cruelty dressed as faith."

I nodded. "It always starts with light. But it's so easy to lose the warmth and keep the flame."

"That's madness," Alaric said.

He nodded. "There are cults that survived after the gods fell. The cult remains hidden and scattered across Aetherra."

"Do they still exist?" Jasira asked.

He glanced toward the darkness behind us. "I think nothing ever truly dies. Especially not belief."

Opening wider now, the tunnel saw the heat fade slowly, like breath exhaled for the last time. The air cooled enough for our steps to echo again. The shrine was behind us. But it didn't feel like it had let us go.

I wrapped my arms around myself as we moved. My skin still buzzed from the mark on my arm. I wasn't burning, but pulsing heartbeat.

We paused to rest where the path bent near a small ledge that overlooked the winding trail ahead. The view was bleak, harsh, and gray, craggy peaks veiled in fog and veins of steam still curling from the valley below.

Bran flopped beside Jasira, who poured a bit of water into her cupped hands for him to drink. Gideon unwrapped something that might've once been bread and offered it to no one in particular. Alaric paced near the ledge, arms crossed, his eyebrow puckered in concentration.

I sat a little apart, letting the cool breeze brush my flushed cheeks.

Erindor settled beside me without a word.

We didn't speak for a long while.

Then, softly, he asked, "Do you believe in them?"

"The gods?"

He nodded.

I turned the question over in my mind. I'd grown up with ceremony, with worship offered more from duty than devotion. But that mark on my arm, the whisper in the canyon, the way the statue had felt, I couldn't ignore it anymore.

"I think," I said slowly, "that belief isn't about being sure. It's about listening. And when something calls out, something sacred, something terrifying, you don't have to understand it to answer."

Chapter Twenty-Six

Erindor

The further we walked, the more the cold crept in.

The heat from the mountain was behind us now, and with it, the smoke-warmed winds. In its place came the sharp bite of winter in our bones. Snow clung to the shadows between the lifeless hills, forming uneven patches along the rocks. The grass was brittle and low to the ground, more cinders than green, and every gust of wind dragged the charred scent of old fire across the slope.

The sky had turned the color of wet stone, heavy and low, spitting flurries that melted on contact. Ice rimmed the edges of our cloaks and lashes, delicate and sharp as a breath held for too long.

Even Bran had stopped bounding ahead. He stayed close to Alaric's heels now, his ears flat against the wind.

The sun hovered behind thick clouds, pale, distant, and cold. A silver coin buried in wool. It gave no warmth, only the sense that something above was observing.

We were two days out from Caerthaine now.

And the land felt like it knew.

I walked ahead, scanning the horizon as the path dipped. Behind me, the others followed, quieter than usual. Gideon's jokes had faded by midmorning, and even Alaric had barked orders in the last hour.

The silence wasn't peaceful. It was pressure.

Wyn moved beside me. She hadn't spoken for some time, her shoulders pulled in against the wind. Snow clung to her hair, and her steps had slowed.

She was exhausted.

The weariness wasn't from the long journey, but a crushing burden built over weeks of tension, haunting visions, dark magic, and inescapable deaths. It was the weight of every unvoiced truth, every shared silence.

"Crevices ahead," I stated firmly. "Stone's splitting from past burn lines. Don't trust the edges."

No one answered, but I saw Jasira adjust her footing. Bran gave a low chuff and nudged Gideon, who was still scanning the slope for movement.

A patch of blackened thorns stretched like claws across the ridge to our left. Beyond them, tucked into the rock, the top of a structure jutted from the hillside, cracked and leaning, half-buried in ice. A collapsed watchtower or what remained of one?

Something had burned through the stone.

I slowed as we approached, narrowing my eyes. Clearly, someone had abandoned the tower decades ago. Rusted spikes still lined the fractured perimeter, although many had fallen. Vines, or the remnants of them, clung to the south-facing wall, their texture brittle like old paper.

Alaric came up beside me. "We push forward. We can make the next ridge by dusk."

"No," I said.

His eyes snapped open. "We're close enough to see the coastline. If we make a push tomorrow—"

"And we'll get there faster if we don't stumble into a crevasse or an ambush by traveling tired," I said, keeping my voice even.

His jaw twitched, but he didn't argue further.

I looked back at Wyn. She had stopped beside a patch of sleet-covered logs, breathing quietly, one hand pressed to her side. Fatigue rimmed her eyes, and her skin was pale beneath the dirt.

That sealed it.

"We stop here," I said, louder now.

Gideon sighed in relief. "Thank every known god."

Jasira gave him a look. "You don't even pray."

"I do now," he grumbled.

We moved into what was left of the tower's yard. The outer wall had mostly collapsed, but the central chamber still had enough of a roof to serve as shelter. I ducked through the broken archway first, sword in hand, checking corners, gaps in the stone, and dark hollows.

No movement or bodies. Only dust, stone, and silence.

I could hear the others enter behind me.

"Oh well, this is charming, isn't it?" I heard Alaric remark.

"This place looks like it caught fire," Wyn murmured behind me, her voice soft but clear.

I glanced at her.

Her fingers traced the scarred mortar of the wall, a faint contact that spoke of weary resignation. Her gaze drifted, lost in thought, shadowed by an exhaustion that settled deep within her bones.

She didn't know I'd stopped the march because of her. A profound ache twisted in my chest at the sight of her so drained, so quiet, aching to grant her respite.

Even if it was in a cursed ruin.

"Let's not light a fire," I said. "Smoke travels too far in flat land."

Gideon groaned. "So much for hot tea."

"Boil it low. Keep the steam covered."

Bran sniffed the cracked stairway and sneezed.

Alaric dropped his pack with more force than necessary and muttered something about weak stomachs. I let it pass.

As the others settled, I walked the perimeter again, scanning the horizon from the collapsed balcony. The hills rolled on, gray and silent. The tower stood like a broken tooth, one more relic from a war no one remembered, waiting to crumble for good.

But something about this place...

The stone didn't feel old.

It felt deep.

As if something had passed through it and left a wound that the world never healed.

Night fell like a weight.

The sun disappeared behind the hills, leaving the sky dim and the wind sharper. What little warmth lingered in the air turned brittle, edged with the bite of winter returning. The tower ruins darkened fast, the broken stone swallowing any remaining light. We lit no proper fire, a low coal burn in a buried tin pit, with a half-cracked lid to keep the glow from traveling. Still, the shadows it cast danced across soot-blackened walls like old ghosts learning how to move again.

Bran wouldn't stop pacing.

He circled the fire three times, then stalked to the wall, ears twitching.

We were all unsettled.

Gideon tried, as usual, to break the tension.

He stabbed a stick into the pot he'd rigged over the low flame and gave it a sniff. "So…we've officially reached the part of the journey where everything tastes like sadness and ash."

"Sounds like your normal cooking," Jasira murmured, lying on her side beside the fire. She had pulled her cloak up like a blanket, but her eyes remained open. Watchful.

Gideon clutched his chest. "Ouch! Wounded."

She arched an eyebrow. "Do you ever shut up?"

"Only in my sleep. And even then, I'm told I mutter charming things."

Wyn sat across from them, knees tucked to her chest, chin resting on folded arms. The hood of her cloak had slipped back, and the coals reflected softly in her eyes. She gazed intently at the low fire.

I sat a little apart, near the tower's outer rim, where the stones cracked open toward the slope. My hand stayed near my sword, fingers flexing against the grip.

I didn't like how quiet the hills had become.

No birds, crickets, or distant owls. Just the brittle rush of wind sliding down the hillside like a blade looking for something to cut.

Gideon's voice cut back in. "Wyn, you're the palace archivist in disguise. Any idea what this place was?"

She broke her trance and slowly turned toward him. "There were no names in the city records. Maybe they never completed it."

"Wrong!" he exclaimed with a grin. "This was the Thornridge Outpost. Supposed to be Caerthaine's first line of defense. Long before the kingdoms signed treaties and kissed rings."

Jasira raised a brow. "Then why's it abandoned?"

Gideon twirled his stick through the pot like it was a scepter. "Because they say it burned from the inside. One morning, patrols passed by and found the entire garrison in ashes. No sign of battle. No fire damage on the walls. The only thing left was dust where bodies used to be."

The flames popped, and for a moment, no one spoke.

Wyn slowly wrapped her arms tighter around herself. "That's not possible."

"That's the thing about cursed places," Gideon rumbled, his voice dark with a knowing grimness. "They don't ask for permission."

Alaric, who had been pacing the outer rim of the wall, scowled and crossed his arms. "Old stories. Campfire rot. You put too much faith in bedtime fears."

"And you don't put enough," Gideon retorted.

Wyn's gaze had dropped to the coals again. Her fingers twitched in thought. I watched her shoulders tense ever so slightly.

"Double watches tonight," I said.

Gideon blinked. "Dramatic."

"Safe."

Alaric looked at me, his expression blank, but nodded. "Fine. Jasira and Gideon take first. I'll relieve them. You two can take the final."

He nodded toward Wyn and me. She didn't look up, but I saw her give a slight nod in return.

. . .

I'd meant to let her rest. We'd been walking for days without a proper stop, and tonight, inside the crumbling shell of the old outpost, was the first real roof we'd had in too long.

When our shared shift came, I rose quietly and took my post alone, hoping she wouldn't stir. She needed the sleep more than I did.

The night pressed cold against the broken ramparts; the wind slipped through cracks in the stone like a whisper you couldn't quite hear. The others soon fell asleep, their breathing deep and uneven in the shadows.

I stood at the jagged edge where the wall had long since collapsed, scanning the hills below, nothing but black shapes and shifting moonlight.

Footsteps approached, light but certain. I didn't turn.

Wyn joined me quietly. She moved like the night—soft-footed, calm on the surface, but swirling beneath. Her cloak brushed mine as she came to stand beside me, close enough that I caught the faint scent of herbs and wood smoke.

"You should sleep," I murmured.

Her mouth curved faintly. "You'd just keep glancing back to check if I was breathing. Might as well save you the trouble."

I huffed through my nose, almost laughing. She was right.

We stood together while mist curled low in the valleys, silvered by the moon. Far somewhere off, a wolf called, the sound thin and lonely. The sky stretched wide above us, stars sharp against the black, scattered like frost on glass. They were too beautiful for this place.

"I always thought winter skies out here would feel gentler," she said after a while.

"They're honest, at least," I said. "Cold. Clear. Distant."

She smiled faintly. "Do you always describe the stars like old soldiers?"

"I describe everything like an old soldier."

She chuckled. It surprised me. I didn't realize how much I wanted to hear it again.

After a moment, she added, "Do you think the gods see us out here?"

I paused briefly.

"If they are, they're terrible at intervening."

She gave a quiet snort of laughter.

The silence lingered, growing taut between us.

After a moment, I added, "Or maybe they have terrible aim."

Wyn blinked. "Was that a joke?"

I didn't answer.

She turned toward me fully in mock seriousness. "Erindor. Was that an actual joke? Have you been hiding a sense of humor this whole time?"

"I haven't, Princess."

"You have!"

"I'm being serious."

"You're not."

"I—" I stopped, shook my head, and looked back at the sky.

She grinned beside me, eyes crinkling slightly at the corners. "I knew it." She added smugly.

"I keep it small. Malnourished. Better kept in the dark."

She gently nudged my elbow with hers. The contact was brief, feather-soft, yet it lingered like warmth from a fire. My chest ached for reasons I didn't want to name.

She was too tired to notice what she did to me. Or I was too stubborn to let it show.

We stood together in silence.

Bran growled once in his sleep across the yard. Somewhere behind us, Gideon muttered in a dream. Alaric had settled near the rubble with his arms crossed.

Wyn shivered slightly. I could still tell she was more than exhausted.

The air offered no sound of their coming, but the ridge above suddenly exploded with light.

Torches bloomed across the ridgeline above us; dozens of them. Their glow spilled down the hills in broken flickers, weaving through the dark like serpents made of flame. My hand was already on my sword before the shouts began.

"Up!" I barked, loud enough to split the dark. "Get up! Now!"

Bran growled, teeth flashing, as Gideon rolled to his feet with a startled oath. Alaric was already up, sword drawn. Jasira grabbed Wyn's arm and yanked her behind a stone post as arrows struck sparks against the ruins.

"Mercenaries!" I shouted. "They're coming from the ridge!"

I caught one torchbearer rushing down the slope, a bulky shape in a rust-red cloak, and I hurled a dagger straight into his chest without hesitation. He dropped without a sound.

The next arrow whizzed within inches of my face, drawing a thin crimson line across Jasira's shoulder before punching into the tower wall with a decisive thock.

Gideon rushed to Jasira's side, blade in one hand, shield in the other. "Stay behind me," he growled, none of the usual humor in his voice. "Touch her, and I'll gut you," he shouted at the mercenaries.

The first wave hit us like a landslide.

Over the crumbling wall they surged, three figures framed by firelight, their drawn blades reflecting the dancing flames. Underneath the grimy swaths of cloth that masked them, their faces hinted at a fierce, unseen intent.

Alaric was there in a blink. His sword cleaved downward in a brutal arc that split the first man's collarbone with a crack like splitting wood. Blood fountained, splattering Bran's fur as the war hound lunged at the second attacker. The man shrieked as teeth sank into his forearm, crunching down to the bone. Alaric pivoted too slowly. The third mercenary's blade swept low, carving a deep line across his thigh. He stumbled, blood flowing down his boot, but he didn't fall. His blade sliced the attacker's neck, ripping through muscle and windpipe in a sickening, gurgling spray.

A fourth mercenary—fast, lean, wielding twin curved blades, rushed toward me. His first strike skimmed my ribs; I felt the heat of it, the hiss of torn fabric. I ducked the second, drove upward with my knee, catching his gut. As he doubled over, I slammed my elbow into the bridge of his nose with a wet crunch, then shoved my sword into his chest. He gagged on the steel, blood bubbling from his mouth before he dropped.

Another came screaming from my left, dagger raised. I caught his wrist mid-swing, twisted until it snapped, and shoved my knife straight into his throat. His blood hit my face, hot and bitter. He spasmed, twitching like a puppet with cut strings, and crumpled at my feet.

Gideon was roaring nearby, drenched in sweat and blood, swinging his axe with feral precision. One mercenary charged him low, ramming a short blade into Gideon's side. He howled, twisted, and brought the axe down so hard it split the man's shoulder and ribcage in half. Flesh parted like overripe fruit, the spray hitting the stone.

Through the chaos, I saw her.

Wyn.

She was running to Jasira, herbs clutched tight in one hand like she didn't know whether to heal or run. Her eyes were wide, stark, revealing the whites all around the iris, while a faint quiver worked its way through her jaw.

And then, heat. Sharp and sudden. The pendant in my pocket seared against my leg, hot enough to make me flinch. For a split second, it felt as though the fire came from inside my chest rather than from the metal. I didn't have time to think about what it meant. Only that it meant her.

Another attacker spun toward her, a blur of motion with lethal intent

I was too far.

He raised a rusty hatchet, grinning.

Wyn grabbed the nearest thing—a blackened iron cooking pan. She swung wildly and struck him in the temple with a hollow crack. His knees buckled, and he dropped without a sound.

She gasped. "I'm sorry!"

Gods.

She had apologized to the man she had knocked unconscious.

"Wyn!" Jasira called, her voice sharp with pain.

A deep gash split her shoulder, spilling crimson in thick rivulets down her arm. Wyn dropped beside her, pressing a cloth hard to the wound, her fingers trembling, breath ragged.

Beyond the ridge wall, more torches flared in the dark. Six. Seven. Maybe more.

One charged me before the thought could fully register. His axe came down in a killing arc. I stepped inside the swing, driving my sword up beneath his ribs. The steel punched through, hot blood spilling over my gauntlet as he choked and collapsed.

Another came at my flank, screaming. I caught his wrist, twisted until the bones popped, and ripped the blade from his hand. I buried it in his gut and shoved him back, watching him fold over it before kicking him to the ground. He writhed once, then stilled.

A third lunged from the shadows, spear low. I parried, turned the point aside, and slammed my shoulder into his jaw. Bone crunched. He stumbled; I finished it with a sharp thrust to the throat. His eyes bulged as blood fountained over my boots.

The clearing reeked of iron and smoke. Steam hissed where blood struck the cold stone. Bodies sprawled in heaps, some twitching weakly, others already slack and pale.

We were holding them.

But barely.

"Behind you!" Gideon shouted.

I spun. Pendant burning hot in my pocket.

A mercenary lunged toward Wyn with a curved blade, raising it high.

I didn't think.

I ran.

Too far to reach him in time. NO.

I threw my sword.

It whistled through the air like a scream, spinning once, twice, and then struck home with a meaty thunk. The blade punched through the mercenary's ribs as he lunged for her, driving so deep the hilt slammed against his chest with a sickening crack.

He staggered once, blood already pouring from his mouth in thick ropes, eyes wide in surprise. Then he collapsed forward like a sack of butchered meat, the sword still buried to the hilt.

The pendant in my pocket cooled from its blistering heat, settling into a steady, lingering warmth, like an ember that refused to die.

Wyn stared.

I ran to her, yanked the blade free, and turned to cover her again.

"You all right?" I asked, voice harsher than I meant.

Wyn sat there.

Eyes wide. Mouth ajar.

Not in fear.

I watched the flush rise in her cheeks before she ducked her head for a moment, pretending to check Jasira's bandages, like her hands weren't shaking for an entirely additional reason.

Her gaze, a blend of startled relief and profound, wordless gratitude, held me captive long after the fallen man's final gasp.

Long enough for me to notice.

Gods, I noticed.

She didn't say a word. She didn't have to.

I didn't leave her side. Not again.

Alaric shouted from the far wall, "They're falling back!"

The mercenaries had retreated, slipping away into the rocks and ash, but not like routed soldiers. Like men who had done their job.

A warning. Not a victory.

I stepped toward the edge of the ridge, sword still slick in my grip.

Then I heard it.

Slow, deliberate clapping from above.

A shape moved out of the shadows near a cragged ledge overlooking the ruins. A man, cloaked in gray and black, with a hood thrown back and a glint of iron at his shoulder.

He moved like smoke.

Confident. Leisurely.

"You're still good," he said. His voice was quiet, but the night carried it clearly as steel.

He looked at me.

"But let's see how you fare against me."

Then he stepped forward into the torchlight.

And I saw his eyes. Gray as ash and cold as stone.

Riven.

My stomach turned to ice.

There was no mistaking him now. The torchlight flicked across his face, too harsh, too pale. His cheekbones cut like blades beneath stretched skin. A scar ran from the corner of his left eye down to his jaw, and though his hands hung at his sides, loose and unthreatening, he radiated danger like a coiled spring.

His presence permeated the space, chilling the air and stealing the warmth

"I expected more," he murmured, his voice a silken thread of menace. "Frankly, I'm rather underwhelmed."

He looked at me.

He wasn't interested in the others. Just me.

"You've gotten better, though, boy," he added. "Cleaner. Calmer."

I didn't answer. I clenched my fingers so tightly around the hilt of my sword that the metal bit into my palm.

He smirked slightly. "But you still hesitate when it counts."

He lifted his right hand, palm open, casual.

The earth beneath the ledge trembled slightly in awareness. The suggestion of pressure.

My grip tightened.

"Why are you here?" I demanded.

Riven tilted his head. "Oh, you know. To observe. To evaluate."

His eyes flicked past me.

To Wyn.

She stood a few paces behind, stiff with tension. Her cloak was still askew from the fight, cheeks pale, eyes locked on him like she couldn't decide whether to run or burn him down where he stood.

The air near her shoulder shimmered faintly, not yet a flame. The echo of what lived within her.

Riven noticed.

But he didn't speak to her.

"You don't belong in this," I said tightly.

"No," he agreed. "But then again, neither do you."

The remark pricked a nerve, a wound too fresh for acknowledgment.

He took a slow step forward. Not down, not closer, but enough to make the ledge creak. "You're still trying to be a sword in a world that forgot how to forge one. Noble and pointless."

I inched closer, blade angled low but ready.

"You will not reach her," I said.

His smile sharpened. "Oh, but I will."

Chapter Twenty-Seven

Erindor

From the blackened remnants, smoke issued forth, a foul, simmering exhalation, suggesting a lingering spirit of decay.

The battlefield lay broken around us, dust drifting across the shattered stone, tents reduced to skeletal frames. The old tower still stood, blackened and cracked, casting long shadows over the courtyard that reeked of blood and heat.

Gideon lay sprawled beside a shattered column, the left side of his tunic soaked crimson with blood. Ignoring her own injury, Jasira dropped beside him, pressing a cloth fiercely against his wound, her lips a frantic murmur of pleas. Bran stood guard over both, teeth bared, tail rigid with tension.

Alaric limped across the clearing, dragging his sword, one leg bloodied from thigh to knee. His gaze flickered to me, a fleeting touch, before giving the slightest shake of his head.

We weren't ready for another fight.

And yet the air told me it wasn't over.

I turned toward the ridge.

Riven walked down slowly, boots nearly silent against the charred stone. Cloak trailing. Shoulders straight. No sword drawn. No urgency in his step.

Just control.

He descended like a shadow returning to its source. Something carved out of vengeance and silence, stitched together with cruelty so old it had forgotten its own shape.

My breath tightened. My blade ready for impact.

Wyn stood near the remnants of the gate. Her cloak had come loose, and she clutched a small dagger as if it were all she had left between her and the end.

Riven saw her. His mouth curved.

"So," he drawled, a smirk twisting his lips, "this is the girl they want to trade for peace." The words, barely a whisper, carried a mocking echo of a forgotten voice.

Wyn didn't flinch, but I saw the tremble in her hand.

"Leave us," she said, her voice too soft for fury, shaking.

He stopped a few paces away. "You've got her talking now," he said to me. "Last time she stared."

My grip tightened on the hilt of my sword.

I inched forward, every muscle tense.

He didn't move. Only his eyes tracked every flicker, every breath, a stillness that hummed with menace.

I could feel the others behind me, Jasira muttering frantic prayers and Gideon groaning through clenched teeth.

Wyn took a trembling step closer.

Riven's gaze flicked back to her. He tilted his head slightly.

"You're trembling," he said. "That blade will slip before you use it."

"Maybe," she whispered.

I stepped between them.

"Don't," I said to her without looking. "He's too dangerous."

Riven smiled, the barest curl of a mouth used to silence. "That's adorable."

Riven's cloak hit the ground before his weapons cleared the air.

He unsheathed a long obsidian blade and a narrow parrying dagger of the same style in a single, fluid motion. Both gleamed with strange veins of metal, something older. Something that hummed faintly as he moved.

There was no flourish or fury; the motion was clean, silent, and devastating.

I stepped forward.

Beside me, Gideon staggered to his feet. Blood gushed from the wound where the blade had caught him, painting his armor in thick, crimson rivulets that dripped onto the stone. But he held his shield high, jaw clenched, defiant even as he swayed on his feet.

Our eyes met for a fraction of a second; no need for words. We'd fought in enough battles to know exactly what the other would do next. The rhythm of survival had its own language, and we spoke it fluently.

He gave me the slightest nod, and I answered with one of my own.

We reached Riven together.

Steel shrieked on steel. My blade met his longsword with a jarring clang, the impact reverberating down my arms.

Gideon lunged, angling for his ribs, and Riven twisted away like smoke, sidestepping with a grace no mercenary should have. His parrying dagger flashed, carving a bloody line across Gideon's forearm.

Gideon snarled but did not retreat. He slammed his shield into Riven's chest, the impact hard enough to make him stagger back a step, following with a brutal slash that grazed his jaw, drawing a spatter of blood.

But Riven's smile widened.

He came at us in a flurry—blade and dagger working in perfect, merciless tandem. I caught one strike on my sword, felt the jolt rattle through my shoulder, while Gideon's shield turned aside the next. We moved in a grim rhythm, one striking as the other defended, forcing him to shift, adapt, retreat a step.

Then Riven feinted left.

Gideon bit, stepping to intercept, and Riven's longsword crashed into his shield with bone-shaking force. Before Gideon could recover, the mercenary pivoted low, his boot smashing into Gideon's knee.

The blow drove him down hard. He hit the ground with a grunt, shield still up but body refusing to rise.

"Stay down!" I barked, stepping over him as Riven advanced, the heat of the fight pounding in my ears like war drums.

I surged forward, blade arcing up toward his throat. He slammed into my swing, steel screeching against steel, and our blades locked in a vibrating, skull-shattering deadlock. The sheer force of it reverberated through my arms, threatening to tear them from their sockets.

We were chest to chest, breaths mingling in the cold air, each of us straining for an inch of advantage. His eyes burned with something feral, a predator sizing up prey, and I knew mine were no calmer. Sweat and blood slicked our grips, the muscles in my shoulders trembling with the effort to shove him back.

The blades shuddered between us, caught in the small, brutal space where one mistake would mean the end.

His face crowded into mine, unnervingly close. What should have been eyes were coals of smoke and chips of ancient stone, harboring a darkness that spoke of something primordial and unknowable beneath.

"Sloppy," he murmured as he leaned into me.

Then the earth moved.

A sickening tremor tore up from beneath us, like a vein had burst under the ground. Cracks spiderwebbed outward from his boots, shoving gravel and broken stone into the air. The pulse hit like a battering ram.

I staggered, boots sliding, but Riven was already on me.

His parrying dagger slashed into my thigh. A stab, puncturing deep above the knee. My vision sparked white. His longsword plummeted, a shimmering arc of death. My blade was heaved up to meet it, both hands braced, but the cataclysmic clash slammed me to my knees. A blinding shower of sparks erupted.

He ripped my sword from my hands, and I hit the ground hard. The wind fled my lungs. Dirt and grit coated my tongue. I coughed blood into the dirt.

He stood over me. His eyes burned into me with an icy fire.

He held no expression, just calculating, disassembling a broken tool as if determining where it had failed.

"Still soft where it counts."

"You talk too much," I spat.

"Better than sulking like a dog under that girl's skirts." His grin widened, ugly now. "She looks at you like you're her answer. That must be exhausting."

Then Alaric roared behind him, sword raised, Bran a blur of teeth and fury at his side. The prince's strike was precise, a diagonal meant to split the bastard from collarbone to hip.

Riven spun. He should've been too slow.

But the ground shuddered under him. A jag of stone thrust upward from the floor like a conjured step, shifting his footing just enough to slip past the blade. The air cracked as steel cut through space.

Alaric snarled, coming in again with a flurry—high, low, a vicious backhand slice. Bran darted in tandem, snapping at Riven's legs. And for a heartbeat, they drove him back.

Riven's hand flexed against his hilt, and the earth itself answered. A ridge erupted under Bran's paws, throwing the war hound sideways into a cracked pillar with a yelp and a bone-shaking thud. The animal rolled, staggered, then relaunched itself, blood at its muzzle.

Alaric pressed harder, forcing Riven to parry three quick strikes in succession. The ring of steel on steel was deafening, sparks leaping between them. But Riven's stance never broke. Another sharp tremor rippled underfoot, forcing Alaric's knee to buckle just enough for Riven's sword to kiss his chest. A shallow slice, but deep enough to draw a crimson bloom across his tunic.

I shook my head clear, the ringing in my ears fading as I pushed to my feet. My legs screamed at me, but I forced them to move. The sight of Bran snapping again at Riven's calf, buying Alaric that sliver of breathing room, was enough to shove me back into the fray.

"Move!" I barked, stepping in as Alaric pivoted away, blood running from his chest. My sword came up high, teeth gritted, and I drove at Riven with everything I had left.

I stepped in, driving Riven back with a vicious overhand swing. The clang shook up my arms, but I didn't relent—strike, pivot, slash for his ribs. He caught the blade on his crossguard, twisting to rip it sideways, and I slammed my shoulder into him, forcing him a step toward the rubble.

His eyes flickered with calculation.

He lashed out with a low kick. I caught it on my thigh, and I responded with a powerful vertical chop, nearly breaking through his guard. But then his heel struck the stone beneath us. The ground answered to him instantly—cracking, heaving, throwing my stance wide open.

He surged into the gap like water through a breach. Steel rang against mine in a furious barrage, the last blow knocking my sword low just long enough for his elbow to drive into my jaw. Stars burst across my vision.

I staggered, teeth gritted, swinging up again, but he was already inside my guard. His blade punched into my ribs; I twisted, barely catching it with the flat of mine. The impact rattled my bones. Then, the stone under my back foot shifted, a slick rise just big enough to unbalance me, and Riven's shoulder slammed into my chest like a battering ram.

The air ripped from my lungs as I hit the ground hard, the weight bearing down briefly before he pushed off.

I rolled, hand clawing toward my sword, which lay only inches away.

Riven stepped on it. He didn't even glance at me. He knew.

A brutal kick slammed into my ribs, the same side he'd hit before. Something cracked. I folded, the dirt rushing up to meet me again. My back arched, mouth open in a soundless gasp, pain flooding every corner of my vision. White. Sharp. Endless.

Above me, Riven exhaled softly, like a child bored with his toys.

He raised his blade.

And then—

Her voice.

"Don't touch him!"

It cracked through the air like lightning.

Wyn.

The instant she stepped into the open, the pendant in my pocket flared. White-hot against my thigh, as if it knew before I did she was in danger.

Riven's head turned toward her.

"No…" The word scraped out of my throat, ragged and useless. "Please…"

She barreled toward him, dagger drawn.

He didn't move.

She swung wildly, and he slipped aside like smoke.

She came again, clumsy and desperate, and he caught her wrist, twisting hard before flinging her down.

She hit the ground with a sickening crack, skidding across scorched stone.

"Princess," he said, almost pitying. "What are you trying to prove?"

She stood, blood streaking from her temple, dazed but upright. Her chest rose and fell too fast; her arms trembled.

"That I'm not afraid of you," she said with a shaky voice.

I couldn't speak. I couldn't rise.

But I saw her.

I saw the shimmer in her eyes.

A pulse of gold curled faintly over her skin, like embers breathing.

Riven hadn't noticed.

He raised his sword.

But then something changed on her face. Determination.

Wynessa

I couldn't feel my legs.

The dirt clung to my skin, and my heartbeat drowned out everything else. My temple throbbed from where I had struck the ground. Blood ran down my cheek in a steady line, warm and pulsing with each terrified beat of my heart.

Erindor lay behind Riven, still bruised, and his chest barely moving.

Gideon wasn't getting up. Alaric had fallen. Jasira was somewhere out of reach, and I didn't know if she was alive or bleeding out in the dark. I wanted to call out. I wanted to cry.

Instead, I stood.

I didn't remember how.

Even when my whole body screamed at me to run.

My hands trembled so violently that I nearly dropped the little belt knife Erindor had shown me how to hold, how to use. It felt useless now, like a twig trying to stand against a storm.

My bones begged me to flee.

But I couldn't. Not with my friends lying there.

Not with them bleeding because they had tried to protect me.

He was going to kill them all. Unless I stood up. Unless I tried.

Even if I died doing it.

Tears blurred the edges of my sight, but I blinked them back. My chest was shaking. My ribs screamed from where I'd hit the ground, but I didn't move. I stood holding my ground.

Riven's presence felt like a cold breath on the back of my neck as his eyes bore into mine.

He cocked his head, almost amused. His sword, long and blackened and stained with fresh blood, hung loose in his grip. The smaller dagger twitched like a flickering flame in his left hand, fast, elegant, precise.

He looked at me like I was an insect that had forgotten its place.

I couldn't breathe, let alone speak. But I forced my legs to steady. My fingers wrapped tighter around the hilt of the dagger until the edge bit into my palm.

"I'm not afraid of you," I managed to whisper, the words catching in my throat, suddenly dry as dust.

But my hands, clammy and trembling, gave away the stark lie.

But it didn't matter. I loved them more, and I would fight for them. No matter what.

He laughed wickedly. "You should be."

Then he lunged.

I tried to move. Dodged left, but I was too slow. The flat of his sword slammed into my ribs, and I flew sideways. I hit the ground with a wet thud; the wind driven from my lungs. My side burned, and I gasped for breath.

He didn't stop.

A hand fisted in my hair and hauled me up like I weighed nothing.

"Cute," he muttered in my ear. "But you're not a soldier. You're a symbol."

Then he threw me against a broken pillar, stone catching my shoulder and spine. My scream cracked through the ruins. I collapsed, and my face pressed to cold ash and blood.

I couldn't move.

I couldn't—

"Stay down," he said, already turning his back.

And that…that was what lit the fuse.

I remembered my mother's voice.

"Softness is a liability. A crown doesn't cry."

I remembered the screaming in the maze. The whisper in the canyon. The light that had bloomed from my chest.

I remembered Erindor's blood on the ground.

"No," I croaked, barely audible.

My knees shook as I pushed myself upright again. I could taste blood. I could feel tears slipping down my face. My vision blurred and split. The dagger shook in my hand as if it didn't want to be held anymore.

But I stood.

Riven turned. His face was blank now, almost disappointed or annoyed.

He stalked toward me, each step deliberate, a predator closing the distance.

Then, he exploded into a strike.

This time, it was the back of his hand across my face, hard enough to split my lip wide open. I fell sideways again; the blade flying from my hand.

"Stop trying to be brave," he said, his voice flat. "You don't know how."

He lunged down, his fist clenching in the front of my cloak, and ripped me upward.

I dangled there, my toes scraping the dirt.

"You're not a threat." He scoffed, the words dripping with contempt. "You're bait. Nothing more."

The world spun. My ears rang.

And yet—

Something deep in my chest stirred.

It wasn't rage or power but love.

All fierce, terrible, and bright.

A need to protect them. Even if it broke me.

Even if it killed me.

Even if no one ever knew I'd done it.

And something inside me opened.

The air grew warm, and light started in my chest.

Like a pulse, a flicker, or a vow.

Golden-white flame blasted from my palm, a scorching brilliance that didn't burn but shredded the mist and sent the shadows recoiling from the stones. The air cracked with a deep, ringing thunder that rolled through the clearing.

The ground bucked beneath us. The same cracks Riven had torn into the earth earlier lit up with gold, searing down into the stone like molten veins.

Riven staggered, teeth bared in a snarl. The shockwave caught him full in the chest, slamming him back into a half-collapsed pillar. Dust drifted down in pale clouds.

Before he could rise, the lingering force of my magic pressed him there, an unseen weight pinning him just enough to keep his blade from lifting clean. He fought against it, boots grinding into the glowing fissures, the muscles in his arms straining.

I launched forward, no time for hesitation. My lungs ignited with the effort.

He swung at me in a sudden blur, his blade clipping my forearm hard enough to send pain flaring up to my shoulder. A tremor ran through my grip, threatening to give way, but I wrestled it back, jaw tight enough to ache.

I slammed my dagger against his sword arm, knocking it wide, and drove in close until the point pressed to the hollow of his throat.

His eyes snapped to mine, blazing with fury—raw, unmasked, and lethal. His lip curled back over his teeth like a cornered predator, every muscle in his body screaming to break free and tear me apart. The golden light crawling over the stones painted his rage in molten fire, but I didn't flinch.

I stood there, hand shaking, fire still blooming from my skin in slow curls.

His eyes blazed against the glow.

"Go on," he said, breathless but amused. "Do it. Let's see what your peace is made of."

I stared at him.

The light brightened again, and then it showed me.

His eyes met mine. And the world flickered.

In the blink of an eye, I saw it:

Stone hands held down a boy no older than eight.

The echo of screams. A girl with silver hair, dragged from his side, her body limp.

They seared a brand onto his shoulder as he choked on charcoal.

A voice whispering: Kindness is death.

I gasped, and my dagger slumped in my grasp.

Riven inhale aborted, a stark mirror of the sudden relief, or perhaps, the lingering dread.

"No," I whispered. "That's not who I am."

The words seemed to pull the heat out of the air. The golden cracks in the earth dimmed, the hum of power fading until it was only the sound of our breathing. My hand loosened. The dagger slipped from my fingers and clattered softly against the stone.

I took a slow step back.

Freed from the weight of my magic, Riven sagged slightly against the cracked pillar, one shoulder braced against it as if testing his own balance. His chest rose and fell in deep, deliberate breaths. For the first time, the defiance in his eyes gave way to something else, something unguarded, almost human.

His gaze swept over me, lingering for a moment too long. The faintest tremor passed through his jaw, as if he were holding back a thousand unsaid words.

And then, in one fluid motion, he pushed off the pillar. He didn't raise his blade again. Instead, he turned and disappeared into the smoke, his figure dissolving into the haze until there was nothing left but the fading scent of iron and ash.

I stayed in place, gulping air until my lungs burned, forcing the tears back until they stung behind my eyes. Then, with a sharp breath, I snapped out of it and turned, stumbling, toward where Erindor lay.

I knelt beside him. His eyes opened barely.

"Wyn…" he rasped.

"Don't move," I whispered, leaning over him. "I'm here."

My hand pressed against the side of his face. His blood was still wet on his cheek. My cloak was torn.

I held onto him tightly, as if that was the only thing tethering me to the world.

The silence after the battle was worse than the chaos.

The sound of wind sweeping over the broken outpost, rustling ash across the stone like a shroud.

I knelt beside Erindor, fingers still tangled in his collar, pressing close to the warmth of his chest. My fire had gone quiet now, but its memory lingered, a phantom ache beneath my ribs, like the ghost of something sacred.

His eyes fluttered open again, unfocused. He looked at me, then over my shoulder.

"You didn't…"

"No," I whispered, pressing my hand firmer against the scorched wound at his side. "I didn't. I couldn't."

The ravaged battlefield groaned beneath the weight of destruction.

The air stank of blood and charred stone. The only sounds were the crackle of something still smoldering and the ragged breaths of the barely living.

Jasira moved first, slowly and trembling. She tried to rise but faltered, knees buckling. Gideon caught her without hesitation, blood still seeping down his side from a vicious gash beneath his ribs. He pulled her close, standing between her and the worst of the carnage as if he could still shield her from it.

"If I die," he muttered dramatically, voice hoarse but playful through the pain, "I want you to wear my armor and avenge me. Gloriously."

Jasira let out a broken laugh. "You're not dying."

"I'm serious," he wheezed. "Sword raised. Cloak billowing. Crying vengeance to the heavens."

"Shut up," she said, but her hands curled into his shirt like she wasn't ready to let go.

Slipping an arm under Erindor's shoulder, I helped him up. He was heavier than I expected, his weight sagging against me. His eyes met mine, pained but steady.

"Go," he said, his voice low but firm. "Help them."

"I—"

"Wyn, go."

My hand froze on his arm, a tremor of doubt running through me. His answering pressure was barely there, a ghost of a touch, yet it urged me on. Every instinct screamed to refuse, but his plea, unspoken yet palpable, tugged deeper. With a ragged breath, I began to ease him back, each movement a battle against rising dread. I gave him one last look, long enough to memorize the set of his jaw, the way the firelight caught in his eyes, before turning away.

I tore open the satchel at my side and pulled out the bandages, the salve jar, and the bundle of dried redflower bark.

"Hold still," I told Gideon, already pressing a clean cloth against his wound. My hands were shaking, but I had practiced the movements. Years of study, of tending scraped knees and bruised ribs, flooded my memory. I knew what to do.

"This'll sting," I warned, as he raised his shirt so I could pour the tincture over the gash. Gideon hissed through his teeth.

"Sting? I feel reborn. Baptized in agony."

I shot him a withering glance, but the corner of his mouth twitched upward, anyway. He was still bleeding, but the worst of it slowed. I packed the wound with herbs and bound it tight with strips of linen.

Jasira sat beside him now, her hand trembling as it brushed his arm. I passed her a poultice and guided her fingers to press it against the slice on his arm. "Keep pressure. Like that. Good."

Alaric limped over next, his pant leg torn and streaked with blood. Bran was nearly carrying him, shoulder to flank. I dropped to my knees at his side, ripped open the fabric, and winced.

"Straight cut, deep. Missed the artery, but it'll need stitches."

"Lucky me. These were my favorite trousers too, you know," Alaric muttered through clenched teeth.

"You're lucky I brought a needle and gut thread." The words were clipped, but a flicker of concern softened the sharpness in my eyes.

I cleaned the wound and sewed it closed, my fingers trembling but precise. He didn't make a sound, though Bran let out a low, protective growl every time the needle pierced flesh.

When it was done, I sat back, wiping my hands on a cloth already soaked dark with blood. My knees throbbed from kneeling, my back burned from hunching, but they were alive.

I looked up. Alaric's usual grin was gone. In its place was something quieter: gratitude maybe, or relief. He gave a small nod. Nothing more, but it was enough to make my throat tighten.

"What the hell happened?" he choked, his gaze sweeping across the blood-soaked wreckage and the battered faces of the survivors.

Silence.

No one looked toward the path where Riven had vanished. No one asked why I'd let him go.

Struggling to stand, and the world threatening to topple with every dizzying shift, I staggered my limp body through the clearing.

Erindor slumped against the fractured column, his breath ragged, one arm pressed tight against his splintered ribs as if his sheer will alone somehow mended the bone beneath. His discarded armor lay in a scattered heap at his feet. Blood had soaked through his tunic in a deep, spreading stain.

His head rose slowly as I approached, his face haggard from weariness, but a gentle light bloomed in his eyes. And in that moment, with the ruin of battle all around us, it said what neither of us could.

"You're hurt," I said softly as I reached him.

"I'm fine," he replied, but he didn't stop me when I knelt beside him and reached for the edge of his shirt.

"Let me see."

His jaw flexed, but he let me lift the fabric. I sucked in a breath. A gash curved beneath his ribs, angry and red, still weeping at the edges.

"Fine!" I echoed. "You're bleeding."

"I've had worse."

"That's not a reason to let it get infected. So, sit down." I demanded, my eyes fixed on him before adding, "Now."

For a moment, it seemed like he might argue. But then his jaw tightened, and he lowered himself onto a chunk of fallen stone with slow, grudging compliance.

He watched me with that unnerving stillness of his, the kind that always made me feel like I was being studied, weighed, and judged all at once.

His skin was hot under my hands. Too hot.

I dipped the cloth into clean water and began to quietly work on the wound. My hands were gentle, but inside I was shaking. His breath hitched when I pressed too firmly, and I caught the subtle flinch he tried to hide, along with the slight, tensed pull of his shoulders as if he was refusing to show me the pain.

"You didn't stop," I whispered, not looking at him. "Even when he threw you. Even when you couldn't stand straight. You still got up."

His gaze searched mine for a moment, then his hand lifted. His fingers lightly brushed my temple, where Riven's action of slamming me into the stone had split and made the skin tender. His touch was feather-light, causing my breath to halt but also flinch a little.

"I had to," he breathed. "He was going to kill you."

A sudden constriction tightened in my throat.

And the silence in the air seemed to hum.

"I would've died," I said. "For all of you."

"I know." His voice was rough. "That's why I couldn't let it happen."

I finished wrapping the bandage and placed my hand on his chest to feel his heartbeat pulse beneath my palm, steady and strong.

"You scared me," I admitted. "You looked at him like you weren't afraid to die."

His eyes met mine, and something in them flickered. "I wasn't."

"Don't say that."

"Why?" he asked. "Because dying should scare me?"

"No," I said, swallowing hard. "Because I fear losing you."

He stared at me as if I'd knocked the wind out of him. Like I was the blade now, cutting too close: "You spared him."

I nodded.

"Why?"

My fingers curled where I had placed them on his chest.

"Because killing him wouldn't have saved us," I whispered.

His eyes flicked to mine. Searching.

"Then what would?"

"I'm not sure," I said, shaking my head.

But I believed in a fire that destroyed nothing. In truth that didn't come at the end of a blade.

Maybe mercy couldn't win a war.

But it could change one person.

Even if that person was me.

I scrambled to my feet. My hands still smelled of blood and herbs. My heart still ached with the weight of what I hadn't said.

But I felt his eyes on my back as I walked away.

And I knew he was still bleeding in ways I couldn't fix with stitches.

Chapter Twenty-Eight

Wynessa

We left the ruined watchtower after dawn, with blood on our boots and smoke still clinging to our cloaks. No one spoke of the fight, Riven, the light that had erupted from my hands, or the way I'd spared him. The only sounds were the shuffle of tired feet over brittle grass and the soft groan of leather shifting as wounds tightened.

Wildervale had vanished behind us. The dead trees gave way to rockier hills, then dry golden brush. Every step forward tasted like dust and salt. The wind changed first—no longer cold and heavy, but warmer, lighter, carrying the brine of the sea.

By midday, we found the river. It wasn't wide, but the water ran clear over polished stones, the current tugging gently at the banks. We all knew we needed to wash away the smoke, the blood, the battle stink, especially with a city on the horizon.

"Boys that way, girls this way," Jasira said, jerking her thumb upstream. "And no peeking." Her eyes swept the group, lingering just long enough to make the last part pointed.

Gideon barked a laugh, deep and unexpected. Alaric clutched his chest in mock horror. "Gods forbid. The scandal." Erindor didn't say a word. But when Jasira smirked, I caught his gaze across the clearing. He looked away so fast you'd think something had burned him; the faintest hint of color touched his cheekbones.

We waded into the water until it reached our waists, shivering as the cold bit at our skin. I ducked under, gasping as the river swept the grit and blood from my hair. The filth swirled away downstream, carried toward whatever lay ahead. My bruises throbbed as I scrubbed them gently, every sting feeling like something loosening inside me—like shedding the last pieces of the watchtower.

"You caught him looking," Jasira murmured, just loud enough for me to hear.

I blinked at her. "What?"

She grinned wickedly. "When I made the peeking joke. He looked. One of those slow ones."

Heat climbed into my cheeks. "You're imagining things."

"Mm. Sure. And I imagine you didn't notice how his ears went pink either?"

I ducked my head, pretending to focus on scrubbing my arms. "You're ridiculous."

"I'm observant," she said, wading further out, her voice lilting. "And if you're smart, you'll start noticing back."

By the time we emerged, the wind had dried us off. We shook out our cloaks, brushed our tunics clean, and combed back our hair. My cloak was a mess: torn along the hem, the embroidery frayed, and a long rip down one side where Riven had grabbed me. I ran my fingers over the damage, a knot forming in my chest.

The boys approached from downstream and also cleaned up. And gods help me—with his wet hair slicked back, his tunic clinging to the cut of his shoulders, and a bead of water sliding down the line of his sculptured jaw, Erindor looked like a temptation I lacked the courage to confront.

My gaze lingered too long, tracing the way his belt sat low on his hips, the faint line of muscle disappearing beneath his shirt. When I realized what I was doing, I tore my eyes away so fast it almost hurt.

He noticed the cloak in my hands. "That's done for."

"It can be mended," I said, the words ringing falsely even in my ears. He reached out and, without a request, his fingers brushed against my hand as he took it gently.

"I'll carry it. No point weighing you down."

"I can—"

"You've carried enough," he said simply, tucking it into his pack before I could argue again. Something in my chest went warm, like the sun had touched it. I just nodded, falling into step beside him as we headed toward the horizon.

By late afternoon, the city walls rose in the distance.

Below the ridge, the world transformed.

The coast unfolded like a painting: the sea spread of liquid sapphire, the cliffs white and gleaming like sunlit marble. A town nestled along the shore, hugging the curve of a crescent bay. Pale stone buildings shone with mosaics and colored glass; rooftops painted in coral pink and sea-foam green. Lanterns swayed from wooden beams, and fabric banners snapped in the breeze.

A gasp escaped my lips as the scene unfolded.

A brilliant, overwhelming rush that burned at the back of my eyes.

Alaric exhaled a low whistle beside me. "Now this," he said, hands on his hips, "is more like it."

He grinned, a grin that meant trouble. I tried to return it, but it didn't reach my eyes. My body was still holding tension from the night before—my shoulders tight, my heartbeat unsteady.

As we walked down the road into the coastal town, the people emerged, and I felt smaller with every step.

The faces of the locals shone with unrestrained joy.

Their clothes were little more than sheer silks and colorful wraps, gold-painted skin dusted with shimmer. Some wore nothing on their feet; others had lace-up sandals or ornamented cuffs with seashells and pearls. Chains looped across collarbones and chests, draped from hair and wrists like woven sunlight.

They were laughing. Singing. Leaning into one another with easy, languid affection. Their skin gleamed. Their eyes were bright. They wore joy as if it were sewn into their flesh.

By contrast, I wore my only good dress left. A sage green, with pale embroidery at the cuffs and hem. It was clean now, the fabric still carrying the faint scent of river water and sun, but its seams had grown soft from wear. My boots were scuffed but free of mud, and my hair, still damp, curled in loose, unruly strands around my face despite my best efforts to smooth it. I pulled my sleeves closer to my wrists, feeling oddly exposed without my cloak.

A group of dancers passed, half-dressed in swirling veils. One of them, a young woman with beads strung between her eyebrows, reached out to touch my wrist.

"You wear your heart like a shadow," she observed, the low resonance of her voice making the words feel heavy. "Has it followed you far?"

But then, she disappeared before I could respond.

Alaric, of course, was flourishing. A different woman came up to him and draped a silk scarf around his shoulders. She told him he had the laughter of a sun prince. He kissed her hand and winked.

Gideon muttered, "We've lost him."

"He was never with us," Jasira said, tugging her own cloak tighter.

I tried to take in deep breaths.

But the noise was rising, music playing from somewhere in the square, market bells chiming, footsteps echoing on worn white stone. The scent of fried citrus and hot spices swirled through the air, thick and cloying. Color flashed in every direction: silks, flags, painted skin.

It was beautiful. Lush. Alive.

And I hated it.

I hated how tight my chest felt, and how every touch from a stranger's hand made me flinch. I hated that I could still hear the echo of swords clashing and bones snapping in the back of my mind. I hated that my hands trembled as I smoothed the skirts of my dress, as if that scrap of fabric could shield me from the crowd's pressure. I hated that even here, in the warmth of color and gold, I still felt cold.

I glanced at Erindor behind us, weaving between the crowd, his hand resting near his sword. He was always watching and calculating.

The comfort was a fleeting breath against my cheek.

But then, as I blinked, the space where he stood was empty.

Alaric disappeared somewhere to my left. Jasira and Gideon were talking to a fruit vendor, their voices muffled.

Suddenly, I was alone.

The crowd pressed in, a suffocating embrace of bodies and booming music, yet I felt a profound, chilling solitude.

My throat tightened.

I turned sharply down a narrow path between vendors, my heart pounding.

The primary thoroughfare unfurled in a wild tangle of stalls, canopies, and painted stands. Vendors shouted over each other in multiple tongues, hawking fruit, perfume, spices, beads, and bottles of glittering oil that caught the sun like molten fire.

Incense drifted from stone censers, smoke curling like pale fingers toward the blue sky. Banners snapped. Coins clinked. Laughter rose. Unfamiliar music played on stringed instruments. Color, sound, and touch greeted me at every step.

It was more than I could handle.

I passed a table where gold-flecked shells shimmered like stars. Someone offered me a cube of candied ginger. A hand brushed my back. Another touched my hair. Compliments chased me in every direction.

"So fair! Are all northern girls like snow and roses?"

"Pretty little bones under all that fabric, I bet. Shame to keep 'em hidden."

"That mouth looks like it's used to saying no, but I'd love to hear it say yes."

I lowered my head, my hands attempting to fend them off.

I was still bleeding, not externally, but internally. I could still hear Riven's voice. I could still feel Erindor's blood on my hands. And here, in this place of sunlight and jewels, I was nothing more than an oddity. A pale doll from the mountains.

A woman tried to wrap a gold-dusted scarf around my shoulders. "This shade matches your hair," she said with a smile.

I backed away. "Oh, no, thank you. I don't want it."

She blinked, surprised. "It's not for want of trying, girl. It's for being."

Her words stuck, like something half-prophetic, but I ignored her, walking away as swiftly as I could.

I searched for Erindor's face, or Jasira's laugh, or Gideon's shape, but they were gone, lost in the crowd. I wasn't far from them, probably. But it felt like an entire world had unfolded between us.

This was something I wasn't meant for. Not the noise. Not the color. Not the attention. Not the pretending.

My pulse thundered. My feet moved without asking permission. I turned onto a quieter lane where the stalls dwindled, and the voices faded.

There, beyond a curve of white stone, a small awning stood in shadow.

It was the only place that didn't shine.

I nearly wept when the noise dulled.

The alley curved behind a row of closed shutters, and suddenly the world softened. No shouting, no bright silk, no clinking coin or perfume. Muted light and the hush of worn stone underfoot.

I followed the scent until I saw the stall.

They tucked it beneath an old wooden overhang, shaded with fronds of woven sea grass. Petals dusted the floor in soft confetti, not the kind that glittered, but the kind that fell. Natural, wilted, authentic. Bowls of flowers lined a long table: some still vibrant, some drying for preservation, all unfamiliar to me.

A small woman stood behind the display, her hair tied up in coils of pale rope cord. Her skin was wind-darkened, her hands stained green at the fingertips. She wore no gold, no silk. Just a pale blue tunic and a wreath of dried tidebloom flowers woven around her wrist.

As I approached, she merely tilted her head slightly, lips tightly sealed.

She smiled, as though she'd known I was coming.

My steps slowed. The ache in my ribs eased a little.

I let my eyes wander across the display.

There were petals like stars. Buds like sea glass. Vines that curled like a sign of doubt.

And then I saw them.

Long, white-stemmed flowers with soft blue and violet centers, their edges dipped in a watery pink hue like a sunset trapped in ice. Someone arranged the flowers in a shallow bowl filled with pale sand, with tiny drops of moisture clinging to their roots.

"Sea lilies," the woman smiled softly. "They only bloom during mourning tides."

I blinked. "Mourning…tides?"

She nodded once. "It's what we call the third moon cycle after a death, when the water pulls harder, when grief weighs more than breath, these only open then. When someone somewhere is still waiting to be loved again."

A dryness gripped my throat, preventing any sound from escaping for a brief moment.

"They're beautiful," I whispered.

"They're stubborn," she corrected. "They bloom when they shouldn't. When the world says stay closed, they reach anyway."

"I'll take one," I said, swallowing hard. "Please."

She nodded, gently selecting one and wrapping it in soft linen. As she handed me the flower, I left the coin on her stall, and she looked at me as if she could see right through me.

"Your soul is louder than your footsteps," she said. "Be careful who you let hear it."

I didn't know what to say.

So, I tucked the flower close to my chest and stepped back into the quiet shade of the alley.

For the first time since we'd arrived in this glittering place, I breathed without pressure. Without bracing.

The scent of dried herbs and salt lingered on my skin. My fingers clutched the delicate sea lily, a desperate attempt to find purchase in a world that felt adrift. I didn't know what I was mourning. Myself, maybe. My freedom. The quiet life I thought I'd lead. Or perhaps the idea that I could go anywhere without being looked at.

But here, in the hush and bloom, I could be invisible.

And it felt like mercy.

The sun had dipped behind the tallest building, casting amber light across the blue-tiled roofs. The breeze had shifted again, gentler now, cool with the scent of tide and stone.

I held the sea lily safely against my chest.

I wasn't sure I was ready to go back into the crowd.

Then I heard the footsteps—measured, slow, and familiar in their quiet weight.

I didn't look until he spoke.

"You disappeared," Erindor said simply, but the quiet tension in his voice revealed a deeper unease.

I kept my eyes on the flower. "So did everyone else."

He didn't answer that. Merley stood beside me for a moment, hands resting loosely at his sides. I glanced sideways. Dust from travel covered his cloak. There was a new bruise across the bridge of his nose, faint and blooming.

"Sorry," I said softly. "I needed to breathe."

He gave a slight nod. "I thought you might."

I blinked at that. "You did?"

"Yes," he admitted, voice quieter now. "I couldn't find you. And it's busy here. Loud."

He glanced down, noticing the sea lily in my hands. His expression shifted slightly.

"Oh, it's a sea lily. Only bloom during mourning tides and all that," I said, holding out the lily for him to look at.

"That suits you, Princess."

I raised an eyebrow. "Because I'm sad and stubborn?"

His lips almost twitched. "Because it's…it's tougher than it looks. Kind of like someone else I know."

The air grew heavy and silent, and my gaze was fixed upon him.

He stepped closer and offered his arm. The gesture was quiet, steady, without expectation.

I accepted, slipped my hand into the crook of his elbow, my fingers brushing the fabric of his sleeve. The tension in my chest eased just enough to let me breathe again. Together, we started toward the quieter paths that wound along the edge of the town, where the stone met the sea cliffs.

We didn't speak for a long time.

The streets thinned, and eventually we walked side by side through a narrow corridor of wind and water. The sea stretched out before us in endless blue, the horizon bleeding gold and violet where the sun kissed the waves. Gulls circled overhead.

I didn't ask where the others were. I didn't want to know.

Here, it was just us—silent and still.

After a while, Erindor said, "I don't like this place."

I glanced at him, surprised. "You don't?"

"Too loud. Too many people pretending to be what they aren't."

I laughed softly before I could stop it. "Since when do you share your thoughts so freely?"

He gave me a look, faintly amused. "Don't get used to it."

We paused at the edge of the stone path, where a small overlook jutted out over the sea. We both sat down on a bench carved from driftwood.

"I felt invisible in the market," I blurted. "And yet, too seen at the same time."

He nodded slowly. "That's because they saw your face, but not your heart."

I looked at him.

He didn't meet my gaze. He didn't need to.

He was here.

"I don't know where I fit anymore," I whispered. "Not with the people I'm supposed to rule, not with these strangers, not with—" I almost said you, but I caught the word just in time.

"You don't have to fit," he said. "You just have to keep walking."

I leaned my shoulder against his.

For a moment, the silence held us in its grip.

A slow, deliberate breath escaped, the sound heavy in the quiet. In a voice barely above a whisper, "I used to run with Riven. A long time ago," he confessed.

I went still.

"I was a boy. Fifteen, maybe. Angry. Alone. He found me like that." His voice wasn't bitter. "I did things I'm not proud of. Things I'll never be proud of."

I didn't move. Didn't press. But he must've felt the way my breath caught.

"I'm not ready to talk about it," he added, his voice quieter now. "Not all of it. Not yet."

I turned my head slightly toward him. "Okay."

"But I will," he said. "One day. I'll tell you everything. I just…need you to let me do it in pieces."

I nodded. "That's enough."

And it was.

Chapter Twenty-Nine

Wynessa

Caerthaine was different.

The air was damp, as if it had just rained, even though the sky was clear. The streets grew narrower, darker. Buildings leaned in too close, their windows shut tight. A ceremonial bell tolled somewhere beyond the rooftops. Dull and echoing. A sound meant for endings.

Erindor slowed his pace beside mine. He said nothing as he looked in the direction the bell tolled.

"What is that?" I asked.

"Execution bell."

I gave a slow, disbelieving blink. "Execution?"

He nodded.

The road bent around a corner, the narrow lane opened into a vast stone square, and I understood.

A crowd had gathered. Dozens of people, all quiet, all watching.

At the center stood a raised platform—the gallows, weathered and straightforward. Beneath it, guards in slate-blue cloaks stood with halberds in hand, their helms shaped like curling waves. Their silver breastplates bore the crest of Kaelor, the god of water: a moon cradled in a rising tide, and the primary god worshipped in Caerthaine.

But the figure on the platform was not waterborne. She stood in what remained of torn white robes, her wrists bound tight with fraying rope. Someone had hacked her hair short and uneven; tufts stuck out like broken reeds. Bruises mottled her skin in sickly shades of purple and yellow, and grime clung to every hollow of her thin frame. She looked starved, with her cheekbones jutting sharp, collarbones like drawn bowstrings. Ash and dried blood marked her bare feet. A sign hung from her neck: "WILD FIRE–FALSE GIFTED"

The air was forced from my lungs in a sudden rush, matching the unexpected, absolute silence that descended upon the square.

A hush fell over the square.

"False gifted…" I whispered, but it came out broken. "But…that's not her fault."

"No," he said. "It never is."

The woman on the platform was young, maybe no older than Jasira. She held her chin high, but her whole body trembled. A priest stood behind her with a bowl of sea salt and a twisted piece of coral, symbols of Kaelor. He spoke a prayer I couldn't understand. The water gifted of Caerthaine believed in control more than anything else. In grief channeled, not worn. In silence and tradition. In drowning, no one can guide.

And fire…fire was everything they feared.

The executioner stepped forward, his voice a chilling pronouncement, cutting through the murmuring crowd. "By order of the

Crown, this woman stands guilty of consorting with wildfire—of harboring imbalance within her blood and soul. Witnesses attest she spoke in her sleep of surviving flame without injury, of hearing it whisper to her. The court sentences her to death for these crimes."

Wyn's stomach turned. "They kill for rumors?" she whispered.

Erindor didn't look away from the platform. "In Caerthaine, they kill for imbalance."

The executioner's voice droned on above them, naming the day and hour someone uncovered her "sins", recounting how neighbors claimed to see sparks dancing across her fingertips.

A man in the crowd—a merchant possibly, judging by his fine coat—leaned toward another and muttered, "Whispers, they said. Whispers in her sleep. The flame spoke back."

My fingers twitched toward my arm, right over the place where the mark lay hidden beneath my sleeve. Bare skin under my touch. I could still feel it—that ember-deep thrum, like a sleeping heartbeat curled in my bones.

I looked at Erindor. He was already staring at me. A moment of raw, unspoken terror passed between us—recognition neither of us dared to name.

The bell tolled.

I tore my gaze away just as the executioner adjusted the rope. The woman stood barefoot, her hair shorn to the scalp, bruises mottling her thin arms. She was little more than bone under her torn robes. She didn't plead. Didn't fight. Only closed her eyes as if she'd already gone somewhere far away.

The bell tolled again.

Erindor stepped in front of me, blocking my view. I still heard it. The creak of wood, the brutal snap as the floor fell away, the rope swinging. And then the sound of cheering.

My breath hitched. The noise was too loud; the air too tight. My eyes burned hot, tears already forming in my eyelids.

Erindor's hand found mine, firm and grounding. He leaned closer, his voice low enough that only I could hear. "Breathe, Princess. Walk with me. One step at a time."

He didn't let go as he guided me out of the crowd, cutting a path through the crush of bodies until the shouts faded behind us. We passed under a narrow archway where damp ivy clung to the stone, but it gave no comfort. Even the plants here seemed to grow under orders.

He looked at me with a hint of worry in his eyes. "You're safe," he murmured, though his tone carried the weight of someone who knew safety here was a fragile thing.

"She was fire-touched," I said eventually. "Like me."

His eyes flicked to me. Then away. "No. That was something else."

I stopped walking. "How do you know?"

He turned to face me fully. "Because what you carry doesn't want destruction. It wants…something else. Something sacred. And you didn't steal it. You bloomed into it."

Words died in my throat, replaced by the chilling phantom touch of a rope and the constricting grip of fear. What if they saw it in me?

We continued to walk. The farther we went, the more the noise thinned into distant echoes, replaced by the steady rhythm of our boots on stone and the hiss of wind funneling between the buildings.

I kept my head down, but he stayed close. Half-step between me and anyone who passed too near. His fingers brushed against mine again, not quite holding this time, but lingering, as if to remind me they were still there.

My breath snagged, and he eased his pace until our steps fell into a shared rhythm.

"Look at me," he said low and firmly.

A prickle of resistance ran through me, yet I complied. His eyes, unwavering and stark, locked onto mine.

"They cheer because they don't understand," he murmured, softer now. "But you do. And that's not weakness, Wyn—it's the reason you'll survive this."

The knot in my chest loosened. His words sank deeper than I wanted to admit, warm and heavy, settling somewhere I couldn't quite name.

We turned down a sloping lane that spilled onto a quieter path at the base of the hill. Sunlight filtered between tall stone walls, catching on the wet ivy clinging there, droplets still slipping from the morning rain. The air smelled faintly of brine.

"In here," he said, nodding toward a narrow archway. "We'll cut through, and it will take us to the meeting point."

The meeting point was a place my nerves had been too raw to approach earlier.

In the arch's shade, he slowed again, his voice a near-whisper. "One more breath," he said. "Then we face the others."

I nodded, drawing in air until the tremor in my hands eased.

Before I could step forward, his hand rose hesitantly, and he brushed the side of my face, his calloused fingertips skimming from my temple down to the line of my jaw. It was fleeting, nothing more than a touch, but it rooted me in place. His eyes searched mine, as if he was making sure I'd truly come back to myself.

Then he let his hand fall away.

We stepped out into the open and found them in a shaded hollow beneath a leaning cypress. Alaric was leaning against the trunk, swiping at his jaw with the back of his hand, trying to erase the faint red smudges of lipstick. Gideon was crouched low, tossing a stick for Bran while Jasira laughed softly beside him.

They looked lighter. Happier. Unaware of the noose and the cheering crowd on the hill above.

No one asked where we'd been. No one needed to.

The air here felt different, loose, though for me, it still carried the echo of the bell, and the warmth of Erindor's hand lingered against my skin.

The road that led to Caerthaine's inner wall curved up through a ravine, hemmed by pale cliffs and guarded not by watchtowers but by stillness. The castle perched above like a predator, all silver and slate, its turrets sharp-edged and faceless. Even the birds seemed to fly in wider arcs around it.

As we climbed the final slope, the wind shifted once more, colder, slipping through my cloak like it threatened to tear it away.

Finally, the gate loomed before us, marking the end of our arduous journey.

It wasn't like Elyrien's: no open arch, no heralds, no banners unfurling. A blackened portcullis flanked by twelve armed soldiers, their armor immaculate, faces unreadable behind water-forged helms.

One stepped forward. His clipped and disinterested voice cut through the air.

"Name and purpose."

Alaric stood taller before answering. "Crown Prince Alaric of Elyrien. Accompanied by Princess Wynessa and an escort. Traveling under diplomatic treaty, by Caerthaine's own invitation."

The guard gave a small, practiced nod and raised two fingers as a signal.

Another soldier stepped forward, younger, mouth twitching with amusement. His eyes passed over Gideon, Jasira, and then landed on me. His gaze lingered, fixed and unwavering, until a shiver of unease traced up my spine.

"So, this is her," he muttered, loud enough for his companions to hear. "Pretty enough to keep the peace, I suppose."

My stomach churned, a sudden wave of nausea washing over me.

The wind cut sharper through the stone arches, and for a moment I felt it again, the noose, the silence, the cold eyes in the square.

Before I could respond, Erindor stepped forward.

He moved slowly, deliberately. His boots crunched over the gravel path, his expression unreadable.

A flicker of surprise crossed the soldier's face as he blinked. "Is there a problem, sir?" he asked, straightening, a subtle edge to his voice.

Erindor just stared.

A stare that didn't threaten violence but promised it.

The guard looked away first and opened the gates without another word.

We passed under the portcullis without fanfare. No cheering, bowing, or warm welcome.

Inside the walls, I nudged my way up beside Erindor. "You didn't have to glare at him like that."

"He was wrong," he said, eyes fixed ahead.

I raised a brow. "You think I need defending?"

"No," he hissed. "I think you don't realize what you are."

I frowned. "And what am I?"

He didn't hesitate.

"Not just pretty enough to keep peace. You're…distracting enough to get a man killed."

"That's not really an improvement," I murmured, cheeks burning.

He looked at me then, and for the first time all day, something in his eyes softened.

"That was not intended as a compliment."

I huffed. "What was it, then?"

"A warning. To myself."

I turned away before I said something foolish as my pulse roared in my ears, deafening and insistent.

The road to the castle bridge rose like a spine, cutting through the heart of Caerthaine's capital. Everything here gleamed with precision. Someone swept the streets clean. The windows shone without smudges. Silver lanterns hung on iron posts, each one identical in size and distance.

Beyond the hill, the sea whispered faintly, but even that seemed dulled here, like the sound had to ask permission to be heard.

The castle came into view gradually, through gaps in the layered buildings. Not towering like Elyrien's, nor draped in ivy like the temples of Wildervale. It was all angles and order. Sharp turrets of white stone. Slate roofs with no moss. No birds perched on the spires.

Everything was symmetrical. Controlled. Cold.

Even the bridge to the gates was strange. Long, flat, and polished so smooth it almost shimmered like glass. No banners. No flowers. Only the muted echo of our horses' hooves as we crossed.

Inside the gates, rows of guards stood in perfect silence. Not a single cheer or trumpet greeted us. No citizens lined the path. Just watchful eyes behind visored helms and the hush of something too careful.

The courtyard was pristine. White stones inlaid with blue-gray veins formed a pattern like ripples in water, and the palace beyond appeared pale and vast, its marble and silver surfaces bathed in a soft light that flickered like candlelight trapped beneath a lake.

A steward awaited us at the foot of the grand steps, where the stone staircase swept upward toward the castle's towering front doors.

"The reception is prepared for tomorrow," the steward announced, his tone smoothly devoid of deference, his head remaining at its arrogant level.

"His Highness awaits you in the throne room."

My legs ached from the climb, but I kept my back straight as we mounted the last steps. The front gates groaned open, and cool air swept out to meet us.

Inside, the castle was a cathedral of shadow and gold. Shafts of late-afternoon light cut down through high, arched windows, turning the dust motes to drifting stars. The walls were carved with scenes of kings and conquerors, their eyes seeming to follow us as we passed. Gilded sconces held flames that barely wavered, as if even the fire here obeyed the rules.

Our footsteps echoed across the polished stone in a slow, steady rhythm. The air smelled faintly of salt and iron, threaded with incense that clung to the back of my throat.

The steward led us down a long corridor lined with towering columns, their bases wrapped in coils of engraved bronze. At the end stood a pair of immense blackwood doors banded with gold. They opened without a sound, revealing a cavernous hall that swallowed us whole.

The throne sat atop a wide dais, framed by banners the color of midnight.

And there he was.

Prince Kaelen sat on the throne as though carved there—tall, immaculate, with one hand draped lazily over the armrest like the weight of the kingdom meant nothing to him.

His hair, the color of midnight, lay smoothly combed, not a single strand deviating from its place.

The high-collared navy tunic shimmered with silver thread woven into intricate, curling waves, while his boots gleamed like newly polished obsidian, ready for a formal inspection. When he smiled, it was a precise, practiced movement, lacking any genuine warmth.

"So," he remarked, a slow ascent and descent of the steps mirroring his unhurried grace, "this is the bride they've promised me."

He reached for my hand. I gave it slowly as I drew in a breath. His lips brushed the back of my bare skin in a gesture that felt more like possession than courtesy.

As his mouth touched my hand, I flicked my gaze toward the others. Alaric stood at ease, though I caught the faint crease between his brows. But it was Erindor's face that caught me, his eyes narrowed, jaw tight, like a man restraining himself from stepping forward.

"Though I expected someone taller," Kaelen asserted, his gaze scanning the surroundings, settling back on me with a critical flicker in the depth of his eyes.

Before I could reply, Alaric stepped forward, sharp enough to break the moment. "Prince Alaric of Elyrien," he said, his voice deliberately light but edged in steel. "The princess's escort. And yours truly."

Kaelen's gaze slid to him, cool and amused. "Charmed, I'm sure."

He released my hand. "Your rooms are ready. Rest. The welcoming banquet is tomorrow. And"—his smile curved in a way that made my skin prickle—"try to look presentable, won't you."

He turned, flicking two fingers to summon a servant. A man stepped forward immediately and bowed, gesturing for us to follow.

The halls were hushed as we walked, our footsteps echoing across pale tiles.

Jasira leaned toward me and whispered, "Feels like the walls are watching."

I gave her a slight nod. The weight of the air pressed down like I'd stepped into a cage dressed in glass and marble.

My chamber was beautiful in a way that made my stomach twist—lilac-carved canopy bed with white lace curtains, a silver comb set beside a basin of rosewater so cold it misted in the air. The windows framed the sea, but the glass was too clean, as if it had never been touched.

It smelled faintly perfumed. Unfamiliar. The bed looked like it belonged to someone else entirely. Someone softer.

The servant bowed again before leaving us. The door shut, and Jasira and I stood in the thick, perfumed quiet he left behind.

· · ·

Later, a knock at the door.

A servant stepped in, eyes downcast. In her gloved hands was a box of glass and silver. She placed it on the edge of the writing desk, bowed, and left without a word.

Jasira leaned forward to open it.

I peeked over at it.

Inside sat a single flower pressed in mid-bloom, its petals silver-white, ideally encased in crystal. A small parchment note lay folded beside it.

Jasira picked it up and read aloud.

"Beauty only lasts if it's encased. Like peace."

The flower looked real. Too real. Preserved at the edge of life, caught in an amber glass like something hunted and mounted.

A band of tension tightened around the neck, constricting my throat.

Jasira's eyes narrowed.

I reached out and touched the crystal.

It was cold.

That night, I couldn't sleep. Not with the image of that glass flower burned behind my eyes. Not with the quiet weight of Caerthaine pressing in around us.

So, I lit a small candle, took my journal from beneath my cloak, and opened it with shaking fingers. Ink bled more than I meant it to, but I didn't stop writing:

I keep thinking about the way the petals curled like it had been alive one breath ago. Like someone had stopped it.

I've seen pressed flowers. I've made them myself. But this was something else. This was invasive. A message or a warning. Or both.

It reminded me of that moment when someone brushes your hair back too gently, not out of love, but to see how it shines before they cut it.

I'm trying not to jump to fear. I'm trying to be rational. But something about this place is beautiful in all the wrong ways.

And I don't think the flower was meant for anyone else.

-W

Chapter Thirty

Wynessa

I sat on the edge of my bed, half-laced into a pale-rose gown, while Jasira's fingers worked silently behind me.

The gale off the sea shrieked against the castle walls, its relentless force threatening to tear the very stone from its foundations and plunge it into the depths.

Though the sky was perfectly clear, an icy detachment seeped in, leaving a sensation of deep, internal coldness. Even the sun here looked pale.

I didn't ask what time it was. The knock at the door had come after dawn, and the girl who delivered the summons hadn't looked me in the eye. "His Highness requests your presence in the Southern Council Chamber," she'd said, voice flat. "Immediately."

Not an invitation. A command.

Now, with the last pin secured in my hair, Jasira leaned closer and muttered, "I don't like this. No one should ask to speak this early unless someone's dead."

I tried to smile, but failed. "Maybe it's policy."

"Mm," she said, clearly not convinced. "Try not to agree to marry anyone without reading the fine print, alright?"

A sharp knock interrupted us before I had a chance to respond. This time it was lighter. I stepped out into the hall; the servant girl fell in at my side without a word. Her steps were short and quick, her head bowed slightly as if she knew better than to meet my gaze.

The walk through the castle was worse than I remembered. Even with the marble polished to a mirror shine and every torch lit, the halls felt hollow. Guards stood at every crossing, silent as statues, their silver armor gleaming like ice. Sconces bristling with thorns snaked along the arches, their twisted forms suggesting a malevolent growth. Portraits of Caerthaine's ancestors glared down with blank, mournful eyes. Not a single banner moved or was out of place.

The servant's pace never faltered, her soft slippers whispering over the stone as she led me deeper into the keep. She didn't speak, and I didn't ask questions.

The Southern Council Chamber sat high in a tower overlooking the sea. When the door opened, cold light poured across the table, as if it meant to wash everyone clean of warmth.

My eyes connected with Erindor's as I walked into the chamber. He stood stoic in the back with Gideon at his side, still assigned to my personal guard detail. Meaning he had to be here.

The Southern Council Chamber was all sharp lines and cold light. A long, narrow table of black-veined marble stretched nearly the length of the room, flanked by high-backed chairs carved from pale driftwood. Tall, narrow windows faced the sea and were inset in the walls; the clear glass made the water look close enough to touch. Salt wind hissed faintly against the panes. Above, the vaulted ceiling bore a mural of Caerthaine's fleets cutting through storm-tossed waters, their silver sails catching an imagined moonlight.

Kaelen stood at the head of the table, poised and polished in storm-blue robes, hands clasped behind his back.

Along the far wall, three older men in formal gray stood with scrolls in their hands. Kaelen's councilors, by the look of them. They did not speak, only watched.

Alaric sat halfway down the table from Kaelen, leaning back in his chair in a way that suggested nonchalance until his eyes found me. He stood as I entered, pulling the empty chair beside him back without a word.

I glanced at Kaelen, and he gestured for me to sit. I lowered myself into the chair Alaric had pulled out, the cold from the glass behind me seeping straight into my spine. He settled back into his seat beside me.

Kaelen's gaze sharpened. "Princess Wynessa, this is Lord Dorian of Southport. Merchant advisor to the eastern provinces."

"And aspiring scene-stealer," Dorian added with a wink, looking at Alaric.

Alaric's brows shot up. "I—" He cleared his throat, suddenly standing a little straighter.

Kaelen's jaw ticked, his voice cutting in like a knife. "And not here to waste our time with theatrics."

Unbothered, Dorian only grinned wider. "Not yet."

He was striking—tanned skin, chestnut hair tied back into a loose tail, and enough jewelry to shame a high priest. Chains of gold, garnet, and moonstone draped across his tunic collar, and a thin cuff curled up one ear, catching the light whenever he moved.

"Well," he said, smiling as if we'd been friends for years. "The Princess herself arrives."

I didn't respond. Instead, I kept my head low, wishing I were safely tucked up in Erindor's arms, far away from here.

Kaelen unrolled a scroll, its ribbon a pale, perfect blue.

"This is the initial engagement contract," he said. "Your father's council and mine have reviewed the terms. Preparations are already underway. Your seal will be required before the public announcement tomorrow."

My eyelids fluttered, a brief shield against the absurdity. "I haven't even read it," I stated, a defensive edge to the tone.

"You will," Kaelen said smoothly. "Before the signing, of course. But the terms are standard dowry, title inheritance, and ceremonial dates. What matters now is that Caerthaine sees this union as inevitable. Unshakable."

Across the room, Alaric shifted. "She should've known before now."

Kaelen didn't turn. "She knows now."

My mouth was dry. "And if I say I'm not ready?"

"You'll be saying it to an audience already gathered. You'll be saying it to a kingdom watching you walk into power," Kaelen said, his voice calm, yet resonating with undeniable authority. "The time for hesitation has passed."

A quiet surrender settled within me, a subtle crumbling of resolve.

He tapped the scroll again, the seal glinting in the torchlight. "Elyrien's lands are fertile, yes, but fragile. Your people are farmers, not soldiers. You have fields, not fleets. If war came, your orchards and granaries would burn within a week."

His gaze lifted to mine, steady and unblinking. "Caerthaine has ports and ships enough to choke the seas, but our cliffs and salt fields cannot feed us. Without Elyrien's grain, we starve. And then there is Vireth."

The name weighed heavily in the chamber.

"The desert breeds hunger and steel. Their armies are unmatched, their politics a knife's edge sharper than any blade. Vireth presses from the south. Caerthaine holds the sea. Elyrien is caught between—surrounded."

I swallowed hard, my throat dry.

"This alliance is not about a wedding, Princess," Kaelen continued. "It is about balance. Vireth's desert thirsts, Caerthaine's soil fails, Elyrien's strength lies only in its harvests. Alone, we all falter. Together, we endure."

"For whom?" I asked, forcing the words through the ache in my chest.

"Everyone," he said smoothly. Then his mouth curved, just slightly. "Including you."

Dorian rose to pour himself a cup of red wine, likely older than everyone in the room, and said casually, "And of course, the falsely gifted don't exactly help things."

Kaelen's expression tightened. "Two more surfaced last week. A seamstress in the port and a boy, fifteen maybe. Burned down half a barn with black flame. No sigil. No god. No control."

A surge of lightheadedness made my surroundings reel.

"We executed them," Kaelen said simply. "We had no choice."

Alaric's voice was sharp. "You burned a child."

"A vessel for chaos," Kaelen snapped. "False gifts are not divine. They are trauma turned inward until it ruptures. Magic that mimics but never obeys. Corrupted. Cursed. Left unchecked, they tear kingdoms apart."

My hand drifted to my sleeve. Beneath it, my skin remembered the echo of the mark.

"They're not all evil," I murmured.

Kaelen's stare cut like glass. "They are not all safe."

Silence fell.

When Kaelen exited, leaving the scroll behind like a dropped dagger.

Alaric approached slowly, crouching beside my chair. "You okay?"

"No," I said, voice small.

Dorian gave me a softer look than before. "Princess," he said gently. "Not all cages have bars. But you can still learn where the lock sits."

I looked at the ribbon on the scroll.

Pale blue. Tied like a wedding knot.

Erindor

I didn't follow her out of the council chamber.

I didn't catch her eye or ask if she was alright.

What would I have said? I'm sorry they're chaining you in silks instead of iron? I'll fight for you, even though I'm not allowed to touch you.

No, I did what I always do.

I found something solid. Something real.

The stable was quiet at this time of day. Warm with straw and the smell of horses, sharp with a salt air that had slipped through the open slats. The torchlight was dimmer here, soot-stained and flickering low. A good place to disappear.

Bran raised his head as I stepped inside, letting out a soft huff before pressing his heavy snout into my palm. I scratched behind his ears, and he leaned into me; warm, loyal, uncomplicated. I was thankful he had not been permitted within the castle's true confines. He didn't belong in a place like that.

Neither did Wyn.

I leaned against one post and closed my eyes.

I could still see her, sitting across from Kaelen. Her face had gone completely still when he mentioned the contract. Not surprised, not afraid, but quiet. Like she'd stepped out of her own body and left only her smile behind.

Gods, I should've said something. Anything.

A footstep behind me interrupted the spiral.

"Found you," Gideon's voice said, too casually. "Figured you'd be hiding somewhere dramatic. Thought about the roof, but then I remembered you're not the poetic type."

"I'm not hiding."

"Mm-hm."

He stepped up beside me and glanced down at Bran. "He misses the velvet carpets and fancy ceilings?"

"He misses Wyn."

"Don't we all?" he muttered.

I didn't laugh.

Gideon leaned his arms on the railing. "So. You gonna talk about it?"

"No."

"Right. I'll do it for you, then." He angled toward me. "You look like you're two breaths from throwing Kaelen off the balcony."

"I've thought about it."

"I've dreamed about it."

That earned the slightest twitch of a smirk from me, and it vanished just as fast.

Gideon went quiet for a beat. Then: "She looked like she was drowning in there. You saw it too."

I nodded in agreement.

"She doesn't get to choose," I said. "Not really."

"She's still breathing."

"For how long?"

I pushed away from the post and started pacing between the hay-stacked walls, my hands clenched.

"She's a healer, not a bargaining chip. She deserves the gods-damned truth, not a crown held together with documents and fear."

"You think she doesn't know that already?" Gideon said. "You think she doesn't feel it every second she walks through these halls?"

"I know," I acknowledged. "I know."

Silence.

He observed me for a long time.

Then: "You care about her."

I remained quiet. He knew all too well how I felt.

He gave me a crooked smile. "She's not the only one stuck in this castle with her heart in chains."

My jaw tensed. "She deserves better than this."

Gideon offered no argument. His gaze, deep and unwavering, held my eyes with an unnerving degree of understanding. "Maybe," he whispered. "You see her. And she sees you, which is a rare thing. But it doesn't matter what you think she deserves."

I looked down at Bran, who had rested his head on my foot, eyes half-lidded but alert.

"She's going to sign it," I said.

Gideon didn't stop me. "Yeah. She probably is."

We stood there in silence. The wind howled against the high stone walls outside, but in the stables, it was quieter and warmer.

"I should've walked away before any of this started," I muttered.

"But you didn't," he said. "And you're still here. That counts for something."

Does it? I wanted to ask. Or is that what men like me tell ourselves so we don't fall apart?

But I didn't say that.

Instead, I nodded and reached down to scratch Bran's ears again.

I couldn't give Wyn freedom. And I couldn't offer her a future.

But I could stay close.

The castle was quieter at night, but never truly still.

Stone didn't rest the way forests did. Trees held their breath in silence. Walls whispered when no one was listening.

I sat on a worn bench near the lesser servants' corridor, tucked in a pocket of dim torchlight. My uniform jacket lay folded beside me. My sword belt hung loose over my knees. But I didn't move.

Not yet.

My hand drifted to my pocket for something small and delicate.

The flower.

Pressed flat between folded cloth, its faded pink petals still held the shape of her hands. She'd given it to me in the mountains, after I'd nearly drowned pulling her from the river. She'd called it a frostbloom. Said it only grew where life fought hardest to return.

I stared at it now, cradled in my palm.

She smiled when she gave it to me. Like I was worth something.

But I wasn't.

I should've walked away from all this. From her. From the moment the superiors assigned me to guard a girl too good and too soft for a world like this.

But I hadn't.

And now she had promised herself to a man who only wanted her light so he could cage it.

My fingers closed slowly over the petals.

What would it feel like, I wondered, to hold her hand without fear?

To reach for her without guilt, without duty tangled in every touch?

I'd watched her today. Watched her pretend.

She was good at it.

But I saw the tension in her fingers. The way her shoulders locked when Kaelen leaned too close. The way she didn't eat, didn't blink too long, didn't breathe too deep, was as if she made one mistake, the floor would fall out from under her.

She looked like she belonged to him. To Caerthaine.

But I knew better.

She belonged to wildflowers and storm light. To the morning sun and mossy stones. To whatever spark still smoldered in her chest. The one the gods had marked, and the fire hadn't claimed.

The gods had touched her. And she didn't even know what she was becoming.

A slow breath escaped me.

I ran a thumb over the edge of the petal, then tucked the cloth carefully back into the lining of my coat, beneath the leather strap where no one else would see.

She'd given me something fragile.

I would keep it safe.

Even if it was the only part of her I could ever hold.

Chapter Thirty-One

Wynessa

I woke to an unfamiliar perfume lingering in silk sheets and spent hours being measured, brushed, and pinned by women who never smiled with their eyes. Meals passed in silence or half-concealed whispers. Courtiers bowed too low or not at all, and every hall echoed with the quiet that meant you were being listened to. They showed me how to curtsy, how to smile without showing teeth, how to wear rings I hadn't chosen, and speak words I didn't mean. I'd thought the court of Caerthaine would be grand, but it was something else entirely, like being dressed in someone else's skin and told to dance before it hardened.

There was a knock. Before I could answer, the door opened and four women filed in, silent as a shadow line. Not Elyrien handmaids. These were Caerthaine court attendants; older, sharper in their movements, dressed in subdued hues of slate and deep blue. Their polite smiles didn't reach their eyes, instead remaining vacant and unreadable.

"Make her ready," one of them said softly. "His Highness has requested elegance."

The word tasted like saltwater in my throat.

Jasira stepped forward, voice firm. "She'll need a moment to change. Alone."

The nearest maid offered a small smile, the kind that looked painted on. "The Princess has no need for shyness here. We are trained to prepare honored guests."

Jasira didn't budge. "She's not your guest."

Another maid moved past her, already unfastening clasps from a wooden case. "She's Caerthaine's bride-to-be. She must be presented accordingly."

Before I could object, they were already unbuttoning my cloak, tugging at the hem of my tunic, like I was their puppet.

"Wait—" I began, but their hands moved too quickly.

Jasira raised her voice. "She said—"

"Please. Let us do our work." A cool hand pressed against Jasira's arm.

Jasira's jaw tensed. I caught her eye again and gave her the slightest shake of my head.

It wasn't worth it. Not here.

With visible reluctance, she stepped back. The door closed behind her.

The room became very quiet.

I stood there in my shift, bare feet chilling against the polished floor, while the attendants unveiled the gown.

It was not a color I would have chosen.

Charcoal black, like the color of midnight. Heavy silk, cut close to the body, with a neckline that plunged farther than it had any right to.

Silver embroidery crawled like vines up the bodice and twisted around the waist. A high slit ran along the left thigh, hidden by a sheer outer layer of chiffon that shimmered like fog.

"It's a Caerthaine cut," one maid said gently as she held it up. "Stern, but sensual."

"It's…not really what I—"

"Tradition, Your Highness," she said, cutting me off.

They guided me into it with superb efficiency. The corset laced tight, until I couldn't quite breathe right. My breasts, small as they were, were pushed into a shape that didn't belong to me. My arms were dusted with silver powder. A thin chain was wrapped around my waist like a leash made of metal.

Then came the hair.

Another maid approached with a tray of pins and oils. Someone managed my hair with practiced fingers and combed it straight with perfumed oil I didn't recognize. She pulled it back tight, weaving it into a sleek, knotted updo that exposed the sharp line of my jaw and every angle of my face.

I felt like a statue being carved.

"You have a lovely neck," one of them said, adjusting the fall of earrings that brushed my collarbone. "They'll notice that first."

"I don't…think I want them to," I whispered.

The woman met my eyes in the mirror and smiled faintly.

"That's not for you to decide."

My eyes fixated on the girl in the mirror staring back at me. Completely unrecognizable.

Her skin was powdered smooth, and her eyes rimmed in ash-toned pigment. Her lips were painted the color of dusk. She didn't look like a healer or a princess. She looked like an offering.

I thought nothing could suffocate me more than that crystal flower, until they dressed me in this.

I whispered, "It's…not really what I—"

"You're not here to want," she said, stepping forward and draping a completely useless sheer wrap over my shoulders. "You're here to symbolize."

A loud, sharp, and unsettling thud vibrated through the floor, catching me off guard.

"Time," the steward's voice called. "The banquet has begun."

The maids stepped back in practiced unison. The one behind me placed a final pearl pin at the nape of my neck and whispered, "There. Perfect."

The mirror girl didn't smile.

Jasira stood motionless in the hallway. The tension in her shoulders sagged, and her face fell into a grim mask of disappointment the moment her eyes met mine.

"You look—" she tried.

"Don't," I mumbled.

"I'm sorry," she murmured. "I should've stayed and fought harder."

I shook my head and took her arm.

"Get me through the door, please," I said. "And promise not to let me fall."

She offered a tight, fierce smile. "If anyone makes you fall, I'll toss them into the sea."

Jasira walked at my side in a fitted uniform of Caerthaine. A blue tunic, crisp and belted with silver thread that caught the candlelight when she moved. It looked wrong on her. She was a woman made for wild colors, for motion and laughter, not the stiff hush of this palace.

Every step taken in those ill-fitting shoes pressed the weight of unwanted choices upon me. A prickling irritation crawled across my skin, saturated with foreign scents and oils. Meanwhile, an inexplicable tightness squeezed at my throat.

I wasn't dressed for a celebration.

I was dressed to surrender.

Court musicians tuning strings and nobles glittering like coins filled the halls outside. Perfumed air stung my nose. Laughter clinked like crystal.

I walked in silence, surrounded by too many eyes.

And then the Grand Hall opened around me like a gaping mouth.

Slate-gray silk covered every window. Smoky crystal chandeliers caught what little light there was above and broke it into fractured, colorless shine.

Kaelen waited at the head table, already seated, already smiling.

He stood as I approached and took my hand, like we were dancers in a play neither of us wanted to rehearse.

"Radiant," he murmured in my ear.

I said nothing as we sat.

His fingers remained laced through mine as the hall filled with people, tables groaned under the weight of food, and conversation bloomed around us like vibrant, yet fragile, glass roses.

The noblemen here didn't engage with me directly. Instead, they asked questions about me, but loud enough for me to hear, which only made me feel on display even more.

I wanted to peel myself out of my skin. Slip away and dissolve into the marble beneath my feet.

Across the hall, I saw Erindor standing at the wall, straight-backed in his dark guard uniform. His expression carved into stone. But I knew him too well. I saw the tension in his shoulders. The way his eyes flicked every time Kaelen leaned too close.

He was watching. Always.

Jasira was seated among the court attendants, back straight. Her eyes burned toward Kaelen, but she held her tongue.

Alaric, two seats down, toyed with his wineglass and looked like he was debating which noble to provoke first. Dorian, however, was the one already speaking, laughing too loudly at some joke told by a man with too many rings and not enough neck.

The feast dripped with false celebration.

Until Kaelen rose.

He held a goblet carved from a pale, translucent stone, red veins running through it like old blood. The hall hushed.

"To peace," he said. "To unity. And to the Princess who brings it."

He reached down, took my hand, and drew me to my feet.

"To my future bride. May she bring peace, grace, and heirs to Caerthaine's throne."

There was no pause. No question. Just a bitter smile and the flare of goblets raised in practiced rhythm.

I tried to breathe. But I couldn't.

Across the room, Erindor hadn't moved.

But I could feel him there, a pulse at the edge of everything.

And I looked at him.

Just once.

He didn't look back, but he clenched his fists and tightened his jaw.

I didn't taste the food. I smiled when I remembered to. I lifted my goblet with the others when Kaelen did. My hands moved, my face moved, but none of it felt like mine.

I was a storybook figure being read aloud.

From her perch near the musicians, a noblewoman's voice, a rustle of silk and gossip, drifted from behind her fan: "She looks younger than I thought."

Another sipped from a glass cut with emeralds. "Elyrien must be desperate to send her."

They weren't whispering to hide. They were whispering to be heard.

One man with a pinched mouth and a jeweled sash added, "He's a collector. Perhaps she's another trinket for his shelf."

I held my goblet tighter.

Kaelen smiled beside me. That same sculpted, practice-perfect expression. His hand never left mine, resting too firmly, like I might bolt.

And he wouldn't be wrong.

Every instinct inside of me roared a single command: run.

My eyes drifted toward the outer wall.

Erindor stood as still as ever, cloaked in shadows at the edge of the hall.

He hadn't looked away from me once.

Gideon stood beside him, arms folded. Jasira sat quietly near the second table, unreadable behind her lashes.

A gong sounded softly, not a chime of celebration, but a cue. Kaelen stood, his smile widening.

"Come, darling," he said, loud enough for all to hear. "They'll expect us to open the floor."

My legs were already up and moving before I had even realized it.

The musicians began to play slowly, sweeping notes from long silver strings. We moved into the center, and Kaelen's arm wrapped around mine like a snare. We danced.

The steps were smooth. Rehearsed. I let him lead because I didn't know how not to. I moved my body the way they taught me: a glide, a dip, a turn. I could've been anyone.

He leaned in, voice low and too amused. "Smile, Princess. It costs nothing."

So I did.

But not for him.

I smiled because I had nothing else left in that moment.

When the dance ended, the applause was polite. Another pair stepped forward. Then another. Soon, the floor filled, nobles spinning and laughing with gemstone smiles.

Kaelen released my hand. "I need a word with the steward," he said smoothly. "Don't wander too far."

I nodded obediently.

I walked toward the edge of the room, pressing one hand against the wall to feel something solid beneath my fingers.

And then I heard his voice.

"You look like you'd rather be facing a bandit again."

I looked up.

Erindor stood a whole arm's length away. No smile, no humor, but his tone was softer than I expected.

I blinked. "I don't know the steps."

"Neither do I," he replied. "We'll look foolish together, Princess."

He offered his hand.

The room blurred. The music blurred. But his hand was steady.

I took it.

We moved slowly and awkwardly at first. I stepped on his foot. He grunted. I apologized. And he didn't let go.

The hall fell away, note by note.

I kept my gaze on the floor until he whispered, "It's not your fault they don't see what you are."

I looked up.

"What am I?"

He paused briefly. "Stronger than this room. And far too bright for any man who thinks he can own you."

A wave of adrenaline surged, sending my heart racing.

The music slowed, signaling the end of the dance.

I stumbled, and his hands caught my waist, steadying me.

They lingered there for a moment too long.

"I—" I started.

He let go.

The space between us rushed back.

"Thank you, sir," I said, dipping my head.

He nodded once, a knight's bow, but softer.

As I walked away, I felt the weight of eyes on my back.

Kaelen. Watching.

The moment the music shifted again, I slipped away.

A graceful turn, a polite smile, a hand brushed against someone's shoulder as I excused myself from the crowd. I crossed the floor with practiced steps, but every inch felt like drowning in brocade.

Beyond the banquet doors, the corridor was cold. Blessedly quiet.

I leaned against the stone, breathing slowly. Laughter and music were now muffled sounds, as if underwater, distant, and unreal.

My hands trembled as I pressed them to my skirts.

It had only been a dance.

But it hadn't felt like just a dance.

His hand was on my waist. The look in his eyes. That line…

"Far too bright for any man who thinks he can own you."

What did that mean? Why had it meant so much?

Why did I still feel him standing close, like a warmth that hadn't faded?

"I'm starting to think you enjoy lurking in dramatic doorways," came a voice beside me.

I jumped.

Dorian stood there, leaning against the opposite wall. With his arms crossed, multiple bracelets clinked softly as he shifted. He wore deep plum tonight, with gold chains layered over his chest and a single sapphire dangling from one ear. His hair was tied back in a sleek knot, but a few curls had escaped to frame his sharp, amused face.

I tried to compose myself.

"I wasn't lurking."

"No?" He raised a brow. "Because from where I stood, it looked like a tragic princess escaping to the edge of her story for a moment of stolen breath."

I exhaled through a laugh.

"Maybe I was overwhelmed."

"Of course you were," he said gently. "This place is a mausoleum with diamonds. It makes everyone feel like they're drowning, but they throw more jewels at you instead of a rope."

I turned slightly, facing him more fully. "Is that why you wear so many?"

Dorian grinned. "Exactly. If I'm going down, I want to sparkle doing it."

A pause.

Then, quietly: "That wasn't just a dance, was it?"

I didn't answer.

Dorian pushed off the wall and stood beside me. Not too close. Close enough to be kind.

"I'm not here to pry," he whispered. "But I am here to remind you that sometimes, one quiet step off the path is louder than a declaration."

I looked down at my hands. "I don't know what I'm doing."

"None of us do. We fake it better the more embroidery we wear."

Another pause.

"Kaelen's watching you like a hawk," he added, softer. "And your knight? He's trying not to fall apart like a tower hit by a tide."

I swallowed. "I'm trying not to fall apart, too."

"Then I suggest," he said, gently plucking a stray thread from my sleeve, "you give yourself one win tonight. Something that belongs only to you."

"And what would that be?"

His eyes glinted. "This moment. Right now. Where you are not a princess nor a bride. In this moment, you're a girl who stepped away when she needed air."

He turned to leave but paused after a few steps.

"Oh, and for the record?" he added, glancing over his shoulder.

"If anyone asks, I didn't see a thing. But if I had, I'd say your knight danced with his whole soul."

And then he was gone.

Leaving me alone in the corridor's hush, heart thudding.

And for the first time in hours, I smiled.

Chapter Thirty-Two

Wynessa

Caerthaine Castle never truly slept.

Even in the late hours, long after the torches had dimmed and the silk-draped halls fell quiet, something stirred beneath the marble and stone, like a hush drawn too tightly across a mouth that had too many things it could never say.

I lay stiff beneath heavy covers, my eyes fixed on the ceiling's painted relief of the moon goddess, Kaelor's sister, her face hidden in shadow. I wondered if she ever turned away from what she saw below. If even the divine could look at this place and flinch.

Sleep had eluded me for days, but tonight, the weight pressing on my chest felt unbearable. The palace walls were closing in like ribs. Ornate. Polished. Too elegant to breathe in.

I pushed the sheets back quietly and slipped out of the bed. My bare feet touched the cold floor in prayer. I moved in silence, the way

Jasira had taught me when we were small and sneaking pastries from the kitchens.

I didn't need to think about where I was going. My body remembered the steps.

The stairs to the servant quarters were hidden behind a tapestry on the eastern side of the wing, past the portrait of Queen Solen the Just.

I'd overheard Jasira mention it, and I had tucked it away like everything else I wasn't supposed to hear.

The hallway outside was cold and dim, lined with flickering sconces and shadowed alcoves. Tapestries hung like silent judges. I slipped behind it, and the air changed.

Stone. Old, damp, and close. The narrow stairwell curled upward like a spine. It smelled of forgotten candle smoke, cold iron, and dust, not the kind that dirtied but the kind that settled after years of silence.

Each step creaked slightly underfoot as I climbed. I held the candle high, its flame bobbing with my breath. There was no banister. No windows. Just the stone, and the hush, and the sound of my pulse echoing in my ears.

Each step felt less like forward motion and more like an emotional excavation, leaving behind the weight of expectation, the pretense.

As I reached the top, an ironbound arched door loomed like a maw. I pressed my hand against it, expecting resistance, but the door groaned reluctantly and opened, revealing a cold breath of air more chilling than anticipated.

The rooftop garden spilled out like something caught between a dream and a graveyard.

It wasn't like the castle's lower courtyards, manicured and prim. This space had been left to the wild breath of the gods. Stone planters lined the balustrade, overflowing with strange white roses and thorny vines that curled like ribs around statues long worn by weather. The gods carved into them were unfamiliar. Not Kaelor. Not Vireya. Their faces had been devoured by time and moss, their features erased as if the stone itself had forgotten.

Frost glazed the pathways.

Clouds veiled the sky above, violet-tinged and heavy, but the stars still blinked faintly, above the low-hanging moon.

I moved through the garden slowly, running my fingers over vines as I passed. A few roses had already withered, their petals curling inward like secrets.

The frigid air bit at my cheeks, but I didn't care.

Because I could finally breathe.

I walked to the edge of the terrace, the cool balustrade beneath my fingertips. Far below, the sea lapped at the rocky shore. The lights of Caerthaine shimmered like broken glass reflecting the stars.

Up here, I didn't have to smile. I didn't have to wear silks or rings or fear.

No one was touching me. No one was watching.

No one was asking me to become anything. I was just me.

"I miss who I was becoming," I whispered aloud.

And for a moment, the wind didn't answer.

But it didn't argue either.

Behind me, a soft sound broke the hush.

A footfall. Measured. Familiar.

I turned toward the sound, half-expecting a guard, or worse, a shadow where no person should be.

Instead, it was him.

Erindor stepped into the garden's moonlit hush like he belonged there. Though his stance was tense, his arms were crossed over his chest. His breath steamed slightly in the air, but he wore no cloak, only his undershirt and the weight of a long day.

"I didn't expect to see you out here," I said, trying to swallow the flutter that rose in my chest at his physique.

He raised a brow.

"Didn't expect to be followed," I added more softly this time, unsure why my voice had dipped.

"You didn't cover your tracks very well." His tone was light, but his gaze searched my face. "Even Jasira would've noticed."

I laughed, a soft, breathy exhalation of surprise escaping me before I could contain it. I hadn't laughed in days, not like that.

His eyes softened. "I miss that," he said.

I gave a disbelieving blink, and my heart lurched, a frantic, tripping rhythm. His gaze darted away almost instantly, as if he hadn't meant to say it aloud.

A comfortable silence stretched between us.

Erindor moved to the balustrade a few feet away from me. He didn't lean on it, but stood steady, silent, the way he always did when he didn't know how to put something into words.

I turned back to the view, but my hands wouldn't stop fidgeting in the folds of my cloak. The words pressed against my teeth.

"He touches me," I said at last.

Erindor didn't move, but I saw the tension return to his shoulders.

"Kaelen," I clarified, my voice flat. "He touches my wrist. My shoulder. Not always in obvious ways. But it's constant. Quiet. Like it's his right."

A pause. A breath.

"And I don't know how to say no without…without it costing someone something. Jasira. You. Elyrien." I looked down. "Maybe even me."

He didn't respond at first. I glanced over. His jaw was clenched, his mouth set in a thin line. His hands had curled slightly at his sides.

"It's not your job to protect me from that," I whispered. "I wanted to speak of it freely for a moment, that's all."

He turned to face me finally. His voice was low and rough at the edges. "Then why does it feel like it is?"

My breath caught.

Not because I was afraid. But because I wanted to lean into the warmth I saw flickering in his eyes.

But I didn't know how.

I didn't know how to move toward something that might disappear the moment I reached for it.

I looked down, blinking so fast it felt like a silent plea for the tears not to fall. "I don't belong here," I whispered, the words catching my throat.

"You're not the only one who feels that way," he said quietly.

His voice held no pity, only something that sounded like understanding.

We stood there like that for a while, both of us watching the sky, both pretending we didn't want to say anything else.

The silence between us stretched, silver and fragile, like a thread caught between stars.

I shifted slightly, brushing the back of my hand along the stone railing. His hand was already there, fingers barely touching the surface, and the light contact between us sparked like frost cracking under sunlight.

I stilled. So did he.

Neither of us moved. Although our hands weren't truly joined, they were close enough to share warmth. Close enough to make my pulse trip over itself.

His voice was low. "You know…" A pause. "If I were a braver man, I'd say something wildly inappropriate right now."

My heart hiccupped. I turned toward him slowly. "Like what?"

He glanced at me sidelong, with that rare, crooked half-smile playing at the corner of his mouth. His eyes gleamed.

But he didn't answer.

Instead, he leaned forward slightly, a breath closer, enough for the air to shift. Then he let the moment dangle there, teasing.

I stared, stunned, heat crawling up my neck. "You're doing it again."

"Doing what?"

"Looking at me like that."

His brow rose faintly. "Like what?"

"Like I'm…" I trailed off, realizing I did not know how to finish the sentence. Like I'm something worth staying for. Like I'm not meant to be locked in someone else's cage.

He said nothing, his eyes looking intently into mine.

The fire stirred beneath my skin.

The heat a steady pulse, like something ancient and golden waking in my chest. It wasn't demanding or loud. But…aware. Present. Like a flame waiting patiently to be chosen.

I curled my fingers around the edge of the railing to ground myself.

A bell tolled somewhere far below, signaling the change of shift for the night guards. The soft chime echoed across the stones like a breath let out.

We both stepped back as if summoned back to ourselves.

He turned away. The closeness unraveled.

The stairwell back to my chambers felt colder on the way down.

My palm brushed lightly against the rough stone wall, a small point of contact and reassurance on the way down. My fingers skimmed patches of frost, caught briefly on a chipped edge where time had worn the stone soft.

We both walked in silence, like we'd both dropped something invisible between us and quietly agreed to leave it there.

At the bottom landing, he stopped. One step behind me.

I turned to face him, my back to the door in the shadowed corridor. The castle, usually a living, breathing thing of sound, was held in a profound and unnerving silence.

"I don't want to go back in," I whispered, surprising myself.

"I'll stand outside. Until you sleep," Erindor offered softly.

A lump formed in my throat. My voice caught on it. "You don't have to—"

"I know."

His gaze flicked to the floor. Then, slowly, back to me. The candlelight from a nearby sconce caught the edge of his cheekbone, the sharp line of his jaw, the quiet storm behind his eyes. All of it steadier than I felt.

Then I saw it—the subtle motion of his hand brushing over his coat, a light tap against the pocket near his heart. Absent-minded. Gentle.

What did he keep there, so carefully guarded?

I gave the slightest nod and turned the handle of my door.

I hesitated as I crossed the threshold.

Hesitation tightened my grip on the doorframe as I crossed the threshold. Without turning, I admitted, "If you ever do say something wildly inappropriate…I don't think I'd mind." My words hung in the silence before I disappeared into my room.

The room was still. Too still. Once again, someone had drawn the lace curtains closed. The mirror reflected only my silhouette, all cloak and wind-flushed cheeks. I let the fabric fall to the floor in a heap and stood by the window, one hand pressed to the glass.

The garden now felt a world away. But the warmth remained low in my chest, like a flame wrapped in ribbon, pulsing quietly as a heartbeat.

I looked down at my hands. They were still trembling. But not from fear this time. Hope possibly?

Chapter Thirty-Three

Wynessa

The next afternoon, I'd reached the landing near the servant stairwell when the page found me.

He bowed too deeply, eyes cast to the floor. "His Highness requests your presence. In the solar. Alone."

A frantic rhythm started in my chest, and a single, stunned word escaped my lips. "Now?" I questioned.

The boy only nodded, then scurried away down the corridor like a mouse retreating from fire.

Gideon looked up from where he leaned against a marble arch, folding a piece of dried fruit into his mouth. He must've heard the exchange because his posture sharpened.

"You're not going up there by yourself," he said casually, but his tone was tight.

"I don't want to cause a scene," I said, my hands clenched at my sides.

"You wouldn't be. You'd be accompanied." He smiled thinly. "That's allowed."

So, I let him walk with me.

The castle had grown quieter since the banquet. A stillness. The kind that comes before a storm breaks. Each sconce we passed hissed softly with candlelight. Long corridors stretched like ribs through the stonework, ribcages of a palace that swallowed its guests and digested them slowly.

When we reached the blackwood door of Kaelen's solar, Gideon offered a look that wasn't quite a smile.

"You've survived Vorrhounds, collapsing cliffs, Mimics, and a sentient maze. Whatever this is, you've got it."

My hand hovered over the iron handle. "Thanks, but I'm not afraid."

"I didn't say you were. But I know the look of someone about to hold their breath."

The door opened before I could knock.

Kaelen stood within, silhouetted by the golden flicker of lamps and the pale shine of the glass windows behind him. He looked his usual pristine self, not a single hair or thread out of place.

His mouth smiled, but the rest of his face remained still.

"Come," he said smoothly. "Just you."

Gideon shifted beside me. "I'm her guard."

Kaelen's gaze flicked to him. "Not here, you aren't. I asked for the lady."

I exhaled slowly and glanced at Gideon. He gave me a tiny nod, his brow furrowed, and muttered, "Knock if you want me to knock him out."

I tried to smile, but it faltered.

The door closed, and the slam of the wood against the frame felt like teeth biting down on my courage.

The solar was spacious but sterile. Pale gray walls. Silver-threaded tapestries depicting Caerthaine's naval triumphs. The shelves were lined with pristine books that looked untouched. A decanter of dark wine sat on a crystal tray, with two goblets set beside it, but they poured wine into only one.

Kaelen circled to the writing table and gestured to a curved-back chair.

"Please. Let's talk like civilized people."

I didn't want to sit, but I did. Reluctantly, I settled into the chair, my body's protest a silent argument with my will.

He sat closely across from me, crossing his legs in a leisurely manner. His collar was open enough to seem effortless, not casual. A man performing elegance.

"I've had the seamstresses begin your fittings," he said, pouring more wine. "We'll need at least two gowns for the ceremony. Possibly more if we want portraits to circulate. I'm also completing the guest list for the ceremony," he said, unrolling a new sheet. "Of course, your god would expect a mention. Perhaps we should also include a display for the coastal temples. Fire draws unease here, best to reframe it as symbolic rather than literal."

"I haven't signed the contract," I mumbled.

He smiled as though I'd said something charming.

"You'll sign it. We both know you will."

My mouth opened, but his voice cut me off, a command sheathed in charm.

"We'll want three heirs ideally. One to bind the alliance, two for contingency. I assume your line breeds true. Elyrien's royal blood hasn't shown signs of dilution, has it?"

"I'm not—" I stopped. My throat felt like it had closed around the words. Kaelen leaned forward.

"Your kingdom needs this. My kingdom needs this. And we're both attractive enough that it won't be unbearable."

His gaze flicked over me then, slow and appraising in a way that made my skin crawl. It wasn't the admiration I sometimes caught in Erindor's eyes. There was no awe, no reverence. Only assessment.

"Are you still a virgin?" he asked, like he was inquiring about a horse he intended to buy.

I felt the blood drain from my face.

His hand slid forward, fingers brushing lightly against my thigh. Not lewd. Just enough to imply ownership.

The room closed in around me.

"I—that's none of—"

"It matters," he interrupted. "To the perception of the union. The purity of our future heirs." His voice was low now, close. "I intend to be king of more than Caerthaine one day, Wynessa. And I need a wife who understands the necessity of appearances."

I jerked my leg back. My breath had gone shallow, fast.

But he only smiled, leaning back as if nothing had happened. As if he hadn't touched me. As if his words weren't stripping the flesh from who I thought I was.

"Don't look so pale," he smirked. "This is what you were raised for, isn't it? To be useful."

I rose to my feet as quickly as I could, scraping my chair across the floor.

"I think we're finished."

"Not yet." His voice followed me to the door, lazy and cruel.

"Shame the wilds didn't take you when they had the chance."

I didn't turn. I didn't give him the satisfaction.

Something kindled within, not with fear or shame, but with the steady, growing heat of a new resolve. It was the deliberate ignition of a fire that had lain dormant, sharper and older than mere obedience.

Gideon was waiting beyond the arch.

His smile vanished the instant he saw my face.

"You've got a terrible card-play face," he murmured. "Want to tell me what he said?"

"Later." I cleared my throat. "I…I need some air."

He studied me with narrowed eyes, then nodded. "You have ten minutes before I come storming through the halls."

I gave him a ghost of a smile and turned away.

I didn't know where I was going yet.

Only that I couldn't stay still.

I didn't realize I'd taken a wrong turn until the sconce light thinned and the walls turned into unfamiliar older stone, the plaster here veined with hairline cracks. No silk hangings, no polished tile. Bare corridors and the smell of old wax and older secrets. I paused at the hall's bend, breathing in shallow gulps. The air felt heavier here, like the castle's bones were thicker in this part of the world.

Behind me, soft footsteps approached.

I spun around in a daze, my pulse spiking, hand darting to the edge of my skirt where a dagger should be but wasn't.

"Easy," came the voice, calm and warm. "It's just me, Princess."

Dorian stepped into view, the glint of his many rings catching the low torchlight. His tunic shimmered faintly beneath his long coat, its embroidered cuffs undone, his hair pulled back as always.

"I didn't mean to frighten you," he said, lifting both hands as if to show he meant no harm. "But you looked like a ghost chasing its own shadow. I was afraid you'd walk straight into a wall."

I tried to give a polite smile, but it felt wrong on my face.

"I needed air," I breathed.

"You chose the one hallway without it," he replied with a soft snort. "The archive wing. No one comes down here unless they're hiding something or hoping to be forgotten."

I narrowed my eyes at him, unsettled. "Are you following me?"

"No," he said easily. "But I've learned to pay attention when someone looks like they're about to splinter."

He paused, glancing both ways down the hall before lowering his voice.

"And you, Princess, are terrible at pretending."

I swallowed, a dry, deliberate act that seemed only to tighten the raw, aching muscles of my throat. The memory of Kaelen's hand still lingered, phantom-heavy on my leg. His voice had followed me like a rot.

Dorian stepped closer. "I don't want to alarm you, but I think you're in danger."

My breath hitched. "Why are you telling me this?"

He reached into his coat, fingers slipping between layers of silk and gold chain, and pulled out a folded piece of parchment.

"No seal. No proof," he said. "But something that shouldn't exist anymore. I found it filed among export records in the new tower. Misplaced or poorly hidden. It didn't belong there."

I took the page with trembling fingers.

Dorian met my gaze. "If you really want answers, there's a room near the end of this hall. Smells like candle flame and secrets. The older archivists used to call it the Deep Shelf."

"What's in it?"

"Things no one wanted remembered," he said. "Letters. Logs. Drafts that never made it into the official record. Things meant to be burned."

I stared down at the paper in my hands, unable to open it. My fingers were shaking too hard.

"Why are you helping me?" I whispered.

Dorian tilted his head. "Because not everyone who smiles at Kaelen means it. And because you deserve to see the shape of the knife before it's at your throat."

He offered a bow, more profound than expected, and then turned without waiting for a response.

I stood there until his footsteps vanished.

Then I walked.

The hallway led to a thick wooden door, slightly swollen from age. The rusted hinge resisted before giving way with a soft groan. Inside, the air turned to a mixture of moth dust and mildew. The room wasn't large, but its shelves were deep, packed to the back with scrolls and ledgers, many of which had remained untouched for decades.

It smelled of damp paper and things long buried.

I moved slowly, guided only by a single flickering candle wedged into a wall sconce. Shadows stretched across the floor like spilled ink. I followed a narrow path between shelves until I found a low cabinet behind a warped screen. Something about it felt out of place. Its wood looked newer than the others. Someone had broken the lock recently.

A knot tightened in my gut.

Inside, there were bundles of letters. Dozens. Some were frayed; others crisp. I reached for the one on top, the parchment Dorian had given me.

It wasn't long. A few lines, written in efficient, courtly script:

"Intercept the envoy before Wildervale. Focus on the soft one. The girl with the healer's hands. If the forest doesn't take her, Riven will."

I could feel my face fall open wide, the raw sting of unshed tears burning behind my eyes.

I opened another letter, this one marked with Kaelen's personal seal; faint, but still visible beneath the cracked wax.

"Ensure the knight dies. He's very loyal. Burn the bond before it forms."

My mouth went dry.

"Payment approved for intercept at Wildervale. Risk is high, reward is higher. Remove the girl quietly. Do not damage the face."

And finally, the last letter and the most chilling: "The girl bears a mark. But her fire is not from birth. Watch her. She is not what she believes she is."

My knees buckled. I sank to the ground, scrolls sliding from my lap like wilted petals.

He knows my gift.

He tried to kill us.

Not random bandits and mercenaries. Not misfortune. Not fate.

Kaelen.

He'd sent Riven, planned the attacks. Approved assassination orders were like diplomatic paperwork.

We were all meant to die before we ever reached Caerthaine.

Instead of a sob, a sound clawed its way from my throat, hoarse and guttural. It was the raw, protesting sound of grief trying to break free.

But no tears came. Crying was something you did when the pain still belonged to you.

This pain belonged to all of us.

A truth burned behind my ribs, terrible and certain.

If Kaelen had his way, we wouldn't be negotiating a union.

We'd be burying the last of my people in foreign soil.

I didn't remember leaving the archive. One moment, I was kneeling on the floor, scrolls splayed around me like broken wings; the next, I was stumbling through a half-lit corridor, my hands trembling, my skin cold and damp.

Now, I tucked the letters under my arm, crumpling them slightly from how tightly I clutched them.

My feet moved of their own accord, taking me nowhere in particular. The castle was silent but not still. Caerthaine always breathed beneath its own stone, whispering through cold halls like a thing alive. The sconces flickered low, casting warped shadows that trailed behind me like ghostly apparitions.

Each step echoed.

He planned this.

He paid for my death. Everyone's death.

I couldn't get the words out of my head. They looped like a fever chant, each time twisting deeper, sicker. My heart was beating too fast and too shallow.

"You'll sign it. We both know you will," Kaelen had said to me. "Shame the wilds didn't take you."

Coward, I thought bitterly. Monster.

I walked faster.

I didn't know where I was going. Only that I couldn't stop.

The door clicked shut behind me.

I stood alone in the cold hush of my room, the scent of lavender and stone trailing in my wake. The letters burned beneath my cloak like coals pressed to my ribs.

I didn't pace. I didn't panic. I moved.

Near the fireplace, there was a seam in the wall. I'd noticed it during my first night here, where the stonework dipped ever so slightly behind the carved screen. I knelt and pressed along the edge, fingers trembling, until I found a groove. The stone shifted under pressure.

The hollow behind it was small enough to tuck something thin and fragile.

The sound of my heart pounded in my ears as I slid the letters inside, still wrapped in the cloth with my family's crest. The moment the stone clicked back into place, it was as if I had buried a body. The weight of the secret settled like earth on a grave.

I stood slowly, brushing dust from my skirt.

The room was silent, but not still. My thoughts howled louder than any wind.

Was it enough?

The letters named him not in signature, but in implication. The wax seals were cracked, and some of the handwriting could be challenged. There were no witnesses, no confession. Just words.

Is that all it takes to end a life? To unravel a peace?

I crossed to the window and placed my palm against the glass. Caerthaine stretched beyond in perfect rows of icy beauty, every spire and square washed in moonlight.

My reflection stared back. I saw my pale skin, hollow eyes, wrapped in silk that didn't belong to me.

This kingdom was a construct of appearances and calculated power, where the masks had been worn so long they had begun to rot into the very skin.

Would they believe me? Or would they say I'd wandered where I shouldn't have? That I was weak. Or hysterical.

The wind rose outside, rattling the panes.

The tears refused to fall once again. Instead, a seismic rift tore through my core, leaving a jagged fissure between who I was and who I would become.

Behind me, the fire whispered in its hearth.

If I stayed silent, I would marry him. If I spoke, I risked everything.

My fingers curled at my sides.

There was no safe path. There had never been.

But in the morning, I would choose one anyway.

I lit a single candle.

I sat at the edge of my bed, the silk hem of my nightgown clinging to my ankles, and pulled the worn journal from beneath my pillow.

Its spine was cracked now, corners curled from damp and travel. But the pages still held me like an old friend. A version of me I wasn't sure still existed.

I opened to a fresh page. Dipped the quill. Let the words bleed out, steady as breath:

I always thought betrayal would come with shouting. With anger. With something loud.

But it came in silence.

It came in ink on parchment. Orders tucked inside a drawer. Words written so cleanly, so confidently, that they didn't even feel like murder. They felt certain.

He was going to kill me. He was going to kill us.

And all this time, I thought I was navigating a court. I didn't realize I'd stepped into a cage.

I keep wondering what I did wrong. What softness I showed, what questions I asked, what part of me cracked open enough for him to slip the blade in.

But maybe it's not about weakness. It's about threats.

Maybe he saw something in me that scared him. Something that still burns.

I haven't told the others. Not Alaric. Not Jasira. Not Erindor.

What would I even say? Did I find proof that our peace is a lie? That I'm sleeping a stone's throw away from the man who wants to kill me? No one can protect me from this. And if I speak too soon, I could ruin everything.

But the silence is rotting me from the inside. And I don't know how long I can keep it. I want to scream. I want to run. I want to burn this whole place down and start again.

But I won't. Not yet.

Instead, I'll sleep with the truth pressed between my ribs. And in the morning, I'll decide whether to stay quiet.

-W

Chapter Thirty-Four

Wynessa

The walls were too white.

Not the soft, garden-bathed white of moonflower petals. No, these were bleached and unyielding. I'd stared at them all morning, pacing between them like some trapped creature circling its own enclosure.

The fire in the hearth snapped as if resenting the silence.

I'd tried to sit down three times. The edge of the bed, the window ledge, the little velvet chair by the writing desk. Each time my body refused to stay still, my bones too tightly coiled with dread.

The letters were still safely stashed in the hollow behind the hearth. That was the safest place for them. Who knows what I would do if they were in my hands?

I had gone for breakfast.

Sat next to Alaric at a long, polished table, gold-fringed and gleaming, while the Caerthaine nobles sipped chilled wine and commented on the mildness of the wind. I'd nodded when spoken to and smiled when required. But my food remained untouched, while my tea, once steaming, grew tepid and left a bitter taste on my tongue.

Erindor had been there too, posted by the pillar, as always. He hadn't spoken, but I felt his eyes linger more than usual, as if he were memorizing my silence.

Lunch had been worse. The clang of cutlery was too loud; the candlelight too bright. I tried to say something to Jasira, anything, but my throat felt lined with smoke and ash.

She had leaned closer, brushing my hair from my shoulder.

"You're too quiet," she'd whispered. "That usually means your brain's on fire."

I hadn't replied. I'd only taken her hand and squeezed it beneath the table.

Because how could I explain what I had found? How could I look my brother in the eye, or Erindor, and say, I know now? I know it was never a chance. The forest wanted me dead, and Kaelen held the leash.

The knowledge wasn't just poison. It was weight. Thick, oozing weight that clung to my skin and pooled behind my ribs.

What do I do?

I had asked myself that question at least fifty times since sunrise.

Tell Alaric? He would burn the entire castle down. And I didn't know yet who might get burned by it.

Tell Erindor? He would act, and gods knew I couldn't bear to see him thrown in chains or struck down for me.

Tell Jasira? She already bore so much. I didn't want to add my crumbling world to hers.

So what? Carry it alone?

My reflection in the mirror didn't answer. She stared at me with pale skin, hollow eyes, and dressed in court-perfect gray silk. My hair was braided back today, tightly wound into a severe style. I hadn't even resisted when the maid styled it that way. I was too busy holding myself together.

I couldn't stay here any longer; wrapped in silence, wrapped in questions, wrapped in fear that hardened into something brittle behind my ribs.

I found Jasira in the reading nook down the hall, fussing with embroidery she wasn't really working on. When she looked up, I smiled too quickly.

"I'm going to get some air," I said. "A small walk."

She frowned. "Now? Wyn, it's almost time—"

"I won't be long," I murmured, already turning. "I just need to breathe."

Jasira stood as if she might follow. But then she paused, studying my face.

"Alright," she said softly. "But breathe smart, okay? Not dramatic."

I gave a laugh that didn't reach my chest. "Dramatic? Me? I think you've confused me with my brother."

"You have a terrible card face," she said, echoing Gideon's words the day before.

Then she let me go.

I didn't head toward the gardens. Not the stables. Not even the chapel.

Instead, I wound my way through the lower halls, each footstep louder than the last in the hush of polished marble. I passed servants who barely looked up. A figure in soft shoes and gray lace. No one is worth stopping.

I reached Kaelen's wing as the bells chimed once overhead, marking the hour like a warning.

My palms were slick, my heart in my throat.

I raised a hand to knock, but the door opened before I touched it.

Kaelen stood in the doorway, his silhouette outlined by velvet and firelight. A flicker of surprise crossed his face, quickly replaced by a satisfied smile.

"Well, well," he said, his smile slow and practiced. "Are you finally going to sign the contract? Or hoping to get a round in before the wedding?"

His eyes glanced over me, uninvited. "Because I'm not opposed either way."

"I…I—" I cleared my throat, trying to shove down my trembling voice. "I need to speak with you."

Kaelen stepped aside with a sweep of his hand, and I entered before I lost my nerve.

The heat hit me first.

Not the comforting warmth of a hearth, but a suffocating heat, heavy and close. The fireplace crackled too high for morning, and the drapes were drawn against the sun. The walls pressed in with velvet and stone, and something in the air smelled sweet, like wine gone sour.

The soft click of the door latch was a period on the suffocating quiet that filled the room. Kaelen strode past me, his attention already elsewhere, and positioned himself at the far end of the solar, methodically adjusting his cuff.

"I was wondering if you'd finally come to your senses," he said casually.

My stomach twisted into a cold, hard knot. My feet were fixed to the ground just inside the doorway, fingers tightening around the forbidden letters hidden in my sleeve like they might anchor me.

"I want to know," I said, my voice quiet but sharp, "why you ordered it. Why you wanted me dead in the forest."

He turned slowly, his smile spreading like oil over water.

"Wynessa," he murmured, his voice a low, poisonous drawl. "Do you truly think you were ever meant to arrive here?"

I stiffened.

He laughed—a sharp, humorless sound—and stepped forward. "You were never a bride. You were a message. The quiet one, the obedient one, the girl they swore would bend like reedgrass in the wind. Easy to lose in the Wildervale. Easy to blame on wolves, or raiders, or a vanished escort. A runaway princess. A broken treaty. And war would come neatly wrapped."

My chest tightened. "You tried to kill me."

He stopped close enough that the gleam of his rings caught the light between us, his smile thin as a blade. "I tried to save us all the tedium. Elyrien is weak—fields and farmers playing at crowns. I wanted its end."

His hand rose suddenly, tucking a loose strand of hair behind my ear. I flinched at the touch, bile rising in my throat.

"But my scouts saw the way the trees bent toward you," he whispered. "The way the forest failed to claim you. The way your magic hums, even when you don't mean it to. The wilds love you, Wynessa. That's what ruined it."

I stumbled back until my shoulders struck the door.

He only smiled wider, calm as still water. "But I adapt. The forest failed. The mercenaries hesitated. You survived. So now"—his gaze raked over me, heavy, possessive—"you'll serve another purpose."

His hand dropped to my arm. His tone shifted; it was lower and more intimate.

"You know, most girls go mad when fire touches them. But you…you glowed. You were always intended for more. And now I get to keep you. So why not make it official?"

He moved to the desk.

There it was. The contract. Waiting. A fresh ink pot and quill beside it.

"Sign it," he said, like it was nothing. Like it wasn't my life laid bare on that page.

Suddenly, I became immobilized, unable to budge.

Kaelen looked up at me and narrowed his eyes. Then he smiled. Not a kind or amused smile, but one of possession.

"Don't tell me you're nervous. Is it the wedding night?" he asked, stepping closer again. "You can tell me, you know. I like innocent things. For a little while. Are you still a virgin, Wynessa?"

I gave him a blank look.

His eyes darkened with amusement. "We can fix that, you know. Sooner rather than later. Make this whole union feel more official."

He reached out, hand gliding down my arm and settling on my hip.

"I hear fire-women are warm all over."

I recoiled, stumbling back. My arm knocked the glass, and it tipped, shattering on the floor. Wine spilled like blood across the marble.

He caught my wrist before I could pull away.

"Don't run," he murmured. "You'll make it worse."

His grip was bruising and practiced. I could feel every ounce of control in his fingers.

"You can scream," he said again. "But no one here will help you. Not in my kingdom."

"Don't touch me."

He laughed. "Not yet? Fine. But you'll learn. The crown doesn't make requests; it makes heirs."

My breath started to come faster now. I stepped backward, and the papers in my sleeve shifted.

Kaelen's eyes dropped. Then narrowed.

"What are you hiding?"

I shifted my body away from him.

But he lunged at me.

In one brutal motion, his hand closed around my throat and pushed me against the desk. Hard enough to choke and sufficient to make my breath catch. Enough to remind me how little space there was between power and pain.

"You will sign," he growled. "Because if you don't, I'll tell the entire court what you are."

He leaned closer, brushing my nose with his, the anger in his eyes burning.

"I'll say you're cursed and that the fire inside you is false. A stolen gift. Do you know what they do to false-gifted here, my little peace offering?"

I tried to pull free. But he held fast.

"They hang them. Strip them bare in the square. Burn them, like that sweet little priestess you passed on the road. I'll put your pretty head on a pike and call it justice."

Tears slipped down my cheeks.

"You're not a queen," he hissed. "You're a fragile little flame flickering in my hand. And I'll snuff you out if you ever try to burn me."

He let go.

I stumbled, coughing and gasping.

He shoved the quill into my hand. Pointed.

"Sign it."

I looked at the page. My vision blurred.

"Do it."

My hand shaked uncontrollably.

His voice shattered the air.

"SIGN IT!"

His fist crashed against the desk, and behind me, crystal shattered like ice beneath a boot.

I jumped and I cried out. Hot, quiet tears rolled down my cheeks as my hand moved with trembling fingers. My name came out jagged, like a wound bleeding across the page.

A crooked line. A shaking hand. The name Wynessa of Elyrien was scrawled in ink and grief.

Before I could step back, Kaelen dipped a thin, black-handled spoon into the flame, letting crimson wax melt until it shimmered like blood. With eerie precision, he tilted the spoon over the parchment. The molten wax dripped in a slow, deliberate stream beside my name, thick and glossy, a perfect circle blooming across the page like a wound. The scent of it rose; sharp and sweet like burning rose oil.

Then he pressed the seal down hard.

The hiss of cooling wax filled the silence, the sigil of Caerthaine stamping itself into the soft red. He held his terrifying gaze, a relentless pressure against me, whilst pinning me between his body and the solid barrier of the desk.

When he lifted it, the mark remained. It was clean, deep, and final.

Kaelen's lips curved, a slow, possessive gesture like a man who'd claimed a kingdom.

He reached down, gently wiping a tear from my cheek with his thumb.

"There now," he said softly. "That wasn't so hard, was it?"

My head bowed, and a fresh wave of tears slipped from my eyes, falling silently to the floor.

The wax seal still gleamed beside my signature. My name burned into the page like a grave marker. The ring he'd pressed into it still sat cooling on the table, the sigil of Caerthaine smirking up at me in silver relief.

Kaelen leaned in closer now, one hand braced beside me on the desk, and the other trailing too close down my arm. I couldn't move. I wasn't sure my legs would hold me.

"You did well," he spoke softly, the words a calm but undeniable command. "You'll be beautiful in the palace portraits. A touch of fire in your eyes. Enough to keep them guessing."

His hand slipped lower, brushing the curve of my waist, then resting deliberately above my hip. His breath grazed my ear.

"I'm tempted to keep you here," he whispered. "Wouldn't that make the gods blush?"

I flinched and turned my face away, barely breathing. "I'd like to go now."

He laughed softly out of amusement.

Instead of stepping aside, he reached out and picked up a lock of my hair, twisting it between his fingers. "They said healers made good lovers. Gentle hands. Open hearts. Easy to control." His smile curved wider. "We'll see, won't we?"

I swallowed a sob. "Please." My eyes fixated on the door.

That word caught him, not in pity, but pleasure. Slowly, leisurely, he stepped aside.

"Go on then," he said. "Run while you still think you can."

I didn't thank him. Didn't bow. I turned and bolted, skirts tangling at my knees as I wrenched the door open and nearly collided with a startled servant. I didn't stop to explain.

The marble corridors blurred as I ran, tears slipping past my lashes, unacknowledged.

No one stopped me. No one followed.

My lungs burned by the time they reached my chambers, a frantic, desperate hunger for air. My hands were not just shaking, but quivering uncontrollably, and every beat of my heart was a sharp, jabbing ache in my chest.

The door shut behind me like a blade sheathed. I didn't light a candle.

I just stood in the center of the cold, perfumed room, shivering under the suffocating weight of it all. My consciousness felt as though it was floating above the scene; I couldn't feel my body. I wasn't even sure if I was breathing.

I stared at my wrist. A red mark illuminated where he'd gripped me, like a bruise still deciding whether to bloom. My other hand trembled as I reached beneath my sleeve and withdrew the letters I had hidden away earlier. The pages crinkled softly, stained at the corners where I'd clutched them too tightly.

I should have screamed.

I should have run.

But I didn't. I signed it.

I crumpled onto the edge of the bed and finally let out the full force of my tears; hot, silent, helpless. They slipped past my lashes and fell against the marble-white fabric of my sleeves, soaking into someone else's idea of royalty. This wasn't my life. This wasn't my crown.

The flame inside me flickered but didn't catch. I signed the line. I let Kaelen win.

Or maybe…he thinks he's won.

The tears stopped, but the burn behind my eyes remained. I sat in silence until the bells tolled midnight and the last of the warmth left the hearth.

Then slowly, I walked to the hearth and tucked the letters back into my hiding space. If anyone searched, they'd find nothing. Not unless they knew exactly where to look.

My signature may have been on the page.

But my will was still my own.

I crossed the room, drawing the curtains tighter over the window, sealing out the fading light. Then I sat, with my back pressed against the cold stone, a quiet fortress built against the world. No more tears came, no sleep offered refuge, only the cold, hard clarity of a plan taking root.

To be Continued in

Book Two of The Oathfire Saga

Acknowledgments

To everyone who believed in me and this story, thank you for keeping the flame alive when I couldn't always see it myself.

To my incredible editor, Sian Morgan, thank you for guiding this book with such insight and care. To Laë Aldin Proofreads, your sharp eye and patience made this manuscript shine. To The BookVeil, thank you for creating a cover that captured my vision so beautifully. And to Seirra Nessel, the very first person ever to read this book, your enthusiasm lit a spark that carried me the whole way through.

To my husband Eric, my mom Erica, my dad Shannon, and my best friend Jade Alaniz—thank you for supporting me unfailingly, cheering me on through every doubt, and reminding me why I write. And to everyone who thought I was worth it: you kept me going when the road was long.

This book was born out of a love for stories that remind us that compassion, kindness, and empathy are powerful even in a world that has forgotten them. To everyone carrying a quiet flame of their own, this one is for you.

Stay Connected

TikTok:

@the.oathfire.saga

Instagram:

@theoathfiresaga

Find all my links here:

Website

Maybe I'll have one someday.

Thank you for reading *The Quiet Flame*! If you enjoyed it, leaving a review helps more than you know.